PRAISE FOR FOX HUNT

Action-packed with a dry sense of humor and a few good one-liners that eases the intensity, this story is easy to get caught up in.

"Crowned Heart" distinction, – InD'Tale *Magazine*.

"A high octane, pedal-to-the-metal, adrenaline-fueled read."
– Jill, GoodReads reviewer

PRAISE FOR UNDERTOW
(THE UNDERCITY CHRONICLES #1)

The writing duo of S. M. Stelmack have mashed their creative talents and imaginative minds together to create this sci-fi, romantic suspense which has the ability to appeal to horror and paranormal fans alike." – *InD'Tale Magazine.*

"...well-written and atmospheric, incorporating a steamy romance between Jack and Lindsay. The underground cultures are interesting and well thought-out. ...a very enjoyable and thoroughly entertaining read with some nice touches of humour to lighten the often dark tone and setting."
– *Jill, GoodReads reviewer*

GINA TAKES

THE FEMME VENDETTAS

BANGKOK

S.M. STELMACK

Copyright © 2013 by S.M. Stelmack
Editing by Alyssa Palmer
Cover Art by CrocoDesigns

http://www.smstelmackauthor.com

Printed in the United States of America

First Edition: October 2013
Library of Congress Cataloging-in-Publication Data

Stelmack, S.M.
    Gina Takes Bangkok / S.M. Stelmack – 1st ed
    ISBN-13: 978-0991869879
    ISBN-10: 0991869877

    1.Gina Takes Bangkok—Fiction. 2.Fiction—Romantic Suspense
    3.Fiction—Action & Adventure

To Carol,
Your enthusiasm for life is matched only by Gina's

(Authors Moira and Serge Stelmack)
http://www.smstelmackauthor.com

A NOTE FROM MOIRA

Dear Reader,

This is a story about family, as the tagline states, and within the myriad families that populate the story are two very special father-daughter relationships, each of which involves either Gina or Kannon. Serge can relate to Kannon's relationship. Both are fathers with precocious daughters. But for me, it was all about Gina and her father, Vincenzo Zaffini. You see, during the writing of this novel, my father died. He was ninety-one, and had lived his days. He tidied up loose ends, got the story of his life straight, said his goodbyes and went on his way. His death was, as he used to say of so much of the serendipitous, the unfortunate and the tragic, "one of those things".

Yet, I mourned him and still do. He was my dad, after all.

My love for him is lodged in the small memories. In the roll of Lifesavers we shared on the Tuesday drive home from my piano lessons, the razz berries to the back of his neck and later the massages I gave there. It was me playing his favorite waltz on the piano right when he came in from chores. It was the quiet pride in his blue eyes as my baby daughter, his one grand-daughter sat on his knee, his big hand like a chair back to hold her steady.

He didn't want a funeral. He wasn't much concerned what the rest of us did with his remains. As nurses and family fussed around him on his last day, he whispered, "Too much." It wasn't but he would see it that way. He'd probably be mortified to have me speak of him this way before strangers. But insofar as it's possible to teach something without knowing it yourself, what I learned from my father is that you don't have to be remarkable to be loved or, upon your passing, to be missed.

And the other thing is to know how to bring your story, including that of your life, to a good conclusion.

Best,
Moira

CHAPTER ONE

GINA THWACKED THROUGH the racks at her favorite store in all of Los Angeles. She came here often, so often that the owner had slipped off to do some banking, leaving her alone to mind the place. Small, simple, and filled with retro clothing, it was her number one hunting ground when she needed A Find.

Most people, and all men, entered a store with something particular in mind. She preferred to think of shopping as an experience in which she would let the universe guide her purchases, so she only shopped when she felt the urge. Never mind that the urges came with nymphomaniac regularity.

A slight cosmic shudder passed through her as her hand brushed a hanger. She tugged it out. A mid-thigh creation in red with gold slashes. Wowza. She had shoes, bags, bracelets and boas to accessorize this beauty. Then—whoosh—the feeling vanished.

What the—? Seemed like she and the universe were out of sync, the second time in as many days. Yesterday, on the other side of the world, her father had celebrated sixty-five years of staying alive, and being a dutiful and loving daughter,

1

she'd phoned to wish him a happy birthday. Her stepmother had answered, saying that he'd gone fishing. Her father had spent nearly a quarter-century in Thai waters and had never fished. The millisecond the call ended she was in the grips of a mega-urge. So today, right after work, she'd hit the store.

Now, a solid hour later and nothing. She should go but leaving empty-handed was not the way things worked. She wove through the spinners, her wanderings edging her to the front. That's when the tingles started again, hot and heavy, pulling her to a rack close to the window. The tingles swelled into a near orgasmic sensation of A Truly Amazing Find aimed at one G-spot on a rack. There. She swept it out and held it aloft.

A black dress with elbow-length sleeves, a hemline at the knee and a neckline at the collar bone. No slits and no buttons.

The universe wanted her to buy a boardroom basic?

She looked at the price tag on the destiny dress. One hundred and twenty bucks! That was all her cash. Really?

Her body thrummed and warmed in a kind of afterglow. Okay, something was seriously out-of-whack.

Tossing the dress over her shoulder in a fireman's hold, she slipped her pink bag from her arm, rummaging for her money clip. Where was it? She shouldn't carry all this crap. After all, it had been months since she'd used the mace. Tucking a shank of her black-and-purple locks behind her ear, she set the purse on the floor to better get at it. Engrossed, she didn't notice the car hurtling toward the store until it smashed through the front window.

The explosion of masonry, glass and ceiling tiles threw Gina against a rack, and she fell to the floor in a tangle of clothing. She laid there, stunned. Not five feet away, the mangled hood of the car sizzled and steamed. Whoever was inside had to be hurting. She struggled to her feet, secured her purse and wobbled to the driver's door, just in time to get smacked hard across the chest as it swung open, knocking her back on her butt.

A young Asian female, blood zigzagging from a gash on her forehead, staggered out and, eyes full of fear, looked over her shoulder. Picking herself up for a second time, Gina followed the girl's gaze outside to where an unmarked van had screeched to a stop in the center of the street. The driver, clearly not cop material, drew a powerful handgun from his jacket as he got out.

This would be a good time to run.

Taking the girl's arm, Gina pointed through the wreckage. "Come on! There's an exit at the back."

The two of them sprinted through the stockroom, rushing out the back door to the alley. The young woman made to continue running, but Gina pivoted her toward a dumpster. "Get in there and hide!" She boosted the girl, forgetting that Asian females were made of bamboo, and with a squeal and windmilling of arms, the girl fell inside with a crunch of cardboard.

From her bag, Gina pulled out a little piece of insurance she always carried with her. With a flick of her wrist, she extended the pink-handled telescopic truncheon her father had mailed to her three Christmases ago, and positioned herself by the door.

The gunman burst out, and with a samurai cry, Gina swung her baton at his wrist. There was a snap of bone as the titanium tip scored a direct hit, and the man dropped his weapon, howling in pain. Gina didn't let up. Whacking away at the thug for all she was worth, Gina struck him across the face and head once, twice, three times, until he dropped to the ground, twitching and bleeding.

Panting for breath, Gina snagged the man's gun from the pavement and was about to make a citizen's arrest when she heard the roar of a motorcycle. Her attacker had backup, and it was headed right for her. With a yelp, she yanked open the door as the bullets started flying, and slamming it shut behind her, clicked the deadbolt into place. She backed up, keeping her gun aimed and ready. The motorcycle squealed to a halt outside, and, a heartbeat later, someone pulled violently at the door.

Gina fired, putting a bullet hole neatly through the center of it, and waited. Hopefully that ought to be enough of a deterrent. The seconds ticked by and all was silent, then the girl cried out.

"Ah, dammit." What part of 'hide' didn't she understand? Tiptoeing to the door, Gina peeked out the bullet hole, but could see squat. She snapped back the deadbolt and opened up, gun at the ready.

The girl stood in the dumpster, apparently unharmed. Her two attackers weren't so lucky. The clubbed one was lying very still, dark blood pooling around his head, and the other was spread-eagled, her shot having pierced the door and struck him straight through the heart.

She'd killed. Again. And well. Like she was meant for the life. Everything tilted and blurred around her. No. She couldn't lose it. Not this time.

Gina looked at the gun, shaking in her hand, then at the teenager. "Don't worry, you're safe. We've done nothing wrong. The cops will be here any minute."

The girl shook her head, her straight black hair whipping about as she climbed out of the dumpster. "No! I need to find Gina Zaffini. Please, do you know her?"

Gina blinked in surprise. "I'm Gina, how did you—?"

"Yes! I'm Tasanee. Your father and mine are friends, and they're both in big danger! I have to get back to Bangkok."

"Tasanee?" Alak Montri's daughter. She hadn't seen her god-sister in ten years, and given the kind of business their fathers were in, the last thing she could afford to do was get the police involved. She steered the girl over to the motor-cycle. "Get on and let's get out of here. You can fill me in when we get somewhere safe."

"Oh thank you, Ms. Zaffini! Thank you."

"Don't sweat it. Just hold on tight, and call me Gina. We're sisters after all."

With Tasanee perched behind her, Gina took off down the alley. They were a mile away when she remembered the god-awful dress. It'd been a narrow escape in more ways than one.

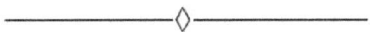

John Wakai resisted racing for the phone the second it rang. There was nothing he wanted more than to return to the serenity of order, to have his inner state reflect his Bangkok penthouse—clean, simple and of unimpeachable quality. This call would determine if the control that had slipped from his grasp was his once again. If his plans, as rushed as they'd been, had worked.

Rolling his wheelchair to the coffee table, he picked up his smartphone. He breathed out, and with the voice of a Zen master, answered, "Is it done?"

"No. We're in trouble," his sister squeaked, her tone somewhere between rage and panic.

"How bad?"

She wavered close to hysteria. "The men I had working for me...they weren't able to finish the job."

"She got away?"

"Yes. No. I mean they won't be able to finish the job. Ever."

This could not be happening. "I thought you said they were right on her tail."

"They were. I don't know what happened. One minute they had her, the next they were both dead. I can't believe they came recommended."

Wakai bit back a curse. He hadn't been privy to all of Montri's secrets; his former boss had kept an ace up his sleeve. Someone to watch over his daughter. Someone dangerous enough to protect her from even his sister's vicious associates.

"I have no idea where she went to. How do I find her now?"

"You can't," he answered with forced calm. "Whatever happened, I'm sure she'll be back in Bangkok soon enough, and that means we have a challenge. A very serious challenge."

"So the plan failed?" she asked.

"No," he assured her. "And I'll make sure it doesn't. I'm not going to let anyone harm you." And of course he wouldn't, even as disturbed as she was. How could he, with all she meant to him? After everything and everyone he'd sacrificed to protect her. "You did the best you could. Come home, Victoria. Catch the first flight you can, and meanwhile I'll sort this out."

He ended the call. As suddenly as the threat to her had developed, he'd masterminded a plan tight with checks, balances and contingencies to keep her safe. Now thanks to the incompetence of a pair of mercenaries, it was unraveling.

Two years ago a man named Erawan Boontan—not an especially smart individual, but a very feared and dangerous one—had attempted a similar power play against Montri. The coup might have succeeded had his boss not retained the legendary assassin, Kannon Takahama, to punish the usurper's audacity. At first, Erawan hadn't worried—after all, he had many friends and supporters, and was no stranger to violence. Two months later he, and all who had collaborated with him, were dead. Kannon wasn't a man. He was a force of nature.

Still, nature could be tamed. All he needed to do was find the girl and capture her, as he'd done with her father. With her prisoner, he'd easily control Montri, and even an enemy as relentless as the assassin would be brought to heel.

Resting the phone on the arm of his wheelchair, he closed his eyes. His meditation was short-lived. Though the number was blocked, Wakai knew who it was. His plan would never have worked without so formidable an ally, yet such pacts were a double-edged sword. Displeased friends could be far more dangerous than enemies. Especially friends such as these.

"Get her?" said a deep, cold voice, thick with a rural Cambodian accent.

"No. She had some security I didn't know about," replied Wakai, with studied firmness. "Killed the useless gunmen Victoria hired. Apparently they came recommended by some idiot."

"I recommended them."

Wakai had insulted him. Worse, he'd made it sound as if Victoria had insulted him, too.

The man was angry now, the kind of anger that got people brutally murdered. Or much, much worse. "We couldn't have made this any easier for you! With the girl, we could have taken the city in one stroke!"

Arrogant psychopath. How convenient to forget that it had been his knowledge and strategy that had afforded them such a quick and decisive victory, albeit an incomplete one. "I said I'd take care of her and I will. Unfortunately, it's going to take a little more time."

"You're so smart you're stupid," came the scathing reply. "Kannon's tracking you down right now, him and his boss's friends. He'll come knocking, and you'll get tossed off your fancy penthouse, just like Erawan."

Wakai grimaced. Back then, he'd still had use of his legs. Had been there when the assassin had thrown Erawan to his death—with one hand.

"You have one week to solve this problem. After that, there's no word for the kind of punishment you'll receive."

Punishment? After all he'd done for them? His new partner's inability to reason made him as volatile as his former boss. He'd have to find some way to muzzle the mad dog. Until then, he gave the only answer he could. "Consider it dealt with."

The line went dead, and Wakai released a loud curse. No way to zen his way back to peace now. Seven days was all he had to put out the fire his sister's vices had started. Fail, and it would explode into an inferno.

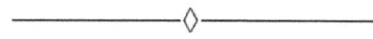

Kannon was running out of time, but not as fast as Jarun who he had tied to a chair in the stockroom of the man's own grocery store. Taking the cigarette from his mouth, Kannon stubbed it out on the prisoner's forehead, eliciting a shrill cry of pain as it hissed against flesh. He re-lit the cigarette and took a puff. "I'm starting to get annoyed with you. Tell me where my boss is."

"For the last time, I don't know," Jarun spat, blood

trickling down his sweat-slicked face. "And even if I did, you'd kill me the second I told you."

There was every reason for his prisoner to believe that. After all, Jarun had never shown any mercy to those who he'd brought to the back of his shop. The man was an enforcer. A fighter. A torturer. One look at his hands, knuckles enlarged and calloused, told that story.

"You helped Wakai kidnap Mr. Montri, murder his lieutenants and hunt his daughter. The question is not whether you're going to die. It's how unpleasant I'm going to make that process. Now tell me what I want to know."

The man gritted his teeth in stubborn determination. "Fuck you."

Behind Kannon, a door opened to admit his apprentice, Ryota. The tall, wiry man nodded to his boss, his expression a mask of cold indifference. He held up a phone. "I have a few numbers that might be leads, and he has a message on his voicemail. Other than that, the place is empty. No sign of where they're keeping the boss."

Kannon removed his cigarette and held the burning tip close to one of his prisoner's eyes. "Where is he?"

Jarun clamped his mouth shut, as he struggled at his bonds.

Kannon growled. "You think you know how to torture? Compared to me you're an amateur. By the time I'm done with this cancer stick you'll curse your father for not pulling out of that ten-baht whore you call a mother. Now. For the last time. Where is—?"

His cell buzzed. Not breaking eye contact with Jarun, he pulled it from his suit jacket. "You better pray this is good news."

He stepped away to take the call.

"Kannon?"

Tasanee. "Where are you?"

"I'm in Los Angeles. I got away from the apartment like you told me to, then somehow Wakai's men still found me. They would have had me for sure except Gina saved me. She killed them, and we're at this workshop, and—"

"Slow down. What did you say? Who killed them?"

He heard the phone being handed to another person. "Hi, Kannon. Remember me?"

Part of what made him such an expert manhunter was that he rarely forgot a face. Or a voice. And though it had been three years since their last run-in, the receptionist he'd completely failed to intimidate was fixed in his memory. "The pink-haired woman."

Of all the people in the world, she was Vincenzo Zaffini's daughter?

"Actually, my hair's black-and-purple now, but it's awful sweet of you to remember. We're at the same place you blew up on your last visit," she rattled on. "I couldn't believe it when Tasanee told me who she was, and who Alak had hired as muscle. You really should step up your security, y'know? Next time I might not be around to do your job for you."

Her squirrel chattering grated. "Put Tasanee back on."

"Fine," she said, "only don't expect me to bail you out again with that attitude." A moment later, Tasanee was back.

"Kannon, I'm at this place called—"

"I know where you are. The people there are...associates of mine." He looked at his watch and scowled. "I'll be there tomorrow night. Stay where you are and who you're with." He added what he knew the girl needed to hear. "You're safe now."

"That's what Gina keeps saying."

Gratitude mixed with his irritation, and the two didn't sit well. "She's right. Don't call anyone else."

"Kannon? Is...is my dad okay?"

No way was he saying otherwise when he couldn't be there for her. "He's good. Don't worry."

Her breath blew out. "Thank you, Kannon. Thank you so much."

His jaw tensed with emotion, though he kept his voice even. "I'll be there soon."

Kannon slid away his phone, and withdrawing his silenced pistol, strolled over to his captive. "Tasanee's safe. Seems like you're getting less useful all the time."

"I don't want to die," the man said, his body dripping blood and sweat. "But I can't tell you what I don't know."

Kannon pressed the gun up against Jarun's chin. "What's the access number for your voice mail?"

Jarun let it go. "3579."

In one lightning stroke, Kannon pistol-whipped the man, knocking him out. He wouldn't kill him. Not yet, at least. He was an old friend of Wakai's, and might still be of some use. Ryota retrieved Jarun's voice mail, and with the click of a button, played the message on speaker.

"Jarun." It was Wakai. "I need you to come and talk to Montri. Victoria screwed up the job and I have to get as much information as I can on who's protecting his daughter. I'll send someone around first thing tomorrow to pick you up. He'll be there at seven." The man who'd betrayed his boss, the man Kannon had bowed to as a superior, softened his voice. "Jarun. I know what you think of all this, but I know you'll stand by me. I know I can count on you."

Kannon regarded Jarun's slumped form. "Ryota, if they get Tasanee everything's lost, so I have to fetch her. Keep

Jarun alive, and when that driver comes by in the morning, take him, too."

"Couldn't he lead us back to where they're keeping the boss?"

Ryota was twenty-four, young enough to be Kannon's son. A good man. An excellent student. If Kannon did his job well, he'd turn Ryota into a hard, calculating killer. Someone who recognized the naiveté of that question.

"Not without Jarun," Kannon explained. "Even if he did, we're not equipped to stage a rescue. Besides, Wakai will move our boss as soon as the chauffeur doesn't return. No. You hold them. Once I'm back with Tasanee, we'll pick up from here."

"So…she's okay?" Ryota asked tentatively, and Kannon realized he'd not told him. "Yes. In Los Angeles. She's with Mr. Zaffini's daughter."

His assistant's eyes widened with surprise. "Gina Zaffini? What does she know about what's going on here? Can we trust her? What if it's a trap?"

Kannon remembered a pair of light brown eyes, fearless and full of life. "This is no trap."

It was past midnight when Kannon pulled up at the special effects company, the full moon shining down on the building. The lobby was lit, and another room on the same level. Outside security lights at the corners showed nothing. Good. Maybe this visit would go smoother than his last one. Back then, he'd been hunting the woman he'd believed to be another killer, though as it had turned out she was merely a thief wrongly accused of murder. That said, the place was an unwelcome reminder of the only time he'd been bested. Delta Fox had not only got him flat on his back, but taken his gun. Had she been a real killer, his story would have been over. It seemed fate had decided that he'd come knocking here again.

He didn't get the chance. As he reached for the buzzer, the door swung wide and he was confronted by a thin older woman in a severe gray suit, her countenance like a constipated drill sergeant's.

"So," she said in a heavy Austrian accent, inspecting him like he was a new recruit, "you're the one responsible for the explosion."

Kannon looked beyond her as he entered. Leaning against the receptionist's desk with smirks on their faces was the little blonde thief, Delta Fox, and judging by their matching wedding rings, her husband, Brian Chanse. They looked like your ordinary, genial California couple. Until you crossed them. The gray suit shoved a sheet of paper in his face.

It was a bill for all the damage Kannon had caused when one of his bullets had missed Fox and instead, hit a locker full of explosives. The blast had trashed the company's back bay, and according to the bottom line, bolded and underlined, caused a high five figures in damage.

Kannon looked to Chanse. "No insurance?"

"It's the principle of the matter," the female commandant answered before her boss could. "If you were any kind of man, you'd take responsibility."

He brought the full weight of his regard on the woman, the same look that made most slink away. She sucked in her breath, her face flushed, and stood her ground. With employees like this, Chanse could set up his own enforcement racket. Chanse cleared his throat. "If it's any consolation, I didn't have Ursula charge you for my car. I figure I had a hand in it getting damaged, seeing as I'm the one that ran you off the road."

Although Kannon had a distinct memory of his boot connecting with a tender part of Chanse's anatomy, he didn't care to continue the conversation, especially since he couldn't see Tasanee anywhere. Or the Zaffini woman, for that matter.

"Funny," Kannon responded, his tone making it clear that it wasn't. "Where's the girl?"

Fox pointed down the hallway. "This way. In Brian's office. Tasanee was lucky Gina was there. She had to kill two men." She pinned him with her bright blue eyes. "So far no cops have come calling. You owe her, Kannon."

He knew that. Two women, two lectures. And two more females to go yet. He needed a cigarette.

Tasanee sat on a chair getting her long black hair braided. Gina, frowning and smiling, in concentration and pride, had the same look his wife had had when fixing their daughter's hair so many years ago. Tasanee rushed into his arms. He returned her hug, then brushed the hair from the bandage on her forehead. "You said you were okay."

"A bit of storefront came through the windshield when she crashed," Gina explained, perching on top of her boss's desk. Her long legs dangled down forever, and Kannon had to force his eyes upwards. She wore tall white boots with plat-form heels, a short dress splotchy with pink and yellow blossoms. It was to this flower child that he was forced to say, "I'm indebted to you, Miss Zaffini."

Fox, Chanse and Ursula had all filed in behind him, and Fox made a surprised noise. "Hang on. Zaffini? I knew that was your last name, but Gina, after what you did today—are you one of the Miami Zaffinis?"

Gina shrugged. "Yeah. My father was a made man. I kind

of took a different path in life."

"Okay, I'll bite," said Chanse, leaning against the office wall. "Who are they?"

"Italian mafia," Fox supplied. "One of the last traditional crime families."

"And here I assumed she was as harmless as she is incompetent," Ursula said.

Gina brightened under the insult. "Don't beat yourself up about it. Menopausal women often experience lapses in judgment." The older woman made choking noises, and Gina carried on to the room at large, "We liked to think of ourselves as the American mafia. Sounded more patriotic that way. Not that there's really any of the family left. My dad's about the only one who's not dead or serving a life sentence, and that's because he took off for Thailand."

"Thailand?" asked Fox. "So what's the connection there?"

Gina played with a red hair clip, snapping it open and shut like jaws. "Well, after my mom died, he got together with a Thai hooker, and when the FBI got too close they took me to live in Bangkok. Anyway, my dad met Tasanee's dad there and the two became friends. Only now it looks like there's been some trouble." She looked squarely at Kannon.

No point denying it. He turned to Tasanee, taking her by the shoulders. She was his daughter's friend, a young woman he'd come to care for. And now he had to dump fear and worry on her. He glanced at Gina Zaffini. And just like that, she slipped off the desk and stood close, so close she could've touched them both. She didn't, of course. Still, for whatever reason, it made what he had to say easier. "Tasanee, I'm afraid there's more than trouble. Your father has been kidnapped. He's being held hostage."

Tasanee froze. Only her lips moved. "What...how? When?"

"One of your father's bodyguards managed to get a call off to me saying they were under attack. That's when I phoned and told you to get out of your apartment. To find Gina. Your father's advisors weren't so lucky—his inner circle were all assassinated."

Tasanee went pale and under his hands, he felt her slump. He realized his mistake. "All except Ryota and me, of course."

It was as if he'd pumped air into her. She straightened, expanded and concentrated. "Who could have done something like that?"

"It was your father's top lieutenant, John Wakai. He betrayed us, and now he's trying to control the city. That's why he wants you. He knows your safety is the only thing that could ever make your father bend, and if your father bends then so will the gangs who follow him."

Tasanee was nineteen, still a girl in many ways, but she was also the daughter of a major crime lord. She bit hard on her lip and gave a quick nod. "I see."

Kannon released her. "Don't worry. I'll get him back. Right now I have to make some arrangements with our... friends here, okay?"

With Ursula left to tend to Tasanee, the rest of them stepped out into the hall.

"You're not in any position to protect her if Wakai's men track her here," Kannon said. "I'm taking her back to Bangkok."

"I'm going too," said Gina.

There was a difference between owing her and being owned by her. "No, you're not."

Gina crossed her arms over her chest. "First of all,

Tasanee's my god-sister. That makes her part of my family, and that makes this personal. Everybody in Bangkok knows Alak Montri and my dad are best friends, so if this douchebag takes over his organization, the first thing he'll do is strip my father of everything he owns. It doesn't matter that you're tough as nails, Kannon, you need some serious backing and you don't have time to screw around. Kun pôot paa-săa tai bpen măi?"

"What?" he replied, irritated.

"I asked if you spoke Thai, and you just answered my question. How do you expect to track down this guy quickly without some help?"

"I've got people."

"People you can trust?" she shot back. "With Wakai in charge, don't you think at least some of your guys might switch sides?"

Kannon made a deliberate pass over her appearance. "I don't think you're cut out for the kind of work that needs doing."

"I knocked off the two killers they sent after her." She said it like a statement of fact but he saw the way her eyes widened, the tensing of her jaw. Killing them had shook her. He had a sudden idiotic urge to take her by the shoulders and tell her, as he'd told Tasanee, that everything was going to be okay.

He stiffened. Not his place. And not a place he wanted, either.

Those clothes, that hair, that attitude. She didn't take her job as a receptionist seriously because she didn't need to—she came from a world of privilege, even if it was an underworld. There she stood, like a purple-haired cat that had eaten his canary, and he had to take it.

She poked him in the chest. "Give me all the dirty looks you want. I'm the one that saved Tasanee's life, and I've got the connections to rescue your boss. I know Bangkok, speak fluent Thai, and with that bastard threatening my family, this fight is as much mine as yours. I'm coming to help you, and that's that. You owe me and this is what I want as payback."

The happily married couple had silently listened to the exchange, arms looped around each other. Now Fox contributed. "I don't think that's how debts work. You're supposed to get something in return."

"I do. A trip to Thailand with my own personal body-guard who scares the skin off everybody." Gina glanced around. "Present company excepted."

Kannon grimaced. Fox and Chanse had both got the better of him at some point, the Witch of Finance couldn't be cowed, and Gina, being a Zaffini, had probably never feared anyone in her life. Other than the days he had with his daughter, it had been a long, long time since he'd been in a place where no one was terrified of him.

A pair of honey brown eyes was fixed on him in bratty defiance.

He sighed. "Call your father and let him know we're coming."

She blinked. "I already did."

Chanse snorted. "Man, welcome to my world. Women ask permission, then do whatever the hell they want."

Kannon knew it only too well, but played it out anyway. "It's your father's decision. He heads the organization. If he says so, you go back to Los Angeles. Agreed?"

"Kao jai láew."

That was it. He was getting language lessons. "Which means?"

"We've got a deal. Now if you'll all excuse me, I'm off to pack." She cut away, back down the hall to the lobby. "Wish me luck," she called over her shoulder. "Too many clothes, too little room. I'll be a mess before it's done."

Kannon observed the swing of her body and knew it was all talk.

CHAPTER TWO

GINA HAD A crick in her neck from all the times she'd twisted it around the privacy screen in the first class cabin to see if Kannon was awake.

He was as he'd been twelve minutes ago, stretched on his back under his airplane issue blanket. He was so tall his feet poked out. His socks were smooth, unrumpled, probably the ones with the special elastic at the top, the kind Ursula had gotten Brian for Christmas. His suit jacket was hung on a padded hanger, his tie loosened, his hands folded across his chest, his shoes, black and polished under his fully reclined seat. He'd been in that exact position for the past eight and a half hours.

There was at least another eleven hours left in the flight. Tasanee was sleeping, finally. The two of them had seen all the movies worth seeing. She'd showed Tasanee the scenes Brian and his stunt crew were in. She should be sleeping herself, except she was restless and bored.

Bored. Bored, bored, bored.

She flicked open her phone and played a game based on the Periodic Table. She beat her old time. Again. Somebody needed to discover some new elements. She glanced at the flight monitor and—surprise, surprise—the plane was still a dot on the Pacific Ocean.

Everything was quiet in the cabin. The attendants were off doing whatever they did between the feedings. Not even any headwinds to buck the cabin. Nothing to wake up somebody in a sound sleep. Gina tucked her phone into the seat pouch and stealth-walked to Kannon. He was a gorgeous man. He must be pushing forty from the lines around his eyes, his body wide and thick and strong. And his hands...she wanted those hands on her.

Hmmm...had she found a way to beat back her boredom? She was pretty sure he would go for it. She'd become something of an expert about whether or not a man was into her, and Kannon had fulfilled all the requirements on her checklist. She went to his feet and drew her finger along a sole.

It only took the one touch.

His eyes snapped open and he was up on his elbows. He shot her a look. Then one at Tasanee. Gina rushed to his side and whispered, "It's okay. Nothing's wrong."

Those dark-as-night eyes honed in on her and narrowed.

"Oh, come on." She wiggled her butt to claim a portion of his seat and bumped up against his hip. She felt him stiffen. Hopefully there were other places he was stiffening, too.

He didn't move, continued to glare. "You've been sleeping for more than eight hours. Do you want coffee? Water? I know where it all is, so I can get a drink for you without waking anyone up."

"Go back to your seat and stay there."

Okay, that wasn't an auspicious beginning. He was angry and irritated, hugely irritated. She recognized those symptoms. "Oh, oh, hang on, hon." She hurried back to her seat and rooted through her stash of essentials. She came back with a pack of nicotine gum. "From the way you were smoking in the parking lot I thought you might get a nic attack on the flight. Here, have some."

He looked at the gum, looked at her. "If I was asleep, I wouldn't need it."

Was he still sore about that? "That's true," she conceded. "But since you are, have one."

"Go away."

He sounded so cross. "Gum and coffee," she decided aloud. "That will loosen you up."

"I don't need loosening up. I need you to go back to your seat."

She went to the kitchenette and poured him a tall black one. When she came back, he was flat on his back, eyes closed. She leaned across and put it on the tray. She glanced back to comment on the airline's fine china and caught him taking in her ass. Yes!

She pulled back slowly, letting him take in the girls, too, which thanks to a built-in pushup, were super perky. She settled herself back down beside him and this time, took the logical next step of leaning her torso over him, tucking her hand on his other side. This would allow him to take in her full package without doing much, and she kinda liked the feel of him between her hip and hand. She stretched her legs because he'd eyed them back at Cause & FX.

She popped out a piece of gum from the cello pack and held it at his mouth. His eyes widened as if it were a poison pill, and he sat himself up against the seat. Good grief. She followed after him. "Open up."

His mouth thinned, though his eyes stayed fixed on the little white offering. "Oh, c'mon. It's gum, for Pete's sake.

Take it. You know you want to."

He caved, nearly taking her fingers with it. He chomped on the gum. "Slow, Kannon. The trick is to let it drip into your bloodstream. Chew it slowly then put it into your cheek and then chew again, maybe in five minutes." Unable to resist, she added, "It's like with any addiction. It's all about the slow release."

His chewing halted, and she watched his tongue pocket the gum into his cheek. "You smoke, too?"

"No, I had a girlfriend who did. She used the gum, and then I had a few pieces, too. And then, yeah, I got addicted to the stuff."

He regarded her with a long, neutral look. The look of a man who has firm opinions he's keeping to himself. "You're addicted to nicotine gum?"

"No! Are you kidding? There aren't many support groups for gum addicts, so I had to go cold turkey. I still get cravings now and again, so I know a little of what you're going through."

Another long, neutral look.

She assumed her previous position of leaning across him. "Soooo, you never said, what do you want to do now?"

"There's nothing to do."

Really? Was he that thick? Maybe it was the privacy thing. Maybe she needed to be way more direct. "You know everyone else is asleep. It's just you and me. "

"Why are you here?"

Okay, she'd overstepped. Everything on the list was checked off, maybe there was something missing in the blank marked 'Other'.

"I'm sorry, Kannon, I didn't realize. Are you monogamous, then?" In some relationships, she knew there was no sex with other partners. She was okay with that. Sometimes couples like that almost made her envious with their closeness, their utter belief that all they needed was each other. "Brian and Delta are so into that lifestyle. They get separated on the premises, and soon enough one or the other comes up to my desk, like a lost kid at the mall, wondering if I can page the other. And they won't carry their phones because they don't see the point when I'm there. And it's true. I'm never without my phone. I realized on this flight how addicted I am to it. Then again, is it an addiction if it's something nobody, absolutely nobody, can live without? Even Brian and Delta count on me to have a—"

"Not here." He pointed to the place between them. "Why are you coming to Bangkok?" He jabbed his thumb toward the dark rectangle of the window.

The calming effect of the nic gum clearly hadn't kicked in yet. "You know why. To help my dad."

"There's been trouble in the ten years you've been away. Why now?"

"How did you know I haven't been back in ten years?" Then she answered her own question. "Right. You work for my dad's best friend."

"I didn't know you were his daughter. I knew he had a daughter he hadn't seen in a decade."

Was he implying she'd deserted her father? She'd gone with his blessing. He'd understood. And she'd understood why he'd stayed in the business.

"We keep in touch, you know," she said defensively. "If my father needed me, I'd be there for him. Only he wouldn't tell me if he did and—and I'm thinking this is one of those times."

She snuck a look at Kannon. His face and eyes were as

hard as ever. Okay, she wouldn't be extending her membership in the Mile High Club on this flight. He took a sip of coffee, apparently having resigned himself to sparing her some attention.

"I called Dad for his birthday a few days ago. His wife answered. Said he was out fishing. Only Dad doesn't fish."

"You haven't seen him in ten years. He could've picked up a hobby."

"No. Dad believes in the specialization of labor. He won't do for fun what another works for. It's disrespectful, he says."

"He should say he doesn't like fishing, and leave it at that."

She liked that he'd said that. "That's what I keep telling him."

"You think your father's in trouble?"

"Yes. No. Maybe. He's supposed to be there to open his birthday present from me. It's a tradition. We do it over the phone. It's been like that since forever. Well, for ten years, anyway. And this year—this year, it didn't happen. "

"You're flying home because he didn't show for a gift opening?"

"That makes me sound oversensitive and irrational. Is that what you think?"

His tongue went to his cheek as he fished out his gum. Of course. He wouldn't insult the daughter of his boss's friend, because that wouldn't be smart. Then another thought occurred to her. "Alak Montri. Did he say anything about my dad?"

She could hear his teeth grind on the gum. "No. He hasn't. Mr. Montri doesn't talk to staff about his friends." He made it sound as if she'd insulted her dad, his boss and him all at once.

"Then I'll ask a different question. Do you know what's

going on with my dad?"

"I couldn't tell you."

"Couldn't or won't?"

"Yes."

A single word of affirmation that might be taken as flippant, except his dark eyes held hers steady and long. Put all together, that one-word affirmation meant that he knew something, that that something wasn't good and that he wasn't answering questions.

"Does Tasanee know anything?"

"You'd have to ask her."

"I did and she says she doesn't."

"Then you got your answer."

"Okay. Can you at least tell me if he's alive or not?"

His careful regard of her didn't change. "As far as I know, yes."

That wasn't a confirmation. "Is he injured?" There was always a chance he'd betray himself and actually give her an answer.

The gum went back into his cheek, and his chin dipped the tiniest fraction to indicate his low opinion of her continued interrogation. Gina shrugged. "Can't blame a girl for trying."

She crossed her legs and laced her fingers over them. "So then, tell me about the love of your life. You married?"

"Widowed."

She opened her mouth to follow that up when he expanded, "Not in a relationship, either."

"That must be kind of tough on your daughter."

"How do you know about her?" His voice was even sharper than usual.

"Tasanee told me. We were talking about friends and she kept bringing up Zoe this, Zoe that. I asked her and she told me."

"Don't talk about my daughter. That's none of your business either."

What was his problem? She wasn't pushing for sex, she was talking about family, which was about as universal a topic as could be. "God forbid we should enjoy each other's company. And don't pretend you're all that. I saw the way you've been checking me out."

She was ready for him to deny it. Instead, he said, "I check out deals all the time. It doesn't mean I'm buying."

"That because I'm Vincenzo Zaffini's daughter?"

"It's because you're Gina Zaffini."

"Ah. So you're rejecting me for who I am. And what is it about me you don't like?"

"We don't need to get into that."

"No, Kannon. We don't. You haven't had to tell me anything, but you have. You've told me that my father is in trouble, that you're a single parent, that you're addicted to cigarettes, and that while you're attracted to me you're not going to act on it, which makes no sense whatsoever considering I've been clear about my intentions."

"You want me?" His tone was one of total disbelief.

Why would he think she wouldn't? Was he not sentient? "Duh."

"I'm old enough to be your father."

"I'm thirty."

"I'm sixty."

"No, you aren't. You should just say you don't want to have sex with me and leave it at that."

"Not saying that, either."

"Then what are you saying?"

Unexpectedly he wrapped his hand around her neck, so

gently it was almost a caress and said in a low, low voice. "What I'm saying is that I'm a killer. It's what I do, it's what I am." He said it with flat acceptance. And with the thinnest edge of defiance, as if expecting her to deny it. Or deny him.

She leaned right in. "Kannon, I kinda figured that out. What I'm interested in is what else you are."

Something flashed in his eyes and she was ready to work her opening when the flight attendant appeared with a carafe of coffee. All pressed and pretty, she took in Gina's pose over Kannon and hesitated. You'd think she'd worked enough overnight flights to be used to this by now.

Oh well, back to being bored.

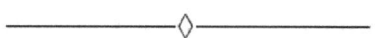

Gina flipped through the tourist brochure she'd picked up from the airport at Kota Bharu. "Seems the main entertainment's a Kentucky Fried Chicken," she said to Tasanee. They were the only females at the seaside café, the male patrons uniformly wiling away their time with newspapers and sweet coffee. "No bars, no nightclubs, nothing."

Tasanee shrugged. "The rickshaw ride was cool."

It was the mode of transportation Gina had insisted bring them the final stretch to the waterfront, overriding Kannon's protests. She had to do something fun, and the rickshaw decked out in a pink butterfly theme was perfect. She and Tasanee had enjoyed being part of the stream of three-wheeled vehicles lazily pedaling down the streets, passing by the vibrant markets and ornate mosques. Kannon had led the way in his own manly rickshaw, scanning the streets through his mirrored sunglasses for anything suspicious. He didn't seem to appreciate it when she'd pointed out that with his suit and scowl he was the most sinister presence around.

Even now, sitting a few feet off, puffing away on his millionth cigarette, he looked like a reincarnated dragon. Dry as one, too. She wiped the sweat from her forehead and adjusted her tudung, the silken headscarf that was the norm in the Muslim city. Although her long dress was pretty, in a medieval kind of way, the tropical heat made it stifling, excruciating for a woman who rarely bothered with panties.

She raised binoculars to check out the bright blue waters of the Gulf of Thailand for any sign of her father's yacht. There were plenty of flights direct from Los Angeles to Bangkok, but her father and Kannon had felt it prudent to meet in neighboring Malaysia instead. That meant they'd landed in Hong Kong, caught a plane to Kuala Lumpur, then another connector flight to Kota Bharu. Gina felt as if they'd been traveling for weeks.

She turned to Kannon. "Do you think I should call Darae? Just to see how long they'll be?"

He didn't look at her. "No."

She didn't get it. What was wrong with making a quick call rather than sit here for who knew how long? Keeping the binoculars in position with one hand, she reached for her phone inside her purse.

Then she saw it.

"Ah, there she is!" Gina stood and pointed to a pale pink yacht that had appeared on the horizon. Kannon held out his hand, and Gina passed him the binoculars.

"*The Pink Pussy*," he said, reading the name emblazoned in golden script on the bow.

Gina slung her purse over her shoulder. "*The Pink Pussy*cat. Check out the smaller font. Port authority made him add 'cat' so it wouldn't be so raunchy."

Tasanee giggled which escalated into snorts and girly laughter that drew disapproving looks from the males. Kannon drew a finger across his throat, and she instantly quieted. When he gave word that a powerboat had disembarked from the yacht, they gathered up their luggage and headed to the dock, a stray dog loping behind.

"I forgot about you dogs in Asia," Gina said to it as she set her bags down at the edge of the pier. "Always coming to keep me company."

"It could be rabid," Kannon cautioned.

Oh, really. She let the animal sniff her hand, then gave it a good scratch behind the ears.

"Or have fleas."

She tipped some water from her bottle into her hand and offered it to the dog. It lapped it dry and wandered off.

A few minutes later the powerboat eased up to the dock. The woman at the wheel was in her fifties, tall and busty for a Thai, her skin the color of cinnamon and her hair drawn into a high ponytail. Darae. One look at her and Gina wondered how it was that she could've stayed away as long as she had. She didn't know how she got inside the boat but all at once she was there, hugging the woman who'd played mother and mentor.

"Sorry, Darae. Sorry," she mumbled into the woman's hair.

Darae pulled them apart and searched Gina's face. "What are you sorry for?"

"I should've come sooner."

A certain closed stillness passed over Darae, and after giving Gina one more affectionate squeeze, she opened her arms to Tasanee. "Oh, Tas. It's so good to see you in one piece. We aren't going to let anyone hurt you. And we're going to make sure that Wakai pays for his crimes."

"He certainly will," said Kannon as he stepped aboard, bowing to Gina's stepmother. "Hello, Mrs. Zaffini. I'm Kannon Takahama. I take it my assistant is already on board?"

"He is. And so are his two guests. We have Jarun in the hold, along with the driver that came to pick him up."

Darae throttled the engine, wasting no time in returning to *The Pink Pussycat*. Gina pushed in close to her, stripping off the tudung that flapped uselessly about her head.

"Your father's happy you came," Darae yelled over the roar of the engine.

Gina steadied herself against the slam of the boat on the waves. "How is he? He wouldn't tell me." She gestured at Kannon.

"He's looking forward to seeing you again," replied Darae, sidestepping the question. "Ten minutes and you'll be talking to him."

Tingles, as fine as the water spray, misted down on Gina. Except it wasn't the urge to shop she felt but the desperate need to get to her father. She fixed her eyes on the yacht.

"Your timing is good. We need you here, Gina," Darae shouted on. "This is no ordinary scuffle. Alak's very respected. You remember, few years back, Bangkok was cut up between so many foreigners, not to mention those horrible pedophile groups. He's the one who put an end to them."

"So he has a lot of enemies. That's pretty standard for a crime lord."

"He's got a lot more friends," Darae countered. "The people, especially those in the slums, love him, and the Thai gangs all either respect or fear him. Now overnight, Wakai's murdered everyone in Alak's inner circle and slapped him in chains. One way or another, order's got to be restored. The trick is keeping his daughter safe while that happens."

"So Tasanee's a princess in peril?" Gina asked.

Darae turned her attention from the water to focus on Gina. "Yes," she said quietly. "Don't forget you are a mafia princess, too."

Her stepmother had always been of the opinion that Gina belonged with her father and his world. The paradox was that the very act that had proven Darae right had also been the one that had caused Gina to choose another path. "No," Gina said. "Not a princess. Not in peril."

"Then, who are you? A receptionist? A single woman? A killer on the run?"

Gina absorbed each of the labels, wincing at the last one. She looked out across the water as the pink yacht grew closer and more real.

"Right now," she said, "all I want to be is a daughter."

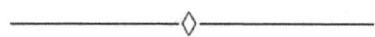

Once her feet hit the deck of *The Pink Pussycat*, Gina flew up the stairs to the sky lounge where Darae had said her dad was waiting. By the time she cleared the stairs, the tingles were crackles and sparks, her entire body a live wire.

Vincenzo Zaffini sat in the shade of an awning, surrounded by young, brown, bikini-clad women. His loose shirt and pants couldn't hide what had happened to his once big, strong body. His frame was skeletal and pale and so weak it couldn't seem to hold itself up. His face was sunken, his hair gone. But his dark eyes still shone up at her the way she remembered.

Slowly, painfully, with the aid of his cane and two of his girls, he stood and opened his arms. "Welcome home, bambina."

And as it'd been with Darae, she didn't feel herself cover the distance, only that she was there, his thin arms wrapped around her, her arms holding him and holding him up. She felt him sway and loosened her hug, trying to find a way to let him sit back down on his own and yet give him the help he needed. When he was seated, she sank to her knees beside him.

"Thought a bullet would catch me before the cigarettes did," he said softly to her. "Doctors say I got a while yet. Time enough for us to sort things out."

She would not cry. She had no right to cry when she couldn't be bothered to visit him in ten years. "I would've come earlier," she whispered. "For you, I would've."

He squeezed her hand, his grip tender in its weakness. "And I shouldn't have smoked a pack a day. Point is, you're here now. And for the time being, so am I."

"You should hear your voice, Daddy. You really sound like The Godfather now."

He leaned close. "Gina, bambina. God made me an offer I couldn't refuse."

Her vision blurred and she swallowed hard. She touched her forehead to his hand and felt his other hand smooth her hair. "Purple, huh?"

"Yeah," she choked out. "I wanted something different."

He chuckled, a throaty exhalation. "You always wanted something different."

She lifted her face to his. "Never wanted a different father."

"It was another story when you were fourteen."

"You can't believe anything a fourteen-year-old girl says."

He stroked her cheek. "Good. Sometimes—sometimes I wondered."

Why? Why had it taken her ten years? For a decade she'd done nothing, not been there for him. He never ever smoked in her presence, a promise he'd made to her mother and kept even after she'd died. If she'd been around more, he would've smoked less, maybe he would've even stopped.

There were footsteps behind her. She turned her head enough to see Darae's gladiatorial sandals, Tasanee's flip-flops and a pair of black polished shoes. She stood.

"Give them to me." She stuck out her hand. "Your cigarettes."

Kannon's face got very neutral. Just as she was certain he'd refuse her, he relinquished them. She sent the pack like a Frisbee over the railing.

Zaffini's organization was made up entirely of females and transsexuals, their turf the city's gentlemen's clubs, massage parlors and upscale bordellos, of which they owned the lion's share. Known as The Pink Stilettos, they dealt in sex and secrets, with more than one of them turning a blade in the back of her father's enemies. They regularly mingled with the fringes of society, yet every one of them was staring at her as if she were a lit stick of dynamite.

She was aware of the futility of what she was doing, that it was all too late. Then again, when had she ever accepted any authority, even that of fate?

Kannon tore his gaze from the railing. "That was my last pack."

"Don't care. I don't want anyone smoking on this ship."

"Does that apply to me, too?" Vincenzo Zaffini rasped.

She ignored his question and sailed on. "Daddy, I'd like you to meet my good friend, Kannon Takahama. We go back years."

If her father wondered how that was possible, he didn't let

on and instead bestowed on Kannon his blazing wide smile, the smile everyone said she'd inherited. In his emaciated state, it looked ghoulish, though he spoke steadily enough. "Your reputation precedes you, Kannon. Your boss spoke very highly of how you took care of Erawan Boontan."

"I owe Mr. Montri a great deal. I'd appreciate any assistance you can give."

Vincenzo Zaffini folded his thin hands over the jade head of his cane. "There's a reason he chose me to be Tasanee's godfather. Alak Montri and I have been friends for twenty years. My organization prides itself on discretion and information. My best girls are already on the job, and I have associates who'll help, too."

Kannon bowed, and Vincenzo's attention turned to Tasanee. "Your father is a great man, Tas. No matter what happens, I want you to know that you still have a family. And you will have vengeance no matter what the cost. You understand?"

Tasanee pressed her hands together at her forehead and bowed deeply. "My father has always called you friend, Mr. Zaffini. Thank you for helping me."

Good grief, Gina thought, all this kowtowing. It really was like a scene from *The Godfather*.

Kannon spoke. "My assistant and I have business to attend to below. Please excuse me."

"That a nice way of saying you're going to break out the thumbscrews?" Gina said.

Kannon addressed her father. "The sooner we do, the sooner we can learn what Wakai's done with Mr. Montri."

With an approving nod from her father, Kannon turned to walk away.

Gina stood. "Fine then. I'll go with you."

Kannon stopped, and looked to Vincenzo.

"Bambina," her father said. "Let the man do his work. We both know you're not tough enough for this."

"Tough enough? I used to hang out in the worst parts of Bangkok!"

Vincenzo shrugged. "Sure. Under my protection."

"I took care of the guys that were after Tasanee!"

"Must have been amateurs."

Gina now remembered why she used to have the hugest fights with her old man. "Oh, is that so? What do I have to do to prove I'm as tough as you ever were?"

Vincenzo rolled his eyes. "Girl, you're not as tough as I am now."

That was ludicrous. Darae stepped forward. "How about we give Gina a chance, Vinny? Let her go down and help Kannon with the—questioning. Let's see what she's capable of."

Vincenzo Zaffini twisted his mouth in reluctant agreement. Before he could change his mind, Gina marched away. "Come on, Kannon. Let's go downstairs and get some answers."

On the stairwell that led down to the yacht's underbelly, she found herself blocked by a tall Japanese man, his frame lanky but still well-muscled beneath his suit.

"Ryota, this is Mr. Zaffini's daughter, Gina," Kannon said by way of introduction. "She's here to help with the questioning."

Gina didn't miss the dubious look they exchanged. "What, you two have a system I'd be messing with? Good cop, bad cop?"

"More like bad cop, worse cop," Kannon replied.

The two men thought she was going to screw up and she

very well might but, at the moment, she couldn't stand for there to be one more ounce of pain anywhere. Not while she could prevent it. "So you're going to try to beat it out of them, are you? You don't think by now Wakai would have figured out we have them? Even if they spill their guts, he'll have covered his tracks. Any information is going to be worthless."

"They'll name names. People. Places. Leads we can use to hunt him down. Nobody can cover their tracks completely, especially now we have eyes and ears throughout the city."

"That'll take time, and following a trail of breadcrumbs only invites an ambush. Besides, once you two start hurting them, they'll say anything they think you want to hear to make the pain stop. Torture doesn't work. We have to be smarter than that."

Kannon's hands tightened into fists, his chest swelling in an effort to intimidate. Gina almost smiled at his bullying. He was so used to others doing what he said that he really didn't have much of a repertoire when it came to getting people's cooperation. He added words to his actions. "I have a lot more experience with…extracting information than you do."

Gina didn't back down. "And I can sweet talk better than a whore on Wednesday. We don't need those men as punching bags. We need them as bloodhounds. Get them on our side, and they'll lead us to Wakai way faster than we could get there on our own." She wondered where that theory had originated. Probably from Darae's teachings a lifetime ago. "Anyway, there's no harm in letting me try, now is there? Not like you can't kick the snot out of them if I fail."

"We don't have time for stupid games."

"Give me fifteen minutes," she insisted. "You can spare that." She got in his face. "You have to spare that."

"Out of respect for your father I'll allow it, but Ryota and

I will be there with you."

"I wouldn't have it any other way." She tugged Ryota's tie. "Now move, handsome. Clock's ticking."

CHAPTER
3
THREE

THE TWO MEN sat in their underwear against the back wall of the hold, their wrists handcuffed to a large concrete block. Their skins were painted with angry welts, and aside from a dish of water and a bedpan, neither looked like they'd been afforded any care whatsoever.

While one had typical Thai features, the younger man was a strange one. His features were sharp and brutish, eyes wide and manic. He pulled his lips back like a wild animal to reveal teeth filed to points. Most disturbing to Gina was the scarified script that had been cut into his forehead, not a word of which she could decipher.

Kannon nodded at the ordinary one. "This one's Jarun."

The man turned pleading eyes to Gina. "Please...something to eat."

Kannon tapped the bedpan with his shoe. "There's your last meal."

Gina glared at him, then instructed Ryota, "Go empty it out."

Ryota looked wide-eyed at his boss, but after a grunt from Kannon, he left with the pan held out at arm's length.

The prisoners looked warily at her, and Gina appreciated how strange she must look—a white woman in Muslim garb, hair purple and wild. She considered where to begin with the two wretches, acutely aware of Kannon's eyes on her. She needed to channel more of Darae's teachings. She straightened and addressed them in Thai.

"My name's Gina, and I want to know where Alak Montri is being kept," she began. "I don't care what role you two played in Wakai's plot, and I'm not going to allow Kannon here to torture you anymore. Instead I'm going to give you a choice. Either we work out a deal to find Mr. Montri and you go free, or I have you thrown overboard to drown. You want to cooperate or not?"

Jarun eyed Kannon. "You'll toss us overboard, anyway."

"It's not what you know right now that's of any interest to me. It's what you can find out when you're back in Bangkok. I don't believe either of you have any idea where Mr. Montri is right now, though I'm sure you could find out if you had the opportunity."

"And what would keep you from killing us as soon as you had him?" Jarun clearly wasn't the trusting sort.

Gina stepped closer to, causing him to flinch, then kneeled so she was on eye level with him. "Do you know how my father took over so much of Bangkok's nightlife, so fast?"

Jarun shook his head.

"Because he kept his word. And that's why people like to deal with him—because they know that when he makes a promise, he keeps it."

Despite Jarun's skeptical expression, Gina pressed on. "You and your buddy here are pawns. Henchmen. I'll happily let you go if it means I can rescue Montri. And I give you my word that if you help us, we'll set you free. I can't make a better offer than that."

Jarun's jaw clenched, his eyes shifting back and forth between Kannon and Gina. They settled on Kannon. "Before we make any deal, I want talk to Mr. Zaffini himself to—"

With a snarl more animal than human, the younger man lunged forward, knocking Gina aside, an instant away from sinking his shark-like teeth into Jarun's jugular. Before Gina's butt could hit the floor, Kannon's foot connected with the attacker's jaw.

The man's head slammed with an audible crack against the back wall, teeth breaking. Jarun scuttled away as far as the handcuffs would let him, at the same time Kannon followed up with an iron grip on the assailant's throat, cutting off breath.

Gina scrambled to her feet, her eyes wide as she and Jarun exchanged shocked looks.

The door to the hold burst open and there was Ryota, gun in hand.

"Unlock Jarun and get him some food and clothing," said Kannon impassively as the man in his grip turned a bright red. "Take her with you."

"And what about...him?" asked Gina, her heart pounding. Were it not for Kannon's reflexes, Jarun's throat would have been ripped out in front of her.

Kannon tilted his victim's head a bit, inspecting him as he thrashed. The redness of his face began to darken to blue, blood and saliva dripping from his mouth. "I don't think this one's going to respond to reason."

Gina placed a hand on Kannon's shoulder. "We need to keep him alive." She swallowed. "*I* need him alive."

Kannon's grip shifted suddenly from neck to face, and whacking the prisoner's head into the wall, knocked him unconscious.

Gina supposed that was a fair compromise.

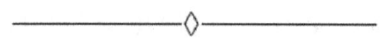

Tucked into his sky lounge chair with Gina and Darae seated on either side of him, Vincenzo smiled thinly at Jarun who was in a short-sleeved red dress shirt and beige shorts, an outfit he'd been partial to in his pre-cancer days, and one, along with dozens of other pieces of clothing, he ordered to be removed. Instead, he now realized, they'd only been removed from his sight. Damn women.

"Jarun, tell us what you know."

"Wakai and I grew up in the slums. He was always smart. Always a good friend. A natural leader. But his sister, Victoria, she was a psycho. Never played with the other children. Always hung out with weird scum. Street shamans. Back alley abortionists. Old Khmer Rouge war criminals. She was drawn to whatever was twisted—and wrong."

Vincenzo noticed Gina squirm in her seat. She always did have a hard time with tales of ugliness. "And you're telling me this why?"

Jarun looked him square in the eye. "Because I know John Wakai. I'm not a member of any gang. Make my living as an independent enforcer. But I'm loyal to him, and I'm not going to betray him no matter what you do to me. His sister, though, that's another story. I bet you anything she's behind why John turned on his boss. Kill her and you'll be doing everyone a favor."

From the blaze in the man's eyes, he clearly believed what he said. Vincenzo glanced over at Kannon who stood off to one side with Ryota.

"The phone message Wakai left for Jarun mentioned that

a woman named Victoria botched up Tasanee's kidnapping," Kannon confirmed.

Interesting. Vincenzo resumed his conversation. "And how close are Wakai and Victoria?"

Jarun twisted his mouth in disgust. "Very close. That's the problem. She's had her hooks in him ever since their mother died. He feels responsible for her, and she uses that to manipulate and corrupt him. She'll know where Mr. Montri is being kept. We can both save our friends."

"You're asking me to forgive Wakai?"

"Exile him," Jarun proposed. "He's in a wheelchair. A cripple. No friend in the world except me. Isn't that enough punishment?"

Hardly. It didn't matter if he pardoned Wakai. His fate would be decided by another. "I can't promise what Alak will do when he gets free, but tell us where to find Victoria and both you and Wakai will have my mercy, for what it's worth. That's the deal we can make. Take one step out of line...."

"I accept, and I swear I'll do everything I possibly can." Jarun raised his hands high in a prayer pose and bowed to his waist. "Thank you, Mr. Zaffini."

Vincenzo's fingers curled a little more tightly around the head of his cane. "Seeing as we're now friends, I think we should start with you telling me a little bit about the man in my hold. Strange scars, filed teeth—I'd have thought that I would have heard of any gang like that. Especially one with the muscle to ambush Alak. Tell me what you know about them."

"When Victoria was a teenager she made friends with that man's gang," explained Jarun. "Back then, there were just a few of them in the slums, but their organization extends into the wilderness areas of Cambodia. For years she's had ties to them, and it was their group that raised a small army to help

Wakai. Came across the border to help him take Mr. Montri and kill his inner circle."

No wonder nobody had seen the plot coming. This was yet another invasion of ruthless foreigners into Bangkok, aided by the treachery of his friend's most trusted strategist and advisor. Vincenzo suddenly felt tired. Had he and Alak accomplished nothing in life? Could it really all fall to ruin so easily? "And what was your part in the betrayal, Jarun?"

"Nothing. It came from out of the blue. Like I said, John and I are close friends, but it was sudden, and I had no part of it. I swear to you I tried to talk him out of it."

Vincenzo knew in his gut that the man was telling the truth. In this business, however, you'd been a fool to say it. "I'm not certain you're as innocent as you claim, Jarun, though in the end I don't suppose it makes a difference. We have a deal, and I think we're done here. At least for now."

Ryota escorted Jarun out, and Kannon made to follow them. Oh, no. Vincenzo wasn't quite finished with Alak's man. "Kannon, a word. What did you think of my daughter's handling of Jarun?"

Kannon didn't pull punches. "I think he'll either flee or betray us the moment he gets a chance."

Gina made an indignant squeak. "And go where? There's nowhere in the city he could hide from us, and you think Wakai would take him back at this point? Friends or not, he'd assume Jarun betrayed him. The only way our buddy can make it out of this situation is by getting on our good side."

She looked so put out, so much like she'd been as a teen-ager, that Vincenzo laughed. "Don't ride Kannon for telling it as he sees it. Few people left like that. Anyway, I actually approve of your plan, bambina. We'll see how things go."

Gina smiled. "So, you're okay with me helping Kannon

then?"

Vincenzo sighed. "Absolutely not."

"What! You said—"

"I gave you a chance to impress me, and you have. I like how you handled the situation. Like your plan. You're smart and you're fearless and you've got heart."

Gina rolled her hand impatiently. "But?"

"But you're also an undisciplined brat. You'll be getting in Kannon's way. I can't see it working out."

On a howl of frustration from Gina, Darae spoke up from the other side. "So you plan on living forever?"

He cranked himself awkwardly around in the chair to face her. Damn, it was hard to do anything anymore. "What do you mean?"

"You know exactly what I mean. When you go, are you expecting me to carry on alone?" Her voice hitched on the last word, then swept on. "And then when I'm gone? Who's going to keep the businesses going and protect the girls? Who's going to be Tasanee's friend, and help her keep order if Alak doesn't make it out of this? Hmm?"

"So you're saying it should be Gina?" he asked. "She's still barely more than a girl herself. Just look at her hair."

Gina scowled. "I'm right here you know."

Darae didn't relent. "Then let her grow up, Vincenzo. Give her a chance. I know you don't want to be the last of the Zaffinis, and if Gina were a son you'd have her involved."

"It's nothing to do with that," he answered, turning away from his wife.

"Then why?"

He closed his eyes wearily. "Because I may have already lost a good friend to Wakai. I'm not losing my daughter to him, too. And besides, I was under the impression Gina didn't want to live the life of a criminal. She made that abundantly clear when she moved to California."

Before Darae could speak again, Gina raised a hand to each of them.

"Look, the last thing we need to worry about right now is my future career. That bastard's a huge threat to our family. To us, Tas, and all the people who work for us. Both of you taught me that nothing's more important than family. That you fight for family to the very end, even if you know you're going to lose."

Vincenzo chopped the air with his hand. "Yes, yes. That's all very eloquent, Gina. You've got your mother's silver tongue. She could have sold sand to Arabs."

"It's easy to sell an idea when you know you're right," she shot back.

Why couldn't they let him die in peace? Not having any children of her own, Darae loved his daughter every bit as much as Gina's mother had. Despite her delicate appearance, Darae had the balls of a brass monkey. And she'd passed those brass balls onto Gina.

Besieged by the women, he looked to Kannon.

Even though he wore his sunglasses, Vincenzo knew damn well where his eyes were aimed. When it came to his daughter, the man was far from neutral. Gina was no longer alone. And, if she didn't blow it, might never be alone again. Besides which, the girl did have a point. This was no time for argument.

"Promise me you'll be careful, stay smart and do what Kannon tells you."

Gina flashed Kannon the smile that had Vincenzo kicking boys overboard the day she hit puberty. "Well, I promise the first two, anyway."

The man was a goner.

"Then it's settled," Darae crowed, she and Gina high-fiving each other right in front of his face.

Damn women.

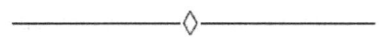

It was late at night when Gina, Kannon, Ryota and Jarun ventured into a part of Bangkok known as 70 Rai, a dark slum that spilled from an industrialized port, pooling beneath a noodle bowl of highway on-and-off ramps. Unlike the glittering towers of commerce at the city's heart, the shanty town had no electricity, the only illumination filtering down from the towering expressways that rose on stark concrete pillars.

Trying not to gag on the stench of raw sewage from the nearby canal, Gina followed Jarun through the narrow alleys, her flashlight beam trained on his back so as not to lose him in the eerie twilight.

"How far is this place?" she asked.

"Only a couple more minutes," he muttered, and he proved to be a man of his word.

The street opened into a kind of courtyard, its borders defined by crumbling walls that likely dated back to the ancient city of Thonburi, the forgotten capital upon whose bones Bangkok was built. Gina might've imparted this little piece of history to her companions had Jarun not drawn their attention to a structure almost as old—a Buddhist temple long since defiled by graffiti and abuse.

Jarun had promised to take them to where Wakai's sister indulged her sick fantasies, and while Gina hadn't known what to expect, this old ruin wasn't it. "Looks abandoned."

Their guide's lips curled back in disgust. "It should be but it's not. Things get started after dark, so this is the time to see if she's here."

"You ever go inside?" asked Kannon.

Jarun recoiled as if insulted. "No. Never. Not even the slum gangs come here. I only know about it because John and I drink together, and he talked about it once when he was drunk. I came here the next day out of curiosity. To see if his story was true. After what the people around here told me, I never wanted to come back."

Gina felt a shiver run down her spine. Considering Jarun was a Bangkok gangster who tortured people for a living, she couldn't even begin to guess at what lay within the temple.

"Well, you're going in tonight," Kannon said.

Ryota tipped his head to Gina. "What about her?"

She rolled her eyes. "Again, I'm right here. I'll come with."

Kannon balked. "We have no idea what's in there. Ryota will stay with you while I check it out."

"If there's going to be trouble it would be better if we stay together," Gina insisted. "Besides, you don't speak Thai. You trust our friend here to do all the translating, or are you hoping they'll all know Japanese?"

"Bringing him was your idea," he ground out, "and I never wanted you translating in the first place. Besides, you promised your father you'd be careful."

Gina looked to Ryota. "Who would I be safer with? You or Kannon?"

"Him."

"Thank you. After we're through with this, I'll fix you up with one of the girls. My treat. Now, enough of this silliness. Let's go see if we can do a meet-up with Vicky."

The candlelit interior of the temple had been converted

into a lounge of sorts, with a red lacquered bar running along one wall and sets of tables and chairs around the rest of the floor space, each with its own hookah. On the black walls was scrawled a crimson script—the same mysterious script Gina had seen carved into the forehead of the freaky cannibal. The temple's golden Buddha was still in its place—with nails driven into its eyes, and barbed wire wound into cuffs around its wrists.

Creepiest of all, however, were the people.

Seated around the tables, surrounded by pale clouds of sweet-scented smoke, were a half dozen sharply dressed patrons. Four were Asians, two were whites, and all had sly, predatory looks. Watching over them was a group of four squat men, their hatchet-like features hardening at the sight of unexpected guests.

Jarun slid aside to reveal Gina, flanked by Kannon and Ryota.

Time to mingle.

She gave the customary bow and addressed them in Thai. "Hello."

One of the hatchet-faced men stepped up, smiling like a lion at a lamb, and returned the gesture of greeting. His Thai tinted with a Cambodian accent, he welcomed her. "I don't believe we've seen you before, Miss..."

"You can call me Ursula," she supplied. "My friend here mentioned that you offer some, um, unusual services. I came here to sample them, if I'm not intruding."

The man took in her tight black outfit and leather boots. "You're a confident woman to visit 70 Rai after dark."

"As you can see, I came prepared," she said. "The neighborhood's not so scary when you've got company."

He offered her a chair. "It's a pleasure to meet you. It's

rare that women come seeking what we offer, though you're not the first. How did you hear of us?"

"A friend I met a while back," Gina replied, accepting the seat. Kannon stood behind her, while Ryota stationed himself to one side, eyes scanning the temple's occupants. Jarun had skirted them all, and hovered nearby. She had to be very careful to disguise her ignorance as she dropped the name of Wakai's sister. She could hear the advice Darae gave her girls for entertaining a client: Talk to get them talking. Then shush.

"She only really hinted at what goes on here," said Gina, keeping her tone relaxed. "Still, I was interested enough to seek it out. Obviously you must know her. She said her name was Victoria."

There was a hum of recognition among the men. "She's introduced several of us to this place," said a man with silver-grey hair wearing a turtleneck, switching the conversation to English, though his accent was cultured French. "Bangkok has so many boring, trivial vices. It's a privilege to meet another connoisseur."

"Likewise," Gina smiled. "So where did you meet Victoria?"

"Through the Elite Twelve," he replied. "Ever heard of them?"

Gina struggled to keep her expression straight. Behind her, she could feel Kannon, feel his power and his anger as forcefully as if they were her own. And rightfully so. The British pedophile ring had been among the very worst, not just trading in young flesh, but actively sadistic in their methods. For them, it wasn't enough to kidnap the children of the poor.

They left unmarked envelopes on parents' doorsteps weeks, or even months later, with pictures of what they'd done, while they'd been doing it. When her father had learned of their atrocities, he and Alak Montri put a bounty on their heads, attracting the interest of the city's gangs and mercenaries. Days later, the 'Elite Twelve' was whittled down to the 'Elite Seven', and the remainder of their horrific organization fled back to the shadows of the UK.

"Oh yes. Never got the chance to get involved. I know people who did, though."

"How about you? Where did you meet her?" asked another patron, a New Yorker from the sound of it. His eyes were cold as a dead fish as he puffed on the hookah.

"We met at a party here in Bangkok," answered Gina, avoiding any specific time or place that might trip her up. "She certainly mixes in some interesting circles."

The French fucker swirled his glass of cognac, and smiled, almost nostalgically, into its contents. "Oh yes, and she's an eager recruiter. Even maintains a website of sorts. Have you seen it?"

Oh, Jesus. A website? Gina swallowed, licked her lips to buy a second or two. Then thinking about what she just did, she licked them again suggestively. "No. Can't say I have. Sounds…inspiring."

Producing a thin silver pen, the man reached for Gina's hand. Instantly Kannon started forward; the man halted; Gina waved Kannon away. Her skin crawled as the pedophile turned her palm upwards, and in precise characters wrote a long Thai web address of seemingly random numbers and letters. "I'm sure you'll find it fascinating. Victoria's an exceptional photographer. Exquisite. She has a certain je ne sais quoi. Much like you."

Gina curled her hand into a fist over the address. "Merci," she said. "I'll be sure to check it out."

The owner gestured to the bar. "We now wait for one

more guest," he said in English, though his words were barely comprehensible, what with his accent and lack of fluency. "Would young lady like drink?"

"Gin and tonic, please," she replied, then turned back to the men. "So how exactly do things work here? Like I said, Victoria didn't go into details."

The New Yorker exhaled a jet of pale blue smoke. "As soon as we're all here, they'll bring out the kids. We pick our favorites, then we head downstairs. Place is expensive as hell, but they've got a world-class setup down there. Bondage yokes, funnel gags, smother boxes, e-stim machines—plus all the usual medical tools. Nice and clean, too."

"Surgically clean," added the Frenchman with a giggle.

That was it. She needed a moment. She averted her face to look at Kannon. His expression was utterly impassive; his eyes on Ryota. He blinked twice, then looked beyond his apprentice to the man who'd gone to fetch Gina her drink.

The New Yorker sank back against the cushions. "So, you a LBL or LGL, Ursula?"

Gina pretended. "LBL here. You?"

"LGL mostly, though I swing both ways. What's your AOA?"

What the hell could that stand for? She noticed Jarun sneak up eight fingers.

"Eight," she replied, hoping she'd answered smoothly enough.

The man raised an eyebrow. "Eight, huh?"

Gina shrugged. "What's yours?"

The man studied her for a moment. "I'm getting the feeling you're a CHSC, Ursula. Would I be right on that?"

Jarun shook his head, wide-eyed.

"Uh, no. Why would you think that?"

The owner arrived back at their table with the gin and tonic, offering it to Gina. "For young lady."

The Frenchman laughed as she accepted the glass. "Now Michael, let's not be paranoid. You'll have to excuse my friend. He's an RSO back in the United States. Makes him nervous of being arrested again."

"Well, you can never be too careful, right?" Gina moved to take a sip, when the situation exploded.

Kannon slapped the glass from her lips with his left hand, his right hand quick-drawing his pistol and firing in rapid succession, bullets finding the chests of the temple's security before they could react. In the same instant, Ryota put the drink server in a headlock, pressing the muzzle of his pistol to his hostage's neck. As a group, the customers and staff raised their hands in surrender.

Kannon trained his gun on the New Yorker, as smoke swirled from its barrel. "Sometimes paranoia is a good thing."

"I don't want any trouble," said the man. "This is a big mistake."

Kannon didn't move. "Where's Victoria?"

The New Yorker shook his head. "I don't even know the bitch. We've never fucking met."

"I believe you," said Kannon. He jammed his gun in the man's mouth and pulled the trigger.

The chair with its contents toppled backwards as Kannon swiveled his gun on the Frenchman, its muzzle dripping with blood and brains. "He was useless to me. Are you?"

Gina leapt out of her chair to grip Kannon's shoulder. "For God's sake, give him a chance to talk."

"I'm a busy man," ground the assassin through hate-clenched teeth. "You've got ten seconds to tell me something useful, Monsieur. Don't, and you join your friend in hell."

The Frenchman pointed frantically at the man Ryota had in a chokehold. "She's friends with these people! She finds customers for them like I told you!"

Kannon's trigger finger tightened, a hair from blowing the man's head off. "Yes, as you've told us. What else?"

"I heard she's into black magic. A Chinese friend of mine met her when he hired some sorcerer to curse his enemies. That's all I know. Please don't kill me!"

Kannon pulled a second gun from his jacket and handed it to Gina. "Take this and keep them covered. I'm going downstairs."

Gina took the gun and did as she was asked, while Kannon strode over to a set of doors at the back of the temple and disappeared through them. Keeping her eyes on her prisoners, she addressed Jarun.

"What the hell was with all those acronyms?"

"The pedophile community uses them so that they can speak to each other without people knowing what they're talking about," he explained. "Helps them recognize each other on chat rooms, too. LBL means 'little boy lover'. AOA is 'age of attraction'."

"And what does CHSC mean?" asked Gina, unable to even guess.

"It stands for ' Cement-headed Straight Clown'," Jarun answered. "Someone who goes out of their way to persecute molesters."

"How do you know so much about it?" Ryota asked, voice calm even as he held his hostage.

Jarun shrugged. "When I was a kid I used to bring guys like these to my friends. That's why I worked so hard to learn English. You learn how they speak so that they'll follow you."

"Your friends prostituted themselves?" asked Gina.

"Hell, no. We'd just ambush and rob them. How do you think I figured out how to cause people so much pain? When you're small, you make every hit count."

The Frenchman glanced at the door Kannon had disappeared through, down at the corpse of his friend, then back at Gina. "Mademoiselle, please, whatever your quarrel, we're no part of it. Each of the men here is someone influential. Kill us and the police will be after you. I already told you everything I know. Let us go and we'll forget this ever happened."

"Shush," Gina replied, annoyed that the man had a point. There were too many people to question thoroughly, and the only alternative to letting them go would be a massacre. Damn Kannon. She'd had everything under control until he'd gone trigger happy.

As if on cue the door at the back of the temple opened up and he reappeared—this time with company. Filing after him was a crowd of boys and girls, poor peasant children new to the city, by the looks of their clothing. All seemed scared out of their wits. None seemed harmed. At least not physically.

Motioning for the children to remain quiet, Kannon trained his gun back on the temple's patrons. "Gina, take the kids outside."

His voice was quiet, eerily serene. "Kannon, what are you going to do?"

He didn't look at her. "I said, take the kids outside."

The Frenchman looked up at Gina desperately. "Please, mademoiselle. He's going to kill us all. I have a family. An important job at the consulate. Please don't let him do this."

"Shut up," snapped Gina, and turned to Kannon. "I know these guys are child abusers, and they deserve to be punished, but we can't gun them all down."

Kannon sighed, and slowly lowering his weapon, he

walked over to Gina. "Fine. Perhaps you're right. We'll tie them up and—"

CHAPTER 4 FOUR

AS GINA REGAINED consciousness, she became aware of two contradictory sensations: the intense pain throbbing in her head, worse than any hangover she'd ever suffered, and the warm rocking movement of being carried. She blinked open her eyes to discover that it was Kannon's arms she was cradled in.

"Wha...what happened?"

He slanted her a look. "I knocked you out. The headache will pass in a few hours. Way I struck you the bruise won't even be visible."

"You hit me?! What the fuck, Kannon! Put me down right now!"

He did as she asked, and touching the side of her head, she winced at its tenderness. The four of them were still in 70 Rai by the looks of it, dawn had not yet broken, and the children were clustered close.

She dropped her head into her hands. "What did you do?"

"Only lawyers should ask questions they already know the answers to," he replied.

"You're a psycho, you know that? I had everything in

57

hand till—"

"Till you drank whatever that man put in your drink. The customers were fooled by you, but the owners saw through your act the second we walked in."

Gina leaned against a wall of corrugated metal to steady herself. "You don't know that."

"I saw him do it. You might have too if you hadn't been so busy chatting."

"I got useful information out of them and you know it," she protested, holding up her hand with the web address written on it. "You didn't have to kill them."

"Can you walk?" he asked, pointedly ignoring her rebuttal.

She was dizzy and wobbly and ready to do a face-plant into the muck. "Of course I can."

She straightened and started off. She staggered, stopped, staggered on.

"We don't have time for this," Kannon growled. He scooped her into his powerful arms as if she weighed nothing, and strode on, leading their motley crew out of the slums. Gina rested her head on his shoulder and closed her eyes, because the way she was feeling, she'd end up barfing on his suit.

"Kannon?"

"What?"

"Who the hell wears a suit to the slums?"

"I'm on the job."

"And you always wear a suit on the job?"

"Yes."

"Why a suit?"

The arms about her tightened. "It commands respect. Besides, I've got a lot of them. Don't want to ruin my good clothes."

She opened one eye. His jaw was rigid, his gaze straight ahead. "What do you consider 'good clothes'?"

"Why are we talking?"

"Because you hurt me, and payback is you get to distract me from my pain."

"Payback is I've got to haul you back to the boat."

"That, too."

He made a grumping noise. She snuggled against him, figuring it was easier to carry a load close than farther away, and because even if she verged on losing her cookies, he felt awesome. She slipped her hand under his jacket to the hard muscles of his upper pecs, and brought her lips against his neck. "Maybe you could distract me other ways."

"I thought you were dizzy."

"Not if I keep my eyes shut. Lots of things I can do by touch." To demonstrate she slid her tongue along the tendon in his neck.

He sucked in his breath. "Cut it out."

"Why? Because you're on the job?"

"Yes."

"So you admit that you find me distracting?"

"Like a monkey."

Stock it up to the pain, or to an evening dealing with the worst kind of scum in the worst part of the city, but Gina decided to call him on this one. She slid her hand from his chest and began to unbutton his shirt.

"I told you, cut it out, or I'll throw you over my shoulder and take you back that way."

"Aren't you in enough trouble with my old man as it is?"

"It'll be worth it."

"Uh-huh. How about I play nice if you just admit that you think I'm hot?"

There was a deep volcanic rumbling from Kannon that finally erupted with, "A Hawaiian shirt and a pair of cargo shorts."

She paused her work on the buttons to take that in. "Those are your good clothes?"

"Yes. Now do up my shirt."

She thought to negotiate when there was a sudden scuffling from behind them. Kannon spun around, and Gina sprung her eyes open in time to see Jarun sprint off into the darkness. Ryota, who'd been herding the children, cursed and drew his gun. There was nothing to aim at. Jarun had vanished.

Ryota moved to pursue. Kannon stopped him. "Let him go. He knows these slums. You don't."

Reluctantly Ryota obeyed.

"I told you to keep an eye on him while I carried Gina," Kannon ground out. "Now he's gone."

Ryota bowed. "I'm sorry."

"If we were still Yakuza, one of your fingers would be shorter. Better hope your mistake doesn't put Tasanee at risk."

Ryota's shoulders slumped as the group trudged on.

"How did you know Ryota has a crush on Tasanee?" she whispered.

He readjusted her in his arms, not very gently at all. "I have a daughter. I know the look."

His jostling and Jarun's escape was doing a number on her, and she quickly closed her eyes. In the comfort of near unconsciousness, she murmured, "You think my father knows the look, too?"

Kannon's answer was an exasperated hiss. "Yes."

"So you're not worried about what my father's going to say when he learns you hit his daughter?" Gina asked. "Or let Jarun escape?"

Kannon didn't answer. Seemed he was done talking for the night.

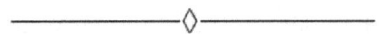

John Wakai brooded while his sister gave him a shoulder rub, surveying the city as he contemplated what more he could do. Her Cambodian friends were prowling the slums and red light districts, searching for any hint of Tasanee's whereabouts, but thus far had come up empty handed.

Odds were excellent she was back in Bangkok. Before he'd wiped out Montri's lieutenants, the Black Lotus had the support of virtually every gang in the city. Tasanee was too young and inexperienced to rally them, but she had Kannon on her side. Already Jarun and one of the Cambodian gangsters had gone missing, confirming his fear that Kannon was trying to find him as hard as he was trying to find Tasanee. Every day she was free the situation became more dangerous, and without her, Alak would remain stubbornly defiant.

Under normal circumstances Kannon wouldn't have been such a problem. He'd outwitted several criminal masterminds in his time. Russians, Chinese, Nigerians, Japanese, Pakistanis, Iranians—all of their respective syndicates had failed to wrest control of the city away from the Black Lotus, and Wakai knew he'd been a key component in Alak's success.

In this case, however, he'd little to work with. Forced to betray a man that he respected and hoped to serve for the rest of his life, he was now pressured for fast results by blunt-minded savages he scarcely trusted. At least he knew where the Cambodians were. Kannon could be anywhere, could be taking out the guards in the lobby right now, could be riding the elevator to put a bullet in him and his sister.

Somehow he needed to regain control of the situation, and fast.

His phone rang. It was a call he couldn't ignore.

"We were hit," said the familiar cold voice. "Four dead in 70 Rai, and all six clients. Kids gone. Didn't know a thing until a customer called. He got there late and found the bodies."

Well, he had his answer about Kannon's whereabouts. Victoria came around in front of him, her eyes wide and worried. He tried to appear calm. "That driver of yours must've talked."

"No. He didn't."

"How else could they have known about the place?'

His question was met with another. "How much did you tell Jarun?"

Wakai's jaw tightened. Perhaps he'd confided in his childhood friend too much. Still, would Jarun turn on him that fast? Perhaps, since Kannon was involved. Wakai felt suddenly sick at what horrific pain Jarun must've experienced at the hands of someone who could unleash a one-man massacre and walk away unscathed.

Apparently his silence was all the thug needed. "We gave you a week to solve the problem. It's been five days now and it's only gotten worse. Lost men. Lost clients. Lost property. We were counting on your brains to take the city quickly, not start a war."

"Unlike you, I'm no sorcerer!" Wakai retorted, no longer able to hold back his sarcasm and frustration. "I've given your people a list of every ally Montri has in this city and they haven't accomplished anything. Fourteen million people in Bangkok, and you want me to find one girl? For all we know she might not even be in Thailand! What do you want me to do, wheel around the city showing her picture? I can't work miracles. These things take time."

There was an ominous silence, and Wakai found himself holding his breath.

"You have two days left." The line went dead.

Wakai set his phone back on his arm rest. "Victoria, we need to take care of this quickly. How's Alak doing?"

Victoria's girlish features twisted into an angry pout. "He's so stubborn. I can't break him. I'm not as good at it as Jarun."

"That's because he's a torturer," said Wakai. "You're a sadist."

He hadn't kept the disgust from his voice and she'd picked up on it. "I can't help it," she whimpered. "Please don't be mad with me, John. Please...."

"I'm not mad," he replied wearily, the same words he'd said a million times over the years. "But I need him brought here, now. Arrange it, please."

Victoria trotted off to fulfill her brother's wishes. She was small, shorter than even the typical Thai girl. If ever looks were deceiving....

He seethed as he watched her go. It was she who had forced him into betraying Alak. She who had botched the simple capture of a teenager. She who'd failed to wring a single word from their prisoner. Yet, even as his anger rose, it dissipated like smoke.

She was his little sister. The last blood he had in the world. The one who'd always encouraged him, admired him and, in her own mad way, loved him. He should have put an end to her sick obsessions when he'd had the chance. Instead he'd only deepened her depravity. It was his fault that she was the way she was. He'd created a monster, one he'd sworn to his mother on her deathbed, he wasn't going to let anything happen to.

Because, God help him, he loved her, too.

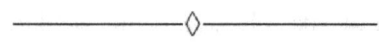

Gina snuggled under the covers of her bed aboard *The Pink Pussycat*, an icepack against her head.

They'd returned to the boat at dawn, and immediately Darae had set about fussing over the gaggle of children, arranging beds and breakfasts for all. The majority of them were from Cambodia, smuggled across the border with the promise of jobs and a better life in Bangkok. Between the lot of them, they hardly spoke ten words of Thai. That didn't matter to Darae.

Being an ex-prostitute, brothel madam and wife of a gangster hadn't stopped Gina's stepmother from having a soft spot for kids. Unable to have children of her own, she doted on everyone else's, and had spent millions funding orphanages, medical clinics, schools and scholarships. Sure it was good PR for the Zaffini's little empire of vice, but Gina knew that whenever Darae gave, the gift was sincere.

With Darae occupied and her dad still asleep, Gina had slipped away, ready to spend the whole day unconscious. Four hours later, there'd been calls for lunch and washing of hands, followed by an excited thundering of little feet past her door to the upper deck. She planned to join them—until she stood. Then, she opted to pop another painkiller instead. God, one hit from Kannon and she felt dead. How did people like Jarun survive him?

There was a knock on her cabin door. "Come in."

It was Ryota.

"Hey there," she said, and stuffed another pillow under her head to raise herself up.

He bowed, and then again, as if for good measure. "Ms. Zaffini, may I speak to you about Mr. Takahama?"

This couldn't be good. "Sure. Shoot." They both winced at her word choice.

"Your father is very angry with him."

She struggled to sit up and failed. "Ow, ow, ow. How did he find out? I asked Darae to call me when Daddy got up, so I could explain things."

"Mr. Takahama told him."

Gina closed her eyes. Of course, Kannon would do the right and honorable and most incredibly stupid thing.

"I was hoping you might speak in his defense," he requested. "Things have reached a critical juncture."

She didn't want to ask what that meant when it came to her father and Kannon. "Okay, okay," Gina tossed aside her ice pack and her duvet. Ryota snapped shut his eyes and turned his back. "Oh, for pity's sake, I do have underwear on."

"Yes, I understand. But my culture is different."

Gina began rummaging through her suitcase. "Give me a break. Your culture has vending machines for dirty panties."

"I have never used them."

"I believe it. What does Tasanee think of your prudishness?"

His back stiffened. "That is not the way it is between us."

Gina located a wraparound dress and wrapped it around. "I can tell." She walked past him to the door. "Tasanee is from a different culture, too. You need to recognize that before you two reach your own critical juncture."

Gina arrived on deck in time to see Kannon about to descend into the yacht's powerboat, her father, leaning heavily on his cane, overseeing the departure.

"Hey, where are you going?" Gina called out.

"I'm sending him away," Vincenzo said.

Gina caught up to them. "What? Why?"

Vincenzo looked pointedly at her head. "If that's not obvious to you then he must have hit you harder than I thought."

"He's the best gun in Thailand!"

"If he wasn't, he wouldn't be leaving this boat alive."

"No, this is ridiculous. You have to let him stay. I need him. I mean I need him to find Alak," she clarified. "Kannon's our best bet to sort out this business with Wakai."

Kannon cleared his throat. "Locating my boss is my business, not—"

"Damn right it's your business," Gina snapped. "And without us, it's going to take you a whole hell of a lot longer to do that, isn't it? In the meantime Wakai isn't going to stop hunting for Tasanee, and who knows what Alak's going through right now. You and Ryota can't afford to go it alone, and neither can we, so let's quit this pissing contest and get back to work."

Two of Bangkok's more powerful men glared at her. It was her father who spoke first. "So what are you proposing, bambina?"

She wasn't sure what she was doing but she did it anyway. "I'm his boss."

"I've already got a boss," Kannon said.

"All you have right now is a man you need to find. And what we've got is a chain-of-command problem. The only way for this to work is if I give the orders."

She turned to her father. "You know Kannon's a man of his word. If he swears he'll do what I tell him from here on in then you know he will."

Vincenzo thumped his cane on the deck. "I know no such thing. He was supposed to protect you last night and instead he knocks you out. Couldn't wait to tell me."

"He told you himself because that was the alpha thing to do," she replied. "And stupid, I agree."

"If he was a real man he'd never hit a woman. That's the first rule of The Pink Stilettos. Every one knows I won't tolerate mistreatment." Each of the last words was thumped out against the deck with his cane. Her father was pale and sweat was beading on his bare head. This was costing him. She needed to bring it to a swift end.

"Look, Dad. You and I both know that the 70 Rai club had to be shut down, and we both know that the only way that could happen was if the reason for its existence was shut down. Those clients, the people who ran that place, they were sick fucks. I tried to stop Kannon and if he'd listened to me, there'd be kids in a lot more pain than me with my little bump to the head."

Vincenzo looked away, shrugged. It was his way of conceding the point.

She angled herself to Kannon so her father couldn't see her bulge out her eyes and aim them at her father. "Do we have a deal?"

His neutral look in place, Kannon gave a barely perceptible nod. "Yes, we do. I swear I'll obey Ms. Zaffini until Mr. Montri is free."

Vincenzo Zaffini slammed his cane down even harder. "You so much as look at my daughter the wrong way, I'll make you wish we'd parted company. You understand me?"

Kannon bowed his head. "Yes, sir."

"Take them damn glasses off and say it."

Kannon did as asked. Vincenzo breathed out. "I need a drink." He bulged his eyes out at his daughter. "And a cigarette."

Kannon gave Ryota a meaningful look, and moving to her father's side, Ryota began to escort Vincenzo away.

"Also, a girl," he said to Ryota.

Oh, hell. Her father had found someone new to terrorize.

"Yes, sir." Ryota said. "I—right away."

As the two walked off, Gina stepped up to Kannon. "Order number one is you don't hit me. Spanking I like, hitting I don't."

Something flashed in his dark eyes before he covered them with his sunglasses.

"Yes, Ms. Zaffini."

"Order number two is for you to call me Gina. Or Gina honey. Or Gina babycakes. Or Gina sugar. Or Gina, you little sex kitten. Or Gina—"

"Yes, Gina."

"And order number three is to go get breakfast while I shower and slip into something that doesn't make me hot and sweaty. Well, any more hot and sweaty than I get around you."

As usual, he ignored her.

"Then we're off to see an old friend of mine."

His mouth twisted. "We don't have time for social calls."

"We have time for this one," she sing-songed.

He took the bait. "And who would this friend be?"

"Nobody special. Just one of the world's most wanted cyberterrorists."

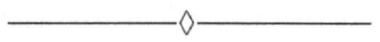

Victoria snuggled against Alak Montri in the back seat of

the limo, setting her chin on his shoulder. She fussed with the cloth bag over his head to ensure a comfortable fit. "You know, when we killed your lieutenants, I thought we ought to kill you, too. I mean, why stop when there's only one enemy left? Doesn't seem to make sense, does it?"

There was silence from the bag and a subtle lowering of his shoulder away from her cheek. Tsk. She cupped his crotch and he froze.

She rolled his soft balls in her hand. "It was my brother that saved you. You know, the man you think betrayed you? He spared you and all he wants in return is for you to be useful, Alak. Don't you want to show some gratitude for his mercy? I mean, you do owe him your life."

She stroked the front of his pants, waking his cock to quivering life. With the handcuffs behind his back, he was helpless to stop her and could only press himself against the seat. The silly, silly fuck. He didn't understand revulsion had nothing to do with sex. In fact, in her experience, the two were quite compatible. "I know I haven't been very kind to you, Alak," she murmured. "Believe me it could have been worse. John didn't want me hurting you. Too much. Nothing that would kill you or do permanent harm. Given the circumstances he was very kind to you. Surely you get that?"

Alak Montri leaned his head back. There, there, relax. And then he head-butted her.

"Duck fucker!" she squealed, elbowing him hard in the stomach. Alak doubled over, and her fingers were dug into his windpipe before she pulled herself together. She shoved him back against the seat. "You're lucky John wants you alive."

She reached into her purse for her compact mirror. Nothing broken, but there'd certainly be a nasty bruise. She dabbed at the blood from her nose with a thick handkerchief she purposely carried for little mop-ups.

Alak Montri hadn't moved, the cloth around his mouth suctioning in and out. She gripped his crotch hard this time and his body jerked. "You better pray that you can be of some use to my brother, because if not, I'm going to tie ten fishhooks on a line, jam them down your throat, and then pull them up out of your stomach one by one."

The man turned his face towards her again. "You may wear the skin of a woman," he wheezed, "but you're a demon inside."

Victoria tilted her head, and unzipped his pants. "You're more right than you know."

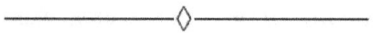

John Wakai watched Victoria yank the hood off his former boss and dump him onto the living room floor. Montri's face was pulpy from bruises and cuts. Several of his fingers looked broken. Dammit. It was always so hard for Victoria to stop once she got going.

Then he noticed his sister's face. "What the hell happened to you?"

"I was playing nice and he head-butted me. Fucker'll pay, don't worry."

Wakai rubbed his temple. "Did you at least give him some water?"

"I tried. He wouldn't drink."

Wakai sighed and wheeled over to him. "Can you hear me, Alak?" He reeked of sweat and vomit and blood, the stench of resistance.

At first there was no response, then slowly their prisoner lifted his head, looking at Wakai with one eye, the other having swelled shut. Wakai worked at showing no reaction to the damage his sister had inflicted.

"I never intended for you to suffer so much," Wakai offered. "In fact I never had any desire to harm you. Despite everything, I've always admired you."

Montri's mirthless smile revealed bloody gaps. "You're a pretty shitty admirer."

So much for the olive branch. "It was you that betrayed me, Alak. You've always had the courage and charisma, but we both know that I've been the brains of our organization. I helped you take this city. Took a bullet for you that left me in this chair. After all that, you couldn't look the other way? You forced my hand. All this is your fault, not mine."

"You expect me to turn a blind eye to that?" Montri spat blood and phlegm toward Victoria.

He had, but Montri's face was twisted in disgust—the same look as when his boss had first confronted him with pictures of Victoria's gross sadism. There'd be no forgiveness, no negotiation. "What's done is done. What matters now is that I'm the one in charge of Bangkok. You need to recognize that power has shifted to avoid further bloodshed. Yours included."

Alak sat back on his haunches. "Power hasn't shifted. If it had you'd just kill me. You're hoping to use me to run things, to get the city to fall in line for your new friends. You lack the means to make me, and sooner or later the gangs of Bangkok are going to organize and crush you."

Victoria darted forward to kick her prisoner but Wakai raised his hand. Several breaths passed before she retreated. "I'll be honest with you, Alak. I've turned Bangkok upside-down looking for your daughter, and so far I don't have a clue where she's hiding. Eventually I'm going to find her, and if we're at war when I do, then whoever was protecting her is going to die. Is that really how you want to repay their loyalty?"

"Even if I wanted to help you, how should I know where she is?"

"Because you know her, and who'd protect her. You know which of your allies she'd run to, and where they'd keep her. We can cut a deal. She can live like a princess, and we can run this city together again. Surely that's preferable to all the carnage you'll unleash otherwise."

Montri didn't even blink. "Fuck you."

Alak Montri really was a heartless bastard. He'd given up everything to protect his sister, and the overlord of Bangkok crime didn't seem to give a damn about anybody. Not even himself, in the end. Only his almighty principles. Never in his life had Wakai felt morally superior to anyone until now. "No, huh? After all Victoria's done to you, and all that she could do to you, your answer is that simple, is it?"

"Of course, it is," Alak Montri said. "If you get hold of her, you'll only use me to set up your own order. Soon as that's done we'd be dead. Tell you anything and I might as well cut my daughter's throat."

Montri's declaration sparked an idea in Wakai. A most excellent one. "Help me or not, Alak, you're still a pawn in this game. A pawn to capture the queen."

CHAPTER
FIVE

5

KANNON LOOKED UP, way up, at the towering skyscraper
to which Gina had brought him and Ryota. The sight of a fifty-
story luxury apartment building in the heart of the city
wouldn't have been unusual, except that this one appeared
completely abandoned. Through the rusty chain-link fence,
Kannon viewed the tangle of trees and vines entwining the
Romanesque archways and columns along its front.

Gina smoothed her neon pink micro-dress as she stepped
up to a padlocked gate, and producing a key from her matching
purse, unlocked it. "Welcome to the Banyan Unique."

"What is this place?" Kannon asked as he and Ryota followed her. He saw Ryota check out her behind, and might've
shot him a look if he wasn't doing the same himself. He'd
never worked for a woman before, much less one this hot—
although it would be a cold day in hell before he admitted it to
her. Her skintight pink get-up—he didn't buy her chatter about
it being gang colors—had made him half-hard for the entire
ride over, and it was a constant chore not to stare at her. It
didn't help that she was so blatant about her sexual overtures.
He would have to find some diplomatic way to put her in her

place but was afraid that place would be between him and a mattress.

"One of my father's few bad investments," she replied, locking the gate before leading them through the overgrown grounds. "Back in the mid-90's the economy in Bangkok was flying really high. Buildings were sprouting up like weeds. My dad thought it would be a good idea to get in on the development boom so he and a bunch of business partners poured tens of millions into this place. Almost got it completed when the financial crisis hit, and suddenly there was zero demand. They mothballed it, and now here it stands—could be the most expensive abandoned building in the world."

Kannon scowled, not liking the look of the structure. Despite the opulence of its design the place had an eerie hollowness to it, its windowless, graffiti-strewn exterior giving the place a distinctly post-apocalyptic feel. "Abandoned, not uninhabited I'm guessing."

Gina grinned. "Well, there are ghosts. Ask the locals. They'll swear to you it's haunted, and that's why it was never completed. Who'd want to buy a place here anymore?"

"How could a building be haunted if nobody ever lived in it?" Ryota asked as they stepped over the threshold into the stark, unfinished lobby. The ground floor was littered with cables, broken tools and old construction debris. At least, it was well-lit, thanks to sunlight pouring through the windowless facade. Above them things got dark fast—two escalators led up into the gloom, remnants of protective plastic drifting like cobwebs from their stainless steel sides.

Kannon caught movement from the corner of his eye, his hand was on his gun before he registered the two dogs.

"Well, look at you handsome things," Gina said, bending over to pat them. As one, Kannon and Ryota took in the pink behind and looked away. "Kisses?"

She let the mutts slobber over her neck and cheeks, giggling like they all had nothing better to do.

"You done?" Kannon cut in. Ryota gave him a surprised, almost reproachful look. His apprentice had spent a full year with him and two hours after getting subcontracted to Gina, he'd switched loyalties.

Gina's answer was to shoo away the dogs and begin the upward climb, addressing Ryota's question as she went. "After the place was abandoned several homeless people moved in. Within a few weeks there were deaths. People falling down stairwells or through incomplete floors in the dark. Suicides off the balconies. One guy hung himself right where we're standing. Then it really started getting weird."

Ryota hesitated as they reached the upper level of the lobby. The place was shadowy, the hallways radiating from it lightless, large portions of the ceiling and walls only half-constructed, exposing pipes and unfinished wiring. "What do you mean? What happened?"

Gina paused, fishing for something in her purse. "People started seeing strange lights on the top floors late at night. Heard screams and crying, but when they searched they didn't find anybody. If that weren't enough a pack of feral dogs moved in. Wasn't long before nobody would come near this place. Locals say it's cursed. Call it the 'ghost tower'."

Pulling out what looked like a small flashlight, Gina gave a jack-o'-lantern grin. "Pretty spooky, huh?"

Ryota nodded.

"To children. Where next?" said Kannon impatiently.

Gina clicked on the light, which emitted a spectral purple glow. Walking to one of the hallways she shone it at the wall, a previously invisible arrow glowing into existence. "UV flashlight and paint," she explained. "Need the first to see the second. Follow me."

Ryota was game but Kannon took Gina's elbow. "You've been away for ten years. How do you know so much about this place?"

Her face caught in the dim circle of light, Gina met his eyes. "I was away, Kannon. Not gone. Daddy and I talked on the phone all the time, and if he didn't tell me everything Darae thought I needed to know, Darae would call me up. I've always been in the loop, even when I didn't want to be."

There was a thread of resigned bitterness in her voice. Had circumstances been different between them, he might've talked it through with her. As it was, he let her lead him and Ryota into near total darkness, the glowing arrows directing them through the maze of the building's interior. Passing down bare corridors littered with debris and up endless stairwells of raw concrete, Kannon and Ryota trudged after Gina to their mysterious destination. With no railings and long, long drops, even he felt wary as they climbed. The air was hot and humid as a sauna, a few filthy windows admitting the only light, and by the time they reached what he estimated to be the 30th floor, Ryota had had enough.

"Stop, please," he called from two floors below.

Gina aimed the light down the rail-free stairs, and Kannon felt the same frisson as when his daughter made a boneheaded move. "Watch it!"

She turned to him, her back heel nearly over the edge. He yanked her away and called down, "Hurry up!"

Gina was looking at him, her purple-illuminated face flushed and invigorated. She was breathing hard, her skin warm and damp and scented, too. Like a hot tropical night. He dropped his hand quickly.

"You're in good shape," Kannon remarked, reaching inside his jacket. He pulled out a pack of nic gum and popped one into his mouth.

"Are you actually going to quit smoking?"

"You threw out my last pack."

"I'm sure you know where to get more."

He concentrated on his gum. He hoped she would turn her pink ass around and keep climbing. No such luck. She shimmied up to him until he only had to wrap his arm around her and they'd be in a tight clinch. "So, did you do it for me?"

"I made a promise."

"No, you didn't."

"To my daughter."

"Why start now?"

"Seemed as good a time as any."

"That's your story and you're sticking to it, huh?"

She wore pink lipstick to match the dress, which didn't look right. The redness of her lips showed through too much. His fingers itched to rub it off. "How come you're in such good shape?"

By some kind of miracle, she stepped back. "I bike to work and run on my treadmill an hour a day. I'm amazed you're not huffing and puffing. And how is it you don't sweat?"

Even though she'd made room physically, she still crowded his mind. "Congenital defect," he replied vaguely.

Gina cocked her head. "So what, you don't have sweat glands or something?"

Looked as if they were parked on the 30th floor until Q & A was done. "I have them. My brain doesn't turn them on."

"So, you don't feel overheated?"

"I don't feel much of anything."

Gina frowned. "What about walking up all these stairs? Your legs don't hurt?"

"No."

"What about when someone punches you? Does that hurt?"

"No."

"What about when you spill something hot on yourself? That must sting."

"No."

"What about—?"

"I don't feel hot, I don't feel cold, I don't feel pain and I don't feel like talking about this anymore. All right?"

Once again she closed those precious inches between them and he held his breath. "What about pleasure? Can you feel that?"

"Yes."

She flashed him a grin. "I'll have to test that for myself one of these nights."

Kannon straightened. This would be a good time to talk about whose place was whose. "I thought we were clear on this. We're not doing that."

He couldn't have been blunter. It couldn't have been more of a rejection. Instead, she stayed put, her body a perfect mold to his, so close magnetic energy might soon snap them together. And he didn't risk moving a stitch, otherwise they'd touch and he'd have her against the wall, her legs not curled softly against him like when he carried her, but wrapped tight around him, her pink heels on him and his hands cupped on the swell of her ass, her dress riding up, opening to where he could press his hard cock to her softness.

"No, as I remember it, the flight attendant showed up," Gina said, so quietly he had to watch her lips to catch every word. "Left me curious why you didn't want to have sex with me, given you are attracted. And don't tell me you aren't. Those sunglasses hide your eyes, not what's going on in those pants of yours. You want me to leave you alone, I will. First, tell me why I should."

He wasn't about to share his reasons. A woman like her would mock him, and it was bad enough she was his boss. She was a Daddy's girl, and she'd manipulated the situation to make him into Daddy's go-boy, and then her own. Now, he had to hunt for one boss while working for another who wanted to scratch her itch for a hit-man.

Job satisfaction would be higher with the second.

So would the consequences.

"My reasons are my own. No clause in the contract says I have to sleep with you."

Gina brought those breasts right up so they were straddling his tie. "If I recall right, you have to obey me...." she trailed off.

Obey me. He'd sucked it back when they'd been on the yacht. A good lesson there about how to kill a man without a bullet. "You want to know the reason? I'll tell you. I'm not interested in being used. You want to get it on with me because you think you can. You think that whatever belongs to Daddy Zaffini belongs to you. Except he doesn't own me, and I'm not your toy to play with."

Her honey eyes widened on him, her lips with the mismatched lipstick parted and she lifted her hand to his face—.

Ryota came into view, and Kannon had never been so relieved to see his junior. He broke away from her and stepped to the stair's edge. "Come on. It can't be much farther."

Ryota's hands were on his knees and Gina made a sympathetic mew, her attention diverted to her other lackey.

Ryota looked up at him, practically begging for mercy. Kannon cut away to lead the ascent. With Gina's backside to follow, the boy would catch his second wind soon enough.

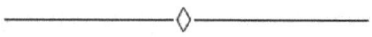

Five more floors brought them to a heavy steel door, the UV light revealing 'B²' written on its surface, and before they could knock, a heavy bolt was pulled back and the door swung open.

Beyond was a large air-conditioned room lit by dozens of computer monitors. The place looked like a low-rent version of a NASA control center, a bunch of youths of every ethnicity manning terminals, surrounded by masses of cables, takeout cartons and spent soda cans.

The man who'd opened the door didn't look the part of the hip urban hacker. He was in the full bristly blossom of middle-age, and was dressed in jeans and a white polo shirt. He and Gina exchanged bows. It was amazing how quickly she'd fallen into this traditional greeting. If Kannon and she had done that back at Cause & FX three years ago, they'd be in a completely different relationship. One where nobody felt owned or owed.

"Hello, Gina. It's been a long time."

Gina followed him in. "It sure has, Dr. Chai. How's life at the top of the world treating you?"

"My enemies haven't found me yet," he replied. "And I'd like to keep it that way. Who are your friends?"

That was classic Dr. Chaiboonma. Always cautious and conservative. Always direct. He and Kannon would get along great, once they got beyond the nasty looks they were exchanging. "Couple of Alak's men," said Gina. "I'm guessing you know the situation."

"Yes. And I see your father has decided do something about it." He practically curled his lip at Kannon and Ryota.

Gina put her hands on her hips. "Wouldn't you if your best friend was kidnapped?"

"Sure. Then again, I wouldn't have Alak as a friend in the first place. To be blunt, Gina, I'm not happy that you've brought the likes of these men to my doorstep."

Kannon's hands flexed, and Gina inserted herself between him and Dr. Chaiboonma. This was not at all like the natural diplomat she'd known as a teen. Apparently there were some things she hadn't been told during her time away. Or some things neither Darae nor her father knew about.

"Have you heard of the temple at 70 Rai?"

The old hacker's expression grew hard and sad. "I've heard rumors."

"The rumors are officially false. It doesn't exist. Not since these two finished with it last night."

"Your point?"

"Last night they made thirteen children very happy. When's the last time you've done that?"

Dr. Chaiboonma met Kannon's gaze, then finally bowed. Kannon and Ryota immediately responded in kind. Gina proceeded with introductions, at the conclusion of which Dr. Chai said, "Let me clear off the boardroom table and we'll have a talk about it, okay?"

The hacker excused himself, and Kannon came alongside her, a full arm's length away and still the space between them was so charged she could almost hear the snap, crackle, pop. "Who are these people?"

He was apparently deaf to the sound of sexual frustration. Gina focused on playing tour guide. "The Bangkok Blondes.

Mercenaries to some, terrorists to others. After this building project failed, Dad agreed to help convert it into a hideout for them. Ran power, water and cable up here, and installed a bunch of satellite relays on the roof. He also spread all those spooky rumors and ghost stories I told you about to keep the locals from snooping around."

"They aren't true, then?" Ryota said it as if she'd burst his bubble about Santa. Kannon sliced him a look, and Ryota mumbled, "The tree of rumor grows from the seed of truth."

Gina had never heard that proverb before and was ready to compliment Ryota when Kannon responded, "Just watch what tree you pluck your fruit from."

Ryota blushed and stared straight ahead. "Yes, sir."

What was that all about? Gina tried to sort through that metaphorical exchange when Kannon carried on as if there'd been no interruption. "They work for your father?"

"What? Uh…no. They're independent, but like all the Bangkok gangs, your boss takes a cut."

"Then why have I never heard of them?"

"The Blondes keep a very low profile. They tap phones, hack police servers and launder money through online businesses for my father, and in exchange he provides them with untraceable headquarters. Pretty good arrangement, seeing as half these people have bounties on their heads."

"From who?"

"Jihadist groups, mainly," Dr. Chai said, returning. "Follow me, while I explain. Back in '08 when India contracted me to help fight their cyber-war with Pakistan, I had no trouble enlisting the best cyber-criminals out there to help me. Only about half the people here are Thai. The rest are Chinese, Russians, Indians, Romanians—even a couple of Canadians. Kind of the U.N. of cyber-crime in the ghost tower."

Dr. Chaiboonma had arrived at a small room where the boardroom table was covered with World of Warcraft figurines.

"Whoa," Gina said. "Now I know you guys are for real."

Dr. Chai gestured to the empty seats. "Part of my recruitment policy. Ensures a common corporate culture. Please sit."

Gina and Dr. Chaiboonma sat, while Ryota stood off to one side and Kannon parked himself behind her, though not so close as he had at 70 Rai. "I apologize if I was less then welcoming, Gina. I really am happy to see you again," Dr. Chaiboonma began. "I'm guessing your father called you back to Bangkok because of his health problems?"

Someone else who knew about her father's condition before she did. Understandable, but—Gina shook it off. "And because Wakai wants my god-sister. It's a family matter now."

"In more ways than one, I assume," Dr. Chaiboonma replied. He looked over Gina's head at Kannon. "Darae always intended for Gina to take over the family business when Vincenzo retired. Groomed her to be a criminal mastermind since she was twelve years old, which is how she wound up meeting people like me at a young age."

She wished Dr. Chai would get to the point and not drag up her old history. Kannon already figured her for a Daddy's girl. Her as mafia princess was icing on his cupcake. "Yeah, well, we all know that's not how things turned out."

Dr. Chaiboonma brought his gaze back to her. "Until now."

Kannon's voice came sailing over her head. "Do you have a problem with her helping my boss?"

Dr. Chai picked up a figurine of a green-skinned brute wielding an enlarged spear. "I consider the effort futile."

"And why's that? You don't think he can be rescued?"

There was something in Kannon's tone that put Gina on full alert. The big bad wolf sounded hostile—and curious.

"Alak's just another mob boss," Dr. Chaiboonma said, setting down the figurine. "Only difference between him and his rivals are their nationalities. They all use the same methods. Commit the same crimes. Spill the same blood. And they all end up the same way."

Gina gripped the armrest, making sure she was in Kannon's way should he take exception. Instead, his reply was mild. "Sounds like your sympathies lie with Wakai."

"Not at all," Dr. Chaiboonma said, randomly picking up another figurine. This one was of a blue vixen in a barely-there purple bodysuit with a set of boobies straight from a pubescent fantasy. "He's cut from the same cloth as well. The only criminals in this city that are any different are Vincenzo and myself."

"And how do you figure that?" asked Kannon.

"Ninety-five percent of what Vincenzo does is legal," Dr. Chaiboonma explained. He set the vixen down in front of him. Despite the totally unrealistic rack, Gina liked the way she was depicted, all bold and in mid-stride as if ready to do battle with whatever monster dared get in her way. "Really, he's a businessman who uses criminal contacts to defend himself against gangs wanting to take over his brothels and massage parlors."

"Nicely put," Gina said, and he acknowledged her compliment with a little bow.

Kannon, as usual, was not impressed. "How about you?"

"Half my money comes from governments," Dr. Chaiboonma said. "National intelligence services employ my team to harass and spy on one another. Admittedly, we're involved in criminal activities, all non-violent. Tax evasion. Money laundering. Digital counterfeiting."

Gina leaned over and picked up the vixen while Kannon continued his interrogation. "You consider yourself morally superior?"

"It's not an issue of morality. It's an issue of sustainability."

Ah, yes, this argument. She spun in her chair to look at Kannon. "What Dr. Chaiboonma means is that most criminal organizations are unstable. Sooner or later they all wind up failing because they rely on fear and violence rather than cooperation and finesse. That's why Dr. Chaiboonma encouraged me not to take the path Darae wanted me to."

"If you had, you'd probably have wound up as one of Alak's lieutenants," added Dr. Chaiboonma. "Which is to say you'd likely be dead by now."

"And none of us want that," Kannon said. He said it so quietly, so damn neutrally Gina was half out of her chair, ready to—what? Kiss him or kick him?

She forced herself to relax and in a quiet, neutral voice, replied, "It's all history or speculation. Right now, I'm trying to help my family, and that's the only reason I'm back in Bangkok."

Dr. Chaiboonma sighed. "And that is why I'll help you, Gina. What would you like?"

Okay, good, they were finally able to get to business. "We're looking for Wakai and we've got a lead, and I—we—were hoping to borrow your expertise." With her phone, she brought up the website address the scumbucket had given her at 70 Rai and showed it to Dr. Chai. "This site is run by his sister, Victoria. Very private and very sick. Death and torture I'm guessing. Find the site, find the sister, find Wakai."

Dr. Chaiboonma squinted at the screen."Darknet, hmm? Sounds a bit like 'Three Guys, One Hammer.'"

Gina winced. "I don't think I want to know what you're talking about."

"An old Ukrainian snuff site. Have you visited this one?"

"Didn't think I'd have the stomach for it."

"Good. They probably monitor traffic pretty closely. Shouldn't be too hard to trace."

Leading them back into the maze of workstations, he brought them to a thin young woman with bleach blonde hair, her skintight black t-shirt depicting an upward arrow with the caption 'I'm with Genius'. She looked up at them through cosmetic lenses that gave her slitted cat's eyes.

"This is Kittyjack," Dr. Chaiboonma said. "Recruited her out of Vancouver a few years back. She'll help you get what you need." He jotted notes on a pad, then slid it over to the hacker. "In the meantime, please excuse me. We're about to release a DDoS attack on the National Command Authority and I really should oversee that."

"I'm sure I don't know what that means," Gina smiled, more than a little relieved to see him go. He was a double-shot of caffeine in that he energized her but also made her edgy. "Good luck, anyway. And thanks again for your help."

"Be careful, Gina," he replied, shooting Kannon a grim look. "Very careful."

"Soyou'retryingtotrackdownsomesnuffsite,eh?" asked Kittyjack, firing out the words as Dr. Chaiboonma walked away.

Gina blinked. Okay, Dr. Chai had that double-shot effect on his employees as well. "Yeah. The website she runs is—"

"GotitfromChaiboonmahangonasec," the blonde replied even as her fingers flew over her keyboard, strings of incomprehensible numbers flashing across the screen as windows snapped open and shut so fast Gina was worried the girl was going to give herself a seizure. "Gotit'sIPsorunningareverse-DNS. Gotit'sDNSsowegotaBangkoksiteonideanet. Confirmingwithtracerouteandwhois. Gotideanetthathackedsolet'sbackdoorandwehaveamatch. Runningitonterraserverand three, two, one...."

Was she even speaking a language? Gina stole a look at Kannon, whose eyebrows were raised halfway up his forehead.

A satellite map of Bangkok opened up, a thin red crosshairs identifying a location. "That'swhereit'srunning-from." Kittyjack scribbled down an address on the notepad, tore the top sheet off and handed it to Gina. "Notawebsitebuta-server. Samedifftoyouthough."

Kannon was still looking at the map on the screen. "What is that place? And speak so I can understand you."

"It's Talad. Rot. Fai," replied the hacker with exaggerated slowness. "The train market."

"What?" Kannon said.

Kittyjack and Gina stared at him. "Seriously?" Gina said. "You live here and you've never heard of Talad Rot Fai? A few years back some antique dealers set up shop in an old railway yard. Word spread, and now the area's the best place in Bangkok to buy anything retro. Clothes, shoes, toys, furniture—even cars."

"Plus," Kittyjack interjected, "I can pretty much guess who's running the server you're looking for. Hacker named Capslock. Used to work for us till Dr. Chaiboonma kicked his butt out of B² for playing too much Starcraft. Guy runs a small operation hosting Darknet sites for spammers, scammers, and pervs."

"Okay. Anything else we should know?" Gina asked.

"Nope," Kittyjack said, her eyes riveted to her screen, fingers a blur. As they turned away, she called out. "Oh, yeah,

I forgot. Take earplugs."

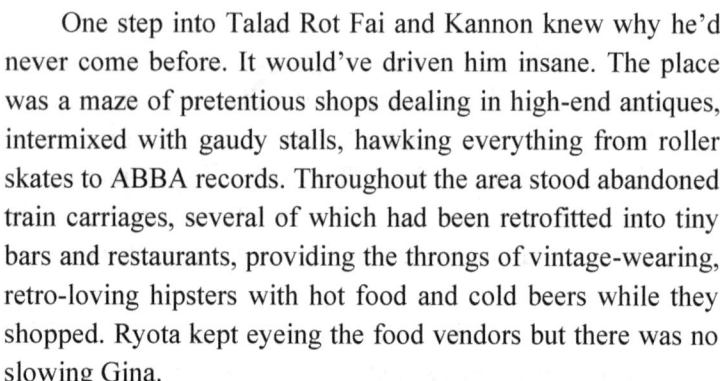

One step into Talad Rot Fai and Kannon knew why he'd never come before. It would've driven him insane. The place was a maze of pretentious shops dealing in high-end antiques, intermixed with gaudy stalls, hawking everything from roller skates to ABBA records. Throughout the area stood abandoned train carriages, several of which had been retrofitted into tiny bars and restaurants, providing the throngs of vintage-wearing, retro-loving hipsters with hot food and cold beers while they shopped. Ryota kept eyeing the food vendors but there was no slowing Gina.

"Oh wow! Check this out!" She held up an ancient Dukes of Hazzard lunchbox. "You know how much this is worth?"

Kannon crossed his arms. "Apparently more than time."

Gina carried on as if he hadn't made a very good point. "This used to be Brian's favorite show when he was a kid. I'm going to buy it for him."

Kannon and Ryota exchanged weary glances as Gina began haggling with the stall keeper.

"An hour of walking around this garage sale and we're still no closer to finding him," Kannon grumbled. Although they were in the general area of the hacker, the anarchy of the market made it impossible to determine a precise location. It didn't help that this was Gina's sixth purchase, he and Ryota already toting bags with vintage dresses, her little spree courtesy of something she called tingles.

"They rush through me like an orgasm," she'd tossed over her shoulder, and Kannon had to shove Ryota in the back to get him moving again.

"Can we please get down to business now?" Kannon said as Gina trotted over to them, lunchbox in hand.

"What do you think I've been doing?" she said, giving him the lunchbox, which he automatically handed off to a reluctant Ryota.

"Buying junk," he replied. One day with her as boss and he'd had it. His only hope for peace was to get her back to the boat so he could get a break from all her…pinkness.

She stuck her face up to his. "I've also been talking to the stall owners about the guy we're looking for. Come on." She was off again, weaving her way through the crowd, one lucky shopper after another feeling the brush of her breasts or her behind.

She brought them to an old boxcar on the far edge of the market, its sliding door securely locked. Gina and Kannon kept watch as Ryota picked it, opening it only slightly slower than if he'd had the key—one lesson the boy had learned well. The inside of the train car was lined with rows of shelves, each filled with humming computers. At the back of the car was a small window, and hooked up in front of it was what looked like a large rifle scope on a tripod, its glowing red end aimed at a cluster of nearby apartment blocks. Ryota kneeled down behind the device and looked through it.

"So, what do we have here?" Gina wondered aloud, taking a picture of the setup with her phone. She forwarded it to Kittyjack, and not a minute later got a call back that she put on speaker.

"Infrared laser. Nifty. Letshimtransmitdatafrom—"

"Slower, please, Kitty."

"I said he's using an infrared laser to send and receive data from his network without leaving any kind of record," said the hacker. "That way he never has to visit the train car.

Never has to access its internet connection. Never has to leave any clues behind."

"It's pointed at a concrete wall," Ryota detailed.

"Means he's ricocheting the laser to another location. Makes him pretty much impossible to find."

Kannon stepped close to the phone, which in turn brought him within the range of Gina's warm scent. He held his breath and said "So this is a dead end?"

"Duh. No," Kittyjack said, with barely controlled patience. "All you have to do is unplug the power. When Capslock notices it's offline, there's a good chance he'll show up to see what the matter is. Problem is, that could take hours or months depending on how often he checks it. If he's really paranoid he might even abandon his little business, but seeing all the work he's put into it, I doubt he would."

"Thanks, Kitty," said Gina. "Give Dr. Chai my love."

"Will do, Gin." The hyper-hacker's voice actually softened. Did Gina have that effect on everybody? Make women go soft and men hard? Kannon focused on the interior of the car. "Fuse box is over here." He ran his fingers down the panel, killing the power. The computers instantly switched to backup batteries. "These shouldn't last long."

He looked at his watch, doing his own computing. "Seeing as this is our only lead, we'll have to take shifts waiting for him to show up. Are you fit to stay here till morning, Ryota?"

His back-up checked his gun before returning it to his holster. "I'll be fine. If he comes, I'll call you immediately."

Kannon was exiting when he saw that Gina was scrolling on her phone. He bit down hard on his back molars. "That work for you, Gina?"

She made a little noise in her throat he was willing to

interpret as agreement.

"Then we should head back to the boat."

Her thumb tapped the phone and she brought it to her ear. "Actually I've got a better idea."

No. Not another idea.

"Hey there, Pensri. It's Gina. Guess who's in town?"

Kannon's heart stopped. It couldn't be. It just couldn't. But given it was Gina, why not? He listened to Gina exchange niceties with her old friend, and then she chirped, "Listen, I'm here with a friend of mine and we need to lay low. Okay if we stay at your place tonight?"

Say 'no', say 'no'. From Gina's sudden brightening, Pensri was soft, too.

Once off the phone, she waggled it at him. "Old friend of mine. We're crashing at her place."

He folded his arms over his chest and took one last desperate stand. "We can't do that. We don't know who can be trusted."

Gina snorted at the idea. "Don't worry, she's one of my oldest friends. If there's anyone in the world I can trust, it's her."

"If she's really a friend, then it's best we don't put her at risk."

Gina peered at him. "Are you okay, Kannon? You're acting kind of weird all of a sudden." She glanced at Ryota, who had his neck stretched so far in the other direction he looked like an owl. Gina switched back to him, looking for clues. Kannon kept his expression like a blank screen.

She shrugged and made for the door. "Never mind. I'll find out sooner or later."

Kannon dug out a piece of nic gum and started chomping like there was no tomorrow.

CHAPTER
6
SIX

WAKAI LAY IN his bed, typing the address of an obscure chat site into his tablet. Every night since his best friend had gone missing, he'd checked it, hoping to hear from Jarun, and every night his friend's pseudonym was absent from the list of participants. Tonight, he ran his finger down the list and smiled. He created a private chat room, empty save for the two of them.

I was beginning to give up hope, he typed.

Managed to get away.

Are you okay?

Yes.

Who had you?

Doesn't matter.

Wakai sat up in bed, dragging his useless legs with him. *It matters if I'm going to stop them.*

I cut a deal with them.

It took a few deep breaths before Wakai could reply. *You changed sides?*

The answer came quick. *Don't be stupid.*

Yes, it was certainly his old friend he was talking to. *If you're on my side then why won't you tell me who's hunting me?*

They won't hunt you if you let Montri go. We could leave the city. Start somewhere new.

Where was this coming from? *That's not an option.*

Yes, it is. Your sister could go to Cambodia with her friends.

Wakai leaned back. Ah, there is was. As much as he cared about his sister and best friend, the two of them had always hated each other with a passion. And he could understand why. Jarun tortured and killed for work, not pleasure. And never children.

It was you, wasn't it? You're the one that told Alak about Victoria's addictions.

No. I should have. Years ago. Now look where we are.

Wakai wasn't sure he believed his friend. Not that it mattered. He needed allies he could trust, even reluctant ones. Jarun and he had saved each other's lives a dozen times over, and if there was one person in the world he could count on it was his old friend. He tried a different tack.

I don't want to hurt Alak. We worked well together for a lot of years. Will you help me protect him from the Cambodians?

There was a pause, then—*Yes.*

Wakai pressed his opening. *Kannon is hunting me. If he catches me, I'm a dead man. Will you help me stop him?*

This time the pause was longer. Much longer. *Yes.*

Wakai released his breath and his fingers flew. *I'm going to give you the address for Montri. Get him and then contact me again. I'll give you instructions from there.*

What's security like?

Wakai filled him in, finishing with, *Is that a problem?*

No.

Wakai paused. Their business was concluded, but he didn't want to sign off quite yet. *It's good to have you back.*

Wish I could say it was good to be back, replied Jarun. Then abruptly, he signed out.

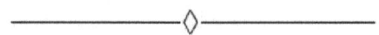

Kannon lagged behind Gina as they walked down the hallway of a lavish apartment building, all plush blue carpeting and silver chandeliers. It was hard to imagine that hours ago they'd been in another high rise, dark and empty.

He wished like hell he was back there again. He'd pitch himself over the stairwell if it meant avoiding what lay on the other side of the apartment door Gina was knocking on.

It was opened by a beautiful Thai woman, her black hair a long sensuous ripple, her body barely concealed by a short silken robe of bright crimson.

"Gina!"

"Pensri!"

The two women hugged each other, and then Pensri caught sight of him over Gina's shoulder. Pensri's hug slackened and Gina didn't miss her cue. She windmilled a hand to hurry him in. Kannon slowly did so, closing and then locking the door.

"Pensri, this is my friend, Kannon." Gina's smile was huge.

Pensri gave a short bow. "Hello, Kannon."

Kannon returned the greeting. "Hello, Pensri."

Gina's smile slipped. "So, you two know each—oh...."

Kannon winced. Of all the people in a city of fourteen million, naturally Pensri had to be Gina's friend. He seriously wondered if there was a person alive who wasn't connected to this woman.

"I see." For the first time in their brief, intense acquaintance, Gina Zaffini seemed at a loss for words. She licked her lip, scraped it and bit it. Then, Gina, being Gina, recovered. She took in Pensri's comfortable pad with its lit candles and warm-colored furnishings, walls hung with artistic, erotic images.

"Wow. Business must be good. I love what you've done with the place."

Pensri shrugged modestly. "I've been very fortunate. Can I get you two drinks?"

"Sure. Surprise us!" Gina answered before Kannon could decline.

As soon as Pensri left the room, he took Gina's arm. "This isn't what you think it is."

"You mean you're not one of her clients?"

"When I went to work for Mr. Montri, he provided me with everything I'd need here in Bangkok. Weapons, money, an apartment—"

"And one of my father's top call girls," she finished for him.

"Yes, but—"

Again Gina interrupted. "Kannon, my family's been running brothels for as long as I can remember, and Pensri and I've been friends since we were teenagers. You really think this shocks me? I know you don't have a girlfriend and, well, people have needs."

"It's not that way," he growled.

"So you haven't been here before?"

"Of course I have. Several times." Why did he feel the need to explain himself? It wasn't as if Gina was upset or judgmental. She seemed to think it perfectly acceptable that he had sexual relations with her friend.

"Tell me, what do you two do together? Play dominos?"

"First time we did," Pensri said, as she returned with iced teas she passed around. "Took a while for Kannon to loosen up."

Gina took a glass, and sighed. "Tell me about it. What's your secret?"

Pensri came alongside Gina, and together they observed Kannon. "You know," Pensri said, "I think our conversation is making him uncomfortable."

Gina tilted her head. "You think? He's just standing there, looking as neutral as ever." She slipped behind Pensri, settling her cold glass between Pensri's breasts at which point she squeezed the soft mounds together to hold the glass in place.

Kannon almost lost his grip on his own iced tea, catching its slippery surface an instant before it spilled. Pensri scooped out an ice cube and fed it over her shoulder to Gina who held it in her teeth as she skimmed it along Pensri's bare neck and shoulder. Pensri made a little mew he knew from experience meant Gina was doing her job well.

Gina tossed back her head and crunched down on the ice. "I think we're going to head to the bedroom, Kannon. I haven't seen Pensri since she visited L.A. last year, and we definitely have some catching up to do."

He nodded dumbly and then found his tongue. "Of course. I'll...see you both in the morning, then."

Gina brought the glass away from Pensri's chest and set it down. They moved in the direction of the bedroom, holding hands. At the threshold, they looked at each other, as if in psychic communication, and Gina turned to him. "You're welcome to join us if you like."

If she'd made her request with the usual grin and hip swing, he could've managed a comeback. Instead she said it with a soft twist of her mouth, an almost shy tuck of her purpled hair behind her ear. It was all he could do to stand there.

Pensri tugged on Gina's hand and the bedroom door shut, cutting off their giggles.

Damn woman. How the hell did she play him like that? His wife, his love, had washed away his cold façade with her grace and gentleness. Gina tore through it with all the subtlety of a chainsaw, leaving him feeling as awkward as a teenager.

His cock was so hard it was almost painful, his ample supply of testosterone raging for him to join them. He gulped down his drink, and picked up Gina's, the outside still warm from her touch and Pensri's breasts.

Through the closed door came a happy moan and sexy little giggles.

Kannon gulped and crunched down the iced drink, and prayed he'd make it through the night.

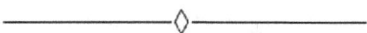

Gina dropped her clothes and slipped into Pensri's bed, her naked friend quickly following. Slim fingers stroked the lotus tattoo that adorned Gina's right breast. At a casual glance the flower seemed typical. On closer inspection its petals contained a stylized crocodile, its expression serene.

"I missed Timmy the croc," Pensri said.

Gina sank into the pillows. "He's been places, that's for sure."

Pensri palmed Gina's nipples, frictioning them to full hardness. "Who's had more men? You or me?"

Gina arched into the sensation—sometimes it was nice to

be in the hands of a professional. "I don't know. I've kinda lost track. I was never sure whether to count blow-jobs. Or if I didn't get an orgasm."

"It's easy for me. If they pay, it's sex."

Gina giggled, Pensri joining in, and she gave her friend a kiss on the lips. "And if they don't?"

"I wouldn't know. They always pay. Some even tip."

Kannon would tip. "Sorry about the awkwardness. I didn't know Kannon was a client." She skimmed her hand down Pensri's side. This was why women were a nice change. They were so soft and smooth.

"Me? Feel awkward? I think you were the unhappiest."

"Me? No way."

"You said nothing. You didn't look at him. You looked" —Pensri paused, thinking, her fingers doing lazy circles on Gina's bare belly—"annoyed."

"I wasn't annoyed. I was more—something that's not annoyed. I mean, he could've told me. Here it was going to be this big surprise to get him in the mood since I don't quite seem to do it for him, and it turns out that he's one of your regulars."

Pensri's fingers paused, a hair above Gina's pubic bone. "Gina Zaffini. Are you telling me he turned you down?"

Gina nodded and wished Pensri's fingers would change the subject.

Pensri's eyes widened. "Why?"

Gina squirmed, directing Pensri's hand lower. "I have no idea. He's showing all the signs of being interested, but he's being stubborn for some reason. Perhaps he's embarrassed about something."

Pensri took the hint and started with a practiced stroking. "Well, I can tell you from experience he's got nothing to be embarrassed about."

Gina let out a frustrated moan. "So much for that theory. How's he as a client? Bet he's a big tipper, isn't he?"

"Yes. Though I tell him it's not necessary."

Gina and Pensri had known each other since the Thai woman had joined them when she was a destitute teenager. Although her profession had brought her wealth, that hadn't stopped Pensri from squeezing out an extra baht given the chance. There could only be one reason she would turn down Kannon's money. "Does he make you come?"

Pensri gave Gina an especially naughty stroke of her finger. "Gina! You know I don't kiss and tell." From the look in her eyes, she didn't need to. If Kannon made the consummate professional come, an amateur like her would be putty in his hands.

"Fine then. Here I am, a friend you haven't seen in years, and you won't share. Even though you know it's the only way I'm going to get a piece of him."

"Get someone else."

"I want him." It came out that fast. Gina sucked in her breath. She could feel herself drying up even under Pensri's luxurious manipulations.

Great. She'd reconciled herself to a night without sex from Kannon, she was with an expert, she wanted sex, and because she wanted it from a man who was sipping iced tea in the next room, she was like the desert.

"I'm so pathetic," she muttered.

Pensri gave a consoling giggle and snuggled closer to Gina, sliding her hand away. "Poor Gina. A man she's known for two days has refused her."

"Three years technically."

That got Pensri up on her elbow. "Really? How do you

add that up? He's been here two years, and you haven't been here in ten."

"We met three years ago at my workplace."

"Let me guess. He was there on business."

"Yes. He was…um, very focused on completing his job."

"Maybe he's focused now."

Gina reached around and pinched her girlfriend's bum. "You're on his side."

Pensri flicked Gina's nipple in return. "I'm pointing out that not everyone has your viewpoint."

"I'm very liberal."

"You accept all viewpoints except from people who don't accept all viewpoints."

"I'm intolerant of intolerance."

"Kannon isn't intolerant. He's very…specific."

"Specific? What man wants sex but doesn't follow through? I'm totally easy. I come with no strings attached. He's making it into a big deal."

"Gina. If all he wanted was sex, he'd be in here right now."

And wasn't that depressing? If he didn't want to have sex with her, there was nothing else. She was just his boss, exactly like he'd told her today.

Gina flipped off the covers and swung open Pensri's armoire. Inside was a row of awe-inspiring lengths and thicknesses. Feathers and leathers, stilettos and more.

Gina took up an especially hefty toy. "Time for the big guns."

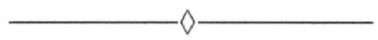

Kannon endured. He suffered the whispering and the

giggling. He swore he heard his name, followed by more giggles.

But when he heard the purr and muted revving of the toys, followed up with Gina's own special purrs and moans, he broke. He strode out the door and took the stairs. He emerged onto ground level and sucked in the hot damp night air, experiencing something that didn't make one iota of sense.

He was out of breath.

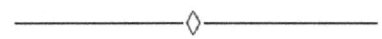

Gina woke to her phone singing *Livin' la Vida Loca*. Pensri rolled and groaned and disappeared under the sheets.

It was her dad. "Looks like we've had a development." He sounded both hopeful and strained, and Gina wasn't sure whether he was referring to his health or Alak Montri's kidnapping. She whipped out of bed. "What's happened?"

"Last night Wakai's thugs started delivering flash drives all over the city. On them is a video of Alak. He's worse for wear, but alive, and they've made an ultimatum."

Where oh where were her clothes? "What did he say?"

"If anyone hits him or his allies again in any way, Alak dies."

Her eyes shot to the door. Kannon needed to hear this. Unable to locate her dress in the darkened room she headed into Pensri's wardrobe and looked for something that could pass for street clothing. "He wants time to hunt us down with impunity. Asshole. Have you told Tas?"

"I have. She realizes that Wakai is using her father as a human shield."

"So what do you think it means? They're not intimidated, are they?"

"I don't know, Gina. Perhaps they have some vulner-ability we don't know about. Or maybe the message is meant for some other enemy. What's your story?"

She flipped through Pensri's clothes as she filled him in on her meeting with Dr. Chaiboonma. All the while, she kept one ear trained for any sound outside the room. When she and Pensri had finished playing the night before, she'd come out for water and Kannon had been gone. Was he back?

Gina settled on a yellow sleeveless buttoned shift, modest enough for a bra which she located by the door. Finishing her update, she added, "Have the Bangkok Blondes had a chance to look at the video?"

"A runner is on her way to Dr. Chaiboonma right now. Hopefully, he can get something useful from the video. Call me as soon as you make any progress." He paused. "Unless, of course, you've got time to visit your old man today."

She stopped trying to struggle into her clothes. "Yeah, Dad. I'd like that. I need to clear some stuff by Kannon and then I'll come see you. Maybe, we'll throw lines off the boat and catch a few."

"Huh. Come home."

Home. A yacht floating around the Bay of Thailand. Always shifting and drifting, anchored to a city that endlessly changed. Okay, Dr. Chaiboonma had a point about stability.

She wiggled her way into the clothing, kissed a comatose Pensri on the cheek and left to see what she could see.

Kannon was in the kitchen, his back to her as he made coffee. He was shirtless. The brightening dawn highlighted every muscle of his body, and in the light she could clearly see the elaborate tattoos that adorned him.

Across his powerful back was a strange chimera with an elephant's head, tusks, and trunk, except with curving horns sprouting from its head, its legs ending in tiger claws. For all its weirdness, its expression seemed at once kind and defiant, and despite its mismatching parts the artist had somehow lent the creature a kind of nobility. It was one of the strangest tattoos she'd ever seen—and one of the most beautiful.

Kannon looked over his shoulder, his gaze roaming over her body a moment before snapping back to her face. She really liked his eyes on her, almost as much as she liked looking at him. "What's the news?"

"You could hear me?"

He took two cups from the cupboard. "Yes. I can hear you even when you try to be quiet."

Which meant that she'd come through loud and clear last night. If she knew how, she might've blushed. Instead she got busy with bringing him up to speed.

"No news from Ryota?" She moved to get a cup of coffee.

"No," he said, turning to face her. "I'm going to relieve him now." He stalked to the living room where he put on his dress shirt from yesterday, and noosed himself into his tie. Okay, somebody needed nic gum. She didn't think it wise to bring that up right now. Instead she carried on. "Will you need me today?"

"Not unless someone shows up at the train market."

"Okay, then. I told Dad I'd visit with him, so how about you call if there's news?"

"You're the boss."

Kannon snagged his car keys and headed for the front door. Just like that. Fine. She was pouring herself coffee when he spoke. "You coming or not?"

"I thought we'd agreed to split up for the day."

"How are you getting back to the boat?"

"I'll take a water taxi to the docks and get Darae to pick me up from there."

"I'll take you."

"Doesn't make sense you going all the way to the docks and then back to the market in rush hour. Ryota's already exhausted."

He held the door open for her impatiently, seeming to think he'd explained himself thoroughly. Gina thought her head would explode. She took up her purse, tagged her phone and strolled after him. She'd call Darae on the way to have a boat at the docks to ferry her to *The Pussycat*.

The car was running by the time she reached it and this morning, now that the cat was out of the bag regarding Pensri, he used a remote to open the gate to the underground parking. He bullied his way into the traffic but then had no choice except to inch along at a snail's pace. It was start and stop, start and stop, making only a few dozen feet of headway at a go.

A dog loped up alongside the car and began to follow them, standing up and sitting down as they stopped and started along the route. Gina looked to a nearby food stall.

"I'll go get some noodles and meet you down the block."

"We don't have time for you to feed a dog."

"I'm not. He's reminding me that it's breakfast time." She got out, even as Kannon rolled ahead.

Gina got a box of noodles, dropped a wormy mess of them on the ground which the dog licked clean and, with a quick pat to its head, she caught up to Kannon.

She held up traffic for the two seconds it took to get into the car and immediately there was the blast of a horn. Kannon threw the car into park and exited, striding to the driver, some unfortunate ex-pat in a BMW.

"Oh shit, shit, shit," Gina didn't know whether to sink into her seat, follow Kannon or run for it. Instead she watched in the rearview mirror as Bangkok's latest incident of road rage unfolded. The driver had clearly taken stock of the situation but there was nowhere to go, his car as boxed in as everyone else's.

She cringed as Kannon pulled open the door to the driver's car, seizing him by the front of his shirt and yanking him half out of the vehicle. The guy was desperately apologizing, and after shoving him back into the car, Kannon strode back to her, his face tight and angry.

Once he got back behind the wheel, Gina kept her head down and her mouth filled with noodles. Only as they crossed yet another bridge did she venture to comment. "For the record, as your boss, I don't think you should be picking fights like that. We've kinda got enough trouble as it is."

"Fire me, then."

"Is that why you did it? To provoke me into firing you? I really don't get you at all."

He adjusted his mirrored sunglasses. "Unless I can get my boss back soon, I'm in trouble with the Yakuza again, and that's to say nothing about how I'm going to keep paying for my daughter's schooling or anything else. Except I can't do anything but wait and wait for some nameless person to stumble into our trap. Or not. Only thing left for me to do is chauffeur you home because I'm supposed to be protecting you, too."

"So you're frustrated."

He gripped the wheel as if aiming to bust it in two. "The situation I can handle. What irritates me is you and a stray dog making a noodle run the second I'm stuck in traffic. You don't need to make my job harder."

"So is that what you think you are? Bodyguard to a mafia princess?"

He rolled ahead, braked. Was silent.

"Look, Kannon. I'm not trying to put you into a spot. I'm not trying to complicate things. You don't want sex with me. Fine. You don't want me as your boss. Fine. You don't want to walk away, either. Fine. Only thing I don't know is what the hell you do want."

He stared straight ahead. He rolled the car forward, stopped. A space opened up and he filled it again. She filled herself up on noodles and said nothing, because really there was nothing more to say.

"A date."

It was a good thing she'd just swallowed, otherwise she would've choked. "A date? You want a date…with me?"

"Yes."

She stared.

He blew out his breath and stripped off his glasses to look her in the eye. "I want to go on a nice, normal date with someone I don't have to keep secrets from. With someone who knows what I do. With someone who's attracted to me, and vice versa. That's what I want from you."

He wore the same defiant look as on the plane when he'd told her he was a killer. He was bracing for her refusal.

"To be honest, I've never really had a normal date either," she admitted. "But I'll give it a try."

You needed to have studied Kannon for as intensely as she had to have seen the slight relaxation of his shoulders, the tight lines around his mouth loosen. "Thank you."

A space opened. He closed it.

She passed him the rest of the noodles, which was more than half. He took up the chopsticks and drove with his knees while eating.

"So, to clarify, did we just agree to go out on a date?"

"No," he explained through a mouthful. "All we've settled is that when I ask you out, you'll agree."

"And when will that be?"

"When I know, you'll know."

They'd cleared the bridge and Kannon swung onto a road that ran along the docks, managing to somehow pick up speed, hoover up noodles and still keep his shirt clean. The man was a superhero. At this rate, they'd be there before she'd cleared things up. "And are we on the traditional 'no sex until the third date' rule?"

"Yes."

"And are we doing the dates in order, or are we going to change it up? Make the third date first, say?"

"First, second, third."

She considered that. "Breakfast, lunch, dinner. We could do a big push and get it done in one day. A Thai-themed three-date scheme."

Kannon swung up to the docks and sure enough, there was Darae and one of the girls waiting for her. He handed her the empty noodle box. "I'll call. Now get out. I've got work to do."

"No goodbye kiss?"

His lips twitched into a near smile. Yes! "Get out."

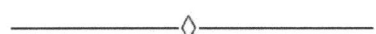

Gina found her father ensconced in his luxurious lounge chair, his frail body wrapped in a vintage smoking jacket that still reeked of the fine Dominican cigars once considered his trademark. Balanced in the corner of his mouth was one of them, unlit.

"You look like Hugh Hefner in that getup," Gina remarked, as she sat beside her father, taking his hand.

He pretended to blow smoke rings. "I don't smoke anymore, but that doesn't mean I can't enjoy the aroma. Besides, it helps me think."

"About this situation with Alak?"

He reinserted the cigar. "I'm leaving that to you and Kannon and Darae. If the three of you can't figure out how to free him, then I sure as hell won't be able to. Maybe it's cowardice on my part. Too hard to see how one man can destroy everything Alak and I spent most of your life building."

"We'll get it back, Daddy. Don't worry."

He patted her hand, as if telling her the same thing. "I only called you this morning because it seems you won't spend any time with me unless I beg for it."

"Dad, that's not true!"

"Then why didn't you come home last night?"

"I went to see Pensri."

"You stayed the night with one of the girls?"

"She's not a girl to me, she's a friend."

"Did either one of Alak's men stay with you?"

"Yes, Kannon did."

Vincenzo Zaffini worked the cigar from one side of his mouth to the other. "That must've been interesting."

"It wasn't. It was boring. What else do you want to talk about?"

"My last words."

Gina felt a lump in her throat. "And who says that you aren't going to beat this? With medicine being what it is today a lot of people manage to—"

"I stopped treatments a couple of weeks ago," he interrupted. "They weren't working, and I didn't want to spend what little time I had left withering in some hospital. I've always made my own decisions, and I'll be damned if I'm going to hand my life over to some doctor right in the home stretch."

"I don't think you should give up," Gina insisted as gently as she could.

"We all die, Gina," he said. "Only thing we control is how we live. And that's why I've been considering my last words carefully. Only one chance to get those right."

"Have you come to a decision?" she asked, trying to remain cheerful despite the morbidity of their conversation.

"When I was a boy," he said, giving her hand a weak squeeze, "the family used to believe that when a person was about to die they gained a special understanding of death and the afterlife. That they could hear the whispers of angels or their ancestors."

"Oh?"

"It's all bullshit. Here I am on death's door and I don't understand anything more about what's to come than I ever did. I haven't the faintest notion of where I'm going, or even if I'm going anywhere at all."

"I'm pretty sure they have a place in heaven for you," she said. "Even if it's in the smoking section."

Vincenzo laughed dryly. "My daughter, the health nut. You're going to feel awful stupid one day, lying in your death bed, dying of nothing. At least my cigars gave me closure."

Gina rolled her eyes. "So sounds like those last words of yours aren't going to be about an afterlife, huh?"

He shook his head. "No. By the time I know what I'm talking about it'll be too late to say anything. Think I'm going to go with a poem."

Gina sucked in her cheeks to keep from laughing. "A poem? You?"

Her father looked almost affronted. "What? You've never written one?"

"Roses are purple, violets are lime, I made up these colors so this poem would rhyme," she reeled off.

"Yes, well, I'm hoping to compose something a little more meaningful. I've been reading a lot of Buddhist philosophy, and these Zen masters recite a poem with their last breath. To share some last bit of wisdom with their disciples."

"You've got disciples?"

"Certainly not Darae," he replied. "I don't think she's listened to a word I've said in all the time we've been married, so it's not likely she'll start now. Besides, I don't want to spend my last moment stuck between wife and death."

Gina groaned at the pun. "That's terrible, Daddy."

"I try. Seriously, I was intending the poem for you. One last little piece of advice before your old man goes to feed the worms."

"That's sick," Gina laughed, trying not to cry at the same time. "But yeah, I'll try to be there for your poetry recital."

"I'll wait for you."

His face was so gaunt, so pale. She swallowed. "You better."

"What then, Gina? What are your plans after we sort things out here in Bangkok?"

Gina wasn't thinking much beyond her first date with Kannon. "Back to my job, I guess."

"I'm surprised you didn't hightail it there already. Being here rekindle old memories?"

"Yeah," she replied. "Good ones. Bad ones. It's been so long since I left I'd forgotten what this place means to me.

Now that I'm here and in the thick of things, well, it feels like I'm finally back where I belong."

"Darae would be happy to hear that. She's always had great ambitions for you."

"Don't I know it."

"She's a smart lady, Gina. If you're going to choose the path I did, you couldn't have a better person in your corner. And that Kannon guy isn't too shabby either."

"Dad!"

"Not that it's any of my business," he continued. "All I'm saying is if a girl were going to have a partner in crime he'd make a good one. Tough. Smart. Loyal. A family man. There certainly are a lot worse choices."

"You giving me a sales pitch, Daddy?"

"From the way you look at him, the way he looks at you, I think it's a done deal."

Gina gave her father a gentle hug. "We're booked for three dates. After that, who knows?"

His arms stayed around her, his stupid cigar poking her cheek. "Who ever does? Only I had to get in my two cents worth before my birth certificate expired."

She batted at his cigar. "I swear you just sit around thinking up new ways to describe your death."

"Yeah, well, that's the life of a poet, isn't it?"

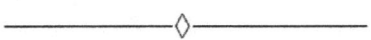

Gina climbed into the boxcar and sighed. Kannon was standing in the room, gun trained on a man in a chair who seemed completely unconcerned by the threat. He was a short, fat, young Thai, horn-rimmed glasses set on his impassive face, his body squeezed into a Starcraft t-shirt two sizes too small.

"Does a day go by you're not pointing that thing at someone?"

Kannon glanced her way, then did a double-take. "Why are you wet?"

"It's not my fault," she said, sliding the door closed behind her. "I was swimming when you called and you made it sound like an emergency. I barely had time to dress and no time to fix my hair."

"Swimming? There's no pool on the yacht."

Gina, refixing her wet knot of hair, stopped. "Kannon. You must be joking. The yacht's in a swimming pool. It's called The Gulf of Thailand."

Kannon flexed his grip on the gun. "The water's got sharks, Gina."

She might've felt flattered by his concern, except that he was being silly. "Pfft. There's not that many, and most of them aren't any bigger than me."

Kannon stretched his neck, like his tie was too tight. "Gina. Hard to date a dead woman."

"I bet. I stick with the live ones myself."

"WHO THE HELL ARE YOU AND WHAT DO YOU WANT?" their prisoner suddenly boomed at them in Thai. That explained Kittyjack's earplug recommendation. Good thing the boxcar was way at the end of the market.

"I take it you're Capslock," Gina said, switching to their prisoner's language. "I'm looking for a woman named Victoria Wakai."

"If I tell you what I know, will you let me go?" he demanded at the same decibel level.

Gina motioned for him to lower his voice. "Sure."

"First, I should tell you that I'm only tech support," the

hacker replied, ignoring her cue to pipe down. "I run sites for all kinds of clients, no questions asked. I'm only a business-man. You understand?"

No, she didn't. That had always been a problem for her. Never understood how to turn a blind eye. "Yeah," Gina said. "Sure. Where we can find her?"

"I don't know where she is," he shouted, "but I know her partner, and the asshole owes me money. If you can find him then maybe you can find her."

Gina backed away a few feet in an effort to save her ears. "What's the guy's name?"

"Ek Choeun," he replied. "Cambodian guy. He's some sort of tribal leader there—calls himself a sorcerer."

Oh, wonderful. "So you're saying he's in Cambodia? That's not a lot of help, now is it?"

"No, he's here in Bangkok," Capslock yelled. "Been here for a few months now."

"Where?"

"I don't know where he lives. He runs a couple of businesses. One's out in 70 Rai called—"

"Been there, killed them," Gina said. "What else?"

The hacker looked at Kannon, then kept on. "Yeah, well, he also runs a kind of black magic service. A lot of business-men in Taiwan and China believe that crap, and they pay him a load of money to curse their enemies. I don't know where he operates from, though."

Gina held up her hand to Capslock and related what she'd learned to Kannon. "What do you think?"

"I think Mr. Microphone here told us everything he knows. The problem is who else is he going to tell if we let him go?" said Kannon, adjusting his aim upwards to the man's head.

When Gina translated what Kannon said to the hacker, he snorted. "Lady, it'd be suicide for me to tell Ek what I told you. I keep out of trouble."

There it was again. The attitude that it was okay to profit from the misery of others. Gina felt her skin crawl the way it had when the pedophile in 70 Rai had touched her. "You seem to think that just because you run things from behind a keyboard you're somehow innocent of the crimes. And I'm not talking about some petty fraud. You have any idea what's on her site?"

If Capslock was in the slightest bit repentant, he did a great job of hiding it. "Yeah, well, you are probably guilty of a few crimes yourself. Like I said, I only host the stuff. No questions asked."

He was right. She had killed two strangers days ago, and before that—. She took a deep breath. No. Whatever her crimes, Capslock couldn't sluff off his own responsibility. Gina stepped up and kicked him in the shin. "You want me to tell my friend what you just said? Because you sound an awful lot like those fuckers in 70 Rai before he put a bullet in their heads."

Although Capslock still looked defiant, his next words were pitched low. "What do you want?"

"You're going to keep on with what you're doing for now. Don't want to tip off Ek. But the next time we're in touch, you'll have forty-eight hours to get out of Bangkok, and stay out. You understand?"

His nod was a jerk of the head and Gina stepped back.

"What the hell was that?" Kannon asked.

Gina made for the door. "An attitude adjustment. Leave him. We need to find out everything we can about this witch doctor, and I know just the person we should talk to." She stopped, realizing something. "That is, if she hasn't gotten herself eaten yet."

CHAPTER
7
SEVEN

LWIN KINJO SMILED beatifically at the Siamese crocodile as she stroked its snout. Though the old woman was an even one hundred years of age, she handled the huge reptiles around her like they were kittens.

Gina and Kannon watched from a safe distance up the bank. "Puts my little dip with the sharks in perspective, doesn't it?"

Lwin cooed to the beast, even as its tooth-lined maw opened in a satisfied yawn.

"Jesus." Kannon cursed with total reverence. For the first time ever, he sounded impressed. "My father had a way with animals, but even he wouldn't do anything like this."

What? Kannon had dropped a bit about his past. Another first. Gina smothered her glee, and pretended that it was natural for him to do that with her. "Oh, she's one tough battle-axe. It's her gang that pretty much runs sporting events in Bangkok."

"I knew about The Smiling Crocodiles, not about their boss. I wouldn't bet against her."

"Not many would." Gina hesitated, unsure whether or not

to continue. Kannon was Yakuza, and he might be a tad sensitive about his heritage, and right now, they were actually having a nice conversation.

"What is it you want to tell me?"

"Am I that obvious or are you that good?"

For the second time that day, he almost smiled. "Let's go with it's obvious I'm good."

"Huh. Okay, this is it. Lwin has killed hundreds of your countrymen."

"What? Her?" Kannon frowned.

"Yep. All by her lonesome. In the 40's Lwin lived on a Burmese island called Ramree," Gina began. "Place was a Japanese stronghold, and the soldiers didn't treat the locals very nicely. Took anything they wanted. Raped the pretty girls. Shot or beheaded anyone who stood up to them. That said, when the Allies attacked she went to the Japanese commander and offered to lead his troops to a place the Americans and British wouldn't dare follow."

Again, Gina hesitated. This time for dramatic effect.

"Gina—" Kannon stretched out her name warningly.

"A mangrove swamp. She led about a thousand Imperial troops right into the heart of it, then when night fell, she disappeared."

The old woman tossed a fish into a crocodile's mouth which snapped shut. "Her pets attacked, I'm guessing."

"Hordes of them," Gina said. "Outside the swamp, the marines could hear rifles firing. Men screaming. Crocodiles splashing and rolling in the water, drowning their catch. In the morning, Lwin led about twenty soldiers out of the swamp to surrender. They were all that was left."

Lwin nuzzled her croc, then stood and walked calmly toward them through the tangle of reptiles sunning themselves at the water's edge.

"Why did she save the soldiers she did?"

"They say she spared the ones that had shown kindness," Gina said. "Apparently a few of them had treated the locals with respect and didn't deserve to die."

The woman arrived at the top of the bank, and pressing her hands together, Gina bowed deeply. To her surprise, Kannon did the same.

Ancient eyes sparkled amidst the deep wrinkles of Lwin's tan face. "Gina," she said in Thai, "So good to see you again. Who's your handsome friend?"

"Kannon Takahama. Alak Montri's man. You heard he was kidnapped?"

"Who hasn't? The work of his best lieutenant."

"It was, and someone else, we believe. Do you know anything about an Ek Chouen?"

Lwin's twinkly softness vanished and she suddenly spat. "Yes. Come."

At the pace of someone half her age, she led them from the pond to a modest thatch house overlooking the water, its light frame set on stilts. How the place stood up to the tropical storms that battered the area had always been a mystery to Gina, but Lwin had lived there for over five decades without issue—ever since she'd married one of the soldiers she'd saved from the Ramree swamp. Gina made a mental note to tell Kannon about that happy ending. Maybe on their first date.

Inside she watched as Kannon's normal deadpan expression was suffused with surprise and admiration. The place was a tattoo parlor, though not a typical one. Every wall was covered with photographs of Thai kick-boxers, some of them recent, others dating back to the 1960's, and all were adorned with tattoos depicting crocodiles in one form or another.

Gina came alongside him. "She does magical tattoos. They protect from bad luck and curses. Give people strength or courage or a long life. That kind of thing. She did mine."

"I don't think many here would need magic to win," Kannon said, looking at a particularly fierce boxer in a black-and-white photo. "Look at his hands. You can tell he trained seriously. Very seriously."

Lwin gestured for them to sit with her at a table. Gina took a seat across from her, expecting Kannon to stand as usual. Instead, he made a series of unusual moves. He sat down right beside her, so close their knees almost touched. He took off his sunglasses and pocketed them. And then he turned his dark liquid eyes on Gina. Looking into those eyes was like plugging herself into a socket.

"Tell Mrs. Kinjo that she does exceptional work," he murmured, his pillow-talk voice making her tummy clench.

"Should I also tell her you make my heart go thumpety-thump?"

The flash of his warm eyes sent more sparks through her. "No."

Gina stuck to the original message and Lwin bestowed him with the same affectionate smile she'd given her pets. "What can you tell us about Ek Chouen?" Gina continued. "I hear he's a very bad man."

Lwin looked ready to spit again. "He is. And very big. They say he's strong enough to strangle an elephant. But it's not just him that you have to worry about. His whole clan is cursed."

Oh no, bad juju. "Yeah?"

"He and his people are descendants of the rakshasas," the old woman explained. "Reincarnations of people who made pacts with demons, polluting their souls and coming back as monsters."

"Sounds familiar," said Gina, thinking of the sharp-toothed berserker held prisoner aboard *The Pink Pussycat*, and the men they'd encountered at the defiled temple.

"Sadists. Cannibals. Black magicians. Very dangerous people. Nothing they won't do."

"They're a clan you say? Like a crime family?"

Lwin shook her head. "No. They raise no children. Rather they corrupt the lineages of others."

"I don't understand. How?"

"Their seed is tainted, Gina," the old woman explained. "They do not know love. They father their children through rape, and when the resulting child grows, it seeks out its own kind. Over the centuries Hindu, Muslim and Buddhist warriors exterminated them, till the last of them hid in the Dângrêk mountains between Thailand and Cambodia.

"Their numbers had almost dwindled to nothing when the Khmer Rouge came to power, and naturally they became part of Pol Pot's genocide. Under their reign they tortured and murdered hundreds of thousands, and they impregnated countless women, creating a whole new generation of rakshasas to plague the world."

Gina didn't go much for ghost stories or black magic, but Lwin was no fool. Whatever the truth behind the rakshasas was, she was probably getting a good part of it. "So Ek Choeun is their leader?"

"Their true leaders are demons that dwell beneath the mountains," said Lwin. "As far as I know, Ek is the greatest of their servants. He came to Bangkok a year ago. Easier to serve his clients, I suppose. Rakshasas make deals with ordinary people all the time, but they only ever form partnerships with other rakshasas. As traitorous as he might be, I wouldn't think this Wakai was one of their kind. Don't think Alak Montri would have ever dealt with a character like that."

Gina turned that fact over in her head. "Are there such things as female rakshasas?"

"Oh, of course," Lwin replied. "Rakshasii. They show their heritage less than their brothers, but they're every bit as corrupted. According to legend they're why the rakshasas have to breed the way they do. The females have a habit of eating their young."

Gina felt sick to her stomach. Thank God she'd abstained from the website. "Even crocodiles carry their babies in their mouth."

Lwin nodded. "Even crocodiles. That was why I've left him alone, and he me."

What? "You knew about what he did and let him carry on?" She expected it of the hacker, not of the woman from the Ramree swamp.

Lwin's expression maintained its usual Buddha-like calmness. "I'm a hundred years old and have killed a thousand monsters. After all your training from so many of us, can you not deal one with one?"

Gina felt the soft rebuke like a blow. On the drive to Lwin's she'd chatted to a mostly silent Kannon about her past. As part of her training with Dr. Chai, he'd sent her to his old friend. Lwin, who'd already seemed ancient to the adolescent Gina, steeped her in the legends and culture of Southeast Asia, taught her the traditions and the superstitions that ultimately had Gina believing nothing but respecting everything.

When she'd left Bangkok a decade ago, Lwin, like Dr. Chai, hadn't said one word to stop her. At the time, it seemed as if she was giving her blessing. Looking into those small dark pools of brightness now, Gina realized that Lwin had waited ten years to speak her mind.

Kannon tapped her knee with his. "What's going on?"

"She's—she's telling me things I need to hear, that's all."

"Something I need to hear, too?"

"I—yes. Maybe, later."

He gave a soft grunt and frowned at Lwin. She smiled and waved.

Kannon's mouth twisted. "I see where you got your deeply rooted fear of nobody from," he said to Gina.

Having dealt with Kannon, Lwin turned back to Gina. "There is a long friendship between Alak Montri and your father. And I understand why your family would seek to free him. But don't underestimate Ek Chouen. Even my markings cannot protect you fully from their kind of evil."

Considering her tats couldn't ward off mosquitoes, Gina wasn't disappointed. "I promise we'll be careful. Very careful."

Her old mentor wasn't yet satisfied. "Ek Chouen is a born killer and leads an army of born killers. To kill him you will need to kill a thousand. You will need to become like me."

Gina bowed her head. She'd left Bangkok because she couldn't accept the life she was being groomed for. Now, a decade later, she was right back in it. Nothing had changed. This time she couldn't run. Otherwise she was no better than the hacker she'd exiled. "A monster hunter."

Lwin reached across the table and touched Gina's chest where the tattoo was. "No. A crocodile tamer."

Gina managed a weak smile. "Ah, much easier."

Lwin sat back and said gently. "For you, so easy." Her voice became brisk. "Ek works out of an underground club called Triple Nine." She rattled off an address Gina immediately inputted into her phone. "He comes and goes, sometimes for weeks at a time. Still, that is where you'll find him. And believe me, you'll know him when you see him."

"Thank you, Lwin. Please let me know if there's ever anything I can do to repay you."

"I will." Lwin pointed a thin, chicken-bone finger at Kannon. "Tell me, is he your lover?"

Gina could feel Kannon straighten, and she put her hand on his thigh to calm him. His muscles there tensed. "Now what's she saying?"

"She wants to know if we're lovers."

Deep lines between his eyes appeared. "How is that her business?"

Gina translated his question back to Lwin whose smile grew as wide as a crocodile's. "Anyone who answers a question with another question doesn't like the answer he'd have to give."

"Are you saying that he wants us to be lovers?"

"Tell me, how does he feel underneath your hand?"

For the purposes of research, Gina let her hand travel down Kannon's thigh which produced very tense muscles. "Hard." She ran her hand down again. "Large." And again. "Twitchy."

With each descriptor, the old woman's merriment grew until she burst into cackling laughter. "You've taken him to the mat, girl!"

Gina couldn't help from joining in. That was enough for Kannon. He set his hand on hers to stop her. "You two laughing at me?"

Gina automatically flipped over her hand, catching his. "She said we're destined to be lovers. No use fighting it, Kannon."

She expected him to snap back at her or even get up and

leave. Instead he gripped her hand tight in his and the look he gave her this time—forget the socket, she was hooked to the grid.

"Tell the tattoo lady this," he said. "Tell her I'm not fighting it. I'm timing it."

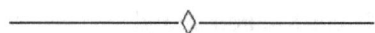

Kannon had seen plenty of women drink from a bottle of sugar cane juice but none of them worked it like Gina Zaffini was doing right now with hers. They were standing down a short ways from Soi Cowboy, one of Bangkok's popular red light districts, and across the street from Triple Nine. Ryota had gone inside twenty-six minutes ago to check the exits and make sure Ek Chouen was there. Twenty-six minutes in which Gina suctioned her full lips around the neck of the bottle, rolled the cold dewy glass across her sweaty upper chest, lapped up spilled drops. And all the while she texted, taking in updates from Ryota and whoever else. She had a different chime for each contact, and so far he'd heard a half-dozen.

"Pensri says 'hi'."

Kannon growled. "Can we get back to business?"

Gina looked around. "We haven't left it."

"How about we focus on it, then?"

"What do we need to do that we're not already doing? We're standing here watching and waiting, and blending in, which you in your suit on a hot, muggy night in Bangkok among thousands of horny tourists doesn't work."

She was right, which irritated him to no end. "You certainly dressed for the part." She'd switched into a party dress. A gold deal that barely covered her butt, and she had enough bling on her to be a walking jewelry kiosk. She'd even glittered her tats. Normally he detested tattoos on women, not in small part because he had so many. But like everything about Gina, she made them into something desirable and totally hers.

She squeezed the bottle between her breasts and the way her dress was wired made it stay in place. His cock shifted. "Ah," she breathed out. "You have no idea how good this feels."

"I think I do."

"Why, Kannon, you need to stay focused."

He looked away. She was right again. He needed to finish this job. Get this rakshasa to spill Victoria's whereabouts, dig out Victoria, find her brother and get Alak Montri back home. There'd be consequences for not keeping Montri safe but not much because he had stayed loyal and, just as importantly, alive. He'd deal with them, bring his daughter out of hiding and then get on with getting it on with Gina Zaffini.

It was hard enough holding out against her constant sexiness, but what threatened to undo him were her sudden exposures of sadness and worry, like when she saw the state of her father and her revulsion over 70 Rai. He wanted to protect her from all that ugliness, as he had with his wife. Except with his wife, she hadn't wanted to know about his life. It was easy to hide what no one wanted to find in the first place. The problem with Gina is that there was no saving her from anything.

Two full-blooded Aussies rounded the corner, their arms wrapped around a pair of Thai hookers in white cowboy hats and boots and little else. So engrossed were they in their purchase of the evening, one bumped into Gina. He immediately apologized and took in Gina's bottle.

"Hey there, mind if I have a sip?" Everyone in the group, drunk or pretending to be, laughed, and Gina joined right in.

Kannon came up beside her. "Drink from your own

bottle."

The Aussie immediately threw up his hands. "No worries. Didn't know she was with you."

"You know," Gina said, as they disappeared into the happy crowd, "I could've handled that."

"You could've but you don't need to when I'm here."

Her phone chirped and she smiled at its message. "Pensri again. She wants to know how our first date is going."

"I may be bad with women but even I can do better than this."

Gina laughed and began typing.

"Don't tell her that."

"I'm telling her we're across the street."

"At Ek's club?"

"No, silly." She lifted her head long enough to point to a flashing neon sign with bubbles floating upward. Outside, Thai girls in skimpy nighties were blowing bubbles at potential males. "The Bubble Boat." The signs carried by two girls read 'Pop my bubbles! Happy endings!'

"Yeah, it belongs to my dad. Pensri made her start there."

"Why am I not surprised?"

"What can I say? Good times are our business."

"What I mean is that it would be right close to Ek Chouen's place. Anybody you're not connected to?"

She bumped her behind against his groin. "There is one."

"You come on to every man like this?"

Gina made a sweeping gesture. "Look around you. Look at the business I grew up in. I'm a product of my environment."

"You don't care about girls becoming hookers?"

Gina tugged out her bottle from its boob holder and took a long pull. "I hope you're not suggesting that hookers don't deserve respect."

"I'm asking what your answer is to those that might think that."

"Here, it's a job. And like every job, it's got its good points and its bad points, and if the bad starts outweighing the good, you leave it."

Her phone sounded, and this one was repeated from before. Ryota. "He's coming out." No sooner did she say it then out he came and crossed the street.

"Only two bouncers inside the door. No guards or cameras from what I can see."

"What about our man?" Kannon asked.

"He's there. And out in the open." Ryota's eyes widened. "He's big. Very big."

Which meant it would be a bitch to get him. "Get Darae. Have her pull up front."

"Got it." Gina was already tapping on her phone. From her unsmiling expression it was hard to believe that one minute ago she was flirting with him. Would she switch back to party mode once they were inside the club, get distracted and get hurt?

"You need to know, Gina, that what we're doing now is something I normally take weeks to plan. Ryota and I can do this because it's what we're trained for. You go in there, the plan doesn't change. It'll still be to get Ek. Me, Ryota, we can't be saving you, too."

Gina lifted her bottle and drained it. "Lucky for you, then," she said, cracking a huge grin, "that I don't need saving."

———————◊———————

Triple 9 was enough to make Gina seriously think that her days as a party girl were over. The club itself was accessed down metal spiraling stairs that opened out into a long concrete basement. She, along with Kannon and Ryota, were immediately drenched in scarlet light that transformed them into altered beings, an effect that she'd once thought cool but then again that was when she'd been the age of its present occupants. The place was packed wall-to-wall with half-naked new adults, bumping and grinding to the deafening beat of rap gone bad.

She could've tolerated the bad music and the worse fashion, if the people were having fun. It was nothing but sneers and glares and droopy eyes. Whatever drugs they were on, it wasn't happy pills.

Kannon took her hand and jerked it, and she followed his gaze across the room. Lwin was right. There was no mistaking Ek Chouen.

He towered over everyone else in the club, way bigger than Kannon, like a circus freak or something that ought to be in a cage. In the pulsating light, she could make out his long, caveman hair, the same cryptic symbols cut into his forehead as the berserker who'd attacked her on the yacht. How the hell they were ever going to take this monster was beyond her.

But apparently Kannon had a plan. He signaled to them that he was going to get closer, and with a frown at her, that she and Ryota were to stay. Why he would go on alone was beyond her, though now was not the time to draw attention by kicking up a fuss, so she let Ryota guide her to a concrete pillar they slid behind as Kannon edged through the press of bodies toward Ek.

He stood by the billiard tables at the back of the establish-ment, observing a skanky pool-shark ply her trade amidst the boozy male clientele. She seemed oblivious to Ek, focused on relieving her playmates of their money. Gina could see that was a mistake. From the look in the sorcerer's cold, dead eyes, unless someone intervened, odds were good that the little shark would be belly up by dawn.

Ek didn't have any bodyguards. Perhaps given his size he figured he didn't need them. But Kannon moved as quietly and carefully as a stalking tiger, staying out of Ek's line of sight as he circled around behind him, till at last he was an arm's length away.

Gina bit her lip as Kannon slid a powerful taser from his jacket pocket, and with a sharp thrust he pressed the crackling tip straight into the base of the giant's spine. Ek's body spasmed. Instead of the giant's legs going out from under him as Gina had expected, the huge man rounded on Kannon, sharklike gaze locking onto his attacker.

"Oh fuck," Gina gasped.

Kannon tried jabbing the taser straight for Ek's chest. His opponent caught the crackling weapon in mid-strike with one hand, the other reaching for Kannon's neck. To her relief Kannon ducked, simultaneously trying to twist the taser free, but the device snapped with a flash of sparks, setting fire to Ek's sleeve.

Ek snarled, kicking out at Kannon as he tore off the burning shirt, revealing a heavily muscled torso crisscrossed with jagged scars, and seeing the opening, Kannon attacked.

Blocking Ek's kick, Kannon got in close and personal, throwing everything he had into a blinding volley of punches almost too fast for Gina to follow. Gut, solar plexus, throat, jaw, face—five perfectly aimed punches in less than two seconds. She smiled at the onslaught Kannon was delivering, but it vanished.

Roaring with fury, the bloodied giant backhanded Kannon like a child, sending him reeling into the crowd, eliciting panicked cries and curses. At least the party-goers had a reason to be unhappy now. Ek lumbered forward with the power of an angry bear, slapping aside people like they were made of paper, then grabbed Kannon by the front of his suit.

Gina cried out as Kannon was hoisted into the air, his head connecting with the concrete ceiling, then thrown into a new tangle of bodies, all struggling and squirming to avoid the fight.

Ek raised a massive foot above Kannon, and Gina's heart stopped. Kannon might be numb to pain, but she felt it for him, a sick sensation of panic roiling through her core. Move!

At the last second, Kannon rolled aside. The party-goer pinned beneath him wasn't so lucky, his ribs snapping like matchsticks as Ek's foot connected like a sledge-hammer. Kannon retaliated with a punch at the one place guaranteed to hurt any male.

Ek stumbled back, as Kannon staggered to his feet, blood trickling down his face. How he was still alive, let alone conscious, was beyond Gina. One thing was clear—there was no way Kannon could take the monster on his own.

"Ryota! Help him!" she ordered, and Kannon's apprentice obeyed.

Ek snarled, thick muscles flexing like coiled pythons, and again he came at Kannon, massive hands curled into claws. Ryota burst from the crowd, throwing a series of long, sweeping kicks to Ek's legs, trying to disable the juggernaut while keeping his distance. The beast reached for Ryota, who gracefully slid away, making use of his lanky frame to stay quick and mobile even as he continued harrying the monster.

It was obvious to Gina that Ryota wasn't doing much

damage, but now it was two on one, and Kannon joined in with his own powerful strikes, dodging and weaving to avoid the counterattacks.

Between the two of them, it should have been easy defeating one opponent, except the rakshasa was exactly as Lwin had warned. Ek turned his back on Ryota, ignoring the weaker enemy to press the attack on Kannon. Absorbing a crushing blow to the face, Ek gripped Kannon by the arm, yanking him forward and bringing up his knee.

Kannon was slammed in the gut with enough force to snap the spine of a lesser man, and Gina's own stomach clenched in sympathy. Now Ek's massive hands were on his throat, crushing the life out of him, even though Ryota had leapt on the giant's back and locked his arm around Ek's thick neck in a chokehold.

Gina was casting about for some way to help when a rear door crashed open, and a group of Ek's clan mates started shoving their way through the crowd. Kannon and Ryota were already fighting for their lives—how could they hope to survive now?

She squeezed through the crowd, desperate to do something—anything—to help. Kannon began punching at Ek's elbows to break the death-grip even as Ryota struggled to cut off their enemy's breath.

Dark blood seeped from Ek's broken nose and split lips, his huge body trembling with effort to finish Kannon off, but with one final punch Gina heard a wet snap, so loud it pierced even the blast of the music and cries of the crowd. For a terrifying second, she thought it was Kannon's neck, then Ek's left elbow bent at an unnatural angle and the brute released him with a howl of agony.

With a spin, Ek threw Ryota from him, puffing and snarling, cradling his dislocated elbow.

Spitting blood, Kannon had readied himself for another round when Gina reached his side. "We have to get out of here! There are more of them on the way!"

Kannon glanced over his shoulder and saw what she'd seen. From the back of the club a trio of Ek's clan members were almost through the crowd, machetes in hand, eyes blazing. Kannon flashed a grim look at Ek, and Gina was scared he'd go another round. She seized his hand at the same time he took hold of hers.

"Run!"

She didn't need to be told twice.

The three of them rammed their way through the club, and tore up the stairwell seconds ahead of their pursuers. They burst out the door, and straight into the open back of Darae's van.

As they pulled out into traffic, Ryota fell back against the side panel. "That guy...he was pretty tough."

Kannon wiped blood from his face. "Next time we'll take him."

Gina rolled her eyes.

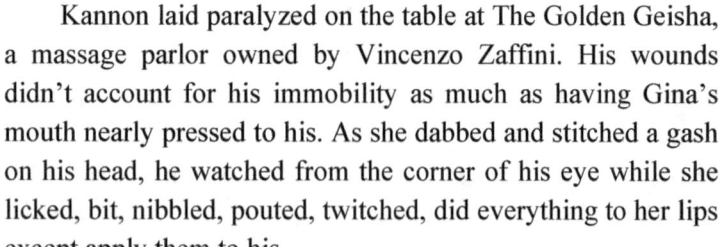

Kannon laid paralyzed on the table at The Golden Geisha, a massage parlor owned by Vincenzo Zaffini. His wounds didn't account for his immobility as much as having Gina's mouth nearly pressed to his. As she dabbed and stitched a gash on his head, he watched from the corner of his eye while she licked, bit, nibbled, pouted, twitched, did everything to her lips except apply them to his.

His self-control was about to snap when she pulled

herself out of kissing range and inspected her handiwork, her fingers skimming cool and quick along the cut. "Lucky your skull's so thick. Anybody else's brains would be stuck to the ceiling at Triple 9 right now. How's the rest of you feeling?"

"Fine."

"Are you sure? You've got these dark red bruises all along here"—her fingers stroked his neck—"and here"—her fingers played over his stomach—"not to mention the ones I know are on your legs but you're too ornery to drop your pants for me to check." She cupped her hand over his right thigh. "We should get a proper doctor. We've got one on retainer, 24/7. You could have a concussion or internal bleeding. You should be at a hospital not a safe house."

And you should be at home in my bed. The words nearly flew from his mouth. Kannon rubbed the back of his neck. "My head and guts got knocked around. That's all. I'm fine."

"And how would you know?"

He forced himself to sit up, swinging his legs off the table. "I've had concussions and internal bleeding before." He eased himself to the floor, the cool tile a balm on his bare feet. "This is nothing a little time won't heal."

She chewed on her lip, her arms crossed, her hair twisted every which way. A real picture of worry. He stood there with no idea what to do. The only other person who cared about his safety was Zoe, and she had only a faint notion of what he did. His wife had been even more clueless. On the rare occasions he got injured, he'd simply not come home until the bruises faded. She'd once asked him if he was having an affair, which he vehemently and truthfully denied. She accepted the answer, as she did with everything he told her.

There was no dodging the bullet with Gina. He wanted to date her because she knew the truth about him but that came with a price: her fear. Her bravery was what set her apart, and his reckless need to end the business tonight had endangered her and the chance to rescue Alak Montri.

He looked into her soft brown eyes. "I'm sorry, Gina. I played it wrong tonight. I got overconfident, impatient. Now the rakshasa will be on high alert. And without a hostage, we'll have to come up with a new angle to find Wakai. I messed up."

Gina stared as if he'd announced his candidacy for US president. "Did you just apologize?"

The monkey was mocking him. At least, it meant she wasn't worrying. "I do from time to time, you know."

"When? When was the last time you apologized?"

Up to now, there only ever was one other person. "To my daughter. Last month. Bawled her out for not calling me but the phone had gone dead because I forgot to charge it like she asked me to."

The mockery turned to genuine indignation. "Crap, Kannon. That's serious. No one should be without a functional phone. I would've made you do push-ups, too."

"I did."

"Of course, you would've." Gina gusted out her breath in a half-laugh. "Listen, don't beat yourself up about it." She made a face at her choice of words. "I'm just glad you guys didn't get yourselves killed."

"Or you."

She quirked a smile. "Yeah, imagine if the great Kannon Takahama lost one boss and got the other one wasted."

There was a smear of blood on her glittery dress. His blood, probably from when she was stitching him up. If Ek could do this to him—. "Both times because they wouldn't take my advice."

She looked ready to shoot off a retort, then slowed down. "Wait. You knew Montri was in trouble?"

"I knew John Wakai was up to something. His patterns were off. Suddenly leaving his place, not showing up at his office. I advised Alak Montri to take along extra security if I couldn't be with him. He asked why, but I wasn't prepared to tell him."

Gina nodded. "No one likes a whistleblower, especially one with no proof."

"Yes."

"Only he didn't listen," she concluded.

"I expected no less." He couldn't keep the frustration out of his voice. Worse, the edge of disrespect. And, of course, Gina heard it.

She sidled closer, scented with perfume and his blood. He held up his hand. "Don't. All I will say is that Dr. Chai's opinion of my boss is not unique among the gangs. I warn you, don't go making trouble. Nobody wants it."

She opened her mouth and again he cut her off. "How about we get you back to the boat?"

She crossed her arms, this time in annoyance. "If you'll let me get a word in edgewise, it's too late. Darae's gone with Ryota, and I don't particularly want anybody moving around the city at this time of night. We're safe here. Daddy's got bolt holes like these all over the place, stocked up for exactly these kinds of emergencies. How about we go to bed and get an early start?"

It was a good idea. Except with Gina, there'd be a catch. Sure enough, she led him upstairs to a bedroom straight from a porn set. Lit in bright neon blue, the place featured a mirrored ceiling, vivid psychedelically painted walls, pink leopard-patterned carpeting and a huge, intense green and anatomically correct teddy bear. At the center of it all was a round king-sized bed, piled high with plush violet and yellow pillows.

"I think I'm going to need my sunglasses," said Kannon.

Gina giggled. "This place specializes in ménages and group sex. Check the cupboards for more bedding. I'm going to clean up a bit."

She disappeared into the bathroom, leaving him to turn down a sex bed. He wondered what she was going to wear since her dress was ruined. She'd better have something on because he was already frustrated enough. Lying beside her, too hurt to do what should be done to a beautiful woman naked in a bed built for orgies, would kill him.

When he heard her come out of the bathroom, he was in bed covered to his neck in a pink sheet, his back to her, with lights out except for one so she'd not stumble. Another sheet and pillow was over—way over—on the other side of the bed. He'd wedged the teddy bear between them.

Teddy was swept away and hit the floor with a thud. Then, the whisper of sheets as she slipped in beside him. *Go to sleep, Gina. Turn off the light and go to sleep.*

There was the airy lift of his sheet and a single cool finger pressed to his back. "Who's this you carry around?"

She never did what he told her to do. Did he really think she'd follow an unspoken command? "A baku."

"A baku?"

"It's from Japanese mythology. Kind of a creature that protects people against evil. Especially children. They call it a nightmare eater."

Her finger glided over his upper back where the head was. "I see. And how did he come to ride around on your back?"

In an effort to block out his circumstances, he talked. "All Yakuza get tattoos. Used to be we weren't accepted in Japan, so we'd get them as a sign that we wouldn't bend to society's rules and norms. But they're more than just that. They hold a meaning or tell a story."

"And what does this baku say about you?"

Even in the near dark, even with his back to her, he had to push hard to get out the next words. "That I was young and stupid when I got them. My father used to tell me that we Yakuza were once lordless samurai back in medieval times. That it was we who defended the cities and towns against marauders that terrorized the countryside. All lies. The truth is, we were the bandits. We've always been thugs and criminals. Nothing more."

Her one finger became her hand flat and solid between his shoulder blades. "What difference does it make what people did or didn't do centuries ago? What matters is what we do now."

"You telling me the past doesn't define us?"

"It doesn't need to."

"I think we also define one another," he replied. "To Vincenzo, I'm a weapon. To Ryota, a teacher. To Zoe, a father. Without them I'm none of those things. In their own ways they define me, and I define them."

With one last long glide along the center of his back, her hand withdrew and he detected the faint brush of its retreat along the sheets. The loss of her touch wasn't the relief he thought it would be.

"Wow. I didn't know I was dating a philosopher."

"We haven't gone on a date yet."

"And yet, here we are on a bed where hundreds have had wild sex."

"Gina, I can't—"

The sheets rustled and sighed as she adjusted her position.

"Neither can I. You're safe from any more mauling tonight. Sleep, baku."

He couldn't. He listened as her breathing eased into the light and even pattern of restful sleep. First, there'd been his wife. Then, his daughter. And now, Gina Zaffini. The third person in his life he'd die for. He'd failed with his wife. So far, so good with his daughter, if only because he'd removed her from the situation. And with this one lying next to him, trusting that there'd be a morning, trusting that he'd keep her safe—he fitted his hand around the gun under the pillow beside him.

With this one, he hadn't a clue.

CHAPTER 8 EIGHT

JOHN WAKAI SAT out on his balcony in the sweltering night heat. The city was primed for a good storm to cool and clean the air. The forecast called for sunny days ahead but his aching legs, useless for their original purpose, messaged something different. There'd be a change. And soon.

Behind him the door slid open, and he felt his sister approach, her body draped in a light silken nightgown.

"Can't sleep?" she murmured, resting her hand, small with taloned nails, on his shoulder.

Even after all these years, her touch still sent a charge through him. He carefully answered, "I don't want to sleep. I'm working."

Her nails pressed lightly into his shoulders. "Have you figured out how to get Tasanee? Is that it?"

Indirectly. The girl was the least of his concerns, what with Ek's threats and Kannon's relentless hunt. "I'm playing poker while they're playing chess. That's the key to winning."

"What?"

Victoria was a simple creature. She wouldn't understand. But she was also vain. This meant that she couldn't accept her stupidity. He'd have to explain or endure a sulk. "There are levels to subterfuge. Anyone can play a game like, say, chess. Unfortunately, there's always going to be a better chess player, so to play fairly is to invite defeat."

Victoria's voice brightened. "So you cheat?"

"Too many risks. You can get caught, for example, or play against someone who's a better cheater than you. While it improves your odds, it doesn't ensure victory."

Victoria's nails pressed harder, her ignorance triggering her impatience. "What does?"

"Making your opponent think he's playing chess, when really you're playing poker. That way it doesn't matter how good a player he is, or how well he can cheat. He loses because he doesn't understand the real objective until it's too late."

"Sure. I get it."

John Wakai pretended that she did, too. "You always did understand me. Now how about you give me some quiet to think on my plans?"

"Okay, John. I'll see you in the morning then." She dipped down to him, and before he could stop her, she brought her lips to his, the kiss sending that same jolt of forbidden pleasure through him as when he'd first tasted her mouth as a boy. It was so wrong. So deeply, obscenely wrong. But he couldn't help what he felt for his little sister. What she brought out in him. What she encouraged.

Their lips parted, Victoria's face flushed in that loving, hungry way that was uniquely hers. He watched her pad back into the penthouse, and no sooner did she slide the balcony door shut then his smartphone rang, the number blocked.

He let it ring till it was about to go to voicemail. "Hello?"

"Kannon hit us at Triple 9," Ek growled.

Why didn't that surprise him? "Odd. I would have thought your magic would have kept him at bay," Wakai said, making zero efforts to hide his sarcasm. "Anyone hurt?"

"He nearly busted my arm," spat Ek.

"Perhaps your sorcery does work. I'm amazed he didn't kill you."

"You think this is funny? The week is up, and I'm all out of patience."

Wakai's mouth tightened into a thin smile. "Then find more."

There was a moment of silence. Wakai could practically feel Ek's anger pulsing down the line, and it made his smile widen.

"What did you say?" Ek exploded.

Wakai moved his phone away from his ear and dialed down the volume before proceeding. "I said that you need to be patient. Without me you'll lose this city in a week, and you and your people will be lucky to scurry back across the border alive. If tonight didn't prove that to you, then you're even dumber than you look."

"When I get my hands on you I'll—"

"You're not doing anything without Mr. Montri," Wakai cut in.

Again silence. The sweet pause as his words sunk in.

"What have you done?" Ek's voice was thick with murderous rage.

"He's been transferred to somewhere where only I can reach him," Wakai said in a deliberately lecturing tone, as if to a particularly stupid child. "And if anything happens to me he'll be freed. Under him the Bangkok gangs will unite to crush you. I suggest that you and I establish a more cooperative working relationship."

There was a roar of anger, a burst of static and the line went dead—probably Ek crushing the phone in that vice grip of his.

Wakai disconnected and returned to his panoramic view. So far his plan was unfolding as anticipated. The Cambodian gorilla had been put in his place, and Kannon the bulldog was playing right into his hands. Soon enough, Tasanee would be captured, and all the city stretched out before him would be his.

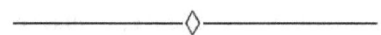

Gina woke slowly, blinking the sleep from her eyes, her hand reaching for her baku. Nothing but slippery sheets, though Kannon hadn't moved far. He was sitting cross-legged on the floor, back straight, his right hand resting in the palm of his left, thumbs touching, eyes closed.

Holey moley. Kannon meditated.

Gina flipped onto her belly and gorged her eyes on some real-live man candy. Well, candy that had gotten dropped once or twice. His neck and stomach were dark purple, and the cut on his head made him a bit like Frankenstein. Never mind. She'd still pop him in her mouth.

His eyelids fluttered open and his dark eyes focused on her. She suddenly felt a little lightheaded, and not because she lacked her morning coffee.

"Gina." And nothing more. He sat there, gazing upon her with an expression both serious and amused.

"Ooookay. Give me back the big mean Kannon because this one's freaking me out."

"You've been the focus of my meditation."

"Didn't know I was so complex. What did you need to

figure out?"

"The problem I'm having, Gina," he said, uncoiling himself, "is that I need to focus. I have to focus with you around me all day and all night, when all I want to do is make love to you until neither of us can move."

Really, really lightheaded now. "But you can't because you need to focus."

"Mmhmm."

"And did your meditation give you a solution?"

He was at the edge of the bed, standing right in front of her so her head was level with his boxers. "No. All thinking about you did is make me horny as hell."

She looked straight ahead. "So I see." She flashed up a smile at him to encounter his solemn expression.

"Gina, I need you to stop driving me crazy with your flirting, with your clothes, with your...your everything. I told you we'll make this happen. But I need you to put it on a leash."

"What do you mean? I'm acting the way I always do." She remembered something. "Okay, that time with Pensri was a little deliberate, I admit."

"Mmhmm. That thing with Pensri was the tip of the iceberg. How about I give you a little demonstration?"

From the look in his eyes, she liked the sounds of that.

"On your back, girl."

She was there. She took in how super sexy they looked in the mirrored ceiling, her in the little thigh-high red robe the girls wore, though with her height, it rode up nearly pussy high. And Kannon standing there with his muscled back, his hard butt, his head bent over her...his hand waving in annoyance over her? She switched her focus to the real Kannon, who was scowling down at her.

"See what I mean?" he growled. "Look at that thing you're wearing. I've seen more material in a bandage."

"There was nothing else to wear! I didn't think you wanted me coming to bed naked like I usually do, and this was the only alternative. Out of respect for you, I put something on and you still say I'm coming on to you."

"What's a girl to do?" he sympathized, getting on the bed. He leaned the thick columns of his arms on either side of her.

He was going to kiss her. He was, wasn't he? She closed her eyes, tilting her face up to help Kannon along.

"Only one rule." His breath feathered her cheek.

"What's that?"

"You're not to touch me."

Her eyes snapped open. "What do you mean, not touch you? How can I not not touch you? That'd be like eating ice cream without my tongue."

"We both know that if you get your hands on me, we'll have sex. And there's no way my first time with you is going to be in some seedy massage parlor."

"Seems this place is perfect for sex. And for the record it's gaudy, not seedy."

"Not good enough"—he brought his lips a shade above hers—"for what'll happen between us." His voice had dropped. "Now, hands flat on the bed. Keep your head and bottom there, too."

"Okay."

"Promise?"

"Promise."

His lips brushed her forehead and withdrew. She gave a huff of disgust. "You call that a kiss?"

"I call that"—he kissed one cheek—"a woman strutting her sweet pink behind up twenty-five floors"—he kissed the other cheek—"I call that"—he licked up the length of her throat to nuzzle behind her ear—"a woman who kisses another woman"—he flicked his tongue inside her ear, tickling—"just to disappear into a bedroom"—he treated the other side of her neck the same way—

"You could've joined us." She twisted to capture his lips, a move he ducked.

"—knowing there was no way in hell I was sharing you." He slipped his hand through the slit in her robe and cupped her left breast. He froze, groaned. Ah-ha! It wouldn't be long now before he relented. He sucked in his breath and resumed stroking her breast, stopping short of her nipple. No matter, it perked up hard and made contact with his palm. He stopped again. His lids grew heavy and a downward glance at the front of his boxers told her she was beating him at his little game.

"Then last night, you in that dress. With that bottle." He plucked at her nipples already so hard—"You're all talk, no action."

She gripped the silky folds of the sheets to hold herself back. "That's not fair. I can give you action. You won't let me."

He swept away the other half of her robe, exposing her entire naked body to him. He studied her, his heavy, heated gaze gliding along her tummy, her moistening folds, her legs. He even stopped at her feet, and she wiggled her pink-painted toes for his viewing pleasure. He took his time traveling back up her body and came to rest at her breasts again, his hand settling between them. "Please take them," she offered. "In your hands. Your mouth. Against your chest." She glanced again at his boxers. "Take them anywhere you like."

He smiled, a soft, slow thing that crinkled his eyes and crinkled her heart into a tight achy ball. And it was this smile that finally, finally touched her mouth.

Its sweetness nearly made her break her promise. One hand twitched and she had to slam it back against the mattress. He must've registered that, because his smile widened on her. His tongue ran along her lips and his mouth spread hers open. His tongue flicked the soft tissues there, then he pulled out and slipped back inside. Again and again. Her heels dug into the mattress and her hands had gathered up fistfuls of pink sheet in an effort to hold up her end of the bargain. Her entire body quivered with the need to grab hold of him.

And then, before she could prepare herself, he drew one finger through the folds between her legs. She yelped, her hands clamped on his shoulders, her leg hooked around his. He went still. His tongue, lips, hands withdrew. He sat up, stood.

She beat her hands on the sheets, drummed her heels on the mattress, the mirrored ceiling capturing her tantrum. Which was so not funny. "Kannon! What sane woman would've done any different?"

"True." His voice was gentle, liquored with humor. "But, Gina, what are we if we can't keep our promises?"

He strolled over to the chair and picked up his shirt—the shirt she'd rinsed out for him so he wouldn't have to walk around with a big blood spot on himself—and slipped it on.

She took a deep breath. "You're a big, fat jerk. With a big, fat hard-on. Remember, I lose, you lose."

All she got was a long, slow smile.

"You wait until our first date," she kept on, in an effort to prove her point. "You think you're cool, huh? I'll get you so worked up people down the block are going to need a cigarette when we're done!"

At that, his smile became a full-out grin. "Promise?"

———————◇———————

Ek stalked up the stairs to the third floor of the rundown hotel where he'd arranged the early morning meeting with his…partner. His battered body ached and his arm throbbed from having his elbow dislocated, and then from his snapping it back into its socket. The second he got Alak Montri back, he was going to hunt down the motherfucker who did this to him and rip him apart. No, he was going to first castrate the motherfucker and feed him his balls. No, feed his balls to John Wakai before he beat the crippled worm to death with his own wheelchair.

But first, the clusterfuck that was Alak Montri had to be dealt with. Reaching his floor, he passed the three men guarding the place, all giving him a wide berth, and banged on the door.

It opened immediately to Victoria, and he shoved his way in. He rammed her up against the wall and put a one-hand choke on her with his good arm. "Your fucking brother has taken Montri."

Her small anticipatory smile at his roughness vanished, and her eyes rounded with shock. "What? When?"

"Last night. One of my men on Montri was shot in the leg, the other beat so bad it'll be weeks before he can walk again. We need to fix this. You need to fix this." He pressed his thumb hard on her pulse so the blood would pound through her ears. He felt her relax. Fuck. That was the trouble with roughing up female rakshasi. They got off on it, which defeated the purpose for doing it in the first place.

"You need to get him to tell you where Alak Montri is, you understand?"

She scowled. "Don't worry, I will. But you're not to harm

John. You need him. He's so smart."

"He's outsmarting us," growled Ek.

"He's not going to betray us."

"He just did!"

"Can't you see, Ek? He's my brother. We're family. Like you and me."

"He still needs to be brought back under our heel."

"He's not some dog to be whipped, Ek. John's always loved me. Always understood my needs. If you two would try to get along you'd see that." Head still pinned to the wall, she stretched her arms and legs toward him, trying to climb him like a monkey in heat.

He threw her to the carpet, and walked away as if she were a bag of garbage. "He's not a rakshasa. He'll never understand your needs."

She crawled after him on all fours until her head was at his crotch. "But I am," she replied. "And you do."

That's right, he did. He took a fistful of her hair with his good hand and yanked back. She yelped in pain and grabbed his balls. Hard. He hissed and didn't let go of her hair. They held onto each other this way, a smile spreading across her face. "The same blood runs in our veins, Ek. Can you feel it?"

Fuck, yes. The pain in his testicles was sharp; it only made him harder. He thrived on pain. Even his own. And looking into her bright burning eyes he saw himself reflected. Like him, she was of his kind, and soon enough the two of them would rule Bangkok.

Her fingers tightened and pain shot straight through his system to his hand gripping her hair. He dug his fingers into her scalp. "A week or two and my brother will have done his job," she gasped and rolled her head against his iron hold. "Then Montri is his slave. We can do whatever we want.

Think of how happy we'll all be. Think of how much our family will grow."

Nothing was as easy as that. Nothing was gained except through blood, sweat and more blood. She might be rakshasi, but she still had a lot to learn.

He slapped her across the face so hard she fell to the floor, letting go of his testicles. He reached down and picked her up by her hair amid her pained and excited cries. And he'd be the one to teach her.

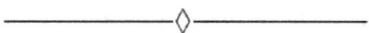

Gina leaned over Kittyjack's shoulder, eyes glued to Wakai's video of Alak Montri as it inched along, frame by frame. Badly beaten, tied to a chair, surrounded by sadistic killers, the man still managed to look defiant. She didn't know how he did it.

"Here'sthepart," said the hacker in her machine-gun voice as a masked man stepped into the picture, a newspaper in his hands to prove the date of the video. With a click of her mouse, Kittyjack paused it, then rolled back her chair a bit so that Gina and Kannon could move in.

Kannon stood a few feet back, chewing gum. "Looks pretty clean. Shot in front of a blank wall so there's no indication of the interior. Newspaper is sold across the city so no geographical location, either. Mr. Montri's hands are tied behind his back so he can't signal in any way. And the man holding the newspaper has his face covered so there's no way to identify him. Looks like Wakai covered all the bases and for the last time"—he glared at Kittyjack—"talk so I can hear what you're saying."

Kittyjack sat there, wearing a faint gloat and a t-shirt that read, 'Intellectuals solve problems. Geniuses prevent them.' "You're right that they didn't make any obvious mistakes. In the end they made three, and they're all in just a few seconds of footage."

She'd delivered a challenge. Gina turned to Kannon. "You up for this, Team Genius?" Kannon apparently understood the reference, because he tilted his head to the screen to give her first-go. Despite plastering her eyeballs to the screen, Gina drew a blank.

She pulled back to give him a turn. "Sorry, Kannon, can't hold up my end." She wagged a finger at Kittyjack's words. "'Pride doeth come before a fall', as a dear nun I know often misquotes to me."

Kittyjack grinned. "It's more pity I'm feeling."

Kannon pointed at the screen, first at the ankles of Montri, then at those of his captor. "The bottom of the kidnapper's pant leg looks wet."

Gina honed in on Kannon's observation. "You're right. There's been no rain, so they were near one of the canals. They could've easily gotten themselves wet stepping off a boat or something." She switched back to Kittyjack, and made the descending sound of a falling object.

Kittyjack set her jaw. "And the second clue?"

Kannon's dark eyes scanned the still video. This time it took the better part of a minute before he picked out the guard's hands. "His knuckles. They're enlarged."

"Yes," Kittyjack conceded. "About twice the size of a normal person's."

Gina made a second descending whistle. "And that means…?"

"It means that he's likely a serious bare knuckle fighter," Kannon said. "And an old school one at that. Remember the photos hanging in the home of Lwin Kinjo? Hands like that used to be common in Asian boxers about fifty years ago thanks to a practice called pinging."

Gina blinked. "Pinging?"

"A boxer," Kannon explained, "would punch an anvil so hard he made it ping. The force of the blow would break the cap of their middle knuckles, and when they healed up they'd be much rounder and larger. Being punched by someone like that would be like getting hit with a hammer. Only the most hardcore fighters did that."

Gina snuck a look at Kannon's hands. Sure enough, his middle knuckles were large, calloused and iron hard. "Or someone who wouldn't really feel it." Here he was in the middle of showing exactly how brilliant he really was, and all anybody would see—all he saw—were those knuckles. "That's all very fascinating, how does it help us find Alak?"

"Not too long ago I saw a man with knuckles like mine on board your father's boat."

Gina thought about it. "Jarun?"

Kannon jutted his chin at the screen. "I bet that's him. Now, we need a where, not a who."

"Until you meet someone like me," Kittyjack smiled. "Bet I can tell you where this Jarun guy is going to be tomorrow night."

Kannon studied the screen yet again. C'mon, Gina cheered him on silently. Don't let the nerd girl win. "I don't see how."

Kittyjack opened her mouth right when Gina cut her off. "I'll find it." She leaned in again.

Kannon sighed. "We don't have time for these games. Let her tell us."

"One minute." She studied the screen, willing something

to appear. And it did. "Lookee, lookee! Jarun's eyes. He's reading the back of it. Like a headline caught his eye."

She whirled in triumph to Kittyjack, whose peeved expression said it all. Gina made a loud crashing noise. "That is the sound of pride breaking into a million pieces," she crowed. "Team Genius takes gold!" She raised her hand to do a high-five with Kannon, who actually did it with her, even though he was looking at her as if she had tumbled off the edge of sanity herself.

"I would've never taken you for the competitive type," he commented.

"Oh, if I play, it's to win." She leaned on Kittyjack's table and let the double meaning hang between them.

"Better shove over, you need to share the podium with me," Kittyjack said. She opened her top desk drawer and pulled out a copy of the same newspaper. "Not a headline, an advertisement."

She flipped it over so that they could see the back, and Gina felt a rush of excitement as she realized what Montri's captor had been looking at. There in the upper right corner was a display ad for a local kickboxing tournament, to be held at an open air arena that night.

Gina laughed. "Okay, I admit it. You're a genius!"

"Duh" was the hacker's gracious reply.

Kannon didn't seem to hear them. "We can tail him back to where Alak Montri's at. A rescue would change the entire situation. And we can be prepared to follow him on water as well as land. It'll be tricky, but Wakai could've given us our biggest opportunity yet." Gina could feel his suppressed energy, so different from his melancholy the previous night and the sexy slyness of that morning. Three different moods in less than a day. Maybe, finally, she was getting to see what else there was to the man who only saw himself as a killer.

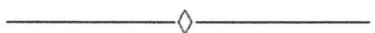

Wakai studied the footage on his tablet, the imaging software smoothing out the pixels to transform the jagged, static-y scene into something for him to analyze. Although cameras were barred from Triple 9 by request of the patrons, they were on the streets, and the local shopkeepers had proved cooperative.

The club doors burst open, and he paused the action. He zoomed in on the trio that had appeared, then set the software to sharpen their features. Kannon and Ryota were instantly recognizable, but who was the woman with them? She wasn't Asian, that was for sure. Too tall. Her features too pointed. Breasts too large.

She didn't seem like a hired gun—women with looks like hers didn't need to resort to violence to earn a living—so why was she with Kannon? With those shocks of royal purple throughout her dark hair, she was far from low key. Certainly no private investigator.

He retracted the zoom to further dissect the scene. There was a shrill metallic chime, and in the top corner of his screen a small image appeared from the elevator camera. It was Ek, and by the looks of him, he was as irate as he'd been last night.

Wakai tapped the button to allow entry. "Victoria," he called over his shoulder. "The wizard's here."

She emerged into the living area from the bedroom. "I wish you'd stop calling him that."

"I think you'd like my other names for him even less."

She kneeled beside him. "He's a valuable ally, John. When we needed him he was there to help us. Him and his entire clan. Why can't you be nice to him?"

Wakai tried to feign a smile. "The man's a bloodthirsty, sadistic, child-raping cannibal. You'll excuse me if I'm a little suspect of his motivations."

Victoria propped her chin on the arm of his chair. "He can't help having the hungers he does, John. No more than I can help mine. I know we seem like monsters to you, but that doesn't mean he's disloyal."

"He just wants to ply his trade in a new territory. At best, he's a mercenary."

Victoria tilted her head. "And what does Montri do?"

Her point was obvious. "Yes, he smuggles, defrauds and kills. Except he rid the city of foreign gangs like Ek's. Put a virtual end to child prostitution. Helped thousands of Bangkok's poorest get a leg up. He's never driven around in big cars or owned fancy apartments. His intentions were always as good as any criminal's could be. Ek's are as bad as they get."

His sister's lower lip came out. "Even after what he tried, you'll defend him?"

"I did what I had to do to protect you," Wakai stated. "That doesn't mean I'm happy about it. As for Ek, you have to give up on this fantasy of us being brothers. It's never going to happen."

On the far side of the penthouse there was a low chime, and Wakai heard the elevator doors open. "We'll finish this conversation later."

Victoria stood as Ek strode over, one arm in a cast. The giant stopped directly in front of Wakai's chair, pausing only to nod in greeting to Victoria before glowering down at him. "You've got some balls talking to me like that last night. I want to know where Montri is right now."

"I left him in the care of you two for a week and he

looked like he'd been run over by a truck," Wakai said, not so much as glancing at Ek. His fingers traced over the tablet screen. Something caught his eye. The woman in the van. He knew her, he knew her...from where, where, where?

Ek railed on. "We were trying to get information out of him. Information you weren't able to, either."

"Yes, I failed. Unlike you, however, I've actually got a plan on how to get rid of our enemies."

Victoria gave a little happy squeal that Ek squelched with a glare. He glowered down at Wakai. "What are you going to do?"

"Not what I'm going to do, Ek. What I've already done. And what I've already done is set a trap for Kannon and his friends. Soon enough you're going to have a chance to pay him back for your elbow."

"When? Where?"

Always impatient, always greedy. "I'll let you know the time and place," Wakai replied calmly. "Remember your role and everything will work out fine."

"My role?" Ek growled.

At last Wakai looked up at the brute, making no effort to hide his disdain. "Our deal is simple, Ek. You're the muscle. I'm the brains. We're partners of necessity. Don't get the idea that you can do what I can."

Ek gritted his yellowish teeth in a sneer. "You think you're so smart. If it weren't for Victoria here you'd already be dead."

Wakai snorted. "If it weren't for Victoria, you and your simian clan would still be cowering in some Cambodian backwater."

"We're rakshasas, not from some fucking simian gang."

"Your answer proves direct lineage."

His sister got between them. "Please, enough fighting. We're in this together. We're more than a gang. We're a family. And Bangkok belongs to us so long as we work together."

It was plain enough to Wakai that his feelings for Ek were returned in full, but he nodded. "We all have our roles to play," he said, extending a small token of conciliation for her sake.

Ek grunted.

"Besides, I have more good news for you two. I know who's been helping Kannon. Who's probably protecting Tasanee."

Victoria's eyes widened in excitement. "Who?"

Wakai angled the tablet to Ek and Victoria, and pointed at the driver of the van. "See that woman?"

They nodded.

"Her name's Darae Zaffini. Her husband controls half of Bangkok's brothels and massage parlors, and he's a close friend of Montri. Should have guessed he'd be the first to cross me."

"Where is he?" Ek demanded.

"I don't know," replied Wakai. "Yet."

CHAPTER 9 NINE

GINA SAT BACK from the small plastic table at the tiny makeshift café and enjoyed the view. It was of Kannon, coming toward her through the crowd of diners and colorful stalls, his mirrored sunglasses blazing like the eyes of an avenging angel. From his right hand hung a large duffel bag, the thick fabric straining under the heavy contents, though he carried it with the same ease she did her purse. Or with the same ease he had carried her from 70 Rai. Or with the same ease he marked her with his kisses.

She scooted out a chair for him. He took it and set the bag down close, tapping it with his foot.

"Quite the interesting toys Dr. Chaiboonma has. We've got this on loan for tonight, and Kittyjack's on standby to operate it. How did you do with Mrs. Kinjo?"

"Lwin called some fighters who'll be competing, and they put me in touch with the arena's owner. They're going to keep a lookout for anyone with 'pinged' knuckles as they collect the tickets, so it's all arranged. Now all we have to do is hope our hunch is right. You had anything to eat yet?"

Kannon looked down at the trio of empty paper plates in

front of Gina. "I'm not hungry. Besides, I try to avoid street food."

"What? It's the very best kind!"

"And how do you figure that?"

She gestured about her as if the answer was obvious. "Look around you!"

He did. "All I see is chaos and all I smell is way too much of everything."

"Kannon, most of the foods around us are delicacies. They're not easy to make, and they take a lot of care to cook. Each vendor only makes one or two specialties, so over the years they become masters at preparing them. A restaurant chef is never going to get that good. That's why I avoid restaurants when I'm here. And the best part is, any day now it will all be gone."

"Come again?"

"You really don't get it, do you? You've been here for how long, did you say?"

"Two years, about."

"And do you know why I asked us to meet here?"

"I don't know. I asked for a nice, quiet, empty place."

"Because this morning driving by, it was! This was a vacant lot and that won't do around here. Probably what happened was a motorcycle with one mini-kitchen in tow pulled up and began serving noodles. Then one after another came more motorcycles and up went stalls and soon you got all this —a half-dozen kinds of noodles, sweetmeats, coconut hotcakes. People coming around with baked goods and bottles. And see, there. A busker. It's like a carnival.

"That's the thing. American and Europeans always want to control, set down laws, tie things up in red tape, but the people of Bangkok, they grab hold of chaos and ride it into whatever adventure it will take them, and everyone accepts everyone else. That's why you can have a skyscraper beside a shrine, and why a hooker and a monk make an offering side by side." Gina scooted her chair closer to Kannon and nudged his shoulder. "And a decent man is out with a wild woman."

She'd said the last bit because as she spoke, his entire pose had changed. He'd become very intense, his elbows were on his knees, and along the edge of his sunglasses she could see crinkles where one eye was narrowed on her. "You belong here."

"In Bangkok?"

"Yes. Like a fish in water."

"Yeah, well, that's what Darae wants."

"Not what you want?"

"I don't know what I want. I know what I don't want."

"To be head of The Pink Stilettos?"

"I'm not any good at it, despite what Dr. Chai and Darae say. I'm no crocodile tamer, as Lwin puts it. I'm a washed-up party girl, and that's it. You know what'll happen to this market tomorrow, maybe the next day? This lot will be swarming with construction workers, and all these stalls will blow to the wind like dandelion seeds and touch down somewhere else."

"You saying you're a dandelion seed?"

She sighed, sitting back in her chair. "I *wish* I was. God knows that's what I've been trying to be. Problem is my whole life has been rooted in this city since before I was even conceived."

"And how's that?" he asked.

She cocked her head at him. "Ask me out on a date."

"What? Right now?"

"Yeah. And tell me we can go anywhere I want."

He looked at her uncertainly, but with a shrug he acquiesced. "Fine. Would you go out with me, Gina?"

"Yep," she smiled. "Where are you taking me?"

"Anywhere you want to go, apparently."

She took him by the hand. "Then come on. I want to show you those roots we were talking about."

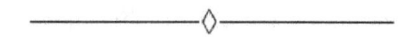

As they crossed a canal, Kannon looked over his shoulder. "We've got seven dogs on our tail. Any idea why that is?"

Gina could understand Kannon's caution about being followed, even if it was by the four-legged. "Beats me. They always follow me around. When I was a kid, I thought they trailed after everyone. Turns out I was special."

"You certainly are." That hung out there and then he added, "My father would've used your talents."

"Oh?"

"It's a bit of a story."

"It's a bit of a walk."

Kannon adjusted his grip on his bag, and took her hand, so they were strolling along like a normal couple, and not a hit-man and a mafia princess killing time until they could hunt down a rival. When he spoke, it was soft and easy, as if they'd all the time in the world. "My mixed heritage didn't make it easy to fit in with the other kids. When I was six I got beaten bad enough by some of the older kids for my mother to pull me out of school."

"Wanted to make things easier on you?"

"They only got harder."

Gina stroked her thumb along his poor beaten knuckles. "How so?"

"My father, he was an animal trainer for the Yakuza. Handled the Tosa breed of fighting dogs. Since I was at home, he started training me right beside them."

"Your dad trained you like an animal?"

"It's not that strange. To win at tōken, which is Japanese dog fighting, an animal can't bark, yelp or lose its will to fight, no matter how hurt it might get. The same applies for someone in my line of work."

"So what did he have you do?" Gina asked, at once shocked and fascinated by Kannon's revelation.

"For hours each day my father would force the dogs to swim back and forth in a deep pool, and naturally I shared the same regime. Puppies that weren't strong enough to make it drowned, and I wasn't allowed to save them no matter how much I begged. A couple of times I disobeyed my father and did it anyway, but all I got for my trouble was a lashing and the puppy kicked back into the pool."

"That's horrible," said Gina.

"That's life," he said. "When I wasn't strong enough to stay afloat, he let me sink before fishing me out. It taught me to keep struggling to my limits. Gave me the kind of strength not many people have."

"That sounds psychotic."

"My father was trying to prepare me for life, Gina. The kind of life I wound up leading. He schooled me in judo. Taught me to punch, kick, grapple and throw till my form was perfect. He showed me how to fight with knives and sticks and broken bottles. How to ambush and trip. To blind and cripple. By the time I turned twelve I even looked as muscled as a Tosa. Then came the real training.

"My father had kept a list of every kid that had picked on me, and one by one he sent me out to pay them back. To break teeth or arms. Or torture them."

Gina didn't even know what to say. The kind of training she'd received was unicorns and rainbows compared to Kannon's upbringing.

"Of course I did as he ordered, and when I started high school I can tell you there was no more teasing. Everyone, even the seniors, gave me a wide berth. Made the Yakuza accept me as well, despite the color of my skin."

"Made you into the man you are today."

"Like I said before, it's all I know how to do."

She bumped against his side. "You're pretty good at kissing, too."

"Not much of a demand for kissers in the Yakuza."

"You're applying at the wrong places. I know lots of places where good kissers are in high demand."

"I should become a male prostitute?"

Gina shrugged. "It's a different way of using your body. For pleasure, instead."

They walked a few steps in silence. "How would that make you feel?"

"What do you mean?"

"Would you feel jealous if I was with other women?"

"You jealous I was with Pensri?"

"Were you trying to make me jealous?"

Gina squinted up at him. "Are we avoiding answering the question by asking other questions? Lwin Kinjo talked about this."

"I don't know. Are we?" He was grinning. She stopped, forcing him to do the same if he was going to still hold her hand, which he seemed intent on doing. She flipped up his sunglasses to see his eyes. There they were, warm and dark ...and on her. Back to feeling mildly electrocuted.

She let the glasses drop back and clucked. "You really think you're something, don't you?"

"With you beside me, I am."

For the second time on their walk, Gina didn't know what to say. Was this the way guys talked on dates? If so, she'd really missed out. Well, no, she hadn't. She was pretty certain she wouldn't be feeling this breathless, if anybody other than Kannon was with her.

"Um…we're nearly there. It's just up against this wall. I mean, on the other side of the wall…" she flustered, and all but dragged him down a street with a high wall that led to an iron gate. Passing under its arch, they entered a sprawling garden, acres in size, following a tended path between tropical trees and orchids. It was as if they'd been teleported from the heart of the city to a remote sanctuary. While most of the dogs had dropped off, three shadowed them: a brown one, a black one, and a black-and-brown puppy.

They finally arrived at their destination. It was little more than an open cobblestoned space sheltered by the boughs of the surrounding trees. All about them were penises. They ranged in size from the realistic to ten feet in length, some carved from wood or stone, some cast from iron or bronze. Little ones sprouted like mushrooms from the green ground cover. A couple of huge ones had legs, the penis angled to look like a torso bent into the doggy position. They were painted in all colors, decorated with everything from bright silk scarves to rhinestones. Lots more had been added in the decade Gina had been gone, and right now she and Kannon had the place all to themselves. A lucky occurrence that needed to be taken advantage of.

Kannon set down the bag and did a slow three-sixty. "What is this place?"

"Two years here and you've not paid a visit?" she teased.

"Oddly, no."

"Well, now for the 'show-and-tell' part of our first date."

Kannon settled himself on the low stone wall that enclosed the shrine. "I can't wait."

Gina and the dogs strolled around, checking out the ornaments. "My mom really, really wanted a kid, only after she married my dad it turned out that she was infertile. They went to every doctor in Miami—nothing worked. Then she read about this place in a magazine."

"And what exactly is this?" Kannon asked.

"It's a shrine of Chao Mae Tuptim—a female tree spirit," Gina explained and pointed to an old gray-barked tree, penises ten deep nestled at its base. "It's said that if a woman is having trouble conceiving she can pray to the spirit and she'll be granted a successful pregnancy."

"So what's with all the…?" He waved his hand about.

Gina noticed a bunch of large phalluses crowded on a short pedestal. They'd been vibrators in another life and she leaned in to examine one Pensri might like. She must've breathed too hard because one jiggled loose and fell to the ground, the jolt causing activation, and it whirred and jerked around the cobblestones, making all three dogs bark and growl at this strange creature. She rescued it and set it back. Kannon was rubbing his temples. Gina hurried on. "If the woman has a baby, it's traditional that she leaves a statue like this at the shrine in thanks to the spirit."

"A lot to be grateful for, I see."

She pointed to a carved stone penis. "See this one? My mother had it carved from Sicilian marble. Dad thought it was all nonsense, of course, but she believed in it completely. Convinced him to fly them here to hand-deliver her offering, a kind of thanks in advance. She took it one step further. She snuck here in the middle of the night with my dad to make love. Twice for luck."

Kannon looked suspicious. "How do you know this? I can't see it something parents tell their kids as a bedtime story."

"Darae, actually."

"Darae?"

"My mom told her. They were BFFs, despite their age difference. Daddy was so pissed when he found out. 'Is nothing sacred with you women?' Funny thing, Darae told me because it was sacred. She thought it was a beautiful story. I'd texted her before you showed up to tell her where I was and she reminded me that this place was close by. She suggested I go visit it."

Gina knew what Darae was up to. Her stepmother wanted Gina to see how much she was still connected to Bangkok, to this warm, colorful, quirky corner of the world. The problem was, she already knew that. It was the dark, unforgiving side that she'd run from. Except in leaving one side, she'd lost both. She slid a finger down the marble phallus and kissed the tip.

Kannon made a noise deep in his throat. "Not what a gentleman on the first date should see, Gina. Messes him up."

Gina was ready for distraction. "You know, this would be a good time to kiss me."

"Then what are you doing way over there?"

She immediately rectified the situation. With no-holds barred, she did a full-frontal assault. She palmed his front, his sides, his back, all the while her tongue and lips nipping and hounding his mouth. He set his hands on her waist but she was pressing in so hard, he had to grip the wall to steady them. She was free to grind against him, which produced hard results.

Kannon didn't fight her, held on and let her have at him. God, he felt good. Wetness leaked into the folds between her legs, and she rocked her pubic bone against his shaft. He gave a low groan she caught in her mouth. The clothes between them were too much and not shifting her mouth or her groin, she tugged at his shirt, successfully baring his dark bruised torso. Now it was her turn to moan at the hard ripple of muscle under her hand. Every part of her swelled against him, her nipples, lips, her pussy.

All their moans and groans were too much for the dogs. They started whining and yipping, bounding through the penises, their wagging tails sideswiping displays, clattering and crashing them to the cobblestone.

Gina broke away and waved after them. "Bad dogs! Look at what you've done. Shoo! Get!" She began setting things to rights. "Oh, crap. I hope this doesn't mess up someone's chances for getting pregnant or even lucky."

"I know it messed up one chance," Kannon said with a sigh. "Just as well. First time's not going to be in a public place."

She rewound the ribbons on a blood-red one. "Geez. Can't be in a massage parlor or a public place. Where, then?"

"At home in my bed." He hadn't meant to say that, she could tell. He immediately tensed and his face became a hard neutral mask. Waiting for that put-down. He was once again a boy sinking, not entirely sure if his father would grab hold of him. He was a young adult, steeling himself as he hurt others. And here he stood now, the man who thought a woman wouldn't want to share his bed.

And the thing was, she wasn't sure if she wanted to. Because now, with his stories and romantic gestures, she understood what he was offering. It wasn't sex; it was a relationship. A relationship filled with passion and walks, but also of absence and danger. And like Bangkok, she couldn't have one without the other.

She tore her gaze away from Kannon and continued on with arranging the penises. When she was done, Kannon was standing off at a distance, shirt tucked straight, bag in hand. "We should go," he said.

"Okay." She needed to explain, tell him that it wasn't him, it was her. Only who believed that line, anyway? "Kannon, I—"

He waited, and she couldn't say what he wanted to hear, deserved to hear. "Thank you for the date."

He gave her nothing. Not a lip twitch, not a flash of the eyes, nothing. "You're welcome."

Their walk back to his vehicle was silent, and after a while, not even the dogs followed.

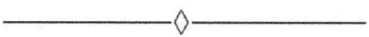

Bright lights flooded the ring from every direction as Kannon sat amidst the raucous crowd of spectators, scorching beams highlighting every cut of the fighters' lean, muscled bodies. The two men, one in black trunks, the other in red, were performing Wai Khru, a solemn pre-fight ceremony in which they thanked their masters, their patron gods, and the spirit of the sport itself for the opportunity to beat each other senseless.

The blaring of Thai classical instruments added to the cacophony of the roaring fans, but despite the energy which rippled through the crowd Kannon remained cool. Calm. Detached.

"Woohoo!" Gina yelled beside him, fist pumping the air as the two fighters transitioned from the contemplative ritual directly into Ram Muay, an energetic dance in which each man demonstrated their skill and style, kicking and punching at the air in a frenetic display. The crowd went wild with excitement at the intimidating acrobatics, eager for the bloodshed about to follow.

"I've got five thousand baht riding on Somrak," she shouted into his ear, pointing to the boxer in the black trunks, his forearms adorned with tattoos of twin angry crocodiles. "Lwin told me he's going to take this fight for sure."

Her energy was a complete turnabout from their silent trek back to his car hours ago. He'd tried to stay neutral, to keep in mind, once again, that she was his boss, no matter what a joke that was. And she'd seemed content enough with that arrangement, sticking to business as they set up the equipment before entering the arena. Then as they were moving to their seats, she was about to step on a spilled drink and he'd put his hand on her waist and steered her aside. She hadn't seen why he was doing it, only that he'd touched her, and she blasted him with a brilliant smile, clearly relieved that he wasn't angry at her.

As if he had a right to be. It always had been him who'd tried to make something more out of their relationship than there actually was. He wanted her, and she didn't want him. Not as a couple working toward a future together. She'd recoiled from even having sex in his bed. Why had he blurted that out? Oh yes, right, she'd asked, and he'd told her.

He didn't know what happened to make her run from Bangkok for a decade, for most of her adult life. It couldn't have been good. She wanted to have sex with him, and sex with her would be hot, would be the hottest he'd ever had or dreamed of having. And that would it be it.

"I hope you're not forgetting why we're here," he said, as a reminder to himself, too.

Although people considered his mirrored sunglasses a trademark of sort, there were several very practical reasons he wore them. One was that the inside of each lens had a corner treated with the same reflective coating as the outside. That allowed Kannon to literally have eyes in the back of his head, and right now his attention wasn't on the fight, but rather on Ryota, who was standing by the entrance, disguised in the casual clothing of the locals.

Ryota in turn was watching the men taking the tickets, and apparently one of them had just signaled him. He nodded to Kannon, and a moment later, a familiar-looking man came into view: Jarun.

Their ex-prisoner climbed the adjacent aisle and merged down a row to take a seat. Leaning into Gina, Kannon said, "That's him. Three rows down, closest to the aisle on the other side of the section."

Gina took stock, her eyes only leaving the ring for a moment. "Okay. Soon as the fight's over, I'll get Kittyjack on his tail."

The fighters, having finished their display, were summoned by the referee to the center of the ring, then he stepped away, allowing the fight to begin.

As brutal as western boxing could be, it was downright gentle compared to the battle that erupted in the ring. Both fighters used every part of their bodies to lash out at one another, punching, kicking and shoving, employing fists, feet, elbows, and knees to hammer each other both above and below the belt. Within a minute blood was flowing, but Kannon's eyes remained set on his target.

Jarun seemed too still for someone who'd come to the arena for pleasure. And the fact that he'd arrived just before the fight and chosen to sit right by the entrance was suspicious. This was all too easy.

Beside him, Gina cringed as her favorite received a kick to the face, staggering back against the ropes. The referee separated the two fighters only long enough to make sure the man wasn't going to fall over, then with a wave of his hand, the battle resumed.

"What do you think?" Gina asked him over the din.

"I think our friend might is bait. We stick with the plan and everything should work."

"I mean about Somrak." She leaned close, and he could feel the gentle give of her breast against his arm. "You think he's got a chance after a hit like that?"

Behind his glasses, Kannon rolled his eyes. What a crazy woman. He should go back to smoking, instead of chewing on gum like a school kid. How was it she got him doing things that he wouldn't do for anyone else, himself included? He couldn't refuse her a thing. He was like the boxers in the ring. Except instead of his body, his ego and emotions were taking a bruising.

He turned his attention to the combatants. "He seems okay to me. It was a little tap to the head." As if to confirm his words, Gina's fighter brought up his knee, connecting with his opponent's stomach in a gut-wrenching strike.

"Ouch!" Gina said cheerfully, as her man pressed his advantage, delivering a volley of ferocious punches, the crocodiles on his arms blurring with the speed of his attack. "You think you could take on a guy like that?"

"He wouldn't be a pushover, but yes."

"You sound confident." She nudged his shoulder.

Kannon shrugged. "He's used to fighting for money. I'm used to fighting for my life. Besides, I've got moves that aren't legal in any ring—not even one as serious as this."

The battle in the ring raged on, both fighters hammering away at one another for all they were worth. Unlike western boxing, the match lasted a maximum of five rounds of three minutes each, so there was no holding back. By the third round, the boxer in red fell to his knees, and with him too battered and bloodied to rise again, the referee called the fight.

The crowd rose to their feet in thunderous applause and jeers, Gina hopping up and down as she joined the roar. Only two people weren't clapping and hollering: Kannon and Jarun. Something was definitely up.

"I'm going to step outside and wait for him," he told Gina as soon as the noise had died down.

Gina nodded. "Okey-dokey. As soon as he leaves I'll make the call to Kittyjack."

He rose out of his seat and then sat back down. "You will keep an eye open. I don't want things to screw up because you're sidetracked with your betting."

"Okay."

"Don't try to do anything yourself. Ryota will be watching, and can take over."

"Okay."

"If, for whatever reason, you can't get—"

Gina flipped up his glasses and leaned in. "Kannon. Okay." She set the glasses back down and poked a finger into his stitched temple. She wasn't gentle about it, either. It actually twinged. "You know, you get all super-protective with me when it's you that's walking straight into trouble. You ever think about that?"

She cared about him. She cared but didn't want to sleep

with him in his bed, in his home. She was fighting what was happening between them, while he'd already given in. Part of him hoped she'd win. There was another part, a bigger part, of him that wanted her as weak as he was.

"I'll be okay," he told her.

"You better be," she warned. "I got a lot riding on that."

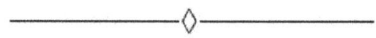

Kittyjack stared at the monitor intently, her finger poised over her mouse. She readied herself, her overclocked mind counting down fractions of seconds, gauging the perfect moment to strike. With the reaction time of a praying mantis, she tapped the button at precisely the right instant.

You won this auction. Congratulations, it's all yours!

"Too slow for the master," she said in a singsong voice, doing a little victory dance in her chair as she clicked the Pay Now button on eBay.

Dr. Chaiboonma looked over her shoulder as she fired in her credit card information. "And why exactly are you buying a vibrating rubber duck?"

"I'mnot," she answered in her rapid-fire voice. "Mystep-fatheris. It'shiscreditcardinfo."

"I'll rephrase the question then. Why would you want a vibrating rubber duck?"

Over her shoulder, the hacker flashed him a sly, meaningful smile.

Dr. Chaiboonma paused, blew out his breath, then walked away.

The smartphone on her desk buzzed, and Kittyjack activated her earpiece. "Speak."

"Kitty, this is Gina. We were right about it being Jarun.

He's leaving the arena now."

Kittyjack finished her transaction in a blur of fingers, then closing her web browser, brought up another screen. "Gotour-toyready?"

"We followed the instruction manual. It's assembled and ready to go on the roof of the building next door. Kannon's outside, waiting for our man."

Kittyjack sent out the signal to activate the machines, and a few seconds later a map popped up on her screen, identifying their location and confirming that they were powering up. Another click and she could see the arena on her screen, the crowd pouring out of it now that the fights were concluded.

"Lookslikewe'regoodtogo. Bye."

Kittyjack disconnected the line and speed-dialed Kannon.

"This is Kittyjack," she said, making a point of slowing her voice. "Where are you?"

"Outside the doors, by the billboard."

Her fingers caressed her mouse, the image on her screen elevating and magnifying its perspective till she could make him out. "I see you."

"He's coming out now," Kannon relayed. "I'll get directly behind him so you can pick him out."

Kittyjack leaned in closer, her cat eyes following Kannon as he joined the crowd then positioned himself behind a man. "I got him. You break away. I'll follow."

Kannon hung back, allowing the target to slip away from him. "Don't lose him. We're not going to get another chance at this."

"What's your IQ, Kannon?" she asked, adjusting the position of her mouse as she worked to keep the man in the center of her screen.

"Never had it tested."

"Mine's one-seventy-nine," she replied. "You know what genius level is?"

"I bet I'm about to learn that."

"One-forty. Shut up and let me work."

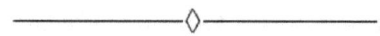

Kannon frowned down at his phone, then up at the sky. High above, he could make out the dot that was the military reconnaissance drone, any noise its whisper-quiet rotors were making lost amidst the ambient noise of Bangkok. With eyes in the sky, he could trail his quarry from blocks away, the position of the drone flashing on his phone.

At a casual pace he made his way after the signal as Ryota jogged up to him.

"She got him?"

"Yes," Kannon replied, "because she's the smartest person in Bangkok."

"Fourteen million people in this city," came the hacker's voice from the speaker phone. "Odds are there's at least three people smarter than me."

Ryota shrugged. "And what's her emotional intelligence?"

Kannon stared at his junior. "Emotional intelligence. What's that?"

Kittyjack snorted. "What people trying to compensate came up with. You might like to know our friend's headed for one of the canals. I'm guessing he's getting on a water taxi."

"Catch up with him if you can," Kannon instructed Ryota. "I'll follow. We'll take turns tailing him to make it look to Jarun that we don't know he's already on to us."

Ryota hurried off. Kannon headed down the street parallel

to the canal, weaving through the throngs of pedestrians as he followed Kittyjack's drones.

"Jarun's just gotten off the boat. Where are you, Kannon?"

"About three blocks behind."

"Pick up the pace. He's heading into some built-up areas and I can't get a clear view from the air."

Kannon broke into a sprint down the narrow streets. Two minutes later, and he was directly under the drone, and a scan of the road pinpointed both Ryota and the man they were following.

Master and apprentice traded places, Ryota now hanging back as Kannon took over the tail, the drone above them circling silently. Jarun turned down an unlit alley, and Kannon paused at the corner. "What do you see, Kittyjack?"

"There's a door at the very end...and he's gone inside. We have his destination."

"A map of the area would be useful," Kannon said. "And so would any floor plans you could get of the place."

"What part of one-seventy-nine don't you understand?" He could hear the click of keys. "Already way ahead of you. Should have some specs in ten minutes, tops."

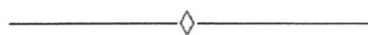

Ek scowled as Jarun closed the door to the darkened warehouse. "Kannon follow you?"

"I'm pretty sure I spotted him and his partner at the arena."

"You better not have made yourself too hard to follow."

"I did exactly as Mr. Wakai instructed," Jarun replied evenly. "If Kannon's half the man-hunter he's said to be, he should be here any minute."

And then there'd be payback for his arm, Ek swore. He turned to the dozen-odd rakshasas he'd brought with him. "Front door's the only way in here," he said, pulling a powerful handgun from his belt. "Let him get a good way inside before you start shooting. I don't want him escaping again."

Jarun stepped up. "What about me?"

"Shut your mouth and stay out of the way," snarled Ek.

Falling back to the surrounding piles of crates and boxes, Ek and his people positioned themselves in a wide semi-circle, readying their ambush. Now all he had to do was wait.

And wait.

Twenty minutes later, everything was still silent as the dead.

"Where the hell is he?" Ek cursed under his breath, fingering the trigger of his gun, his eagerness for revenge melting into dark frustration.

"Maybe seeing if there's another way in?" a rakshasa offered up. "If he thinks Montri's here, he might be looking for another way in."

"You're sure all the other doors are blocked?"

His servant nodded. "Either barricaded with heavy crates or have their bolts welded shut. All the windows are high above the ground. Sooner or later, he's going to have to come through this way."

"It may be later than sooner," Jarun said. "If Kannon suspects his boss is in here, he won't make a move until he's ready. He might even call in back-up."

Minutes stretched into hours, the hours into a whole night, and as the first rays of dawn penetrated the warehouse's high windows, Ek let out an angry curse. Turning on Jarun, he ground his sharpened teeth. "How long does it take this fucker?"

"This is the sixth time, you've asked me that. My answer's the same. I don't know. I did as I was told. If you're unhappy, talk to Wakai."

Ek strode over and glared down at Jarun. "You and Wakai snuck Montri away. And now you fail to lead Kannon here. I should be cutting your heart out right now."

Wakai's little buddy looked up at him, craning his neck back to do so, but his expression remained passive.

"Well?" Ek demanded, the man's silence only enraging him more.

"The Buddha says the ignorant man is like an ox. He grows in size but not in wisdom."

The fucker was insulting him. "And what will your Buddha say when I peel the face off your skull and show it to you?"

Jarun's eye twitched, though Ek couldn't tell if it was from anger or fear. "The message doesn't change no matter how much you whip the messenger."

Ek's phone went off. Wakai. "We've been here all night and nothing. He didn't show. Your trap failed!"

"Did it?" came the reply. "Or is he waiting for you to come out? Why don't you send one of your inbred followers to look around?"

"I've got a better idea." Ek pointed at the door. "Jarun, go outside and have a smoke. Let's see if our friend's been waiting as long as we have."

Ek heard Wakai's hiss of protest and smiled, and the smile broadened at Jarun's sudden unhappy expression. There, that fixed him. Ek and his men watched Jarun head for the door. There was a burst of sunlight as he stepped outside, then the door swung shut and all was quiet.

"Hide again," Ek ordered. "Let's see what fish our bait brings us."

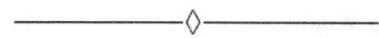

The sunlight was blinding, so the second Jarun emerged, Kannon knew he had the edge. Pressed to the wall beside the entrance, he waited for the door to close of its own accord, then stepped forward and snapped the fighter into a vicious chokehold. Pressing his windpipe and jugular, he stifled the voice, and in a matter of seconds had his victim unconscious.

Hauling the limp man over his shoulder, he hustled down the alley to where Gina was waiting with the van, engine running. She opened the back doors, and as soon as Jarun was safely tied and gagged, he pulled out his cell and dialed Ryota.

"Everything ready?"

"Yes."

"Then, let's give our friends some excitement."

Once he was off the phone, Gina asked, "You sure you don't want me to wait?"

"No. Meet us back at the Golden Geisha," he answered, swinging out a large jerry can of gasoline. "We'll be right behind." He slammed shut the back doors.

Gina didn't move, her bottom lip caught between her teeth. He did not need this.

"Go!"

She jerked, and did what she was told. First time for everything.

As she pulled away, Kannon carried the container to the front door of the warehouse. Thanks to Kittyjack's drone they'd been able to determine exactly who and what was inside it, the machine being able to peer through the windows with its lowlight cameras. They'd had all night to prepare, and now the rakshasas were going to learn just how good a trap their warehouse really was.

Emptying the fuel around the entrance, he set the liquid ablaze. The front of the building was suddenly set upon by a sheet of flame, and Kannon backed away, drawing his gun. Ryota had simultaneously torched the other exits, and within minutes, the old timber warehouse would be an inferno.

Kannon allowed himself a small grim smile. "Let's see you get yourself out of this one, Ek."

CHAPTER 10 TEN

THROUGH HIS LIVING room window, Wakai observed a plume of black smoke rise from a distant neighborhood, his fingers drumming on the arm of his wheelchair. "Guess Kannon's smarter than I thought."

Behind him, Victoria was pacing back and forth. "I don't see how you can be so calm about this. Ek could be hurt. Even dead!"

And wouldn't that be a shame, though he knew better than to say so to his distraught sister. Truth be told, it was worrying. Surely the clues he'd planted in the video of Montri had been subtle enough. And a hunter like Kannon wouldn't have too much trouble tracking Jarun across the city. So what had gone wrong?

And where was Jarun?

Most likely it was some slip-up on the part of Ek, which is exactly why he'd advised the behemoth not to go. There was no point dwelling on that now. Without him, what would the other rakshasas in the city do? Go home? Follow Victoria? Appoint some new psychopath as their chief?

A metallic tone chimed from the tablet on his knee, and

an image from the elevator camera appeared. "You can stop your pacing. The wizard has returned."

The elevator disgorged Ek, his hair and eyebrows almost singed away, his clothing scorched and reeking of smoke. None of that seemed to matter to Victoria. She hugged Ek, smiling up at him in relief. "Oh, I'm so happy you're all right."

Ek set her aside, and shot a murderous look at Wakai. "My men aren't."

"How many did you lose?" asked Wakai hopefully.

"All but one," he spat. "The warehouse was full of smoke in minutes. We had to run through the fire to get away."

Wakai raised his eyebrows. "Lucky Kannon wasn't waiting for you."

"He was!" Ek exploded. "Shot the first man out the door between the eyes. Kept us pinned inside till the firefighters arrived."

Wakai carefully released his breath. "What happened to Jarun?"

"I sent him out to find Kannon. He didn't come back. What do you think happened to him?" Wakai fought for calmness. "Guess we both underestimated him."

He was yanked clear out of his chair, dangling in the air from Ek's one good hand. "You set us up!"

"Ek, no!" cried Victoria, pulling at his arm. "John would never do that!"

"And I can prove it," Wakai managed to choke out, the collar of his shirt tight as a noose.

Ek's grip tightened even more. "How?"

"Because I need you to get Tasanee for me. I know who has her."

Even though Ek clearly wanted nothing more than to smash Wakai like an insect, the news gave him pause.

"You've got a lot to pay Kannon back for," Wakai gasped, taking Ek's wrist in a bid to keep from being strangled. "With Tasanee in our hands, he's done."

Ek let go, and Wakai dropped into his chair with a bone-shuddering thud. Leaning over, the rakshasa pointed an ash-darkened finger straight at his face. "You had better be right. Because this is your very last chance."

Hate for Ek surged through Wakai for his callous treatment of Jarun—and himself. "And you'd better not fuck this up. Because this is your last chance, too."

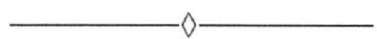

Gina was looking out the window of the Golden Geisha when Kannon arrived in a three-wheeled tuk-tuk. He paid the taxi driver, who looked pointedly at the sign and Gina, and gave him a thumbs-up. What? Was that a general sign of approval between two men or did he know Gina?

He never learned Thai formally because he planned to leave as soon as he could. Ever since teaming up with Gina, he'd changed his mind. He'd changed his mind on a lot of things.

He stepped inside. "Ryota here?"

"Got here about ten minutes ago and dragged Jarun upstairs." Gina moved from the window to him. "This evening's appointments have been shifted to the Magic Mango, so all the girls have cleared out. The place is all ours."

"Jarun wake up?"

She nodded. "Just after I arrived here. Question is, what are we going to do with him?"

He flexed his hands and made for the stairs. "I have a pretty good idea."

"Kannon, I...."

His foot rested on the bottom step. He knew what was coming. "Yes, boss?"

She set her hands on her hips. "That's uncalled for, Kannon. I've never lorded over you, and you know that. I— let's not turn this into another bloodbath, okay?"

"How rough I get is up to Jarun. I'm not a psycho, Gina. I hurt people because it's my job. Back there at 70 Rai was personal, and you backed me up on that, so as far as I'm concerned, it's done and gone. Now, if you want to take a stab at Jarun, be my guest, except that didn't turn out so well last time."

"I did fine! It was that berserker who messed things up."

"Well, then," Kannon said, sweeping his hand up the stairs, "be my guest."

She stalked past him. "Thank you, don't mind if I do."

She was halfway up the stairs when she stopped and turned. "Well, come on then."

He didn't like this. He didn't like being at her beck-and-call and then her daring to tell him that wasn't the way it was between them. He didn't like her ass swing up and away from him, while he had to, once again, trudge behind. "Why do I have to be there? Ryota can back you up."

That made her blink, which was good, because he was feeling a bit testy right now. She retraced her steps down until they were eye to eye. She straightened his tie. "You've pulled an all-nighter, haven't you? And you've had to deal with a gang of baddies and after all that, you get grief from me. It's not fair."

What was the little chit up to now?

"You're right. How about you wait here? Have a snooze, while Ryota and I deal with Jarun." As she turned away, he caught her arm.

"I get you, Gina. You know that I'd not let you in there without me, no matter how good Ryota is. But that wasn't my question, and you know it."

"What was it, then?"

"The question is: why do you want me with you when you don't need me?"

Her teeth set to gnawing her lips and the inside of her cheek. Good. She could chew herself up as bad as he was getting chewed up inside, too. "I guess I was confused," she finally said.

That was it? That was all she was going to give him, the woman who had answers and hugs for everyone else in the world? "Yeah, I guess you were," he said. He pushed past her to take the lead. "C'mon. You've got another interrogation to conduct."

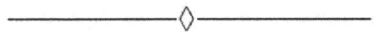

The round sex bed was looking a little different than yesterday morning. For one thing, Jarun was on it. Gagged, blindfolded, and his arms and legs bound. Kannon yanked away the gag and the blindfold.

Jarun looked around the room, at Gina, Kannon, and Ryota, his gaze coming to rest on the anatomically correct teddy bear. "Hell of a place to torture a man."

Kannon turned to Gina. "You're up."

It was the time on the boat all over again. Gina had no idea how to begin. She hoped she reflected nothing but cool confidence in order to fool Jarun—and Kannon. "You told us that Victoria was poison. That she's corrupted Wakai. Yet I find you helping her friends lure my man into a trap."

Jarun was snaking around on the bed, trying to pull himself upright on the slippery sheets. He looked like a landed fish. Gina felt a twinge of sympathy. She knew what it was like to be on that bed and not able to move. He managed to flop his head onto a pillow. "Your man? He was Alak Montri's. You and The Pink Stilettos act outraged while you steal his people."

She didn't dare look at Kannon. Not that she needed to. She could feel his stiff neutrality like a stone wall. "A temporary arrangement. But you haven't answered my question."

"You didn't ask one." Jarun looked ridiculous lying there, yet he had the upper hand. Kannon would've had him blubbering for his life by now, willing to confess to killing Jesus. She forced herself to sound like someone to be reckoned with. "Why were you dealing with Ek's people?"

"Wakai asked me to. Thought if he could get his hands on your man he could find out where Montri's daughter was. To be honest, I was looking forward to paying him back for the beating he gave me. Looks like I'm up for round two."

"There won't be any violence here," Gina said.

Kannon shifted on his feet. A quiet move that communicated deep impatience. She kept talking. "I'm not sure what to make of you, Jarun. You led us to that snuff brothel in 70 Rai, so I have reason to think you're sincere. On the other hand, you seem happy enough to help the Cambodians. Perhaps you could clarify that for me."

He didn't. He didn't say a word. And nobody did anything because they were all waiting on her, and she hadn't a freaking clue. Jarun gave a cool, knowing smile.

"This the best you've got? Thought the Pink Stilettos were supposed to be more than a dying man and his airhead daughter." He twisted to face Kannon. "And some washed-up

Yakuza thug."

It was a deliberate goad. And she fully expected Kannon to pistol-whip Jarun. A beat went by, and another. After several more, she realized that Kannon was not going to do anything. That he was willing to let their prisoner demean him in order to give her the chance to prove herself. And from how he stared straight ahead at the garishly painted wall, she knew what this was costing him. She had to find a way to break through.

"A *question*." She drew breath. "Are you playing Wakai and me off against each other?"

Jarun snorted. "Don't flatter yourself. And I don't play games when it comes to my friends. Wakai knows damn well what Alak Montri will do if he gets free, especially with three dozen gangs behind him. That means Wakai needs Tasanee. Without her, he has to keep depending on Victoria's friends for protection. With her, he won't need anyone but me."

Something started to tweak for her. She took a step closer. "So you're partnering with Wakai, then?"

"No, I'm trying to protect him. From you. From Victoria. Even from himself."

And there it was. The soft hitch in his voice. Ah. Progress. She took it one more step. She crawled on the bed and laid down beside him.

Kannon was right there, standing over them. Jarun's body stiffened, though it was hard to tell if it was from her languid proximity or Kannon's aggressive stance.

Gina propped her head on her hand. "I get it. You and Wakai are…close. You'd like to have him all to yourself."

Jarun's lip curled. "It's not like that between us."

Nearly word for word what Ryota had said of him and Tasanee. "You want to cheapen it," he went on. "Make it into something sordid, like it is with you and your Yakuza lapdog."

Not nearly as sordid as she wanted it. "Believe me, I know what it's like to want someone you can't have. So here's what I propose." She was winging it. "You tell us where Wakai is, where Montri is, and you *and* Wakai go free."

Jarun looked at her as if she was the idiot she felt like. "Montri would never allow that."

"Montri would never have to know," she ploughed on. "We'd get the two of you out of Thailand with enough money to disappear."

"And I'm supposed to just trust your word on that? I bet we'd disappear. Right to the bottom of the Gulf."

Gina's mind was racing. She needed something to sweeten the deal. Something to gain Jarun's cooperation. The moments stretched out to an embarrassing length, before it occurred to her. "Even if I set you loose right now you wouldn't be free. Neither you nor Wakai. So long as Victoria's alive you're both going to be bound to her sick whims. I'm not your enemy, Jarun, and you're not mine. The real enemy is that perverted, sadistic bitch. And with her gone we can all get what we want."

Jarun hesitated. "What are you saying?"

Later Gina found that the most surprising thing was not what she said, but how easily she said it. "That we'll kill her. Montri will get the city back. Tasanee can go back to a normal life. And you and Wakai can go start a new life far away from Thailand, exiled together. Everybody wins. Now enough bullshit. Do we have a deal, or do you want to test your claim that Kannon is washed-up?"

And with their heads together on pillows, and Kannon with pointed gun hovering above, Gina and her prisoner chatted.

————————◊————————

Kittyjack smiled as she guided her drone high above Bangkok, zooming in on a particular apartment tower. "That, my friends, is the Maharaja Xecutive. Fourteen stories tall, containing eighty-four two-bedroom deluxe suites—and one seriously nice penthouse. Technically, the top floor is still unsold, but seeing as the place was completed seven years ago, that's a little suspicious. Only way up is by private elevator and an emergency stairwell, both of which are tightly secured."

In the night-time photo, a lit fountain sprayed up a giant water flower and more halogen lamps coursed white light up the walls. Gina's apartment was in a similar building in L.A. All very chic and modern—and lifeless. You could live there for years and never know your neighbors. Never know if you even had any. "Very pretty—for a fortress."

"That's exactly what it is," Kannon said. "And in the middle of the city, no less. Try and crack that by force and we'll have half the cops in Bangkok after us."

"How do we do it?" Gina asked.

Kannon didn't answer right away, his eyes locked on the screen. "There is a way, but it's risky."

"And what happens once you do?" Dr. Chaiboonma interrupted from behind them, his voice drawing their collective attention.

Oh nice, Gina thought. Dr. Chai was going to take up where he left off, proclaiming her as the prodigal daughter.

"Then the rakshasas are kicked out of Bangkok," she answered. "Once Alak Montri's free, you can bet the gangs will line up behind him."

"And he'll most certainly win," said Dr. Chaiboonma.

"By attrition, if nothing else. But how long before the next gang shows up? Montri's already fought seven turf wars in twenty years. This will be his eighth, and the second one against an usurper."

Gina didn't want to be dragged into a debate. "That's the nature of the business."

"It doesn't have to be," replied Dr. Chaiboonma. "At least half those battles could have been avoided by negotiation. The rest could have been discouraged by intimidation. Your boss considers himself a nationalist, and in truth he loves his king like every good Thai. That doesn't make him any less of a blight on the people of Bangkok. All he's brought is violence and death to this city and no matter how you cut it, that kind of instability is bad for business. Very bad."

Gina threw up her hands. "What would you suggest? Letting the rakshasas win? Of all the foreigners that have tried to take over, they have to be the worst."

"I'm not suggesting we surrender," Dr. Chaiboonma said. "What I don't understand is why the gangs of Bangkok only ever seem to be united under a dictator. The muscle to crush the rakshasas exists right now, yet each gang sits in hiding, none of them willing to support the others without someone to give them their marching orders."

Beside her, Kannon was his usual inscrutable self, which meant that he didn't like the direction Dr. Chai was taking either. Sure, she'd avoided violence with Jarun, only because she'd promised to get another person killed. And who had she implied would do the job? Yes, she was a hypocrite, telling Kannon to avoid violence, and then practically signing him up for it. "The bottom line is that Montri's my father's friend. His daughter is my god-sister. Regardless of what he does after we get him out, those are reasons enough to rescue him. The same would hold true if it was you who'd been kidnapped, Dr. Chai."

The leader of the Bangkok Blondes softened at that. "You've got a good heart, Gina. You should use it for a good purpose."

She was getting nowhere. Time for him to hear the truth. "Ha!" She turned to Kannon. "Tell him how my good heart is useless when it comes to getting things done. Tell him how I nearly blew it this morning with Jarun."

Kannon took off his glasses. "She did fine."

He was being nice because he still felt she was the boss. "No, Kannon. I give you permission. Tell it like it is."

Kannon's head listed slightly towards her before adjusting to continue with Dr. Chai. "Her methods are—unorthodox, but she gets the job done."

Gina felt her jaw drop, actually feel the hinges crack from the sudden release. Did he really approve?

"I agree," Ryota piped up.

"Thanks a bunch," Gina snapped, "for your total lack of support during my time of crisis."

The three men exchanged looks, the kind of gingery glances made around unstable people. Even Kittyjack was staring at her screen as if her life depended on it. None of them understood. She simply didn't have what it took.

She fastened onto Kannon. "You said there's a way into Wakai's penthouse?"

He pointed at the screen to a corner of the building inset with a decorative pattern. "Someone could use those as a series of handholds. See how it runs all the way from the ground floor to the rooftop, and how there's not much light? If someone went at night, they could climb all the way up unnoticed. An expert climber could do it."

Kittyjack snorted in disbelief. "That's about a two hundred foot climb, and even if you're agile, you sure as hell ain't light."

Kannon gave Gina a meaningful look. "It wouldn't be me that would be doing the climbing."

Gina's stomach lurched as the drone passed over the building, giving her a clear perspective of exactly how high fourteen stories really was. "You think she'd be able to do it?"

"The way she climbs, I don't have any doubt," Kannon answered. "The real question is if she's willing to come out of retirement."

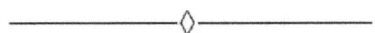

Delta and Brian weren't due for another seventeen hours, and Kannon planned to make good use of the down time. He called his favorite restaurant, and then Gina on *The Pink Pussycat.*

"I've got reservations at Pern Dee for eight tonight. Care to join me?"

He made out happy squeals and chatter in the background. Although the 70 Rai children weren't due to head back to Cambodia until the next morning, that didn't entirely explain the level of noise.

"Tonight?" she blared.

"Yes. If you can't make it, that's fine." And it was, he told himself. Just fine.

"No, I should be able to get away."

Kannon couldn't remember the last time he'd walked into a public place with a woman he didn't have to be careful around. His wife had never known the full extent of his dealings, and after her, he'd always steered his conversations with women away from his work and life. That had two results: half the women he dated quickly began to distrust him, and the ones who were happy to keep the focus solely on themselves weren't the kind he wanted to be with. In the end, he'd gotten so weary of the dating game, he'd dropped out. Pensri served his purposes well enough.

Then along came Gina.

Within a minute of being seated, the short, round waiter and Gina were clacking to each other in Thai like old friends. Kannon intercepted the waiter's downward gaze at Gina.

"What would you recommend?" Kannon inquired, weighting each word.

The waiter waved his hand at the menu. "It is all good," he stumbled in English. He turned to Gina. "You like prawns?"

"Does the sun set in the west? Of course! Surprise me. Whatever you think I should have, and don't worry." She pointed at Kannon. "He's paying."

The waiter turned to Kannon. "And you, sir? The usual?"

"Surprise me, too." The waiter fumbled his pencil. What the hell did the little butterball think he'd do? Kill him over a prawn? "Just no papaya. Make it as hot as you can."

As the waiter turned away, Gina touched his arm and whispered in rapid Thai to him, looking all excited.

"What did you tell him?" asked Kannon.

"Told him this was the first time you've taken me out. And that we wanted it to be something special. Something we'd remember for the rest of our lives."

Kannon narrowed his eyes at the doors the waiter had bumped through. "A case of food poisoning would do that. I should've stuck with my usual."

"Kannon! Really, quit being so paranoid."

"Comes with the territory." He settled his eyes on her.

She looked great. Her hair was in ringlets, the purple tips like ribbon twining through it all. She was wearing a skintight dress, red and yellow—backless and damn near frontless. It was amazing. "You realize that without your sunglasses, I can see you're looking at my boobies."

At a table beside their booth, the husband of an elderly Thai couple glanced at Gina and then at his triple-chinned wife and then back at his menu.

"I know for a fact that you wore that dress so I would."

Gina rolled her eyes. "Duh."

"Zoe says that. But she's fifteen. How old are you?"

"Thirty-one years old." She gave a secretive look. "Today."

"Today's your birthday?"

"Had a big party on the boat. Was going to pull an all-nighter, when you called."

"You left your own birthday party to go on a date with me?"

"When have I ever lied to you?"

"You haven't. I don't understand why you left the party, is all."

A strained look crossed her face. "Daddy was getting tired, and I knew he wouldn't have rested while I was there."

"My call was serendipitous is what you're saying."

Gina grinned. "So I accepted. And I have to say I love the gift you got me."

Kannon looked around. "Well, this place isn't *that* fancy."

"Not the meal, Kannon," she laughed, reaching out to place her hand on his. "I mean our second date. Our first one ended kind of awkwardly. Was a little worried there wasn't going to be another."

The waiter arrived with the appetizer. Prawns, of course.

Gina let out a little moan he felt in his cock. "This looks delicious." She popped one in and sucked spicy red sauce off every finger. "I can't believe how much I love these."

"I'm getting the idea."

Her mouth stilled and she withdrew a finger. "Listen, Kannon, I wasn't trying to—tease you."

He had to say it—and fast. "Gina, I know. I got the message at that fertility temple. It's like what you told Jarun. This is a temporary arrangement, and I can live with that. I'm not going to lie and say that I wasn't hoping for something more. The way things have worked out, I see it wasn't one of my better ideas. So how about we do things Thai-style, and enjoy each other for the time being?"

Gina bit her lip. "We could—"

"Do I know you from somewhere?" The Thai man from the next table had leaned across to address Gina.

From your wet dreams, thought Kannon. "I don't think so," he said, low and final.

Gina ignored him, and started in with twenty questions to place them in her social history. It turned out Kannon was right, but that didn't stop Gina from launching into an extended conversation with the older couple. To Kannon's horror, pictures were soon being called up on the woman's cell phone, and Gina left the booth to lean over the couple's table, gushing over pictures of children and grandchildren. The old man had probably never taken more interest in his progeny, Gina's breasts nearly spilling out from her dress.

The entrée arrived and the date resumed, their waiter obviously eager to please. "Is everything to your satisfaction?"

Gina looked at Kannon with deliberation. She dipped her finger into the sauce and put it in her mouth. She extracted it with a slow pull. "Positively orgasmic."

Yes, they were going Thai-style tonight. The waiter grew heavy-lidded and gazed at her like one of Snow White's dwarves, then opened them on Kannon "And you, sir?"

Kannon gave him a level stare. "Everything's mutually orgasmic here."

The waiter blinked, retreated.

Kannon needed to say one more thing. "One proviso to going Thai. I'm done with sharing you for tonight. Okay?"

"Okay."

Her answer was quick, so he knew she meant it. He got serious about his meal. It was hot and spicy, the way he liked it. One thing he had come to enjoy about Bangkok was its food, though he preferred to sit indoors without dogs and traffic to disturb him. He raised his head to make that distinction to Gina to find her staring open-mouthed at him. He dabbed his mouth with his napkin and glanced down at his shirt-front. Nothing. She still looked as if he'd swallowed a shoe.

"What?"

"You always eat like that?"

"Like what?"

"Like this." She reached over and popped in a pork bit thick with sauce. There then ensued a lot of tongue work and sucking in breath and puckering, building up to a happy sound of pleasure that was too over-the-top to be him.

"That's not me."

She aimed her chopsticks at his mouth. "So you."

"Huh. Guess I can tease, too."

And then they were grinning at each other, like goofs in love. This was as good a time as any. He reached into the inner pocket of his jacket and pulled out a small present. "Happy birthday, Gina."

She dropped her chopsticks. "Kannon! How did you

know?"

"I didn't, actually. I was planning to give you this, any-way. Since it's your birthday, let's call it a birthday present."

She tore it open and he was treated to a second squealing of his name. "Kannon! She's adorable." She set the purple vixen figurine, a miniature version of the one in Dr. Chaiboonma's boardroom, on the table between them. "How did you know?"

"It's my job to watch you." He paused. "Sometimes, it's my pleasure."

Her face brightened and softened, and her shiny lips parted. He had to get them out of there. "So, birthday girl, what would you like to do after dinner?"

"There's a club around the corner from here called 2XS. Best happy hardcore music in the city."

Happy hardcore? "Get the feeling I'm too old for it."

"But it's my birthday." She stuck out her lip.

"I thought my daughter pouted because she inherited the ability from her mother. Apparently it's gender-specific."

Gina laughed, dislodging a drop of sauce from her chopstick onto her open chest where it began a slow trickle down. Kannon blew out his breath. "I'll take you. Only until midnight. By then your birthday will be over and I'll be deaf."

That got her moving—it was already coming up on ten.

It turned out that the only thing sexier than Gina eating was Gina dancing, especially to the frenetic pace of the synthesized music. The way she moved as the lights pulsed around her it was as if she were part of an orgy, especially given the amount of unnecessary bumping from others into her. She touched his waist. "You dance well for a sixty-year-old."

He'd been so focused on her dancing that he hadn't

noticed what his body was doing.

Her front slid close to his. "Do you know any moves?"

It had been well over a decade and the music was all wrong. Then again no one was moving in time. He slid his arm around her warm waist, took her hand in his and whispered, "I do, girl." He spun her away, then twirled her right back.

He and his wife had danced together for years to the point that their movements flowed in perfect harmony. They could move together while they talked or watched others, a synchronicity bred over time. Though Gina was so different from his elegant, petite wife, they were still perfectly matched. Despite the challenging pace of the music her instincts were honed, her long legs and inborn sense of rhythm allowing her to keep up with him even as their bodies whirled and slid and pressed together. And it helped her eyes stayed fastened to him the whole time. Two dances in, and the crowd had cleared a spot for them at the far end of the pulsing dance floor. By the fourth, the younger ones were trying to imitate them, and as expected, Gina didn't mind showing them how to do it. A skinny young punk with spiked-up hair and size two biker boots tried to partner up with her. Kannon practically lifted her away. One look delivered his message, and though half-blitzed out of his mind, the kid backed off.

"Sheesh," Gina started in when he hustled her out on the stroke of midnight. "You kinda went all alpha there."

"He needed to be put in his place."

"Put in place? There's that paranoia coming through again." Gina lifted the hair off the back of her neck, wound it into a loose coil and from the inside of her dress hem produced a doodad she jammed into her hair. Long purple tips shot every which way. "There. That's better." She ran her fingertips across her chest. "I'd forgotten how hot the nights get here.

197

You're so lucky you're not feeling this."

"I suppose."

Gina tilted her head. "Where to now?"

"Back to the docks. I'm tired and it's not your birthday anymore."

Gina threatened him with the lip. "It's still our date."

"We've got a busy day tomorrow. We need to be on our toes. Probably shouldn't have gone out tonight, except—"

Gina got in his space. "Except—?"

"Except it was your birthday."

"You didn't know that when you invited me out. It's because you couldn't wait to go on another date with me. Come on, admit it."

"I couldn't wait to take you out on a date. Now let's go, and don't give me the lip or else—" He stopped because there was no way he could threaten her with anything.

"Please tell me that I'm not too old for a spanking."

He hustled her into a taxi to take them to the docks where he'd parked. And why was he not surprised that the taxi driver thought himself a conversationalist? Gina spent the whole trip back yakking to the man in Thai about their evening together, or so she informed him. Had he not made it clear he didn't want to share? She called the Pussycat when they arrived at the deserted dock, and he knew damn well why she hadn't done it earlier. She turned to him where they were standing at his car. "So, since it's Thai-style tonight, I was wondering if—"

He answered with his mouth on hers and, for the first time that night, she was wholly his. Her body melded against him, her dress and skin damp from sweat and humidity, the already thin material slicking under his hands. "Gina," he said against the wetness of her mouth. "You're wet."

She pressed her lower belly against him. "Lubed inside

and out."

That was enough. His hand slipped under her dress and encountered something hard and rectangular. He set her phone on the hood of the vehicle and made a second attempt. This time, he found her breast, her nipple already a hard point. He licked her neck. "Tell me. When you went into the bedroom with Pensri, what did you two do?"

Gina's clever hands got under his jacket, squirreled under his shirt. "Oh, you know, the usual," she said. "A little rubbing, a little licking, a little experimentation with her toys. Got sleepy before we did any anal play."

Kannon didn't let up with his mouth on her neck. "How about your breasts? Anything with them?" He moved his hand to the other side. There his hand came upon something hard and poky. He pulled out the figurine and set it by the phone. His second attempt produced a breast as perfect as the first.

"Oh. Not much. I'm very sensitive there. You can pretty much tell from the state of my tits how the rest of me is feeling. And…as you can see…I'm ready…to go…though I guess I was from the second…you called."

He'd heard enough. He lifted her up onto the hood of his vehicle and leaned her back against the windshield, her buttocks over the crevice between the windshield and the hood. It wasn't the most comfortable of positions but he was intent on making her forget that.

He pulled down the straps off her shoulders straight to her waist. "I've loved your breasts since I saw them three years ago, you behind that counter."

"You seem focused on your job."

"Focused. Not blind."

"Looked to me as if—"

He bent his head and drew a dark nipple into his mouth.

She gave off a sound like when the prawn sauce had hit the back of her throat. After a few more pulls, the sounds deepened into something that no one in that restaurant had had the pleasure of hearing.

He moved to the other breast, while massaging the freshly suckled one with his hand.

From the corner of his eye he saw her hips take to rotating. He broke suction, touched his lips to hers. "I keep this up with your breasts, will you come for me?"

Her lips trembled under his. "Halfway there already."

Kannon returned south. Her right breast, he discovered, was the most responsive, causing her to squirm, the heels of her bare feet rubbing the length of the hood. The left one wasn't to be ignored either and made Gina's back arch. The trick was to get both working for him when he had only one mouth. The best he could do was squeeze the two together to close the space, and that alone drew a deep orgasmic moan out of her. She wouldn't be long now. He risked a glance to the water and spotted the powerboat coming to pick up Gina. He'd have to make it happen soon. He bent his head again and didn't let up with his mouth even as her body went rigid, her hands clamped onto his head and he got his arm underneath in time to have her pound out her orgasm.

After, she herself pulled up her dress, swung those dancing legs around and hopped down, tucking away her phone and figurine into their usual safe spots. "The boat's almost here. Or I'd return the favor."

Something was wrong. She didn't look as…satisfied as he'd hoped to make her. There was no way she could've faked it. Or had she? He crowded her against the vehicle door, even as the boat idled close. He hitched up her dress and skimmed a finger between her legs. "You're soaked. You didn't fake it."

She gave him an appalled look. "I never fake it. What's the point of that?"

"You don't look…quite done."

She looked at him wide-eyed as she maneuvered space between them to wiggle her heels back on. "What do you expect? I only came once."

He blinked. "How many times can you come?"

She shrugged. "My record is 22 times. But"—she gave him a quick kiss and a pat on the cheek—"I don't expect it from you." She slipped away and did a skip-scurry toward the boat.

Had she handed him a challenge? If so, he accepted. It was going to be one hell of a third date.

CHAPTER ELEVEN

THE SUVARNABHUMI AIRPORT was a marvel of engine-eering. Its vast, bright and ultra-modern construction seemed to defy gravity. Flowing steel arches spanned epic distances while towering hoops of glass provided a breathtaking view of the sprawling public gardens at its heart. The monumental main terminal was decorated with huge, colorful murals and towering statues of Thai dragons, warriors and gods.

It was also very, very, very long. Gina's feet felt as if her shoes were designer vises. "Holy hell, I shouldn't have worn heels today," she shared with Kannon. "How much farther is it to the arrival gate?"

He lifted his chin to the long line of stores, restaurants, spas, beauty salons and way off, bowling alley. "The route we're taking, another twenty miles. The economy won't col-lapse if you bypass a few of these, you know."

"But why risk it?" she said, hobbling toward a stand of comfy shoes. Kannon snagged her elbow. "Come on, girl, or we'll be late."

Gina didn't protest. She could always come again. Maybe when she flew back to L.A. Whenever that was. Her life in

America seemed unreal right now.

By the time they swam upstream through the arriving visitors pouring out the gate, Gina was barefoot. "Do you see them?" she asked as the flow of exiting passengers washed up onto the welcoming shores of friends and relatives.

Kannon scanned the lake of heads. "There." And swam on, Gina in his wake.

Brian, Delta and two backpacks were by a golden statue of one of the many fertility goddesses. Brian squared on them as they approached.

"We're not doing this. She's pregnant."

Kannon took in the statue. "That was fast."

Brian wasn't finished. "Do you know how I found this out? On the plane over. She upchucks after her eggs. She's never been sick in all the years I've known her. She tells me not to worry. 'I'm just pregnant, is all.' Why, you are probably wondering, didn't she tell me this before we got on the plane? Because she didn't want to worry me."

Kannon released a long, exasperated breath, and set his hands on his hips, his suit jacket pulling open to show his wide torso in a royal blue shirt. He looked awesome in that color. As good as the black one last night. She couldn't wait for the third date when she might get a peek of what he looked like without one. A third date also marked the end of their temporary trial period which was all she'd told him she wanted. Only—

Only, she was happy he was with her. He could talk Brian down.

"The day my wife told me she was pregnant I caught her petting a stray cat," Kannon informed them.

Crap, he was on Brian's side.

The rigid line in Brian's shoulders relaxed. "So you agree that Delta can't risk doing this."

"I do." Kannon slid off his mirrored glasses. "Congratulations, Ms. Fox."

"Mrs. Chanse," Brian corrected. "And it's the only 'chance' she's taking from now on."

Delta looked up at her husband with an expression of forced patience. "I already told you, Brian, It's not like I'm suddenly made of glass. I know what I'm doing."

Kannon looked at Gina and gave the barest tilt of his head toward Delta. He wanted her to talk her boss's wife and her friend out of going. Except Delta was their best hope. On the other hand, she could understand Brian's worry. Whatever happened here in Bangkok, risking the lives of the two he loved the most, his wife and his unborn child, wouldn't be worth it.

Gina sighed. "Okay, you guys, you need to come to an agreement, whatever it is. And you need to do this quick, because time's kind of short here."

"We are decided," Brian said firmly. "We're going back to L.A. on the next flight."

Delta turned to Gina. "When's that?"

Gina did a quick search on her phone. "Tomorrow morning. 7:20 departure."

"Okay. We'll go then."

Brian narrowed his eyes at her. "And what will we do in the meanwhile?"

Delta stole a look at Kannon.

Brian exploded. "You haven't listened to a word I've said, have you?"

"Maybe, we should—" Gina started but Delta interrupted.

"I know this is a risk, Brian. I get that. Back at the airport in L.A. the bookstore had this pregnancy manual I flipped through. Turns out I shouldn't have had the shrimp platter last week. Turns out that my pelvis might be too small. Turns out that there are tests for genetic markers we could've taken, so we might have to deal with the consequences of that. Point is, we've already taken the biggest chance by just choosing to have a baby."

"I'm talking about unnecessary risks. And this is unnecessary."

"You were fine with me doing it before you knew I was pregnant."

"At least then it was your body and your decision. Now you're making decisions for someone else."

Delta got in close to Brian and spoke in a way that seemed to close them off from the rest of the world. "I'm not walking away from this one, Brian. I can't. This isn't about springing some Godfather. This is about all the kids those sick bastards are going to hurt if they're not stopped. If anyone can take care of business it's Kannon, and I'm damn well going to get him inside so he can do his job. I know I'm risking our child, but I need to do this before I go home with you and have our baby. Okay?"

Gina didn't know the full story of Delta's past. She wouldn't be surprised if Delta had only told Brian the bare facts. There'd always been a pocket of reserve about her that made her seem aloof, and in a lot of ways Kannon was similar. He'd dropped little stories but, like Delta, would always hold himself back. Being with him would be like Brian's relationship with Delta. Dealing with a stubborn and strong-willed person, used to doing things their own way. And from the seriously unhappy expression on her boss's face, it would suck.

Brian swung up both backpacks. "Okay, I'm buying our tickets home right now. You do whatever the hell you need to do. Come 7:20 tomorrow your butt is on the plane to L.A. Agreed?"

"Agreed."

Brian jabbed a finger at Gina and Kannon. "Anything happens to Delta and I'm holding you two personally responsible because this is your fucking problem that you"—he focused on Kannon—"caused when you let your boss get kidnapped."

Gina felt a sudden flash of anger. "Hey, wait a min—"

Kannon cut her off. "Agreed."

He looked grumpy. Delta looked defiant and tense. Brian looked like a sick tourist. Desperate times called for desperate measures.

She tapped on her phone. "You want to see what I did on my birthday yesterday?" She turned the display to Brian, Delta sliding in beside him. They peered at the screen, their eyes widening, and both looked simultaneously at Kannon.

"Dances pretty well for a man considering he's sixty, huh?"

Kannon slid his sunglasses back on in obvious embarrassment.

There. A distraction, and if it happened to focus on Kannon, all the better.

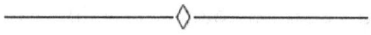

Victoria leaned over the rail of the powerboat and dry heaved, her empty stomach having nothing to offer. She got nauseous from water taxi rides, let alone plying the turbulent estuary of the Chao Phraya river. Within minutes of getting underway that morning, she was seasick, and as the boat crossed the river mouth and headed once again to the open ocean, she let out a low moan of dread.

The radio beeped and crackled, and the static-y sound of Ek's voice reached her. "Anything yet?"

Victoria stumbled past the rakshasa piloting the craft to pick up the receiver. "Nothing," she said. "Where are you?"

"Patpong," he replied, the sounds of the red light district's street noise almost drowning him out. "Spent all night and this morning here, but no luck. Bastard could be hiding anywhere. Let me know if you find anything."

"Will do." Hanging up the radio, she ran her tongue around her mouth. "Agh! I'm so sick of the taste of vomit. I swear I'll flay that old man alive when I catch him."

"I thought that was your plan anyway," the rakshasa said.

Victoria flashed him an irritated glare. "Yes, well he'll deserve everything he gets, making me suffer like this."

Her brother had figured out it was Vincenzo Zaffini helping Kannon, but finding the old man was proving to be a real bitch. Even with the eyes of Ek and his men glued to Zaffini's brothels and massage parlors, they hadn't caught sight of the man or any of his known associates. Word on the street was he was dying. Some said he'd gone to seek treatment abroad. There was even speculation that he was already dead, and his wife was running his businesses now. All their leads were coming up dry, except there was one that they hadn't crossed off their list yet—*The Pink Pussycat*.

According the harbor authority, the yacht had set sail for Australia weeks ago, a claim verified by the fact that its berth at the Ocean Marina Yacht Club was empty. Her brother suspected that the Pussycat wasn't as far away as they were being led to believe. She was assigned the task of searching every nook and cranny a yacht could squeeze into.

The powerboat bounced over the waves, each bump

making Victoria's stomach slam against the back of her throat. She held the binoculars as steady as she could and scanned the waters. The coast was dotted with both fishing and sail boats, with one or two larger pleasure craft making their way toward the city. Nothing big and pink.

"Gulf's huge," the rakshasa muttered behind the wheel. They'd already boated all the way to the neighboring city of Chon Buri and back—a hundred miles of misery. But her John had an instinct for spotting deception, and she wasn't about to give up the hunt.

"Take us over there," she ordered, pointing at a nearby fishing boat, its red paint peeling, its body flecked with rust.

With a grunt the man complied, and a minute later they were pulling alongside the battered old craft. Fishermen, faces streaked with chalk to protect them from the scorching rays of the sun, glanced down at them with cautious curiosity. They were all Burmese by the looks of them, illegal immigrants who'd come to Thailand searching for a better life. Probably little more than slaves, exploited by their captains as cheap, disposable labor. Nothing men like these wouldn't do to get out of their situation.

"Have any of you seen a yacht?" she called to them. "A big one. Very rich. Not too far out to sea."

Most of the fishermen ignored her, except for one, perhaps sixteen years old, who raised a calloused hand.

Victoria held up a small roll of bills. "What color was it?"

"Pink."

Victoria grinned. "Where?"

The boy stretched his arm to the south. "We passed it about a half-hour ago." His eyes were fixed on the money in her hand. "Looked like it was anchored."

A bolt of victorious exultation shot through her, and she

tossed him the money.

Quick as a monkey, he snatched it from the air. He had such a lean and newly muscled body, so wonderful and young, and so many things she could do with it. The dark hungers she'd inherited from her violent father coiled within her like some obscene dragon.

"You've been very helpful," she said, her voice friendly. "You should come and work for me."

His innocent eyes widened. "Doing what?"

"Keeping me entertained," she replied. "I'm sure a strong kid like you could do that, hmm?"

The boy hesitated.

"Unless you're happy working out at sea for the rest of your life."

That got him moving. With a furtive glance over his shoulder, he scrambled over the rail and jumped into the water, Victoria gesturing to the rakshasa to pull the boat around and pick him up. Dripping with water but clearly excited, the young man with his unmarred skin climbed aboard with Victoria's aid.

"Thank you." He pressed his hands together and bowed deeply. "I promise I won't let you down."

Victoria laid a hand on his shoulder, her seasickness quickly lifting. "Don't worry. I'm sure I'm going to just love you to pieces."

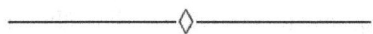

Darae cursed as the bow of *The Pink Pussycat* lurched, almost throwing her off her feet as she hurried down the narrow hallway, klaxons blaring in her ear. The normally whisper-quiet engines were roaring at full throttle, bouncing the yacht off the waves with enough force to make the whole ship vibrate, spray coating the windows as it raced across the dark waters. Arriving on the bridge at a run, she burst in on the captain and first mate.

"What's happening?" she demanded in Thai.

The captain was a Bangkok native who'd been working for Vincenzo ever since he'd purchased the ship ten years ago, a sailor with twenty years experience in the Thai navy. For all that, her face was grim. "Radar picked up a half-dozen small craft approaching from the north, making straight for us at high speed."

Darae's eyes widened at the six dots on the screen the first mate was monitoring. "Can we outrun them?"

"As soon as I noticed them, we weighed anchor and made for open ocean," replied the first mate, the captain's daughter. "We've got her up to forty-eight knots. They're at roughly fifty-five. I estimate they'll reach us in five minutes."

"What are we looking at?"

The captain's answer was staccato sharp. "The three of us, two engineers, the bosun, three deckhands and four stewardesses. Thirteen in total. I say we're outnumbered two to one."

Fuck. The boat lurched again, and this one Darae felt in her stomach. "Ready yourself for boarding," Darae ordered, "and buy us as much time as you can. If they catch us, you know what to do."

The captain and the first mate, mother and daughter, looked at each other and then at her. Together, they nodded.

She made for the ship's armory. There was no time to tell Vinny what was happening. He probably knew already. Last thing he'd said as she tore from their bed was, "Keep Gina out of this." A promise she could keep, because there was no time to get her into it.

The cabinet was being emptied of handguns and gas masks by all hands, and gripping two of the stewardesses by their shoulders, Darae nodded in the direction of the cabins. "One of you on Vincenzo. The other with Tasanee. Take gas masks for them and lock yourselves in the cabins. Don't open for anyone but me, you got it?"

The two women grabbed what they needed and hurried off.

"The rest of you, I want the ship locked down and every-one at their assigned stations," Darae said. "These bastards get on board and being killed will be the least of your worries. We got less than five minutes. Move!"

Darae took to the top deck, the wind whipping at her hair as she peered into the darkness. Through the goggles of her gas mask, she could detect the dark shapes of the speedboats clos-ing in fast, cutting through the water like hunting sharks. All at once, the sharp chatter of automatic weapons filled the air, illuminating their pursuers in flashes of deadly gunfire.

The boats were bigger than she expected, each with a half-dozen men on board. Looked like the fight was going to be closer to three to one, with their enemies more heavily armed.

Steadying herself against the rail, Darae aimed her pistol at the nearest speed boat and emptied the clip at her enemies. She doubted a single bullet found its mark, but hoped it make the fuckers reconsider.

The boat fell back. Then, she realized their true intent. There was a bright flash from the lead speedboat, a brief shrill whine, and the back of *The Pink Pussycat* exploded into a blinding fireball. The engines shredded, the yacht decelerated hard, knocking Darae to the deck.

She ejected the magazine and slapped in a fresh one, then

jumped to the railing. The powerboats had already surrounded them, the rakshasas tossing grappling hooks up onto the rails, their men boarding from every direction.

Vinny. Tasanee. She couldn't keep them safe.

She fired at them, one of her bullets finding the throat of the first boarder, but was forced to scramble backwards by a hail of gunfire. Chaos broke around her as the crew were driven off the deck, gun smoke clouding the air as the whizz of bullets ended in ricochets, shattering glass and screams of pain.

In moments, the rakshasas would swarm the deck. Darae and her crew had one last chance.

There was a sudden metallic ping as dozens of small nozzles extended from the ship's walls, hissing their contents into the air. Within seconds the closest of the rakshasas were feeling the invisible gas. Howls of agony echoed from all sides, and risking a peek at the deck below, Darae watched as several of her enemies clutched at their eyes, wheezing and cursing as they staggered back.

The men behind them hesitated as one fell to his knees, letting out a retching gurgle as bloody froth appeared at the corners of his mouth. Dropping his gun he grasped at his chest, his face turning dark blue.

They didn't know it yet, but they were already dead. The cyanogen chloride they'd inhaled was already plummeting their blood pressure, even as it filled their lungs with fluid. Within a couple of minutes their hearts would either stop pumping, or they'd drown in their own bile.

The reprieve was temporary. The poison would only kill those who got a good breath of it, and the gas would stop spraying in a couple more minutes. Once stopped, the wind would quickly dissipate it, leaving *The Pink Pussycat* all but defenseless. This was their one and only chance to turn the tables on their enemies, and standing, Darae and her crew fired into the rakshasas, as if they had everything—and nothing—to lose.

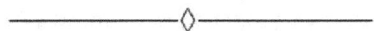

Kannon was used to tense situations, where life and death were a split second apart. Still, he had never experienced what existed in the back of the van as it approached the Maharaja Xecutive.

Delta and Brian sat on one side, he and Ryota on the other. Gina was at the wheel. Except for Brian they were all dressed in black. Delta was in a cat suit, her hands sheathed in custom gloves of rough, waterproof stingray skin, her feet in boots with divided toes for better grip. Black paint coated her normally pale face. She even had oversized black contact lenses that changed the entirety of her eyes into eerie pits. She wore a headset to communicate with them, and a backpack containing a large spool of braided fishing line and a few other useful odds and ends. She sat among them like a watchful alien.

She wasn't the source of the stress, and neither was the danger-fraught mission. It was Brian. His worry was a throbbing presence, worsened by his attempt to contain it. It had leapt out once when Delta had earlier suggested that he wait at the hotel room. That, everyone soon learned, was not going to happen.

He never thought he would, but Kannon sympathized with Brian. Ever since she refused to shoot him when she could've, he'd secretly admired the little thief with her quiet pluck. More to the point, he knew how he would feel if it were

Gina geared up across from him. He'd be wired, too, every fiber of his being strung as tight as Brian's was right now.

The van slowed. "One minute to drop off," Gina said from the front. Her voice betrayed her anxiety, too. Selfishly, he wondered if any of it was for him.

Delta turned his way. "Thirty minutes for me to get to the top and drop the line."

Kannon checked his watch. 2:02 a.m. "Got it."

Delta slid a look at Brian, who was bent forward elbow on his knees, one hand gripping a radio.

"I won't use the channel unless I have to," she said.

He didn't move, except for a short, quick nod. The van crawled to a near stop, and Delta hesitated, her eyes on Brian. Finally, she shifted toward the back doors. Brian caught her up, snagged her around the waist and suctioned her to him, her back to his front. "Hey. You two come back. Hear?"

In the dark, Kannon could see Delta relax. "We will. We've got a plane to catch."

One last squeeze and he let her go. She slid to the back door as Gina brought the van to a full stop and, in an instant, Delta was gone.

Kannon started the timer, then picked up a sturdy climbing harness from the floor of the van, pulled it over his broad shoulders and locked it closed. He next slung a heavy coil of black nylon rope over his shoulder. Brian returned to his elbows on his knees, his eyes bent to the radio as if it could relay messages from God. Four minutes in, Kannon saw Ryota sneak his hand into his pocket and pull out his phone.

"Make sure that thing's off before we go."

"Yes, boss. I was just checking messages."

Kannon studied his junior's face. "What's the problem?"

Ryota shrugged it off. "Tasanee usually texts me before

she goes to sleep."

Kannon thought back to the plane ride over when Tasanee slept through Gina and him. "She fell asleep is all. If there was a problem, Darae would call Gina. She hasn't, so there isn't. Now, turn it off. Time to move."

At the front, Gina was nearly hidden from view. From the light on the street coming through the front of the van, he could see the edge of her shoulder, arm and head facing away. Any other time he would've been relieved that her mind was on the job, but a part of him wanted a part of her.

Her eyes met his in the rearview mirror. One of her light brown eyes closed in a wink. It felt like a kiss. It made slipping out the back door with Ryota almost easy.

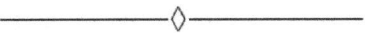

Delta had jumped from the van and hit the ground, running. She sprinted ahead a ways, then leapt upwards, catching the top of the wall, swinging herself over it in one graceful movement, and landing on the other side in a catlike crouch.

She surveyed the garden, and finding it empty, made for the edge of the building, granting herself three breaths when she reached it. The surface was concrete, moist from the humid tropical air, inset with a decorative swirling pattern that repeated upwards, floor after floor. Testing her weight upon it a few different ways, she quickly worked out a sequence of holds for her hands and feet to make the ascent. The moves wouldn't be easy, but the real challenge would come at the upper floors when her strength was ebbing, the wind was its strongest—and the drop was the highest.

"Hope you're good with heights," she whispered to her unborn child, then gripping the first handhold, she started.

In a slow and steady crawl, she scaled her way up. She'd ever attempted this height before, a little fact she'd kept from Brian. The farthest she'd ever free climbed was eight stories, a little more than half this distance. Soon enough the wind was tugging at her, threatening to pull her off the wall. Flattening herself to its face she clung tight, keeping her focus as she inched ever higher. Her feet and hands began to ache as the ground got farther and farther away. She was slick with sweat as her fingertips hooked against the shallow fissures, the edges of her feet seeking purchase on the slightest of support.

Then, suddenly, she was there—her hand gripping the small ledge that ran around the perimeter of the penthouse, a couple of feet beneath the safety rail. She rolled onto the ledge and dropped to her side as she undid her pack and eased out the high tensile line. On the end of it was attached a steel ring, muffled in cloth, and dropping it over the edge, she let the spool unwind till it reached a point marked with a dab of Gina's hot pink nail polish.

She checked her watch. Twenty-eight minutes, fifty-seven seconds. Her mentor, Mr. Hadrian, would be proud.

It wasn't long before there were two distinct tugs on the line, and she began to reel up the spool. It took a while to retrieve the two hundred feet, especially as the weight increased, but at last she received what she'd been fishing for— the end of Kannon's rope.

She pulled up a couple more feet of it before tying it around the base of one of the safety rails in a strong hitch knot. Tug, tug. The double jump of the rope signaled that it was secure. Now she could lie back and relax while Kannon roped up his climbing harness and made his way to her.

Despite the danger she risked a peek at the tiny rectangle of the van far below. She hated to put Brian through the strain but she didn't feel she had a choice. Without a twist of fate in New Mexico, she'd have been long since dead, and by the very hand of the assassin she was now risking her life to help. When she'd had Kannon's gun trained on him, she'd been tempted to pull the trigger. Had been a hairsbreadth away from doing just that when something inside her had begged her to spare him—the very killer Gina looked like she was falling for, and who seemed to be falling for her.

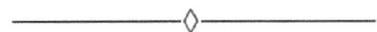

With Delta safe on the top floor, Brian fell back against the passenger seat beside Gina, his grip on the radio easing. He'd moved up there, immediately after Kannon and Ryota had left and together, they'd watched the little shadow scale the wall. Now that she was safe he seemed totally unconcerned.

She whacked his shoulder. "Hey, there's still two more to go up, you know."

"They've got lines, thanks to my wife," Brian clarified. "Ursula could do it."

Gina peered into the darkness. Looked as if Ryota was going up first. That was good because if the line was faulty then at least it wouldn't be Kannon plummeting to his death. She immediately crossed herself for her selfish, callous, bitchy sentiment.

"You know, when I first saw Delta climbing," Brian said, "I thought she was amazing. Thought she would make a terrific stuntwoman."

"And now?"

"And now she's carrying our baby."

"Two incompatible occupations, huh?"

"She doesn't see it that way. You know," he said, "nobody changes, so you better know who you're dealing with going in."

"I see. You're in favor of the long courtship."

At this point, Ryota was high enough that Brian and Gina had to lower their heads to see him advance. "I'm not talking about the other person, I'm talking about yourself. You don't change either, so you got to know if you can live with the situation. Which, in my case, is living with a little ninja daredevil."

"Whereas Delta has to live with a big ninja daredevil."

"Point taken," Brian said. "Now, you and Delta can talk about life with your dangerous men."

"Kannon's not my man," Gina said. Where was he, anyway? She couldn't see him at the bottom. Probably flat against the wall or in a bush.

"What? He hasn't succumbed to your charms, yet?"

"It isn't like that between us," Gina said. Holy. Exactly what Ryota had said about him and Tasanee. And Jarun about him and Wakai. Was she implying that there was more to their relationship?

She could feel Brian's steady gaze on her. "You going to spill?"

"Kannon and I are working together to recover Montri, though we both recognize that there is a chemistry between us."

Brian snorted. "Gina, your PR sounds like BS. No kidding about the chemistry. Delta had a bet going about whether or not you'd make him part of the mile high club on the flight over."

Gina squirmed at the memory of that disaster. "Yeah, well, you're going to have to pay up. I couldn't persuade him."

Brian shot her a quick grin before returning to watch Ryota who was more than halfway up already, aided by the rope. "Isn't me that lost the bet."

Gina chose to be offended. "What? You thought that I couldn't do it? I mean, turns out you were right but thought you'd have a little more faith in me."

"I know how men think."

"I thought men just want to get it on."

"Not with the ones they've got bigger plans for. Then, it's a slow seduction."

"Uh-huh. Like a long con."

Brian shot her another grin. "Now, who's showing little faith?"

Ryota reached the top. Kannon's turn. She could see him ascend in quick pounces. Crap. He was so exposed. *Don't fall, don't be seen, don't fall, don't be seen.*

She swallowed. "Thing is, Brian, I've got faith. In him, not me. I don't have what it takes to be with him. It—it's too scary. You know that with Delta."

"Yeah. I do. Except look where we are. Sitting here, dealing. And where would we be if they weren't in our lives? Sitting and dealing with other stuff."

Gina focused on the climbing black spot.

"I'm going to have to tell Ursula to hire a new office manager, aren't I?" Brian said softly.

"I—I don't know yet." She couldn't concentrate on the conversation. She was occupied with Kannon. *Don't fall, don't be seen, don't fall, don't be seen.* Her silent mantra worked. He reached the top. She leaned her head back against the seat and, for the first time since Kannon's feet left the ground, took a real breath.

Now, for the second stage. Getting to Montri.

Brian reached over and took her hand, squeezed it. "I think you do, Gina."

He had this calm, fond smile, as if he knew something she didn't. Something he claimed she did know. "No, I don't know anything. All I know is that I can't think about anything except that Kannon is in danger. I don't have room for another thought."

Her phone binged. She snatched it up. Darae.

Boat's sinking. Tasanee's taken. Hide.

As the message exploded inside her, Gina realized she had loads more room.

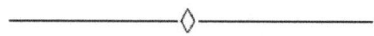

Kannon slid quietly over the penthouse balcony, drawing one of his silenced pistols as soon as his feet were planted. "Wait here," he whispered to Delta. "We won't be long."

Some killers relied on stealth and surprise to get the job done. Others on raw aggression and brutality. He liked to employ both.

With Ryota as his shadow, he slunk to the French-style balcony doors and looked sideways into the room. Two bored-looking rakshasas were watching brutal porn on TV. He considered the door handle. Not having to shoot through glass was preferable, though not likely. Besides, he hadn't custom-made his bullets for nothing.

He stepped up to the glass and fired. He put a neat hole in the temple of one and dropped the other with a bullet in the left eye. Both dead in seconds, with Ryota and him inside and at the hallway moments later.

The shattering glass had brought no one running, and Kannon now knew why. There was what sounded like another movie being watched, a violent one, from the shouting and screaming. Edging around the corner, he saw the light of a monitor coming from a room at the end of the hallway. He and Ryota strode down, and reaching the entrance, Kannon looked inside.

There was Wakai, behind him his sister, both of them watching a streamed video shot with a lowlight camera. He raised his gun to exterminate Victoria, when he realized what they were looking at. *The Pink Pussycat.*

The boat was badly shot up, smoke wafting across its body-strewn deck. The assault wasn't over. The camera focused on Ek as he gripped one of the cabin doors with his good hand, ripping it right off its hinges to let one of his lackeys blast away at the interior with his submachine gun. Vincenzo's cabin.

Gina. Does she know? He switched to Ryota on the other side of the entrance. He hadn't moved but his eyes blazed.

Kannon stepped forward and delivered a sharp kick to the back of one of Victoria's knees, lifting her off the floor with his arm around her thin neck even as Wakai turned, his look of satisfied pleasure dissolving into one of shock.

His gun muzzle against Victoria's temple, Kannon clipped out, "Call off the attack."

Wakai raised his hands. "I'll give you whatever you want. Just don't hurt her."

Kannon tightened his arm until Victoria wheezed. "Waste my time and both of you are taking the express route to the ground floor. Now, call them off."

Wakai shook his head. "I can't. It's over. We're watching a recording they sent us."

Kannon's finger tightened on the trigger.

Wakai reached up. "For God's sake, stop! I can give you

your boss. I can spare the captives. Please, don't hurt her. I'll do anything you want, just swear to me you'll spare her this time."

"Do you have any idea what this bitch has done?" Kannon growled. "Do you know what she is?"

"Please, she's sick," Wakai begged. "She can't help it. She's never been able to help it. It's my fault it came to this. If you have to kill someone, kill me. Please, Kannon, leave her alone."

This was the man who for the past two years had happily sent him on whatever mission was the flavor of his day, never mind the unnecessary danger he put Kannon and Ryota in. And now he wanted mercy? For his piece-of-shit sister? Kannon didn't know what he felt more, revulsion or pity. "Get Ek on the line now."

"First swear you'll let her go," Wakai replied. "I know you're a man of honor, Kannon. Promise me you'll let her go tonight and I'll make the call and see that Montri's released."

Kannon didn't have a choice. God knew what was happening on *The Pink Pussycat* at that very moment, and there was only one way to stop it. "Just this once, Wakai. Next time she and I cross paths she's a dead woman. Now dial that bastard."

Keeping one hand raised, Wakai slowly extracted his smartphone. He punched in the number, put it on speakerphone, then held it up for Kannon.

"Ek, this is Kannon," he said as soon as the line was answered. "I've killed your men and I've got Victoria and Wakai hostage. Release my people or I'll kill them."

Ek's voice came smooth and hard—and surprisingly calculating. "I already got who I came for. Montri's kid is with me and we're on our way back to shore. We've already had our fun with your friends. You can have what's left of them."

This would break Gina. As it was, he could feel rage pulse from Ryota.

"I want the girl back," Kannon replied. "Now."

"No," Ek contradicted. "You want your boss? Then get Wakai to tell you. You get me your boss and then we'll talk"

"No deal."

"Too bad, because it's the only one you're going to get. You kill Wakai and you'll never find Montri. Kill Victoria and I'll make sure Tasanee suffers. I won't kill her, but she'll wish I did."

The line disconnected.

"Where's Mr. Montri?" Kannon asked.

The corner of Wakai's mouth edged up a little. "I don't know how you got in here, Kannon, but right now Ek's calling more of his minions to come kill you. You know you can't hurt us, so I suggest you leave before—"

Kannon shoved Victoria away from him and nodded to Ryota. His junior aimed and shot the bitch in the foot.

"Okay! Okay!" Wakai gasped as Victoria yowled with pain, blood splattering as she fell back into a chair. "I'll make a call and have him released."

"Not good enough," Kannon said. "You're coming with me." Holstering his weapon, he grabbed Wakai by the front of his shirt, hauling the man out of his wheelchair and over his shoulder. Leaving Victoria for Ryota to tie and gag, he headed for the balcony.

"We've got company coming," he said as he emerged into the cool night air. "We have to get out of here quick."

Delta's dark silhouette materialized out of the shadows. "This your boss?"

Kannon dropped Wakai on the balcony. "The next best

thing."

He strode back through the apartment, and pressed the elevator button. The door opened onto the empty car, and he jammed a chair between the doors. That left Ek's scum to climb the stairs.

By the time he returned to the balcony, Wakai's hands were bound with line, his mouth tied with a backpack strap. The whole operation was done in under five minutes.

"I'll go first with Wakai. Then, Ryota, you follow with Delta."

Kannon couldn't remember a descent faster than this one. He didn't have to worry about Wakai holding on. The bastard had him in a death grip. At the bottom he tugged on the line to give Ryota and Delta the go ahead and then he tossed Wakai over his shoulder and moved as fast as he could. Back to the van. Back to Gina. And somehow, back to *The Pink Pussycat.*

CHAPTER 12 TWELVE

THE PINK PUSSYCAT listed in the fuel-slicked water, its once sleek hull lacerated with scorch marks and bullet holes, shattered glass glittering under the pre-dawn light. Ryota pulled a motorboat up to the stairs, and he and Kannon went up first to inspect, leaving behind Gina and the hapless Wakai.

She waited in the boat for the all clear, each second feeling like an hour. At last Kannon's head appeared at the top of the stairs, his expression grim, and gave a nod. The moment she was on deck, she nearly crumpled at the sight before her.

A few seagulls had landed to peck at the corpses that lay strewn around the deck. A dozen or so rakshasa bodies had been left where they fell, some dead from gunshot wounds, others with contorted faces, tongues lolling from choking to death on the poison gas.

As far as the crew, only the captain was in sight. She sat motionless on the deck, her crisp white uniform stained with crimson streaks, her wrists raw from where they'd been tied. Gina knelt beside her. "Captain?"

The woman didn't answer, her bloodshot eyes looking though Gina like she wasn't even there.

"She's in shock," said Kannon. "Your father's up in the sky lounge."

Gina looked at him, eyes wide. "He's alive?"

Kannon's jaw tightened, and again a brief nod.

Gina ran as fast as she could to the upper deck, her heart pounding, eyes tearing. The lounge was a nightmarish parody of its usual luxurious order, and there she found her parents.

Vincenzo lay in his chair, his pale face in sharp contrast to the blood on his torso. A mass of bandages had been pressed to his belly in a desperate effort to staunch his bleeding. Beside him, unconscious and cradled in Ryota's arms, was Darae. Dried blood coated her inner thighs, yet a medical kit lay open beside her, and her arms were stained up to the elbows from her efforts to save her husband.

Hands shaking, Gina gently peeled back her father's bandages, only to let out a sob of horror. A clean swipe of a blade had all but disemboweled him. Despite how close he was to death, Vincenzo's eyes were still open. Still bright.

"I was hoping you'd make it." His voice was barely a whisper.

Gina dropped to her knees. "Daddy...don't talk...we'll get you to hospital...."

Weakly he raised a skeletal finger to her lips. "It's too late. And I was nearly done, anyway. But I need you to listen now. Okay?"

Trembling, face wet, she managed a nod.

"You're my heir, Gina. The last of the Zaffini bloodline. You're all that's left of our family now. As long as your heart is beating we'll still be with you. If you listen to it, you'll always remember who you are. You'll always know what it is you have to do."

She caressed his forehead. "I will, Daddy."

"Then, you've made me very proud. Say goodbye to Darae for me. Tell her I love her. That I'm sorry I couldn't protect her at the end."

"I will, Daddy," Gina choked. "I'll look after everything."

"That's my bambina," he said. "That's my girl...."

Gina leaned her forehead to her father's, and a moment later, felt his last weak breath upon her face. "Goodbye, Daddy."

She remained there as Ryota wrapped Darae in a blanket and carried her gently out of the lounge. She spread another over her father, aware of Kannon standing at her side. When she was done, she asked, "What happened to the rest?"

"Dead," he replied, his voice flat. "Raped. Bound. Thrown into the sea to drown. That's what I got from the captain. They only spared her so that she could watch it happen. Only spared Darae so that she could watch your father die."

Gina wrapped her arms about herself and hunched over. She sat on a lounge chair and stared at the shrouded figure that was once a strong, vital man. Kannon sat close beside her. His arm came around and pulled her close. For a moment she let his warmth comfort her. And then she removed his arm.

"I know you mean well, Kannon. Only it's not what I need from you."

He stiffened. His hand, the one that had just cupped her shoulder, flexed, then retracted into a loose fist. A few beats later, he rose and stood. Silence stretched between them.

"Something happened to me, Kannon. Years ago. Happened right where you're standing now."

Still in his black outfit, he regarded her and in those dark eyes that had melted her with their heat, she now forced herself to stay solid. She owed him that much. "When I was fifteen, I loved this boy. Pricha. He worked for my father. At one of our top-end brothels, he shone the shoes of customers while they were busy with the women. He didn't have any family, so that was how he made his living.

"We all loved him. He was funny and kind, and he had this way of charming the socks off everyone he met. And he was really determined and hardworking. Intelligent and ambitious. And I had this huge crush on him.

"We were never officially boyfriend and girlfriend. Class differences and all. But we came up with lots of excuses to be together. He was the first boy I kissed. The first person who wasn't family that I would've done anything for."

"He was murdered." Gina lost her breath. For a full decade, she'd never spoken of this to anyone. And now in saying those three words, she realized time had healed nothing. Kannon started toward her, then stopped. He averted his eyes, looked out to the horizon where dawn was breaking. Well, wasn't she getting exactly what she'd asked for? She forced herself to breathe and then, to continue. "Wrong place, wrong time, as they say. When Dad told me he was dead, it was more than terrible. By that age I'd already lost my mom. Somehow losing Pricha was even worse. I must have cried for days. Then, Darae tracked down his killers.

"Three of them. They were dragged before me. Made to kneel on the deck where you are now. Three brothers, crying, none of them any older than Pricha had been. They told me how they hadn't meant to kill him. How they'd been hungry and needed money. How they'd only meant to scare him with the knife.

"Pricha had refused to give them anything, but they had seen by the way he was clutching his pocket that he was holding something of value. They tried to take it off of him and that's what led to the fight. To the murder. All over a hundred baht and—" Once again she had to fight to breathe. She fixed her gaze to the spot where Kannon stood. His shoes weren't black and shiny and polished as usual. Instead he wore boots, bloodstained and on one was a green leaf, probably from crossing the grounds at Maharaja Xecutive.

"The stupid boy had gone and spent all his money on a love charm. That's what the fight was over. He'd had it clutched in his hand when he died.

"I remember how my blood was boiling. How I'd been ready to slaughter the three of them. I was so filled with hate. Then the eldest boy, he fell at my feet. Confessed that he'd killed Pricha. Offered up his life but begged—begged that I spare his brothers.

"And then I saw how thin the three of them were. How ragged their clothing was. How dirty their faces. The youngest had wet his pants."

Gina let the memory replay in her mind. "Darae took me by the hand. Put a gun in it. She knew how much I loved Pricha, and she gave me the opportunity to avenge him. But it was more than that, Kannon. It was like a test. To see what I would do. If I was really tough enough to be my father's daughter. If I had what it took to be the heir to everything he'd built."

In Kannon's dark eyes flickered understanding. Yes, of course. "I guess it was like how your father was about your bullies," she acknowledged. "She didn't do it to be cruel. Even before my father married her, she always treated me like her own flesh-and-blood. It was more like a rite of passage. Time to grow up."

"I put the gun to that boy's head. The one that had killed Pricha. And...I pulled the trigger. And just like that, he was gone."

She shut her eyes, bowed her head. "Only then did I realize that I'd made a horrible, horrible mistake. It didn't make me feel better. It made things a thousand times worse. The boys holding their brother's body, sobbing. The blood. The burning smell of the gunpowder. Darae having to pry the gun out of my hand. I'd have given my life to take back what I'd done, and I swore right then that I'd never be put in that position again. That I—"

She couldn't go on. She was too weak, too tired. Too far gone.

Kannon finished it for her. "That you'd never care about anyone that much again you'd kill for them, give your life for them."

She raised her eyes to his. "But it didn't even take that. Tasanee shows up with a couple of gunmen and I shoot like I've been doing it all my life. What does that say about me?"

"Not to mention the company you keep." His voice held a jagged lilt of irony.

"I've never thought of you that way. At least, not entirely."

He faced her square on. "I'm the part of you that you hate, Gina. The killer. The person who doesn't care that he hurts others so long as the ones he loves are safe. I'm also the part you can't live without because without people like me it would all go to hell."

Even as he said those words, even as she saw the truth in them, she also saw another one. "That's not why I pulled away from you, Kannon. You're my Pricha again."

He strode over to her. "You telling me you love me?" His voice, always low and rumbly, was sharp now. "You're telling me you would avenge my death?"

"No, I—"

"Then I'm not Pricha. I'm Kannon. I'm the man who shuts the bullies up."

"No. You're baku."

He sucked in his breath. "Not that. Not anymore."

She was about to contradict that when he sighed impatiently. "You told me your story for a reason? You want me to do what you don't have the guts for? Who do you want me to kill? Rakshasas? Wakai? Who?" Anger and frustration hammered through each question. He wiped his hand down his face, and his voice switched to tired and low. "Tell me what you want, Gina, and I'll do it."

She wanted everything back the way it was. Only that wasn't going to happen. So, there was only going forward. One step at a time. "I need my father put in a boat."

He moved to make it happen.

"Are you sure there are no survivors?" Gina asked, hoping. "In the water or hiding in the closets?"

"We double-checked. You want us to check again?"

"Yes. Is—is Darae going to make it?"

"She should. She's torn up pretty bad but nothing she'll die from. She's on the powerboat. We should get out of here before the coast guard finds this."

That's when Gina became clear about one more thing she wanted. "We'll burn this ship. Send it to the bottom. I don't want them able to use this to terrorize the other gangs."

Kannon nodded as if it was the most natural of requests. "I'll see to it all."

Gina stood. Next step. "Meanwhile, I'll check to see how Ryota is doing with the captain."

Not well, as it turned out. The captain was now crying, a deep keening wail.

Ryota turned to her, his face pale and haggard. "I can't

get her to move."

Gina placed a hand on his back. "Find Kannon. And hey, we'll get Tasanee back for you. Okay?"

His eyes flashed in gratitude, he bowed and retreated. Gina crouched down, and got close. "Captain. I know you're hurting. It means you're alive. And so is Darae. I need you to get up and help her get to a hospital. Think you can do that?"

The captain rose to her feet, battered and bruised, and Gina helped her into the powerboat. She glanced at Wakai, and realized what a dangerous combination it would be to have the captain anywhere close to the man partly responsible for the death of her daughter. "Here, captain. Could you hold onto Darae? Keep her as warm as possible."

Gina turned to John Wakai, all trussed up. "We're going to back to the shore, and when we get there you're going to release Mr. Montri. We spared your sister, and now you're going to keep your end of the deal."

"I will," he replied.

"Good. As soon as we have him we'll let you go. Are you comfortable enough in the meantime?"

Wakai gave her an uncertain look. "Let me go?"

"Your friend Jarun cut a deal with me. When you see him you can tell him I keep to my agreements. Every single part of them."

He looked up at her, his expression at once relieved and confused.

"You have a question?" she asked.

"Given the circumstances. You don't seem..."

Gina stared at him, unmoving. "I don't seem what?"

"As upset as I thought you'd be."

"Oh, I'm way beyond upset, Wakai. I'm now in charge of something I never wanted thanks to you and your sister. Then again, at least I'm not flopping around in the bottom of a boat."

Kannon appeared at the top of the stairs with her father's body, and minutes later, they were heading back to Bangkok. The light of dawn illuminated the towering column of smoke and flame that engulfed *The Pink Pussycat*. The magnificent ship listed farther and farther, then sank beneath the waves, down into the inky depths below.

Gina didn't see it happen. Her eyes were to the shore, her thoughts on what to do once Alak Montri was free. She turned to Kannon on the seat beside her, to ask him what their next step after Montri should be, when she realized that she and Kannon were done. Once Montri was released, he had no reason to be with her. She was on her own. She had Darae and the rest of the Pink Stilettos, and that was it. *Tell me what to do and I'll do it, Gina.* Well, that was short-lived. Whatever she decided, she'd have to do it alone because Kannon would no longer be hers to command. Not that he'd ever been.

Spray splattered on her face, and wiping it from her eyes, she turned to him and said above the engines and slap of the water. "I guess there'll be no third date."

He twisted to her. He wasn't wearing his glasses, and the early light burnished his cheek. "What are you talking about?"

"You'll be Montri's again."

"How is that a problem?"

Didn't he get it? She leaned so her lips were against his ear. Wakai was at the back of the boat, and couldn't hear them. Still she wasn't taking chances. "Because I've got friends, Lwin and Dr. Chai, who are kinda peeved with your boss. So you in the company of me might not look so good."

"We could work around it," he said into her ear.

They could, too. Meet up somewhere, have a night of it.

One night where they could have a few hours of good, hot sex, and in the morning say their proper goodbyes. And then what? They couldn't have a relationship, and an affair was risky, too. No, it would be too frustrating, too—heartbreaking.

She said something that had never fallen from her lips before, that up to this night she'd never considered. "Let's not. It wouldn't be worth it."

She expected him to go neutral, the way he always did when pushed. Instead, his face clouded with sadness, and the smile he gave her was small and bitter. She'd hurt him. And there was nothing she could say or do to make it better.

She set her gaze once again to the shore. She could make out the solid extension of the dock now. Soon there'd be the wooden thumping of footsteps down its length. Soon there'd be orders and directions, and Montri's release. There'd be all those things and not what she could now see from the corner of her eye—Kannon bent over, elbows on his knees, rubbing at his swollen, beaten knuckles as if they were a drawing he could erase.

Gina pressed her hands together, bowing to the hundredth or so guest who entered the grand hotel ballroom where her father's eulogy service was about to take place. A couple of hours earlier the crowd had filled the Assumption Cathedral, the main church of the Archdiocese of Bangkok, and now that the somber Catholic rites had been completed, it was time to gather together once more—but not in remembrance.

The people who had gathered were the who's who of Bangkok's underworld. The city's top smugglers and madams, counterfeiters and hackers, conmen and killers. Many were genuine friends and associates of her father. All had come to hear what Alak Montri had to say. After all, if Bangkok had a Godfather, it would be him.

The elevator at the end of the hall opened, and the man of the hour appeared, flanked by Kannon and Ryota. Gina braced and forced herself to keep her eyes on the man in the middle and away from the more imposing Kannon. She'd not seen him since they'd docked on the shore six days ago. She'd gone to the hospital with Darae and the captain, and he and Ryota with Wakai to retrieve their boss. No contact whatsoever in six days. No matter how often she'd stared at her phone, it was never him who called. And she was left to scroll through the few pictures she had of him. Dancing. And one of him, glasses off, his expression saying, "You've got to be kidding me."

Well, what had she expected? She'd broken up with him. She didn't know much about dating but she figured if you told someone being with them wasn't worth it, then they were through. At least with a guy like Kannon, you would be.

Although Alak Montri still sported a few bandages, the remnants of his mistreatment at the hands of Victoria, his dress was impeccable, his stride full of purpose. He headed straight to her, and they exchanged bows of respect.

"I know this is a bad time, Gina, but I wanted a word with you before the ceremony begins," he said in Thai. "Ryota can greet the guests if you can spare a moment."

She'd half-expected this. She gestured to a smaller adjoining room she'd already set aside. "Of course."

She would've walked right in but Kannon cut in front and inspected the room first before giving a nod to the waiting Alak Montri. The head boss was cautious and justifiably so.

As soon as she and Montri were inside, Kannon closed the door and stood next to it. He crossed his hands in front of him, immaculate in his suit. He wasn't wearing his glasses, though she could've wagered they were in his front pocket.

Not that she was thinking of him. Not at all. She focused on her father's dear friend.

"First of all, I wanted to extend my condolences. Your family made the ultimate sacrifice for me, and I'm not about to forget it."

Gina nodded. "You and Tasanee are as close as blood to us, Alak. We'd never abandon you."

"And you've more than demonstrated your loyalty," he replied. "This is why I want to offer you a position at my side, Gina. Kannon has told me how instrumental you were in freeing me. How you risked your own life several times for my daughter and me. I'll need people like you if I'm to wage war on Wakai."

It took everything she had not to look at Kannon. He... admired her. Later, when she was alone with her phone pictures, she feel the pleasure of that but not while Alak Montri stood in front of her, ready to announce his move. "You have a plan on how to rescue Tasanee?"

Montri's expression tightened. "For twenty years I've fought to keep this city. I've taken on all comers. Enemies from every corner of the earth it seems, and I've beaten them all. However, victory requires courage, Gina. It requires bloodshed. And more than anything, it requires sacrifices."

Gina blinked. She wasn't understanding him. She couldn't be. "You're not suggesting that you'd leave Tasanee to—"

"I'm saying," interrupted Montri, "that your father gave his life so I could take back Bangkok from these monsters. How can I sacrifice any less and still be a man of honor?"

"But she's your daughter," Gina replied. She might've

felt sick if the shock of Montri's words hadn't left her numb.

"And it's because she's my daughter that she must now play her part. Today I am going to call for war on Wakai. I'm going to unite the gangs and crush these Cambodian vermin. They think they can control me. Today they're going to learn just how badly they miscalculated. Will you fight with me?"

Gina couldn't help it. Her gaze flew to Kannon. He didn't move, continued to observe them as if cut from stone. His expression was neutral. More neutral than humanly possible. It would take a tremendous effort to look that unmoved. She switched back to Montri. "I'll fight to drive the rakshasas out of this city, Mr. Montri. I swear I'll fight them with everything I've got. But I won't fight for a man who'd leave his own daughter to die, especially at the hands of monsters like those."

There was a long, dangerous pause. When he spoke his tone was all cold politeness. "Thank you for your honesty, Gina. I'm disappointed, but there are other allies. Perhaps you'll reconsider your position later."

He gave a curt nod, and strode for the hall, no doubt ready to make his speech to the gangs. Kannon fell in behind his boss, not sparing her a glance.

She was sure he didn't approve of his boss's abandonment of his daughter. She also knew that to defy his boss meant endangering his own daughter. He said he'd kill anyone to protect the ones he loved. She understood what he had to do. She expected no less of him. And she hated the man who had turned her and Kannon against each other.

"Bastard," she muttered, fuming at the heartlessness of her so-called ally. If he gave that speech, Tasanee was as good as dead, and soon enough the streets of Bangkok would be bloodied by yet another turf war. Dr. Chaiboonma had been right all along, only she'd been too naive to listen. Still, as

Montri himself had said, she'd risked her life for her god-sister several times already, and she wasn't about to give up on protecting her now.

Only, what to do? She tugged at her black dress in an effort to make it more modest. When the urge to shop had overtaken her after completing arrangements at the church earlier that week, she'd expected the universe to send a replica of the black dress from her favorite store in L. A.. Instead, it had delivered a knee-length, body-molding cocktail dress with a single strap across one shoulder. Gina thought it entirely inappropriate. She'd cringed when she put it on that morning, her bare shoulder revealing the curves of her crocodile tat. Every time she tried to put on something else the tingles crackled through her so bad that in the end she'd given in. She'd styled her hair so that it fell over her twisting blue ink but even now, she felt it burn through, clawing for her attention and everyone else's.

Attention.

She had it. She never asked for it. It was like the dogs who trailed her around. Kannon had pointed out how she seemed connected to everyone, and she'd dismissed that as something she couldn't control. Yet, here she was. The universe or God or some god had made her the center of attention, and this time she'd take full advantage. She flipped back her purple-streaked hair, exposing Timmy for the world to see, spun on her four-inch pink stilettos and strode through a second entrance that opened onto the front of the hall.

She crossed to the podium before the sea of guests, and surveyed their faces. There was Montri and his lackeys, expressions already impatient, waiting for her to finish saying her piece so that they could declare war. There were other people, too. Darae and her father's girls, their sheer number a good indication that there was scarcely a brothel or massage parlor open in Bangkok that day. She saw Pensri and Lwin. Dr. Chaiboonma and Kittyjack. They too were listening, as were numerous gangsters who must be weary of the endless conflicts that had bloodied them over the years.

She flattened her hands on the podium, ignoring the neat stack of cards that was her father's eulogy.

"Today, my friends, we have a traitor in our midst."

Shock rippled through the crowd. Whatever they'd been expecting, it wasn't this.

"And like all traitors," she continued, "this person presents a face of loyalty. He claims that he is our friend. Our mentor. Our protector. But whose interests is he really looking after? His own."

Montri's face was rapidly growing bright red, and without flinching, she turned to address him directly. "Alak Montri. Bangkok is once again under siege by ruthless foreigners. Once more you, your families, and your businesses are going to be ground under someone's heel. Tell me, whose judgment was it that resulted in this situation? Whose incompetence allowed John Wakai to seize power? Who was it that now wants that power back, no matter what the cost to those who have demonstrated true loyalty to this city?"

She paused, turning her gaze back to those assembled. "Bangkok is not one man. This city is our shared territory, and all of us should have a say on how to deal with the threat we now face. My father was smart, brave, rich, and well-prepared, yet we all know what his fate was. Rush to fight now, and how many more funerals are we going to have to endure? That is the lesson my father died to teach us."

There was silence in the room.

To go on, would only lessen the impact of her words.

She'd had no time to prepare, speaking only from her heart. Had it been enough to save Tasanee's life?

She was about to find out.

The program was for Montri to be the first guest to speak, but she had the podium, and instead she looked over his head to someone else. "I know that many of you have words to share regarding my father, so I'd like to begin with one of my father's most trusted colleagues, Dr. Chaiboonma."

The leader of the Bangkok Blondes stood up, and made his way to the front. As she relinquished the podium to him, he gave her a short bow—and a discreet thumbs-up. He turned to her father's mourners and echoed her words, pointing out that this was not the first time the city's stability had been jeopardized by an usurper and the poor decisions of one man.

As soon as he finished she called upon Lwin, who spoke with wisdom about the value of biding one's time, studying one's opponent before stepping into the ring against them.

And as her allies spoke, Gina studied the crowd, trusting her instincts as to who was with them, and one by one she called them forth. Some were lowly criminals, others respected gang leaders. Some she knew. Most she only knew by name and reputation. All called for caution and moderation, and the mood of the crowd smoothed from churning anger to calm reason.

Bit by bit the wind was taken from Montri's sails until the man was almost trembling with rage. When there was nobody left to call upon, Gina stood before the crowd again, her hands fisted. "Thank you all for coming today to share your thoughts and good wishes toward my family. That concludes this service. Luncheon is served across the hall. Good day to all of you."

Just like that she shut the door in Montri's face, denying

him any chance to undo what she'd staged.

Their eyes met as he stood, his jaw tight as he strode over, not stopping until he was almost nose to nose with her. Kannon had followed, keeping his distance, and now stood to the side, his expression implacable. "Vincenzo was my friend. I should have been allowed to speak."

"My father died defending your daughter," she spat back. "And you honor him by throwing her life away? You have no idea what friendship is, Alak Montri."

"I'm not going to allow Wakai to take my city."

"It's not your city anymore," she replied, pointing to the crowd, pointing out the window to the city itself. "It's theirs."

Montri paused, looking over his shoulder at Kannon, then back to her. "We'll see about that."

He was going to sic Kannon on her.

Montri spun on his heel and stalked off, Kannon in tow. Why didn't he give her a sign? Something to let her know that he approved of her stand. Or even that he disapproved. Or that she best leave town. Something.

"I'm sorry," Gina called, "but I'm unable to extend you an invitation to the luncheon."

Alak Montri kept moving, as did Kannon.

"I recommend you try street food," she continued. "It sums up the best of Bangkok."

She could've sworn there was a hitch in Kannon's step before he walked on.

CHAPTER 13 THIRTEEN

SPIRIT HOUSES WERE everywhere in Bangkok. Stationed next to homes, businesses, schools, parks, and even shopping malls, they resembled large doll houses. Thousands were scattered throughout the city, but Gina's favorite was a very obscure, very old one where Pricha used to leave offerings of little figurines to the resident spirit.

Since the spirit was seldom visited by anyone except a few elderly locals, Pricha had figured it might be bored, so he'd provided some entertainment. With bits of wood, wire and metal, he'd fashioned beautiful little figurines of horses, elephants and dancers, as well as some more exotic diversions he'd taken from Gina's stories of life in America—cartoon characters and pro-wrestlers.

And they were all still there, lovingly tended to by the infrequent visitors. Kneeling in the tiny ancient courtyard, the bright morning tropical sun simmering on her back, Gina placed the purple vixen figurine amongst the other offerings, then closed her eyes, palms together. She wasn't praying, exactly. She'd never been religious, though she'd always sensed that everything in the world was infused with some kind of vast, underlying power. It was in this presence that she meditated.

She'd come alone because she hadn't wanted anyone with her. No, that wasn't true. She'd wanted Kannon, except he'd followed Montri from the hall yesterday. He had made his choice, and so had she.

But the choices each had made put her in his crosshairs. Montri wanted her dead, and who better for the task than his personal assassin, the man who knew her better than anyone else. This man who wasn't her lover exactly, this man she was...dating? Had dated? Was he now her enemy? Was she now his—target?

She heard footsteps behind her. A deliberate scuff of heels on the paving stones. She opened her eyes, turned her head. Sure enough, it was Kannon. He looked down at her, eyes concealed behind her reflection in his mirrored sunglasses.

"How did you find me?" she asked, then nixed the question. "Never mind, you're not Asia's top manhunter for nothing. Did Montri send you to kill me?"

"Yes." His voice was flat.

Weird that she wasn't scared. Kannon never had scared her, even now when he was threatening to kill her—again. "And are you going to?"

He didn't answer, his gaze traversing the small area. "No guards?"

She glanced at the yellow dog that had followed her in. "Meet your replacement."

He adjusted his stance, and Gina knew it was to get a better view of the yard's rear and side exits. A hit-man checking out his escape route. The dog, seeming to think he was relieved of his duty, dropped to his belly and rested his head on his paws. Apparently loyalty couldn't be bought with a pile of leftover hors d'oeuvres.

At last he looked down at her. "You drew a line in the sand yesterday."

"Montri did. I tried to erase it."

"All you did was make him angry. Angry and paranoid."

Her own anger at Montri for abandoning Tasanee was what had rode her through the confrontation with him. And what of it? She had no plan for rescuing her god-sister. Didn't know who to turn to, now that the one man she could've gone to was set to kill her.

"And so he sent you out to earn the big bucks he pays you."

"Revenge can be expensive."

She exhaled the breath she didn't even know she was holding. "Kannon, I'm not exactly the most patient of people. And you found me on my knees, already. As a final request, could you get on with it?"

Instead, he squatted beside her. The front of his jacket fell open and she glimpsed his gun inside. "You didn't see your father when I brought you back from 70 Rai. You know what his health was. He rose from his chair and came to me like a new man. Carried you to the bed you woke up in. He only stumbled after lying you down. I got him into a chair and he asked me what had happened. I told him, and I knew he wanted me hurt for hitting you, which I understood. I'm a father, too. And it's because I'm a father that I couldn't let him do what I deserved. I need to stay alive for Zoe. My daughter's a strong girl, but like Tasanee, isn't ready to go it alone yet. Remember how your father was going to banish me? That hurt."

What? Wounded pride? Was that it? "I thought you

couldn't feel pain."

"I felt that."

"You felt the pain of humiliation?"

He cut her a swift look, irritated. "No, I felt the pain of you not being there. All I'm telling you is that for someone who doesn't know the pain of the sun or a knife or hot water, it felt like a miracle. I'm saying you make me feel things I haven't felt in a long time. Maybe ever."

Gina definitely felt warmth surge through her. Hope. Excitement. Connection. "So you're not going to kill me?"

Kannon gave her the same look of dry disbelief as on her phone pic. "You ever wondered why I told Brian I'd target you if he didn't deliver up the killer of Matsuda's son?"

"I've wondered that myself. I dunno, it was your way of showing how much you liked me," she teased.

His lips curled into a quiet smile. "Actually, in a way, yes."

"Now, this I got to hear," she said.

"I took a look at Delta and I thought there was a lot to like about her. Maybe it was even true, as Brian said, that he loved her. But I saw you and I thought that there was someone a man might give his life for. So I figured between the two of you, Brian would do his damnedest."

Someone a man might give his life for. And was he that man? "And if he hadn't, what then?"

"Lucky for us, it didn't come to that."

Crap, what did she have to do to get a straight answer out of him?

"Okay, are you going to kill me or not?"

"Woman, I just told you. No. I'm not going to kill you."

"There. Was that so hard?"

He glared at her. "Now I'm reconsidering."

She grinned, and his frown deepened then relaxed. There was a shimmering between them, a lightening, and if it had been any other way between them, they'd be kissing right now, holding and being held. Kannon had chosen her over Montri, even if it meant making Montri his enemy.

"I guess I owe you," she said.

"Big time."

"What did you have in mind?"

If the look he gave her before was full of heat, the one now made her feel as if she were about to walk on burning coals—hot and dangerous and exhilarating. He wanted sex from her, and she was more than happy to give it to him. And if he still wanted more, well, then—could she share a life with him and Zoe?

Oh God, Zoe.

She gripped his arm. "What about Zoe? What does this mean for her?"

He grunted. "She's safe, for now."

"Does Montri knows where she's at?" Gina persisted.

"Yes."

"Then you can't defy him, Kannon," she said, looking into his eyes. "You're a father. You can't choose me over—"

"I choose both of you," he interrupted, and reaching into his jacket pocket, produced a smartphone, offering it to her.

"What's this?"

"It was Montri's," he explained. "That's why I came to find you. He's not going to be a problem anymore, and we have a lot of work to do if we're going to save his daughter."

Gina's eyes widened on him. "Oh God, Kannon. You mean you…killed him?"

"No," he replied. "I still owe him a great debt for shelter-ing Ryota and me from the American Yakuza. And how could

I rob Tasanee of her father, even if he's a poor one? Zoe would never forgive me."

"So…where is he?" asked Gina.

"Don't worry. He's safe and sound with Lwin."

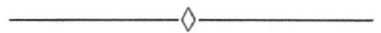

Montri stood on the raised porch of the small riverside bungalow, glowering down at the huge mass of crocodiles that surrounded him. "You're making a serious mistake holding me prisoner," he growled at Lwin in Thai. "A serious fucking mistake."

The old woman continued to stroke the snouts of her pets as she stood among them. "Don't be silly, Alak. You're free to go whenever you want. Just mind your step on the way out."

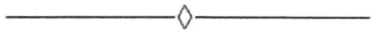

"First thing Mr. Montri did when Ryota and I got him out was start drawing up a list of everyone he was going to have killed." Kannon filled Gina in as they puttered through morning rush hour traffic. He pulled up to the rear bumper of a bright orange tuk-tuk that had just cut into his lane. That was his next vehicle, a tuk-tuk. He, Gina and Zoe could all fit and they'd always be one ahead of everything else on the road. "Before he even showed up at your father's memorial he'd already managed to find out where several of them were. It was his intention to send me out to collect their heads as soon as he declared war. Wanted me to get things rolling, as it were."

"You knew what he was up to?" asked Gina.

"Not until we were on the way to the service. In the car he

handed me the files. Explained what he was going to do. If I'd known any sooner I would have tipped you off. Lucky for Tasanee you were able to handle the situation. Have to say I was very impressed."

She retuned his compliment with a squinty-eyed look. "So impressed you couldn't give me a sign you were still on my side?"

"So distrustful that you thought I had to?"

Gina blew out her breath. "Touché."

And grinned. The cheek of her. A week without that grin and he'd felt himself drying up. He was going to bust if they didn't get all this sorted out. Because after seven days, he knew one thing for certain: he wasn't going through the rest of his life without her cheek.

"Let me guess," she said. "Wakai was at the top of the list."

"Yes."

"Except you let him out on his own reconnaissance."

"Yes, as per our agreement with Jarun. Hurt like hell to let him walk." Kannon winced. "Or the equivalent thereof. Dropped him in the elevator and sent it to the penthouse."

"That wasn't very kind."

"Wasn't kindly disposed."

"You going to tell me where we're going?"

"You going to stop asking me a whole bunch of other questions so I can?"

"Technically—"

He cut her a look.

"Yes, I am. Right now." And another grin.

He had to look away or he'd pull over and drag them together, and they wouldn't be driving anywhere for a good long time. "Only way to save Tasanee is to get her from the rakshasas fast. Only way to make that happen is to have Wakai's cooperation, and to get that, we're going to need an ally both sides trust."

"Who is?" she prodded. His turn to smile. Let her feel a little frustration, too.

Turning down a narrow lane he parked in the first available spot. "Jarun."

Gina looked around. "Jarun? We're practically in Chinatown. He lives here?"

"That's what we'll find out." He opened his door. "Best to walk the rest of the way. Come on."

Sempeng Lane was a very long, very narrow street that bisected Bangkok's Chinatown, its dimensions so tight that in parts Kannon could have touched both sides by stretching his arms. The winding passage was flanked with small shops running in a seemingly endless procession, selling every conceivable kind of product—though mostly shoes, cheap jewelry and hair accessories—all at prices lower than anywhere else in the city.

"Wherever you're taking me, looks like you've been there before," said Gina, walking in Kannon's wake. Even in the cramped quarters people made room for him.

"Not specifically," he replied over his shoulder. "I've walked this cursed street a hundred times before."

Gina's brow wrinkled in surprise. "Really?"

"This is Zoe's favorite place to shop," he explained. "I used to chaperone her and Tasanee almost every weekend."

"Isn't that a little overprotective?"

"They wanted me to come. Seems they got better deals when I was around."

Reaching a small stand selling freshly-squeezed pomegranate juice, Kannon paused, looking down at the old woman who was running the place. The woman stared with an apprehensive smile, her eyes swelling with fear. Like the waiter in the restaurant, he scared people, even when he didn't intend to.

Luckily, he had Gina. "Hello, ma'am," she said as soothingly as she could over the noise of the crowd. "We're looking for—"

In the reflective corner of his sunglasses, he caught sight of Jarun. "There!" He charged into the crowd, scattering the densely packed shoppers like squawking chickens. Jarun had apparently been heading back to the stall with a large basketful of pomegranates when the two men had spotted each other, and now he was striding toward him like an irate rhino.

"You've crossed the line this time!" Jarun yelled, his face as red as the fruits he was carrying.

"I'm here to talk."

"Oh yeah? Well, talk to this!" Snatching up a hard fruit from his basket he hurled it at Kannon, then setting his load down, commenced firing away.

Kannon deflected the fruit with his hands and forearms, one of them exploding, scattering both him and surrounding bystanders with bright red juice. Ducking, he darted to Jarun to kick aside the basket. He seized Jarun's wrist before a punch could connect. "Will you calm down! I'm not here to fight!"

Jarun yanked his hand free. "Then what were you doing scaring my mother?!"

Was this what it was all about? He glanced over at the old woman who whispered something to Gina. She translated. "She says he's really a good boy." Her gaze skittered to the surrounding shopkeepers who in a show of support or outrage, had started to surround Kannon brandishing canes, bottles and a cricket bat.

"Stay there. I'll take care of this," he told her. So, of

course, she came to his side, and began public relations with the mob, gesturing at him and other shopkeepers. In minutes they were chatting and laughing, and any who might've still had a bone to pick with him now settled for dirty looks before wandering off.

Kannon turned to Gina. "I'm not going to ask what you did because it worked, and that's all I care about."

She smirked. "You might care next time you come here shopping with your daughter. Then you'll be paying."

Jarun was still looking murderous. Gina brought her lips to Kannon's ear. "I think he'd like an apology for threatening his defenseless little mother."

"I didn't—" Kannon exhaled and turned to Jarun. He manufactured as contrite a face as his fuming mind permitted. "I apologize for any misunderstanding that has arisen as a result of my behavior."

Jarun looked over at his mother who was staring with shoulders sagged at the mess of pomegranates. "You should make it better by cleaning up the mess."

"I didn't—" Kannon exhaled again. If it wasn't that he needed the scum's cooperation, he would've shoved the entire basket down his throat. As it was, this was all payback for his earlier interrogation of Jarun. Without waiting for his answer, Gina began hustling around the fruit, tossing undamaged pomegranates in one basket, damaged in another, ordering him to take the baskets back to the stall. It was all done in no time flat.

"Now," Kannon gritted out. "Now, can we please sit down for ten minutes? To talk."

Jarun pointed to the stall. "Fine. But this better be important."

At the back of the stall, Gina sipped on a glass of juice as

Kannon tried to get the worst of the sticky red fluid off his suit.

"I thought you said you were going to arrange for Wakai and me to leave," Jarun complained. "It's been nine days. Nine days!"

"I said I would and I will," Gina said.

"And what about Victoria? I thought you were going to deal with her."

Gina slammed down her glass. "Jarun! I said I would and I will. Now, can we talk or do you need something other than your pomegranates squeezed?"

Jarun looked from one to the other of their faces, and agreed.

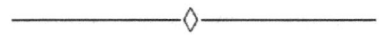

Wakai contemplated the mummified corpse of the infamous Si Quey Sae Urag, arguably the worst serial killer in Bangkok's long and sordid history. Worst one ever caught, anyway. The monster's shriveled body stood hunched, enclosed in a glass case resembling a white telephone booth. The killer's leathery skin was dark from the embalming process, the face bearing an expression of morbid interest in whoever gazed upon it.

After being cooped up in his penthouse for a full week, with only Victoria and his thoughts for company (rakshasa didn't count), it would seem peculiar to others that his first excursion was to a medical museum. The place was housed in Bangkok's oldest hospital, and abounded with bizarre medical curiosities. All around him were preserved bones and organs, stillborn babies in jars of formaldehyde and a hundred other grotesque displays.

His mother had once worked as one of the hospital's

groundskeepers, and left in charge of his little sister, he'd snuck into the museum with her. Both had been fascinated by the place, though for very different reasons.

For him, it was a welcoming departure from the chaos that marked their lives in 70 Rai. A sterile and ordered sanctuary from the filth, violence and misery that was his home and neighborhood. He could look at the body before him and take comfort that even such an abomination as Si Quey—murderer, cannibal, child killer—could be contained. That cold intellect could prevail over chaos, and that even a nightmare could be neatly boxed up and put on a shelf if one was disciplined and dispassionate enough to do it.

His sister was a different story. Whereas he longed for control over the horrors of Bangkok's underbelly, she ached to become one of them. She'd gazed upon the mummy with solemn admiration, like a pilgrim visiting the sacred remains of a saint. He'd known even then that she was insane, but the museum had inspired him. If he was smart enough, he could protect her. Veil the worst of her desires from the authorities, neighbors and, most importantly, his psychologically frail mother.

Now he realized that Victoria was the reason their mother had been so brittle, and why suicide had been, for her, the logical conclusion. Life, Wakai had learned as he'd looked at the bleeding corpse of his mother, really was an option.

An option the man he most feared had extended to him. After revealing Montri's location, he'd not expected Kannon Takahama to set him free. Not even with Tasanee as their hostage. Not even with Gina Zaffini underwriting Kannon's own promise. Yet he had, and Wakai had spent the week considering the whys and wherefores of it.

His phone rang, shattering the silence of the exhibit room.

Montri. Well, well. It had only taken a week. "Good to hear from you, Alak."

"This isn't Montri."

Gina Zaffini. It took a moment for Wakai to find his tongue. "May I ask why you're on Alak's phone?"

Despite the hatred she must feel for him, the woman's tone remained as calm and collected as when they'd been on the boat. "I'm afraid both of us have miscalculated, Mr. Wakai. You thought you could control Alak by holding his daughter hostage, but he is ready to sacrifice her to take you down. That isn't something I can tolerate."

The news hit him like a hammer. "You...killed him?" Wakai tried to keep the shock from his voice. "How did you get by—?" Of course. "Kannon Takahama."

"Kannon's a friend of mine," she asserted. "As are several of the most powerful gang leaders in Bangkok. And that makes me believe that we can both still get what we want. Let's cut a deal, shall we?"

He took a deep breath, trying to steady himself. No sooner did he seem to have control than it was snatched away from him. Would Alak have truly been so ruthless? Could his daughter have meant so little to him? Perhaps in his desperation to protect Victoria, he'd projected too much of himself onto his old boss, expecting the same kind of familial devotion. He remembered what Montri had said while on his knees in Wakai's apartment, remembered Montri's ruthless observance of his principles. Wakai loved Victoria, and had mistakenly believed that his old boss was capable of the emotion, too. What would happen when Ek found out? He eyed the grisly displays, the sight depicting any number of unpleasant possibilities.

"Who else knows about this?"

"Aside from you and I, only Kannon and a couple of trusted others," she replied. "I know that this must upset your plans, Mr. Wakai, but I believe that we can still work together."

There was something about Gina Zaffini that made him want to believe. "And what makes you think that?"

"Because I'm guessing our motives are similar. I want to protect Tasanee. You want to protect your sister. We've both done what we've had to do to keep our families safe."

"Then we've both got a major problem," he said. "I've promised control of the city to the Cambodians. That's the only reason they haven't laid a finger on Tasanee so far. Without Alak, I don't see how I'm going to deliver on that, so things aren't looking very good for either of us at the moment."

"They'd have been a lot worse if I hadn't stopped Montri before he declared war on you," she countered. "He was ready to do exactly that at my father's memorial service."

She was implying she'd saved his life, that therefore he owed her. He wasn't playing that game. He was sticking to chess. "All you did was buy a little time. I left Alak alone this past week so that he could heal from his injuries and bury his friend." This was partly true. The other part was he didn't want to make the first move, in case it was the wrong one. "The Cambodians are already impatient with the delay."

"Then we'd best come up with a plan PDQ," she said. "Otherwise we're both going to wind up as dead as the people in that museum you're in."

Wakai almost dropped his phone in shock. "How did you—?" Again, he answered his question, with a variation. "Your lover."

Her quick inhalation confirmed it. So, Kannon had

developed a weakness, one who thought she could blackmail him. He let her prattle on. "Like I said, Kannon's a friend of mine. And so are a lot of other dangerous people. If I'd wanted to harm you I could have easily done so. The fact that you're still breathing is a show of goodwill. You're a very smart man, Mr. Wakai. But I'm pretty smart myself. If we work together, I think we can both benefit."

There had to be a catch. "What about your father? Don't you want vengeance?"

"I want Tasanee back more. Can we meet?"

How gracious of her to pretend he had a choice. "Where? When?"

"How about at the museum café?" she replied. "Right now."

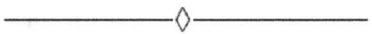

"Watch him. He's what you call a smooth talker," Kannon warned Gina as Wakai glided his wheelchair toward them in the café.

Kannon sat beside her, Ryota stood nearby. She could feel hostility rise off both men. She took a sip of tea, though at the moment, she'd have preferred something stronger. Forget about cutting the tension with a knife. She'd need a chainsaw.

Once, she'd sympathized with Wakai. It must suck to have a psycho for a sister. It must doubly suck to be confined to a wheelchair as a result of taking a bullet for your boss. And then to have the boss hunt you because you were trying to protect your sister from him.

But she had not appreciated his jibe. Your lover. As if Kannon was a despicable choice. As if he were beneath her. How dare he? Smooth talker. Yeah, right. More like hypocritical, snobbish, conniving…underling.

Kannon was watching her. She could see the direction of his eyes behind his glasses. He was worried that she was worried. She gave him a big smile and saw his lips twitch in response.

Wakai came up to the table, his eyes flickering back and forth between them. The corners of his mouth pulled down in disgust. Let him look, let him draw whatever conclusion he wanted. "You have some kind of plan you want to discuss."

He made it sound as if he was doing her a favor. She knew it was all talk. Still…she reached over with her cup of tea and sloshed it over his crotch. Kannon sat up straighter. Wakai gripped the arms of his chair and glared at both of them. She waved a finger. "Attitude."

Wakai's face went tight and he stayed quiet.

"Now. I like to know a little bit about the people I do business with. Especially with one who double-crossed his boss."

"I didn't want that," Wakai burst out. He snapped his mouth shut but Gina rolled her hand for him to continue. "Alak found out about my sister. He did what he always did when he discovered one of his people had family who was his enemy. He offered me the chance to kill her myself. Given my service to him." He gestured at his legs. "Cleanly. Humanely. If I didn't, then he'd get him"—Wakai jerked his head at Kannon—"to kill us both. Simple as that. We both know how—inflexible he is."

Yes, didn't she? "Why didn't you just run? Why drag the whole city into this?"

Head jerk to Kannon. "Again, because of him. There wasn't anywhere I could have taken her that he wouldn't have followed. And after Alak found out about my sister's website

—after he saw what she'd done to all those children—I knew he'd hunt the world for her."

"And how did Alak find out about it?" asked Gina.

Wakai squirmed in his seat, whether from her question or his wet crotch, it was hard to tell. "Don't know. Once he did, I didn't have long to act. I did the only thing I could do and cut a deal with the Cambodians. They were the only ones with the muscle to protect Victoria and me, except they wanted a lot in return."

"They are allies of yours?"

"Hardly. They were my sister's friends, not mine. They kept such a low profile in Bangkok I didn't even realize their numbers until Victoria told me."

Gina leaned forward. "So it was she that suggested you go to them for help?"

Wakai snatched up napkins and patted himself, sopping up the tea puddled between his legs. Gina let him, though she could tell by the faint narrowing of Kannon's right eye that he would've hurried things up. Wakai tossed the sodden napkins back on the table. "I know what you're thinking. That she's the one that leaked the website to Alak. That she orchestrated the whole thing to get me to help them."

"Sounds like what you were thinking, too," Gina lobbed back.

"I know Victoria. She'd never do that to me."

Was he really that naïve? "You're saying the pedophile serial killer wouldn't betray your trust?"

"You don't understand our relationship," Wakai replied.

Naïve or loyal to the point of stupidity. "I sure as hell don't."

"Perhaps you should consider how many people your 'friend' here has killed over the years." He cocked his head at

Kannon. "I'm willing to wager Victoria's tally is smaller. The only difference is that your hit-man only knocks people off after they've turned eighteen, so don't preach morality to me. We're all killers at this table."

Ah, there it was. There was the danger of Wakai's words. He didn't unbalance others with lies but with the truth. Yes, they were all killers, despite whatever distinctions she had hoped to make between them. Between people like her who were given no choice or Kannon who chose his victims or Victoria who enjoyed the killing, in the end the result was the same. People died. She felt Kannon slant a look at her. Like the time with Lwin, he was carefully tracking their Thai conversation, monitoring her responses, all her nonverbal signals. She should hate herself for not being any better than Victoria. Then again, it also meant she was as good as Kannon. "I suppose we'll have to agree to disagree on that point. Time's short. Let's get back to business."

Wakai gave a little smile. He thought he'd scored a point. "Let's. I'm dying to hear what you've come up with."

Gina laced her fingers together on the table. "You and I both know that there was only two ways the gangs of this city could have been bullied into falling in line with the Cambodians. One would be if Montri seized control again and you used him as a puppet. The other is if your sister's friends had the muscle to enforce their will."

Wakai nodded. "Correct. My plan with Alak apparently backfired, and the Cambodians don't have enough resources to take the city."

"And since you can't deliver on your promise it seems likely Ek's going to kill you as well Tasanee," Gina continued. "So you're back to square one—make a preemptive strike and decapitate your enemy before he realizes his position."

Wakai gave her a wary look. "Only where would that leave Victoria and me? Defenseless."

"Not if you had an ally that could protect you," Gina countered.

"And why would you do that after I helped kill your father?"

"Because you still have Tasanee to bargain with. She's my sister, like Victoria is yours."

Wakai waved a dismissive hand. "Only she's being held by Ek, not me. Besides, Victoria wouldn't go along with it."

"Not even if she knew it was the only way to save your life?"

Wakai hesitated, and Gina pressed the point. "Seems to me that if you're as close as you say you are, she would. And if Ek and she are such good friends I bet she could easily rescue Tasanee, too. At this point, it's the only viable option." She paused and then conceded, "For all of us killers."

Wakai rubbed his chin. No doubt it was meant to convey thoughtfulness, but Gina was sure she could see something else in his eyes.

Fear.

She leaned back, crossed her arms, and waited.

CHAPTER
14
FOURTEEN

COMFORTABLE IN HER lounge chair, Victoria wormed out
the last flecks of dried blood from under her fingernails with a
cuticle trimmer. The boy from the fishing boat hadn't disappointed her, but he'd had his vengeance—her fingertips were
aching almost as much as the stump of her missing toe.

A shadow fell across her, and looking up she saw that
Wakai had wheeled out onto the penthouse's balcony. "Try
hydrogen peroxide," he suggested.

"Oh, you're back," she replied, setting down the trimmer.
"Ek's been trying to get hold of you."

"I blocked his calls while I was out."

Victoria sighed. "Why are you two always tormenting
each other? He just wants to know when you're going to get
started with Montri."

"I told him I'll handle it and I will."

Her brother's voice was final, and she knew better than to
argue the point. She pulled up her leg to pluck at the dressing
over her mutilated toe. She couldn't wait to change it so could
check on the rate of healing. At least her accident had given
her useful knowledge. "Fine. I'll leave you to sort it out.

Where did you go? I didn't even hear you leave."

"The museum."

Ah. She had fond memories of that place. She and John alone together, while their pinch-faced bitch of a mother had dug dirt. "Haven't been there in years."

"It's still the same. Good place to go and think."

"Think about what?"

"About you and me. About maybe taking this chance to get out of Bangkok. Maybe settle down somewhere else."

His face was set in a way that worried her. "Get out of...John, what are you talking about? Why would we leave now?"

"I promised Ek the city. Now that he's got it, why does he need me anymore? Why does he need you?"

"He needs you for exactly the same reason Montri did. To keep things running."

"And what if I'm not interested in doing that?"

No. He always turned the situation into one that he could control. She'd always let him think that because it suited them both. "John, this isn't just a deal. I keep telling you, we're family. And family hunts together. Mates together."

John's body went solid, his face inscrutable. "So you love him?"

Love was alien to the rakshasi, an abstract she no longer had to pretend at feeling. "I share blood with him. That's why it's so important that we all get along. Why we can't up and leave."

Her brother sat there, holding her hand, his expression one of troubled contemplation. The silence was becoming uncomfortable when at last he spoke. "So be it. If we're going to carry on with this operation, then I'd best get started. First, I want to see Tasanee. Make sure she's being properly cared for.

I wouldn't trust Ek to water a houseplant."

Victoria shook her head. "Ek doesn't want you knowing where she's being kept. He's afraid you'll steal her like you did with Montri."

"So you're keeping secrets from me?"

Really, when would he understand that he wasn't the alpha male? "If I tell you, Ek's going to be upset with both of us and, besides, I promised him I wouldn't. I know where she is, and I know she's safe. Can't you trust me on that?"

"I suppose I'll have to. If I'm going to be kept in the dark then I need you to do something for me right away."

"And what's that?" she asked.

"I want you to pick up a copy of today's paper and go take a video of her holding it. I'm going to a meeting with Montri tonight, and I'll need it."

Montri? That was progress. "I can do that. Will you tell Ek you're seeing Montri? He wants to see action, and this'll cheer him up."

Wakai smiled. "Deal."

She kissed him, a long, lingering goodbye. She'd been away from Ek's people for a week now, and she was getting revved. She ended the kiss—it was always her who did—and reached for her crutch. "I'm going to change the dressing, and then I'll go. Be back soon. "

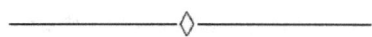

As soon as the elevator closed behind his sister, Wakai tapped on his phone.

Jarun answered on the first ring.

"She's on her way," he said. "Make sure you take it easy. If she finds out she's being followed, then they'll move the girl. There won't be any second chances."

"Don't worry. I'll take care of it."

Though Wakai had trained himself to repress his emotions, even he couldn't ignore the lump he felt in his throat. "Thank you so much for helping Victoria and me. I swear I'll make it up to you."

"We're brothers," Jarun said. "I'm sorry I didn't help you sooner. Now get yourself out of there. I'll be in touch once I have her in a safe place."

"Just be careful."

"You know me," Jarun replied, and disconnected.

Wakai set aside his phone and wheeled to the elevator, relief rolling through him. If there was one person in the world he could still trust, it was Jarun.

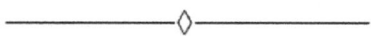

Tasanee pressed her feet to the rough brick wall of her cell as she gripped the chain, her slender legs quivering with effort, her body dripping with sweat, as she tried to pull it free from its anchor. Yet, she barely managed to loosen it. With a choked sob of frustration, she fell to the floor and kicked over the electric lantern that was her only source of light. She lay there, panting on the bare stone as bloated flies buzzed around her attracted to the scent of fear and pain and death.

Swatting them away, her gaze drifted to the bloodied hook that hung from the ceiling on the other side of the chamber. Victoria hadn't hurt her. Hadn't so much as laid a finger on her. Instead she'd spent the previous night watching the horrors inflicted on the Burmese boy, felt the warm flecks of his blood splatter on her. She'd begged Victoria to stop, pleaded with her first to let him go, and then to just let him die.

The torture had gone on for hours—until finally, finally, the boy had expired and he was spared what Wakai's sister had done to him, then.

She'd wanted Ryota. His quiet voice and gentle touch. But it became too much to think of him and listen to the sounds from across the room, and she'd curled into a ball, clapped her hands over her ears and tried to block it all out.

Beyond her cell, she heard a rusted metal door squeal open, and she dragged herself into a squat. She heard the click of Victoria's crutch as the woman made her way down the stairs, then a voice spoke, deep and gravelly, infused with a rural Cambodian accent. "What are you doing here?"

Then that low drippy sweet voice from last night's nightmare. "Not happy to see me?"

"Surprised to see you back so soon."

"John didn't call you?"

Tasanee heard the man spit. "No. He finally getting off his ass"—there was a mean chortle at the cruel joke—"and doing something?"

"That's why I'm here. Got to take a video of the brat. Proof to Montri she's still in one piece. What are you doing here?"

"What the fuck does it look like? Guarding. You sure you weren't followed?"

"I kept one eye on the rearview mirror the whole way here. Besides, the last couple of miles it's open road. Nobody could have followed unless they were invisible."

The man grunted, apparently satisfied.

"So you fed and watered her yet?"

"She's got a bottle in there. She didn't want to eat anything."

After what she'd witnessed, Tasanee doubted she'd ever

be hungry again.

"Well, might as well get to work then. Don't want her looking too skinny in the video."

Tasanee retreated to the corner of her large, airless cell, huddling there as she heard a heavy bolt pulled back. It opened to Victoria, her body scrubbed clean of blood, wrapped in an attractive amber sundress, perfume covering the stench of another's agony which otherwise would have clung to her.

"Good morning." She smiled, waving away the flies with a newspaper as she hobbled into the room. Although he worst of the gore had been washed down a drain in the center of the floor, Tasanee could hear the slight stick of the woman's feet to the stained stone floor. "Time to prove to your father that you're still alive."

Tasanee stifled a whimper of fear as Victoria shuffled closer with the tabloid.

"Take this and hold it in front of you." Victoria gave the paper an impatient wiggle. "I don't have all day."

Tasanee did as she was told, and Victoria held up her phone. "Have anything to say to your Daddy?"

She shook her head.

"Not even after what you saw last night?" Victoria prompted. "Don't you want to tell him about all the fun we had?"

"My father knows who you are," she replied. "So does Vincenzo Zaffini."

"The Italian's dead," Victoria said and clicked, then stepped back and aimed the phone again.

Tasanee knew it was likely, but still it hurt. "The Pink Stilettos will come after you. Kannon Takahama, too." And so would Ryota.

Victoria clicked and moved to get a different angle. "No,

they won't. They work for Montri, and unless we get every-thing we want, when we want it, we're going to start mailing little bits of you back to your daddy. So, you see"—click!—"one way or another, you two are going to be reunited."

Tasanee's fists clenched on the newspaper to keep the tears away. Her father would not see pictures of her giving into these bastards. He would see her strong, and worthy of him.

Her silence seemed to bore Victoria, and she dropped her phone back into her purse. "I think that ought to do."

As Victoria turned to go, Tasanee couldn't stop herself. "Why did you do that?" she blurted. "Why did you torture him?"

The woman looked over her shoulder, her crutch pivoting on the wet grime. "If I were you, I'd be more worried about myself than a dead fisherboy."

"But why?" Tasanee repeated. She could understand gangland violence. She grasped the concepts of threats and intimidation and the elimination of rivals. She even fathomed the necessity of torture to extract information. Even in the brutal circles her father ran in, she'd never heard of the depravity she'd witnessed.

Victoria leaned on her crutch. "From the time I was a little girl I remember wondering the same thing. Why I needed to hurt and destroy things. Why it made me feel so good to throw poisoned food to stray dogs, then watch them as they died in the gutter. I knew it wasn't normal. I knew that everyone except my brother was afraid of me. Even my own mother used to wince at the sight of me. That's why I went in search of answers. In search of others of my kind. And I found them. We're rare, but we have the common instinct to find each other. And I learned the reason we do what we do. It's because that's what we were made for."

Tasanee shook her head. "I don't understand."

"How could you?" Victoria thumped her way to the door. "You're not a rakshasi."

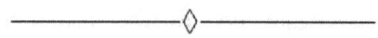

The outskirts of Bangkok couldn't have been more different from the heart of the metropolis. Here, the skyscrapers and urban sprawl thinned to small wooden houses set along the edge of the jungle, connected by narrow dirt tracks and ancient canals, each with its own orchard or rice field farmed by the same family for generations.

Pulling onto the shoulder of the muddy road, Kannon got out of the SUV, looking across the tropical farmland at a distant ruin, its crumbling brick structure overgrown with vegetation and tree roots. According to Kittyjack, it was a former Portuguese trading house, now centuries old. Right now, he was downloading all the rest of her intel.

"I see it," he said into his phone.

"Thenhappyhuntingkiller," Kittyjack chirped.

Above him her drone flew back towards the city, its rotors a faint hum in the still country air.

"And here I was thinking you had some kind of sixth sense," Jarun grumbled as he, Gina, and Ryota followed him out of the vehicle. "Turns out you just cheat."

"I do what works," Kannon replied, as he scrolled through the drone photos of the place on his phone. "And what works allowed me to catch you twice and rescue Mr. Montri."

He looked at Gina, who was leaning over the hood of the vehicle as she scanned the Portuguese ruin through binoculars. "What do you see?"

"Not much. Victoria's car is parked out front, and so are a

couple of Land Rovers. Your buddy Ek might even be there."

If he was, there was about to be a rematch. Hopefully, bullets penetrated the giant. Gina lowered the binoculars, her face tight with worry. He did not need to see her like that.

"Any dogs?" Kannon slid off his mirrored sunglasses. The last thing he wanted was reflection off the lenses to give them away.

Gina checked. "Nope."

"Then the three of us will go on foot," Kannon instructed Jarun and Ryota, before turning to Gina. "As soon as we have her, you drive in and pick us up. Agreed?"

Gina rounded the truck to stand beside him, shielding her eyes from the sun. "And what happens if they get away with her?"

"They won't," he said. He wasn't entertaining any other possibility. He'd get this job done, and he'd focus on getting Gina into his life. And not the Gina facing him right now. She wore cargo pants, a gray t-shirt and hiking boots. When *The Pink Pussycat* sunk so had her wardrobe, and she'd replaced it with this practical junk. Her hair was back in an utilitarian ponytail and she didn't have a lick of makeup on. She still had a beautiful face without it, only she wore makeup for fun or when she was taking herself to a place of fun. This...this was as if he had a different woman with him. Then—and he could see how much effort it took—she tugged up the corners of her mouth into a smile.

"Wanna kiss for luck, baku?"

He glanced across at Jarun and Ryota, standing a short ways off. He figured Ryota suspected the relationship between Gina and him wasn't entirely professional, but Jarun didn't know anything. And he wanted it kept that way for now. The more people who knew that he cared about Gina, the more vulnerable she was.

"Don't need luck."

Gina's smile wavered. The next thing, the lip would come out.

"Things go sideways in there, don't come after us. Leave."

The lip didn't come out. Instead the chin came up. "To hell with that."

"You need to be around to make another plan."

"If I'm not willing to leave Tasanee behind, why would I leave you behind?"

"I'm not an innocent, that's why."

"Neither am I."

He didn't know what to do so he glared. That had its usual effect. Her grin was blazing. "As I see it, there's only one solution," she said.

He waited. She got up close so her perfect breasts made contact with the sleeve of his suit. "Don't screw up."

Each of the three words was said with her lips puckered and pouty. He felt his whole being contract with the need to grab her up and kiss her. More than that. Plant himself inside her and feel the soft clench of her around him, listen to her noises—

"Third date," he said. "Then you get your kiss."

The fact that nobody was in sight meant one of two things. The rakshasas were either sloppy, or hiding, lying in wait to ambush anyone who attempted a rescue. Seeing as they were experienced guerrilla fighters who prowled the dense jungles of their mountain homeland, Kannon's money was on the latter, and he whispered as much to Ryota and Jarun as they observed the ruins from behind a fallen log.

It had taken them the better part of an hour to make their approach, staying low as they made their way along the bank of an irrigation canal, then creeping though a grove of jackfruit trees, to get to their present position, a few hundred feet from the crumbling brick walls of the trading house. Getting this close hadn't been much of a challenge, but ahead of them was a flat overgrown grass field.

Ryota's eyes were fixed on the house. Where Tasanee was. Kannon had watched him closely, but so far Ryota hadn't let his emotions interfere. Without turning from the house, Ryota said, "So how do we take it?"

Kannon studied the maps on his phone one more time to make sure he was properly oriented. He hated being unprepared. This was exactly what had happened at Triple 9 when they'd gone in too quickly. Only this time there wasn't any choice. At any moment Ek might discover that Montri wasn't under Wakai's control, and Tasanee would be tossed to the rakshasas like meat to wild dogs. "I'm going to cross the field, then climb over the wall. On the other side should be a small courtyard. From there, I can get into the main building."

Ryota's lips thinned. He wanted in, Kannon knew. All his apprentice said was "And what about Jarun and me?"

"You two are going to circle around to the road and, very quietly, take out any guards they've posted. Then make your way to their vehicles and prepare an ambush. If they attempt to run, that's where they'll head."

"And what if they have the girl?" asked Jarun.

"Then do whatever you have to do to keep them from driving away with her," Kannon instructed. "It shouldn't come to that."

The two men nodded their understanding, and Kannon began to crawl through the field, allowing the tall, waving grass to conceal him as he inched forward.

The going was painfully slow; he constantly searched his surroundings as he advanced, and when he was halfway across he finally spotted something. There, in the shadows of a clump of bushes, was a rakshasa, all but invisible as he sat cross-legged, rifle in hand. There appeared to be only one of them.

Kannon froze, hunkered down and plotted out the field for every scrap of cover, then crept onwards. Foot by painful foot, he flanked the guard, edging out of the man's field of vision until he was a scant twenty feet away. Carefully he leveled his silenced pistol.

Silencers themselves didn't make a gun particularly quiet. As soon as a bullet surpassed the sound barrier it made a bang more than loud enough to raise an alarm. That's why he made his own ammunition. The exact amount of gunpowder to bring the slug up to the threshold without breaking it. The result was a bullet that could only be used at close range, but was very, very quiet.

There was a soft pop, and the rakshasa fell backwards, a neat hole in his temple.

One last look around, and Kannon burst from his hiding place, reaching the wall in a few strides. His pistol in his belt, he scaled the wall, the missing bricks making the job easy, and poked his head over the top to survey the courtyard. Deserted.

Dropping down, he got to the nearest door. Kittyjack hadn't been able to find any details of the interior, so from here on in he was working blind, his only advantage being that nobody knew he was there.

A gentle tug on the door. Unlocked. It creaked open and he slipped into the darkness.

———————◊———————

Ek growled as he fucked Victoria up the ass, fingers gripping her hair as he thrust, not caring if it was too hard. She took whatever he inflicted, which pissed him off at times. He preferred them with a little more fight.

Over the sounds of her moans he sensed something. In his time, he'd been the target of numerous assassination attempts, the byproduct of the rape, robbery, and violence he inflicted as a matter of course. Only once had he ignored his instinct, having had a bit too much to drink and being distracted by the tight rear of a sexy pool shark at the time, and the result had been a fight with Kannon that had nearly done him in.

He pulled out of Victoria and yanked up his pants, his finger to his lips as she twisted around. He retrieved his submachine gun and skulked to the door to listen.

A soft pop. A rattling breath. A dull thud. Someone had come to visit.

Ek shoved open the door and stalked through the shadowed passages, keeping his steps light. Edging around a corner he saw one of his men lying face-down on the stone floor, a hole in the back of the head, which meant that the bullet had come from—

He spun and squeezed the trigger.

Kannon Takahama gripped the muzzle of Ek's submachine gun, deflecting it away. The noise of the rapid-firing and strafed masonry was explosive in the closed space. Montri's man jammed his pistol against Ek's chest and fired. Heat and pain ripped through Ek.

And underneath it all, he detected the scent of his own death.

A roar broke from him, and with an almighty shove, he

sent Kannon flying backwards into a wall with bone-jarring force. He'd die creating even more death. Lurching, he slammed his fist into the ribs of Montri's number one hunter, heard the crunch.

The effort cost him, and weakness rushed through him. Iron hard knuckles mashed Ek's throat; he sucked air on a rattling gasp. One, two, three punches to the face and then a kick to his damaged chest and he felt the sharp squeeze of a lung collapsing.

Ek fell to his knees, and snarled at Kannon like a cornered dog. Kannon picked up his pistol, leveled it at Ek, and there was a loud bang—not from Kannon.

His vision dancing with spots, Ek shook his head to clear it. It was Victoria, smoking gun in hand, smiling down at him.

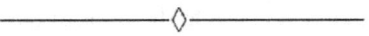

Gina chewed her lip as she waited, the endless silence unnerving. Just as she checked her phone for the twentieth time in twenty seconds, it chimed with a text from Kittyjack.

prolly 2 l8 bt atachd r d plnz of d NcyD. gud luk.

"Seriously?" She mentally translated the message, then pulled up an attachment of a crude map showing the building's interior. The place was a maze of rooms and corridors, but on its western side, she spotted a stairwell to a cellar. Gina tightened her hold on the phone. The perfect place to keep Tasanee—underground, there'd be no way any cries could be heard.

The message had already been copied to Kannon. Fat lot of good that was with his phone muted.

Automatic weapon fire echoed across the field.

"Oh, fuck." She trained her binoculars back on the building. Nothing and nobody. Another distant bang.

Blood trickled into her mouth, she'd bit her lip so hard. She ached to go help. Except Kannon had made it very clear that she was to stay put until called. Maybe it was all going according to plan, and she needed to stick to it. Maybe she needed to have a little faith. Her gaze skittered to the phone. "Phone, baku. Phone."

All was quiet, then the front door of the building opened to three rakshasas struggling to carry a huge, bloodied man over to the nearest Range Rover. Ek. Halfway there, more gunshots rang out, cutting all three down, and Ek collapsed to the ground.

All was still again.

The binoculars jiggled in Gina's shaking hands and she strained to focus on the bodies. Ek was moving. Hand over hand he dragged himself towards the Range Rover, leaving behind a bloody trail. At the driver's door he struggled to his feet, then Ryota strode up. He pressed his gun to the back of Ek's head and pulled the trigger, dropping the rakshasa leader execution style.

Gina bit back a shout of happiness. Yes!

Ryota raced to the building door, Jarun materializing out of the underbrush to join him.

Where the hell was Kannon?

"Fuck this," she cursed to herself, and climbing into the SUV, threw it into drive. She flew down the road. Kannon had to be okay. He had to be. "Don't worry, baku," she said. "I'm coming."

But in the pit of her stomach, exactly as she had when she'd pulled the trigger on that poor boy years ago, she knew things had gone all wrong.

———————◊———————

In fear and hate, Victoria clenched her teeth as she heard the gunshots at the front of the building—the direction the last of Ek's men had carried her lover.

So Montri had decided to get his daughter back, had he? Well, that was a mistake. Gripping her gun, she hobbled forward, eye squinting as she tried to follow Kannon's blood trail through the shadowy interior. Kill Kannon. Then, kill Tasanee. It was a shame she wouldn't have the time to cut up Daddy's little girl.

She peeked around a corner down a corridor. A bullet instantly ricocheted off the wall beside her face.

"Duck fucker!" she cried, pulling back. She'd injured Kannon enough to make him drop his gun, but apparently he had another.

The front door banged as it was kicked open. Montri's men. She'd no time left. She had one advantage—she knew the layout of the ruin, knew exactly where Tasanee was, and they didn't. Switch the order. First the girl, and then if Kannon didn't bleed out from the bullet in his gut, him second.

She angled through the place fast, and limped down the worn stairs to the cellar. She slid back the bolt and opened the door. The girl was huddled in the corner, flies buzzing all around. Pathetic spawn.

Victoria aimed her gun, lips twitching with rage. "This one's for Ek," she hissed. Her finger began to squeeze the trigger.

"Victoria!"

It was Jarun.

"Victoria! Where are you?"

Had her brother sent him? If so, how had he found the place?

"Victoria!" he called again, his voice closer, urgent. "We

have to get Ek to the hospital or he's going to die! Where the hell are you?"

Ek was alive? Then, what were those gunshots she'd heard?

She stepped back, turning to look up the stairwell. "What are you doing here?" she called out

"We have to get the girl and get out of here. Come on!"

No, something wasn't right. Her brother didn't know where this place was. And that meant that Jarun couldn't have either, unless he was in league with Montri.

"Duck fucker." After all John had done for that worthless street rat, this was how he was repaying them? Well, she'd show him. She'd show all of them. She was a rakshasi, a daughter of the Nirriti, dark void of the underworld, and she'd make them suffer like—

All at once a heavy chain slipped over Victoria's head, yanking tight against her throat. Tasanee screeched in anger as she braced her foot between Victoria's shoulder blades, pulling for all she was worth.

Losing their balance, the two of them tumbled backwards into the cell. As Victoria tried to aim her weapon over her shoulder, the chain went slack. Gasping, she staggered to her feet in time for the solid metal door to slam in her face, the bolt thrown shut.

"Duck fucking bitch!" she screamed, blasting away at the door, her finger pumping the trigger in rage until nothing but clicks emerged.

By the looks of it none of the bullets had penetrated the thick steel. Beyond it, she could hear Tasanee scrambling up the stairs, begging for help.

"Fuck!" With all her might, Victoria hurled her gun at the door. It bounced off and rattled across the floor.

Wait, someone was coming. Slow, steady steps that halted on the other side of the door.

"Well, this is ironic," came a woman's voice. A woman Victoria had never heard before.

"Let me out!" Victoria pounded her fist on the door. "Let me out right now!"

"I'm really tempted to leave you here," said the voice. "After all the misery you've caused. All the suffering you've inflicted on my family and me. I should leave you in there to starve in the dark."

Victoria stepped back, eyes wide with horror.

"But I won't," the voice said softly.

The bolt was pulled back, and Victoria sighed with relief.

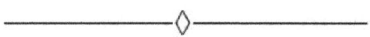

As she pulled open the door, Gina fired. Victoria clutched her chest and looked at her in shock, obviously not having any idea who'd just shot her, then slumped onto the bloodstained floor, the flies already circling.

Slowly Gina lowered her gun. "Odds are all these gunshots were heard by someone," she said calmly. "Couldn't risk the police finding you here. Letting you free."

"You think this is over?" Victoria gurgled.

"No, I don't," Gina said. "Because I'm going to make sure every last one of you sadistic bastards is hunted down. No matter how much it costs. How long it takes. I'm going to make sure every single one of you is exterminated."

She aimed and pulled the trigger again, then once more for good measure. She hurried up the stairs to where Tasanee was waiting, sobbing quietly beside Jarun. "Where the hell is Kannon?"

Her answer came an instant later.

"Gina! Jarun!" Ryota called. "I need help now!"

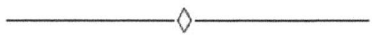

Kannon's normally sharp vision was blurry as the SUV jolted him around, Ryota driving like a madman, almost putting the vehicle on two wheels as they rounded one tight corner after another. Above him Gina pressed a blood-soaked cloth to his torso, the front of her own clothing red from him.

He was dying.

"Zoe has Ryota's number," he said, his own voice sounding distant as he tried to focus on her tear-streaked face. "When she doesn't hear from me, she'll call. Please look after her."

"She is going to hear from you," Gina choked out, and he felt the sudden deep pressure of her on his wound. "You're going to be okay."

He took her arm, his grip as weak as a child's. She shouldn't worry. Especially not for him. "I'm already okay," he said. "Because all of you are safe."

"We're almost there," said Jarun, trying to focus on his phone as the SUV went airborne for a few seconds before landing with a jarring thud. "There's a clinic less than two kilometers away."

"Hear that?" Gina said, her lips nearly touching his. "You're going to make it."

His eyes felt so heavy. Every breath felt labored. If he could feel pain he was sure he would have died from shock by now.

"Sure," he said as darkness crept over him. "Can't miss our third date."

CHAPTER 15 FIFTEEN

GINA FELT AS if she were in some kind of alternate universe.

She, and the leaders of the eleven major gangs that ran Bangkok, were sitting in a circle on the floor of the forgotten temple in 70 Rai. Gone were the bar and chairs where pedophiles used to lounge, painted over in sunny yellow was the bizarre script which had defaced the walls and, most importantly, restored was the statue of Buddha, symbolizing the triumph of wisdom, ethics and action. The temple even had a new name—Wat Namchai.

Namchai was an ancient Buddhist virtue, encompassing spontaneous warmth and compassion, the making of sacrifices for friends and family, and the courage to extend hospitality to strangers—and enemies. It was a bizarre name for a den of thieves and cutthroats; a perfect one for the new peace and stability she was determined to introduce to the Bangkok underworld. And, as it was, the first meeting of the newly formed Namchai Circle had gone along as smooth as a meditation pool. Only one more piece of business to conclude.

Dr. Chaiboonma, the meeting chair, nodded to Ryota,

who stood by the temple doors. Opening them, he admitted Alak Montri into the chamber, along with the cool rush of rain-swept air. "Please join us, Alak," said Dr. Chaiboonma, gesturing across from him to a place deliberately left open in the circle.

Montri strode over to the group, regarding the assembled as if they all stunk. And from the look he gave her, she reeked to high heaven. "I see you've formed a new organization."

Dr. Chaiboonma replied as if he was channeling Buddha himself. "Alak, you have long been a respected member of this community, but you are neither cooperative nor inclusive. Though you are a great warrior, violence is not the only way. We are here to offer you a place in something much larger than any one of us."

Montri snorted. "Is this meant to appease me?"

"Don't mistake kindness for weakness," Dr. Chaiboonma replied, still sounding divinely inspired. "If you do not accept your place among us, you'll suffer the same united wrath that drove the rakshasa from Bangkok these past two months."

"So join or die? Is that it?" Alak scoffed. "Hardly a choice."

And still Dr. Chai spoke from on high. "A vote was held as to whether to offer you a position among us. A motion put forth by Gina, the woman responsible for rescuing you, beheading the rakshasa leadership, capturing John Wakai, and saving your daughter's life. The vote was even until Gina decided to sway it to give you the opportunity before you. I suggest you demonstrate some humility and take it."

Montri looked about the circle, and he couldn't have liked what he saw. The most inviting response was Lwin's poker face, so when his gaze shifted to Gina, she gave a little friendly wave.

"I accept your offer," he said through clenched jaw.

Dr. Chaiboonma smiled and bowed. "That makes you the thirteenth member of the Namchai Circle. I will now update you on two important orders of business that have already been addressed. The first is concerning John Wakai."

"I'm amazed he's still alive," replied Montri.

"And he'll remain so," Gina added.

She couldn't tell if Montri was more angry or astonished, but he was certainly a good amount of both. "Why?"

"Because Jarun was instrumental in the defeat of the rakshasas," she expanded. "In return for his service, both he and Wakai will be exiled from the city. Come the end of this meeting, they'll be driven to the airport and put on the first plane to anywhere else."

"Wakai's a dangerous traitor!" Montri protested. "Let him live and he'll only stir up trouble."

Oh, the irony. "Wakai's broken in body and spirit, and he's friendless save for Jarun. He's of no danger to anyone anymore."

"Well, isn't that forgiving?" Montri sneered. "I suppose it doesn't matter that he contributed to the murder of your father."

Gina straightened her back and locked eyes with the father of her god-sister. "It's not an issue of forgiveness, Alak. A deal was made with Jarun, and we Zaffini keep our word."

"You mean you Zaffini. You're the only one left."

He'd omitted Darae. "I am one yet many." There, she could Buddha-talk, too.

"And who are you to hold a position in this circle?" he countered. "You think that just because your father was a friend to Bangkok that makes you some kind of princess?"

There was divine intervention from Dr. Chai. "That's the

other item you should be apprised of. Gina has been elected as the first head of the Namchai Circle. For the next year she'll be the chair of our monthly meetings, and be in charge of determining our agendas, mediating between our members and speaking on our behalf when dealing with other syndicates."

"And what, may I ask, did she do to deserve such an honor?" Montri demanded.

"She sacrificed," came Lwin, her ancient voice fierce. "A man she loved died in the effort to defeat the enemies you let past our gates. What more would you ask of her, Alak? What more should she give us to prove her loyalty?"

The memory still seared her. The blood. The pain. Saying goodbye. She gritted her teeth, and forced herself to focus on the present. All she could do now was to be strong. To honor him.

"Come next year we'll have another election," Dr. Chai said. "If you think she's done a poor job, vote against her then, Alak. In the meantime, I believe we've covered our agenda for this first meeting. Thank you, everyone for attending. If there're no objections, we'll adjourn."

Quietly the group stood, each bowing in respect to the Buddha, and one by one they filed out of the temple until only Gina, Lwin and Ryota were left. Gina plunked down on the Buddha's foot. Lwin edged to her side and took Gina's hand into her own.

"Would you like to come for tea?" she asked.

Gina shook her head. "I'm sorry, Lwin. I'd love to another time, but I have something very important I need to do. I hope you'll forgive me."

Lwin tilted her head. "Going to see someone?"

"Yeah," Gina said. "You could say I've got a date to keep."

———————◊———————

Gina kneeled before Pricha's spirit house, her hands together in prayer, eyes shut tight. It wasn't her first sweet love that squeezed her chest today, but a loss far more recent. The world would probably remember him as a bad guy. Some villain they were better off without. Only she'd known him. Loved him. And she knew that in his heart he'd been honorable. Decent. Kind.

"I wish we'd had more time together," she whispered. "Wish I could have been there sooner. I'll look after things for you, I promise. And I'll never, never forget you."

Her phone chimed.

Third date. My place. Map attached.

Kannon.

What was he doing out of the hospital?

Forget that. Where did her man of mystery live? She clicked on the map and scrolled up, down, sideways. Crap. Halfway to Malaysia from the looks of it.

She went back to the first part of the message. *Third date.* Two words that felt as if she'd won the lottery.

No one had expected him to live. Not the doctors, not Darae recovering on another floor, not Ryota, pale and tense. Not Lwin, not Dr. Chai. Nobody.

In the beginning, every breath Kannon took, every heartbeat, was a miracle. She found herself staring at his chest, willing it to rise and fall, rise and fall, listening for the hoarse wheeze of the respirator in and out, in and out. After the surgery, he was placed in a private room. Gina knew what that meant. He wasn't going to live, and they were giving family and friends privacy.

Only they didn't know Kannon, and they didn't know her.

After the first two days, the staff brought in a cot for her. After the first five days, an admin staff approached her about how his stay was going to be financed, and Gina hugged the insensitive bastard because it meant that not just she thought he was going to make it.

While she wanted nothing more than to be by his side, she was needed elsewhere to deal with the rakshasas. Her time was soon consumed with plotting, planning, wheedling, worrying. She tried to visit Kannon when she could. For lunch or after supper. Hospital fare made him convert to street food until he nearly died again from heartburn. But damned if he was going to give up his hot and spicy.

Once it was 2 a.m. before she could visit him. She had needed to see him, even if it was only to look at him sleeping. He anchored her.

She'd snuck in, actually had a pair of scrubs for this sort of situation. The bodyguards posted outside Kannon's room giving her nods of recognition as she'd come down the hallway.

Kannon had been awake, the overhead light set on low.

"Hey," she whispered. "Why aren't you sleeping?"

"At least I'm in bed. What are you doing up?"

"Had to tuck you in, baku. Sorry I'm late."

"That's not answering my question."

"There was a hit tonight. Ten more of the bastards sent to the morgue."

His hand covered hers at the same time he ground out, "You didn't tell me. Ryota know?"

"He led the charge. I told him not to tell you. You'd worry."

"Me not knowing what I'm supposed to worry about worries me." His hold remained gentle, a counterpoint to his sharp words. "There'll be consequences."

"Fewer and fewer each day. We're killing them twice as fast as they can send reinforcements. Got the home ground advantage and the way you trained Ryota, he's like a one-man army."

"I should be out there."

"You should be healing up," she corrected. "You're exactly where you need to be."

His hand became restless on hers, his thumb playing over her palm. His dark eyes, warm and troubled, rose to hers. "Thank you for taking care of things while I've been laid up here."

"I'm glad to do it."

"I'm just sorry you had to deal with Victoria. She was my responsibility. I don't want what happened to drive a wedge between us. I've been worried that it has."

For a split second, Gina wondered what on earth he was talking about, before she realized he was referring to her confession on board *The Pink Pussycat*. She wiggled her butt onto his bed, stretched herself over him, her hand tucked against his hip, her exact position on the plane ride over. Except this time, seduction wasn't on her mind.

"Is that what's keeping you up, baku? Truth is, I'm glad it was me. I'm the one who made the promise to Jarun, so it was right I be the one to keep it. And that's the difference. That was always the difference. Darae pushed me to do something that I knew was wrong. Killing Victoria was anything but."

Kannon grunted, apparently still unhappy with himself.

Gina bit the inside of her cheek hard to keep away a sudden smile. He could be such a grouch. She bent close, her lips hovering over his. "Well, how about you do something else for me then?"

Their kisses in the hospital up to now had been dry taps on the mouth. This one was different. Here in the illicit quiet, they came together in a long and thorough and tender kiss. By its sweet end, she had melted into him, warm and damp, one leg cramped up on the bed, her heart pounding.

"One kiss from you," she said, "is like a round of hot sex with anyone else."

"I don't think so." He took her hand and guided it down the sheets. "Don't think we should be feeling this after a round."

Okay, seduction was back on her mind.

"I could take care of that for you." She began to edge the sheet down but he pulled it back up. "Not until the third date."

That was the first time since the shooting he'd mentioned the third date, the first time he'd indicated that they had any kind of future beyond the hospital. "Still got big plans for us?"

"I do."

"Tell me."

He skimmed his hand over her ass, up the bend of her spine till his fingers nestled in her hair. "You'll find out soon enough. For now, you've got a city to save, and I've got wounds to heal."

She'd left that night, in love. Of course, she had loved the infuriating man for a while now. She loved him and wanted to be with him forever. And she hadn't even had sex with him. Not that she needed to; they'd be way compatible. It was that the Gina from L.A. wouldn't ever have considered going long-term with anyone unless a solid foundation of good sex had been laid. The Gina from Bangkok was good with a promise.

Or so the Gina of the 2 a.m. kiss thought. Then Kannon started to really recover. He got hold of a phone.

"Where are you at?" he'd say and she'd fill him in. He

gave advice when it came to her dealings with the gangs. When it came to her personal life, it was nothing but orders.

"You wearing that bulletproof vest Darae got you?"

"Ryota's on his way over with motion detectors for your balcony."

"You eating right?"

"Go home."

"Go to sleep."

Third date. My place. Map attached.

Sheesh. Was this what it was like to be in love? Putting up with a bossy, grumpy, secretive man who deliberately withheld sex? Given that one part of her brain was already calculating how long it would take to get to his place, it was.

She rose up on her knees and took down a square of laminated paper propped up against the vixen figurine. It turned out her father had written her a poem that she'd discovered in a safety deposit box along with his will.

Her father was no poet. The rhythm jolted, the phrasing was awkward, but it spoke of their love of small things. Their walks through the markets, her face tucked to his side, the fruity smell of her hair, the shared iced mango. And her laughter that made him feel that he'd done at least one right thing in his life.

She returned the paper to its rightful place. She stood, blew a kiss to her father, another to Pricha, then typed a message: *Coming, baku.*

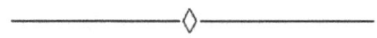

Kannon's home was a clearing in the jungle. A narrow twisting track brought her to an opening where his SUV faced out for a quick getaway. She parked nose-to-nose in front of it.

The house itself was a white stucco bungalow surrounded by a modest orchard of orange trees. As she rang the doorbell, a giant dog loped across the yard, lifted his leg on her back wheel, then joined her on the welcome mat.

They weren't kept long. Kannon swung open the door and the dog stepped in. Gina stared. Her date wasn't wearing a suit. He wasn't even going for semi-formal. He wore a Hawaiian shirt, light brown cargo shorts, and sandals. His good clothes. He gave her a huge smile, and his eyes were on her in a way that made her feel she'd drunk a glass of wine. Or two.

She gave a low bow. "Uh, hello, there. I was looking for someone named Kannon. Badass in a suit. Wears sunglasses. Know where he's at?"

Still smiling, he bowed in return. "Maybe I can help you." He stepped aside and gestured for her to enter.

Gina did, glancing around, then moseyed on over to Kannon. "I was instructed to meet him here. Sounded very urgent."

Both of his arms wrapped warm and solid around her. "I'm sure he won't mind if—"

There was a loud crash and a shriek from the back of the house. Kannon closed his eyes and reopened them on a sigh. "Time for you to meet my daughter, Zoe."

He led the way through the open layout to balcony doors at the back. Gina quickly noted a pink bean bag chair, a deep cushioned leather couch, a wall picture of a little girl on a giant tortoise. Then they were on the back deck, Kannon moving to the railing. "Everything okay out here?" he called.

Gina caught a glimpse of a sliver of blue water, a swath of thick jungle and then she was at the railing, too, looking down into the backyard. It was punched out from the surrounding jungle and dipped sharply away from the house into a kind of zoo. A tortoise with a shell the size of a manhole cover strolled about, a tall white leggy bird had a beady eye on a fish pond, two parrots cawed and ma-cawed from posts above the scene. Geckos scurried and songbirds hopped. In the middle of it was a young woman with black braids wearing a wide-brimmed straw hat and tall rubber boots, and looking up at them.

Zoe's eyes darted to Gina and her mouth dropped open.

"Hi," greeted Gina, "Quite the menagerie you've got back here."

Zoe appeared dazed. Then, she surveyed her surroundings. "Oh, I don't keep them. They come and go. It's feeding time." She glanced down at the tortoise. "Except for Darwin. He won't leave, like ever. And the animal police came and wanted to confiscate him and fine us but then Daddy"—Zoe stopped—"but then they changed their minds."

"What was that noise?" Kannon said.

Outrage flooded Zoe's face. "Those freaking monkeys tore through and grabbed Darwin's papaya. Again."

Kannon stretched his neck the way that Gina had always put down to his tie being constrictive. "And where's that damn snake of yours?"

"Don't know exactly. I think she's up there." Zoe pointed to the roof. Kannon leaned his elbows on the balcony railing and turned to Gina. "How do you feel about wildlife?"

Gina kicked off her high heels and headed for the steps. "I don't know. Let's find out." And in a louder voice to Zoe, "Could you show me around?"

She came across the backyard barefoot, and Zoe squawked, "Careful! There're scorpions everywhere. Not the real poisonous kind. It's just that if they sting, your foot will swell up."

A pair of men's rubber boots landed at Gina's feet. "Put

them on," Kannon ordered, and Gina didn't argue.

Properly attired in a skimpy sundress and rubber boots, Gina began her tour with Kannon's girl. Zoe was so alive, her face so animated, her hands dancing in the air or busy stirring up the birdseed or twisting her hat about. With all her movement it was no wonder she was as skinny as a chopstick. Once when Gina was peering into the bushes to spot the elusive 'stick' insect, she caught Zoe staring at her with the same awe as earlier. Zoe reddened and switched her focus to the balcony. Kannon was still there, still resting his elbows on the rail and looking down at them with a soft expression.

"I think he's looking at you," Gina whispered.

"Uh-huh. You."

At that moment, something long, green and very snake-y spiraled through the air and landed on Gina. The recently appointed chair of the Bangkok underworld screamed long and loud as a meter-long snake slithered and wound itself about her shoulders and arms. Zoe, too, joined in the screaming.

"Careful, she's agitated. No! Don't touch her tail. She doesn't like it. Here, let me—careful!"

All at once, Zoe grabbed the serpent about its head and midsection, and shoved it into the nearest bush.

Kannon was slumped over the balcony railing, laughing his head off.. Zoe's mouth pressed into a thin line.

"He thinks the stupidest stuff is funny," she informed Gina out of the side of her mouth.

Gina side-mouthed back, "I wouldn't know. I've never heard him laugh before."

Zoe reached for an overturned metal pan Gina had stepped into during her snake struggles. "Get used to it." She froze at what her words implied, and her eyes went wide. "That is—if—you want to." Her voice was a whisper.

Kannon was doing a poor job of trying to get a hold of himself, his attempts at coherent speech seriously impeded. Gina didn't know how it was she could feel so exasperated and so connected to him. She whispered back, "I want to."

Zoe immediately unfroze and returned to her former hyper-animated state. "Next time, I'll hold the snake and you can get a better look at her. She's a paradise tree snake. They fly in this swirly, spirally way. It's quite amazing, consider-ing—"

Her eyes went owl-ly again. This time in horror. "Shit. Shoot. Daddy! Look at my phone. Are there any messages? It's on the table."

Kannon sobered enough to get on with it. "Tasanee. Ten minutes ago. Said she was on her way."

"Shit! Shoot!" Zoe sprung away, peeling off hat, gloves and shoes as she went, her dad barking at her to pick them up so the scorpions wouldn't get inside them again, her retracing her steps to obey, racing inside, Kannon in tow, dispensing lessons in time management and sartorial advice that would've had Zoe dressed like a Mennonite.

Gina stepped into Zoe's bedroom and drew a deep, steadying breath. "I'll take care of this," she said to Kannon, and shut the door in his face.

It was a challenge. Zoe's wardrobe was chaotic to say the least. In the end, she had Zoe outfitted in something that would do for going to a movie, hanging out with friends of mixed gender and walking Sumkhovit Road. There was a knock on the bedroom door. It was Tasanee, looking like a runway model in her short dress and heels.

With Tasanee's help, they got Zoe out the front door, where her father put her through the drill regarding itinerary, curfew, cell phone usage, and a general reminder about the perversity of all males and the importance of determining one's own path, concluding with a tender message of support: "Movie. Dinner. Market. Darae's by 11:30. Call me. Boys are stupid. Don't be stupid. Hug, kiss, go."

Zoe fulfilled the last three orders automatically, and was halfway to Tas's car when she stopped and turned. "Bye, Gina. It was nice meeting you."

"The pleasure was all mine," Gina responded, and then added on a whim, "I hope we get too see more of each other."

"You will," Kannon confirmed. "Tomorrow. For brunch. We'll pick you up at 10:30, Zoe. Tell Darae and Ryota they're invited, too."

Zoe looked to her friend. "What about Tas?"

"Tasanee's family," Kannon answered. "She's always invited."

The second the car disappeared, Kannon turned to Gina, and she to him. She felt the heat of his gaze on her lips, the swell of her breasts. He stepped close so that the fibers of her dress brushed his shirt and bent his head until his mouth almost touched hers. His arm curled around her and he pulled her with him as he sat on the railing, forcing her to straddle him as his legs stretched between hers. "So what do you think," he said, looking about, "of all this?"

Gina felt her short skirt rise up and up. His hand came down to clasp her inner thigh, high up, and he squeezed the flesh there as his finger stroked inside her panties. What was she thinking wearing underwear, even if it was an itty bitty lacy thing?

"Zoe thinks that there is something more between us, you know," Gina said. "Something more than a third date."

"You're the first woman I've ever brought home to meet her."

"Sounds...serious."

"You okay with that?"

"Yeah, I'm okay with that." That was the understatement of the year but she thought it was too early in the evening to lay out exactly how okay she was with getting serious. Besides, his stroking was making the bottom of her feet tingle.

"You always get this wet?"

"Kannon, I've been wet for you since the day you showed up in my life."

He didn't answer. Instead he plied his fingers along her folds, rolling and rotating on and around her clit until she had to grip his shoulders for support. Her lower belly warmed and tensed.

"I need to come," she whimpered.

He made it happen. It was not her usual wild bucking orgasm but a long, shuddering, whole-body one that melted right to the core of her bones, a gasp erupting from her that he clamped quiet with his mouth on hers, pulling her against him so her wetness was pressed to his hard cock. They kissed, a smooshing of tongue, teeth and lips.

But there was still the sweet clawing ache to have him enclosed within her. "Can we go inside now? Take it one step further?"

He lifted her, and her legs wrapped around him. He carried her inside, down a hall and into a room with a ginormous bed, mattress wrapped in white sheets with two white ginormous pillows.

"Blankets can come out later. Right now, they'd get in the way." He set her down on her feet and tugged on the back of her dress. "Like this thing." She crossed her arms and skimmed it off. The second her breasts came free, he lifted her by the waist until her right nipple was in his mouth. Like everything about him, he was hard yet gentle with it.

She wrapped her legs around his torso. "Kannon, you need to get your own clothes off."

He spoke around her nipple. "We got time." His mouth suctioned on her again, and that was that. "This is so unfair," she whimpered. "You know if you keep going I'm going to come again?"

He lowered her to the bed, him following, his hand gliding up her inner thigh to her pussy. "You complaining about getting another orgasm?"

She took in his hand on her, his gorgeous face bent over her perked nipples, and her head fell back against the pillow. "You're right. What was I thinking?"

In moments, she wasn't thinking at all. She was thrusting against him, her back arching off the wall and Kannon's mouth had lost hold on her breasts as she bucked out another orgasm. She hadn't come all the way down from that when she was tugging on his shirt.

"Okay, baku, time to shed. I mean it. "

Kannon brought her hands above her head and encircled her wrists. "Before things go too far, what kind of protection do you need?"

"None. I'm covered." She thought about how he might view her previous lifestyle. "And clean, too. Bet you are, too."

Kannon sighed. "After my wife, it was Pensri. That was it."

"Really?"

"That was all I wanted till now."

"So, this is a big deal for you."

His eyes warmed on her. "You're a big deal for me."

She swallowed. "You're my big deal, too."

He swept her into a long, powerful kiss. "Why is it that I

want to keep sweet-talking with you and have sex at the same time?

She tilted her hips up invitingly. "We could do both. Climb on and get in."

He grinned and shook his head. "You sure know how to romance the guys."

"Okay, the Big Tease is over." She pushed him onto his back, and straddled him. She unbuttoned him, revealing the surgical scar across his stomach. "You sure you're up for all this tonight?"

"Things get too tender, I'll tell you. How's that?"

"Deal. The best one I've made since coming to Bangkok." She flipped off him and dispensed with his shorts, as fast as he'd done with her panties. And what was revealed—"Wowza. Considered a second career in porn?"

She clamped her hand around his hard dark length, and his entire body jerked in response. "Gina!"

She heard his urgency, felt her own, and slowly slid onto his cock.

Despite all her fantasies of him, despite having had sex with a hundred people, despite knowing exactly what turned her on, she was not prepared at all for how powerful it felt to have Kannon inside her. They fell silent, and very, very still.

"If I so much as wiggle my toe," she whispered, "I'm going to come."

He clenched his jaw. He seemed to be experiencing the same difficulty.

It was like a pressure system that hung hot and heavy, a tropical storm about to break.

His whole body tightened underneath her, his hands flexed at his sides and gripped the sheets. "I want to make our time together special."

She cupped his face and kissed him. "You and me are together. Alive and well and safe. It's special."

His eyes snapped open. His hands locked onto her hips and he thrust upwards. The sudden movement inside her was enough and her body began convulsing, and finally, finally their long wait was over, and he didn't hold back any more.

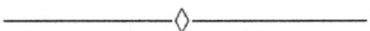

Orgasms four through to seven came with licks, flicks, swallows, commands to lie still (Kannon's), sweat (Gina's, mostly) and an inadvertent clip to the side of his head with her heel ("I'm sorry, baku, I always lose control during my climaxes."). Eight and nine involved a late dinner and cayenne pepper.

They were back in the bedroom where Kannon was setting things in motion for number ten when his phone rang. Zoe's check-in time. Kannon watched Gina snag his shirt on the way out of the room. Where was she going? It was probably the shortest call on record with Zoe but she was smart enough to know not to prolong it. The second he disconnected, Kannon was hunting Gina.

She was on the balcony, leaning back on the railing. He pulled her into his arms.

"You've got a great home, Kannon. A great daughter." She gestured to her side. "You even have a dog."

The mutt sat up and smiled at Kannon.

"I don't. Thought he was with you."

Gina grinned. "Told you I have a way with animals."

"You and Zoe both. Between the two of you this place will probably get overrun. Be lucky if a herd of elephants doesn't show up."

Gina went still. "Did you just say I was moving in with you?"

After weeks of planning, it was time to make his pitch. "I'll always be a killer, Gina. No escaping that. What has changed is Bangkok, thanks to you. It means I've got options. I have a mind to start a school. Teach the gangs of the Namchai Circle what I know, like I did with Ryota."

"I can picture all these kids in business suits and sunglasses filing into Baku's School for Assassins."

Kannon grinned. He could, too. The image Gina had created gave him the lift to carry on with his most nerve-racking question. "What are your thoughts? About us, I mean?"

"When you were dying, Kannon," she replied, "I swore that when you were out of danger, I'd grab hold of you and never, ever risk losing you again, but all you've ever asked for is a third date. My thoughts are I'm ready for a fourth, and a fifth, all the way up to a twenty-fifth wedding anniversary if you'd have me."

In his wildest dreams, he hadn't expected that, had thought she'd make him work for it. She *deserved* to have him work for it.

"The twenty-fifth, huh?"

She nodded.

"I hadn't figured it out much beyond the honeymoon."

Gina let out a whoop like when her fighter had won at the arena. "You love me! I knew you did under all that grouchiness! And I love you, Kannon! I love you."

His arms banded tight around her as she jiggled up and down. Before he could pose the question she beat him to it.

"Kannon, will you marry me?" she asked, looking up at him with puppy dog eyes.

He sighed. "You got the shot off first."

Even within the tight circle, she bounced, then pulled back to study his face. "You weren't planning the third date. You were planning how to propose to me." She gave a hoot of laughter. "What, were you planning to seduce me into marriage?"

It was a good thing he loved her so much, otherwise he might be embarrassed. She gave a louder hoot. "Brian told me about this. Called it the slow seduction. You've been working it for two months now." Jiggle, jiggle. "The long con."

He grinned. "It worked, didn't it? You're practically begging to marry me."

"It did. And I'm not too proud to say it, if it means getting what I want. See?" She went on her tiptoes, nibbled at his neck. "Feel me begging you?"

He did more than feel. He dropped into a crouch and pulled her into a fireman's hold, giving her behind a playful swat. "Time to beg for mercy elsewhere."

She squealed all the way to his bed, finishing up with a special high-pitched one when he tossed her on the mattress, him following, trapping her bounces underneath his body. They kissed and touched, their caresses slowing, their limbs twining and growing heavy. Then, they murmured goodnights and slept.

Bright and early the next morning, amid sunshine and bird calls and a dog barking, they woke and, still caught up together, it was Kannon's turn to beg and she granted him his pleasure. And while he conducted a private celebration upon his fiancée, she snatched up her phone and announced to the world that Gina Zaffini was officially, and thoroughly, taken.

S.M. STELMACK

REVIEW REQUEST

Your opinion matters. Here's your chance to tell us and other readers what you think of *Fox Hunt*. Readers will get a better idea about what to expect, and we get valuable feedback about what you like and what you want.

Come to our website <u>S. M. Stelmack: Cars, Guns, Skin and Sunsets</u> and sign up on our email list at <u>S. M. Stelmack Pillow Talk</u>. Sign-up means we'll periodically send you exclusive stuff, like love letters and research findings, and we'll alert you to our upcoming releases.

We are on Goodreads! Come to our author page at <u>S. M. Stelmack</u>.

WHAT'S NEXT?

Pensri's Pink Platypus…the third in THE FEMME VENDETTA series.

Billions are being made in the resource-rich outback of Queensland, and setting up a brothel, Pensri and her quixotic girls are determined to snare their share. But wherever there are riches, there's trouble, especially when she crosses a vile gangster with his own horrific way of creating wealth. Luckily Pensri's also caught the eye of stockman Zach Donovan, a former outlaw with secrets to guard, and his own stake in Pensri's business—The Pink Platypus.

Add it to your Goodreads list: *Pensri's Pink Platypus* on Goodreads

Release date Spring 2014!

Also, below, is the opening to *Undertow*, the first in our urban horror romance series, *The UnderCity Chronicles*, available now!

All of these excerpts are available over at our website, too

UNDERTOW

THE UNDERCITY CHRONICLES

The City is deeper than they know.

S.M. STELMACK

PRoLoGUE

Lindsay desperately wanted to hold Jack's hand. Her breath came fast and shallow, and her every muscle had stiffened into near rigor mortis. And still the elevator dropped beneath the city streets, down into the dark guts of New York, its metal lattice floor the only barrier between her and the shadowy depths below.

She wasn't about to admit her fear of heights to Jack. Sure she had a crush on him, as bad as any fifteen-year-old could have, and would've considered herself the luckiest girl in the world to hold hands with him. Yet, she also knew he hung out with her because she could keep up with him. To confess her vulnerabilities now would make her no better than all the other girls, and she was determined that he would remember her as someone exceptional.

Sam Cole, Jack's father, gave her a lopsided smile. "This crate's on the slow side, but we'll be there in a minute. That hardhat fit okay, Lindsay?"

She managed a nod, and the oversized yellow helmet slipped over her eyes.

The other side of his smile shot up. "Good. I'm glad Jack invited you. Another couple of weeks and we'd be finished down here. Not many people ever get to see the real underground."

As if on cue, the elevator reached the bottom, making Lindsay's already queasy stomach lurch.

"You okay?" Jack asked.

Great, she probably looked like the vomit she was trying to keep down. "Yeah. I'm–I'm a little nervous of heights."

His golden eyes shone. "So I noticed." He looked down. Her hand had his in a death grip.

Lindsay gasped and let go, her face burning. "Oh, jeez. Sorry. I didn't even realize that I...sorry."

She hurried off the elevator—and stepped into a fresh hell. The subway tunnel was dark and filthy and reeked of grime and oil, and she could feel claustrophobia begin to crush her. The halogen lighting created a pool of civilization in which the workers called to each other, and there were the strong noises of steel striking steel and generators throbbing out energy. Beyond that, in the world Jack was going to take her, there was only darkness and silence. Yet he and his father looked content, as if this dank scene was a veritable wonderland.

Jack had used that very word when he was talking her into coming. A wonderland. She described it the same way to her parents, and to her brother, fifteen years her senior, and his wife around the dining room table. Her niece, two going on irrational, wanted to go right away, and when Lindsay explained that wonderland didn't mean Disneyland, she said it was okay, that Jack could lift her on his shoulders and take her to the playground there. Due to her gender, Seline adored Jack. Lindsay's mother melted when Jack came over and ate through the fridge and pantry, and Lindsay had the distinct feeling that it was Jack's charms had played a large part in her mother had giving her permission to go underground. Her father, being male, had only given the go-ahead once he knew Jack's father was going to be nearby. Then her brother, male and bossy beyond belief, had called up Jack's father to confirm the dos and don'ts. Gracie, her sis-in-law, had winced in sympathy. "You should see him with the babysitter. The poor girl is stiff with worry before we've even left, and then she's got an evening of Seline. I always give her an extra ten as stress pay."

Sometimes Lindsay envied the casual bachelor relationship between Jack and his father. Sam Cole was pretty laid-back as far as parents went, and actively encouraged his son to explore the tunnels. He'd done the same thing in London when he was a boy, and was overjoyed that his only child shared his lifelong passion for places deep and dark.

"Be back within the hour, and no taking Lindsay off the track," he said. "I don't want to go searching for you again."

Jack laughed, sharing an in-joke with his father. "We'll be careful. Let's go, Linds."

He flicked on his helmet light and waited long enough for her to do the same before leading her down the tunnel, away from the swarm of tradesmen and engineers. Jack was always ready to chart unknown territory, and he wasn't one to check if anyone was following. He was always the first to take a dare, not to show off but because he couldn't resist a challenge. That she was his regular buddy filled her with pride. That he was leaving for Hong Kong in a month, and likely never coming back, filled her with a profound sadness.

Right now with him so real and solid beside her, Lindsay wasn't going to worry about the future. The immediate present was freaky enough. She could feel the darkness here. It had a kind of smothering thickness to it, so alien to anything on the surface.

"What's this about sending out a search party for you?"

she asked off-handedly, as if this was no different than walking the streets above.

"They did, but I made it back on my own and they got lost. In the end, I was part of the group that found them."

That was Jack. Total master of his surroundings. Lindsay looked about, her light cutting a pale swath over wet concrete walls, iron rails, graffiti. "Sounds like you know these tunnels pretty well."

"No, I've barely scratched the surface. One day I want to come back here and map the whole underground."

He wanted to come back. Okay, not to see her. Still, there was no way he wouldn't look her up. She squashed down her excitement. "How long do you think they'll take to map?"

Jack gave a short laugh. "A lifetime."

She stopped in her tracks. "You want to spend your life in tunnels? Don't you think that would get old after a while?"

"Not for me. Come on, I want you to meet someone."

"What?"

"There's this guy who lives down here. Name's Tim."

"Who the hell lives in a tunnel?"

"People with nowhere else to go, Linds," he said quietly and, to her ears, reproachfully. "Used to be a lawyer or judge or something. When the transit authority kicked him out of the tunnels, I got him a copy of the keys so he could get back in."

Lindsay wondered what the men in her family would say if they knew Jack was taking her to visit a bum. Or that he'd done something shady for that bum. Maybe she'd skip this part.

"Tim knows everything about the tunnels. My dad told me they've had people down here since the 50's. Tim says there were people underground before that. Way before. You wouldn't believe the stuff that goes on down here."

Lindsay looked over her shoulder, uneasily noticing how far they were getting from the work crew, and bumped into Jack, who'd stopped immediately ahead of her.

"Sorry…"

Jack didn't seem to notice, his gaze focused down the tunnel on some point beyond the beam of his helmet light.

"What is it?" she whispered.

"I thought I heard something up ahead. Like a yell or… something."

Lindsay strained to hear anything. Nothing but the faint dripping of water. "One of the workers?"

"No," he replied hesitantly. "They'd be wearing a light." He started forward again. She couldn't stop herself. She caught his arm.

"Shouldn't we go tell your dad?"

Jack kept his eyes on the darkness. "It's probably just Tim. He said he has nightmares sometimes. Sees things that aren't there. Come on. There's nothing to be afraid of."

Then why had his usual confident pace slowed? Wordlessly, she followed on Jack's heels down the tunnel for what seemed like a mile, each step taking them further into the gloom of the underworld until the lights behind them had almost faded to nothing. Cold crept over her, a vapor that twined about her limbs.

She was about to suggest again they return when Jack pivoted to face a small side passage that branched off the subway line. The opening didn't reach Lindsay's shoulders and was barely as wide as her body, and it was so obscured by pipes and cables that she never would have noticed it on her own.

"In here," he said, and crouching, disappeared inside.

Fear rooted her feet to the ground. Something was wrong

here. Very terribly wrong, and though she trusted Jack, her intuition screamed at her to run back to the safety of the surface, away from whatever lay beyond. But Jack was waiting for her, and she'd never abandon him even if she knew that disaster lay ahead. Especially then. She took a deep breath and followed.

She stayed right on his butt so she was beside him when the cramped passage emptied into a chamber the size of Lindsay's bedroom.

It was the smell that hit her first. Warm, metallic. Blood. Jack's hand clamped around hers, the beams from their helmets skittering about as they frantically scanned the room. Lindsay took in scattered newspapers and paperbacks, an overturned folding cot, pop bottles and a kerosene lantern.

Then Jack made a soft pained noise, and she turned so that her light ran alongside his. Blood was smeared along the wall by the entrance, left by hands that had clawed futilely at the concrete before being dragged off into the darkness.

"Oh my God," Jack whispered. "They're real."

CHAPTER ONE

Eighteen years later

Lindsay sat alone in Captain Monroe's small, drab office and tried not to be sick all over his desk, a mishap that might not have mattered much since it already looked as if raccoons had been set loose on it. The fluorescent lighting flickered, emitting that mosquito-like frequency as it prepared to burn out, though it wasn't loud enough to drown out the death rattle coming from the computer hard drive. On the printer sat a delicately balanced styrofoam cup of cold coffee, perched there like a bad deodorizer. She might've opened the window with its view over the slate gray waters of the Hudson River, except he doubted that would be appreciated given the freezing temperatures that had gripped the East coast during the past week.

Deep down she knew it wasn't her environment that was making her nauseous. It was why she had to be there. Her eyes drifted, as they did every time she visited, to the maps plastered on the walls. Faded from long years of use, they were, except for the one of the New York subway, all byzantine in their complexity. They depicted tunnels and sewers, air ducts and water mains, forgotten train lines and long-sealed garbage pits. There were maps of cable, gas and steam lines, each representing vast labyrinths buried deep beneath the streets, systems that joined and overlapped, multiplying their complexity.

If that were not enough, many of them were incomplete, inaccurate or both, rendering navigation in some sections of the city's bowels virtually impossible. She'd learned as much from several private investigators, all of whom had turned down her case.

After an eternity, Captain Monroe entered, steaming cup of coffee in hand, and sat across from her without a word of greeting. She bit back the urge to tell him about the precarious position of the abandoned cup. She wasn't here to regulate his coffee consumption.

"Thank you for seeing me, Captain," she said as evenly as she could. "Again."

He grunted, and began shuffling through the papers on his desk, clearly searching for something. "You here for an update?" His dismissive tone made it clear he wanted her out the door as quickly as possible.

She tried to keep the frustration out of her voice. "Yes. I'd like to know why nobody is searching for her."

Monroe examined a sheet, frowned, tossed it back and kept rooting around. Lindsay itched to jump in and make square corners and open spaces on his desk.

"Ms. Sterling, do you know how many miles of tunnels there are beneath New York?"

"No. I don't."

Monroe squinted at another scrap of paper. "Neither do I,

or anybody else. They run for hundreds of miles, and go down as deep as twelve stories. What I do know is how many men I have to patrol those tunnels, and that number is exactly thirty."

There was a stapled sheaf of papers suspended over the edge of the desk, and the way the Captain was bulldozing around it was going to slide off. "Nevertheless, it's your duty to search for missing persons."

He pinned her with a look no doubt reserved for punks and do-gooders. "I don't need you to remind me of my job. I've been on the force for thirty-four years. I know my responsibilities."

Clearly being nice wasn't going to work. "Then, why aren't you doing anything?"

"Ms. Sterling, how many times do I need to repeat myself before you get it? The people down there are not like the people up here. Most of them are drug addicts. Many have extreme psychological problems. Unless we get some kind of solid lead on this investigation, I'm not sending my men down in a blind search. It's too dangerous."

"But you're the police!"

The captain's face reddened in anger. "Last year we had an officer knifed to death down there. Another one was beaten so badly he'll never walk again, and do you know what he was beaten with? His own nightstick. And that's in subway and maintenance tunnels we regularly patrol, not in the lower levels. We'd need an army to conduct a thorough search, and—surprise, surprise—we don't have one. I explained this to your niece before she went down. She decided she knew better."

Lindsay sucked in her breath to snap back, and then slowly released it. If she was going to find Seline, she needed his cooperation, no matter how unwilling he might be to give it. She rescued the slipping report and set it safely on his desk. He peered at it, then snatched it up.

"Well, at least you found something that you were looking for," she commented with emphasis. "Look, I understand my niece was no great friend of the NYPD. I understand she was conducting her research despite your warnings, and despite *my* warnings, to be frank. I understand that you're undermanned and don't want to place your men in danger. But Captain, I can't just forget about her. There must be something we can do."

Monroe stared coldly across at her. She held it. "Ms. Sterling, I really don't think I can help you..." he began, but his eyes darted to a battered old Rolodex tucked against his computer. She pressed for the advantage.

"Please, Captain," she pleaded, "if you can think of anybody who could find her, anyone at all, I need to know."

Monroe stared back, setting his jaw as if weighing his options. "There is one guy," he said after a moment, though by his expression he was already regretting his words.

"Who is he?"

"His name is Jack Cole. Used to be a professor."

Lindsay froze, went as stiff as the bodies of the homeless that turned up every day now on the city's icy streets. "Did you say Jack Cole? Jack Andrew Cole?"

Monroe's hand hovered over the Rolodex. "You know him?"

"Yes," she replied, fond memories softening her initial shock. "We used to be best friends back in high school. I haven't seen him in"—she did the math—"eighteen years. He's a...a scientist?"

"Anthropologist. Expert in urban subcultures." Monroe set the Rolodex in front of him and began flipping. "Did a lot of work around the world. London, Paris, Rome, Moscow and here in New York. Nobody knows more about the underside of cities."

Lindsay shook her head in wonder. "That's the kind of work he always said he was going to do. He could find Seline, couldn't he?"

"If he wanted, though I doubt he will," Monroe said. "I guess you could say he's retired."

"Retired?" Lindsay echoed.

"About three years ago, Dr. Cole went missing in the underground during one of his expeditions. We searched for him as best we could. After a couple of weeks, we simply didn't have resources to keep it up. He was presumed dead, and that's the way things stayed till early last year when he finally surfaced."

"He spent two *years* underground? What happened to him?"

Monroe eyed one of the cards, then shook his head and kept flipping. "He didn't say."

"What do you mean he didn't say?" Lindsay asked. That wasn't the Jack she'd known. He would've popped up, those lion-like eyes of his bright with enthusiasm, and begun telling the world of his adventures.

"I'm saying he didn't say," Monroe growled. "End of story."

Not for her. She'd find him and he'd help her. He wouldn't let her down. She knew that much about him.

"Yeah, here it is." Monroe stopped at a card and began patting the papers in the hunt for a pen.

Lindsay produced her own pen and paper.

Monroe smirked as he jotted down the address. It was a few blocks from Gates Avenue, in Bed-Stuy. Though parts of

Bedford-Stuyvesant were wonderful places to live, featuring beautiful tree-lined rows of century-old brownstone homes and tight-knit communities, Gates Avenue was infamous for its poverty and crime rate. She didn't need to be a psychologist to see Monroe doubted that a professional white woman, dressed like she'd stepped off the pages of a fashion magazine, would dare set foot there.

"You have his phone number?"

"No," Monroe said flatly. "Now if you'll excuse me, I have a lot of work to do today."

Lindsay had the address memorized before she reached the door. As she was leaving, the captain called out to her.

"Make sure you go yourself."

She turned in the doorway. "I beg your pardon?"

"I said you'll need to go there yourself. Cole isn't likely to help you, Ms. Sterling. He definitely won't if you hire someone to go talk to him."

What did he take her for? Thirty years on the force and he hadn't figured out that appearances meant nothing. "I learned long ago that if I wanted anything done, I'd have to do it myself. Today you just reminded me of that."

At that precise moment, the fluorescent light burned out, leaving Monroe in twilight. It was her turn to smirk. "It's hell being left in the dark, isn't it?"

***

Seline woke to a sudden squeal, letting out one of her own as she bolted upright in the blackness, the sleeping bag provided by her captors twisting around her legs. She unzipped it, the opening of the nylon teeth sawing on her ears. She tried to determine the direction of the noise, or if there had been one, and not yet another hallucination. The chain that stretched from the thick collar around her throat to a concrete pillar clunked and scraped against the floor with her every move, messing with her ability to gauge sound. God, she hated the chain. Early on she'd measured it using her hands and estimated it to be fifteen feet long, not long enough to reach any of the walls in the tiled room, walls she knew existed because if she stretched her legs her feet barely brushed against them. She craved to have a wall at her back.

She sat cross-legged on the bag and breathed deeply, the smell of cold iron and stale air filling her, and willed her racing heart, the beats impossibly loud, to slow. It took longer each time the panic attacks hit, but she calmed herself enough to allow for rational thinking. She'd been down for about a week, though time was fast becoming a shredded concept in this world of perpetual night. She'd tried using the number of times she slept to gauge the passage of days, until she realized that the lack of light and noise made her sleep too often. Or maybe not. All she knew was that she was far from the surface, in the lowest levels of the tunnels, and that despite the silence that surrounded her, she wasn't alone.

She could only guess how many captors there were. She hadn't even gotten a glimpse of them before they'd pulled a sack over her head and dragged her through endless passages, her screams muffled. There were at least two of them to start with—one had held a knife at her throat while the other had bound her wrists behind her back. She now sensed that there were more. Many more.

"Hello?" she called, her voice echoing through the chamber. She always called out after waking. It was a way of establishing contact with her captors, of reaching out to possible rescuers, of proving her humanness. She'd heard somewhere that the best thing to do if kidnapped was to try and make friends with your captors. If they saw you as a person, as opposed to just a hostage, it made it harder for them to harm you.

"Hello?" she tried again. As usual there was no response, and it was the silence that made her more afraid than anything. She wished she'd listened to Lindsay, to that Jack Cole, to everybody. They all said the tunnels could kill. She'd gone down before, twelve times, and nothing had happened, not a whisper of anything. And then this. For the thousandth time she thought of Lindsay's story about when she and Jack went into the tunnels as teenagers. Was she going to be ripped apart like that poor man?

No. No. Against all odds she was alive. They would've killed her outright, if the stories were to be believed. Whoever or whatever was keeping her prisoner actually seemed intent on keeping her alive. She hadn't been beaten or raped. While she slept, the provided bedpan was emptied. A stringy meat stew, palatable after hunger had hollowed her out, was regularly provided along with a bottle of fresh water.

Only they hadn't uttered a single word to her.

"Listen," she called out, repeating once again her offer. "If you contact my sister, she'll ransom me. If you let her know that I'm alive, she'll pay for my release."

Silence.

"Her name is Lindsay Sterling," Seline continued. "You can reach her at Sterling Restorations. Or you can call her home." She rattled off the numbers.

Behind her she thought she heard the slightest rustle and twisted around.

Blackness.

"Please. I'm no threat to you. I'll go away and never

come back if that's what you want. I won't tell anyone about you, promise. Please let me go."

Silence.

"I only came down here to help. I'm not with the police. I'm not even a real social worker, just a student. I wanted to make the people who run this city realize that you're down here. To make them stop ignoring you."

Then, a sound. It came in hushed vibrations all around her, making her heart thump wildly. From every corner of the pitch-black chamber she could hear her keepers. Ever so quietly, they were laughing.

***

The street where Jack lived was all but deserted when Lindsay reached it, the rows of cheap shops and slum housing standing stiff and battered in the chill morning. A bunch of young men gathered around a junker turned as her Lexus cruised by, their expressions sullen and calculating. All seemed too cold to do more than look.

Jack's address turned out to be a dilapidated grocery store, its barred windows smashed and brick facade layered in crude graffiti. Pulling over to the curb, she double-checked the address. Had Monroe played some kind of cruel trick on her? Surely to God, Jack couldn't be living in a place barely fit for a rodent.

She locked her car and wondered if she would ever see it again. Oh well, that was why she paid the outrageous insurance premiums. You shouldn't have what you can't afford to lose. It's what her father had always said, and she'd made it her personal motto. She walked across the street and was about to step onto the curb when the heel on her right Blahnik got wedged in a pavement crack. She tugged with her foot, and nothing happened. The heel was sensible, a full inch across, and still this.

"Fine," she muttered. She unzipped the boot, slipped out her nyloned foot and hopped on the other as she began prying out the heel. From down the street, she heard the men snort in laughter.

Yes, she could afford to lose her six hundred dollar boots. Her pride was an entirely different matter. She was not going to meet an old high school friend with one shoe. Besides, it was freezing. She went at it again with renewed vigor.

The heel popped loose which sent her hopping madly about in all directions to keep her balance. The crowd laughed raucously, and Lindsay jammed her foot back into her boot, closed it with a most satisfying zip, and straightened. Then gasped.

She was looking up at the biggest black man she'd ever seen in all her New York life. He was a tree, a building, a mountain. He wore a knit hat, a parka that could've covered her car, and tundra boots that had to have been custom-made to fit him. A brown paper bag full of groceries hung from his bear paw of a hand with no more effort than she'd hold an empty envelope. Down the two-lane bridge of his nose, he looked at her with the mild disdain normally reserved for pigeons.

He took in her boots, her coat, her car, and no doubt, her skin color. "You lost?"

Lindsay tried for a friendly, brisk tone. "Not at all. I'm meeting a friend. He lives right here." She attempted to skirt around him. "I mustn't keep him waiting."

The giant pulled a face and narrowed his eyes. "Here? What's his name?"

She dropped the friendly and kept the brisk. "Why would I tell a stranger my friend's name?"

His eyes widened and apparently conceding the point, he stepped aside to let her pass.

"Thank you," she said. "Have a nice day."

She got past him and headed up to the rusted metal door of the shop. She tapped on it, then banged on it. Nothing. Aware that her every move was being watched, she tried the handle. It was unlocked—didn't, she realized, even have a lock. She glanced back to where the winterized wall of humanity stood watching her. He smiled, flashing a set of gold teeth, clearly not intending to walk on.

"Uh, looks like he left it open for me. Must be home, then."

His smile glittered. "Must be."

"I'll have to remind him not to leave his door open." She paused deliberately. "Who knows who might wander in?"

"Yeah. Good idea."

Lindsay didn't know what to do, so she pushed open the door and tried to close it quickly behind her. It took a couple of goes as the door didn't sit square with the frame. She waited, listening for the Yeti of Bedford to follow. Nothing happened, and she turned back to the shop's interior. Or what there was of it.

Crumbling white plaster exposed wires, and the floor was stripped straight to the plywood underlay. A patchwork of old linoleum tiles, mud-stained carpet rolls and cardboard trailed from the front door to a reinforced metal one at the rear.

"What the hell happened, Jack?" she said under her breath. She crossed the gutted store and knocked on the metal door.

No answer. Lindsay went straight to the door knob. It was

locked. She knocked again, harder this time. Behind her, the shop door crashed open and in came the giant.

"You ain't getting past that one," he said, nodding.

"Wha—?"

He strolled towards her, shifting his bag to one arm, while his hand dug around in the pocket of his parka. "Locked it on my way out." He pulled out a set of keys so full that they formed a stiff three-quarters arc and selected one.

He stepped forward and she stepped aside.

"You live here? Not Jack Cole, then?"

"That the name of the friend who's waiting for you?"

The game was up. She sighed. "Yeah, it is."

Again the man's mouth broke into an amused smile. "He'll be back soon. You want to, you can come down and wait." He moved sideways to hold the door open for her.

Lindsay tried not to look as scared as she was. What the hell had Monroe gotten her into? The cop had warned her to talk to Jack herself, but hadn't mentioned anything about his living in the basement of some abandoned building with Bigfoot. Perhaps it was a kind of test. After all, if she didn't have the guts to go down there, how could she expect others to face New York's real underground?

"Sure. Sounds good." Carefully she walked down the stairwell, him clumping behind her, filling the one escape route. They emerged into a clean, spartan apartment. No, not spartan. Spartan was its own kind of style. This was absence, the kind of deprivation found in a prison cell. There were no bookshelves, no television, no phone—not even a single picture on the cracked plaster walls. The only illumination was the weak beams of sunlight that fell through a pair of small street-level windows high on the back wall. Lindsay had no sense of Jack in the bleak apartment, nothing to make it seem as if this was where he belonged.

The black man kicked off his boots, carpeted the floor with his coat. "Sit down. He'll be back soon."

Her seating choices were two chairs, an uncomfortable-looking plastic one by a small formica kitchen table, and a worn mud-brown leather armchair pushed into the far corner. Lindsay crossed the room to take up the latter.

"So...my name's Lindsay."

The man took two cartons of eggs from the paper bag, placed one on the counter and the other in the rusted fridge. "That right?"

Lindsay was tired of being played with. "Yeah, that's right. Now could you stop with your I-know-something-you-don't-know game and act like a normal human being?"

His eyes positively gleamed. "Man, I can't wait for Jack to come back and see what I brought home."

"You make it sound as if I were a bargain at a garage sale."

He gave a soft hoot. "More than what Jack bargained for, I'll bet." He turned to the sink and began washing his hands under a sputtering tap. "Reggie," he tossed over his shoulder. "I'm Reggie."

"I take it you're a friend of Jack's

Reggie dried his hands on a towel that Lindsay wouldn't have washed her floor with and took a large frying pan from one of the small cupboards. "Yeah. Something like that."

Lindsay took in his familiarity with the place, and had to ask, "You and Jack are...roommates?"

"Yeah." Reggie scrunched his forehead in sudden thought. "You asking if I'm gay?"

The directness of his question threw her, and she reacted with her own bluntness. "I don't care if *you* are. I'm just wondering about Jack, is all."

Reggie let out a whoop of laughter, and he fell back against the ancient yellow fridge, rocking it and holding his gut. He chugged out a succession of long motor-like guffaws. "Oh, man, I can't wait. I can't wait." Gradually he subsided and began cracking eggs into the pan.

He was on his seventh when he theorized, "Might explain why he's so off women, but I doubt it."

Lindsay watched as Reggie broke all twelve eggs into the pan and proceeded to scramble them on a two-burner hot plate, his back to her.

"How do you know him?" Lindsay said, shedding her jacket and folding it over the back of the chair. The place wasn't as cold as it looked.

"How come you say you're a friend of Jack when you've never come around before?" he asked right back.

He had a point. "We were friends in high school, then he and his dad moved away, and I haven't seen him since. I didn't know until today that he was back in New York."

"You're here to say hello?"

Lindsay wasn't about to go into it with Reggie. "Yeah. Something like that."

He snorted at having his line thrown back at him. "I like you, girl." He shook his head. "I can't wait."

When the pan had heated to a steady hissing, he tipped half of the yellow globby contents onto a plate, and ate the rest out of the pan, staring off into space as if he were by himself.

"You live alone?" he suddenly asked.

This time Lindsay was prepared for Reggie's abruptness, maybe because he was a straight-shooter like her. "No. I have a niece."

He stopped chewing. He looked ready to ask another

question when the door at the top of the stairs opened. The light from the store above briefly cast a man's shadow down to the dim apartment. Gold teeth appeared in anticipation. "Must be him now."

Lindsay stood automatically. Her hand fluttered to her pale hair and she wished she'd thought to check herself in the mirror instead of watching Reggie shovel egg into his face.

Not that she was here to rekindle a high school crush, her ears tracking the descent of the booted footsteps. Still, there was no denying it. She was looking forward to seeing Jack Cole again.

WANT TO READ IT?
If you're on Goodreads, here's the link to adding
Undertow to your bookshelf.

www.goodreads.com/book/show/17564454-undertow

Also find there
Midnight Everlasting (The UnderCity Chronicles #2),
set for release in Spring 2014.

www.goodreads.com/book/show/17831831-midnight-everlasting

ABOUT THE AUTHORS

S. M. STELMACK IS OUR pen name, short for Serge & Moira Stelmack.

We aim to give what we like in a story—gutsy men and women, high stakes and LOL lines. Serge is the storymaster who blasts out the beginning, middle and end. Moira comes behind, clucking and hemming, as the story undergoes countless rewrites till it meets our vision. She's also the media relations manager, senior editor, marketing VP, director of operations (domestic and foreign), comptroller and the one who makes sure that Serge has a steady supply of cola while he works.

We live with our two kids, and several other strange pets, in a land of wintertime sunshine and snow and summertime mud and mosquitoes. Actually, it's not that bad. The snakes in the local lake aren't venomous.

We really need to move.

Authors, Serge & Moira Stelmack
www.smstelmackauthor.com